The Upper Room

MARY MONROE

The Upper Room

www.kensingtonbooks.com

DAFINA BOOKS are published by

Kensington Publishing Corp.
119 West 40th Street
New York, NY 10018

All Kensington titles, imprints, and distributed lines are available at special quantity discounts for bulk purchases for sales promotion, premiums, fund-raising, and educational or institutional use.

Special book excerpts or customized printings can also be created to fit specific needs. For details, write or phone the office of the Kensington Sales Manager: Kensington Publishing Corp., 119 West 40th Street, New York, NY 10018. Attn. Sales Department. Phone: 1-800-221-2647.

The Dafina logo is a trademark of Kensington Publishing Corp.

ISBN: 978-1-4967-3916-2
ISBN: 978-0-7582-6772-6 (e-book)

First Hardcover Printing: October 2001
First Trade Paperback Printing: July 2002

20 19 18 17 16 15 14 13 12 11 10 9

Printed in the United States of America

This book is dedicated to
Jacqueline Susann Monroe, Michelle Monroe,
Eric B. Holtsmark, and James M. Leefe

Dear Readers,

I love all of my novels, but *The Upper Room* is special because it opened doors I'd been knocking on for decades. It was the first book I published, and it introduced my favorite character, Mama Ruby. It's been thirty-six years since it was originally released, and Mama Ruby is as popular as ever—even more so with some of my die-hard fans.

People often ask me how I came up with a character like Mama Ruby. They are amazed when I tell them that she is a composite of three family members: Mom, Aunt Berniece, and Cousin Florence. These queens are no longer with us, but they will live on through Mama Ruby. Unfortunately, as far as they were concerned, the only book worth reading was the Bible. Even when I went to New York to be interviewed by The Associated Press and our hometown newspaper featured the lengthy interview on two pages; Mom, Aunt Berniece, and Cousin Florence clucked their tongues and shook their heads. They'd read a few chapters of *The Upper Room* and couldn't figure out what all the fuss was about. According to them, Mama Ruby was like a lot of the down-home southern matriarchs we interacted with.

My road to success contained numerous detours. I endured whuppings, scoldings, and ridicule when I was a child for "fiddling around with a typewriter trying to be a writer" when I should have been reading the Bible or doing my chores. When I got older, the naysayers tried to discourage me even more. They strongly advised me to pursue a future with sensible things: a husband, motherhood, church, recipes, and a "real" job (post office worker, cashier, waitress, etc.). I am grateful for their input over the years. My relatives and other people in my life unwittingly gave me mountains of rich material to work with!

I am proud to release *The Upper Room* again.

Peace and blessings,

Mary Monroe

PART ONE

1

Dotted with thick forests of gray cypress, tulip, and magnolia, the territory known as Florida rests vaingloriously amid opalescent southern waters. Wild, long-stemmed flowers sway gently in the summer breeze, as damp moss that seems to fall from the sky clings to the trees. Along the Tamiami Trail across Florida's Everglades, alligators sun themselves on the banks, ready to scramble into the muddy water at the slightest provocation.

Maureen Montgomery was born in Silo, near the Everglades, on a humid evening in July during dog days, that period of inactivity between early July and early September when the sultry summer weather comes to the northern hemisphere. It was so warm that day that the lazy alligators, seduced by pleasure, lay lined up along the swamp banks in orderly fashion, waiting.

In the midst of the swamp stood a crudely built shanty. Inside, on a living room sofa, lay a woman who was almost as big around as she was tall. Ruby Montgomery, wearing a long, shapeless black flannel duster, rested on her side sipping her twelfth can of beer that day, a thirty-year-old black woman with a round face, small brown eyes, heavy black eyebrows, and generous lips. She had a nose that was too wide for her to be considered handsome.

Her house smelled of boiled pork and steamed cabbage.

She had just lit the coal-oil lamps, and the dim light illuminated the walls of the living room with huge distorted shadows. The furniture was cheap and shabby, but everything was neatly arranged, for Orderliness and Godliness were part of southern tradition. An immaculate home, no matter how humble and plain, would surely please the Lord, it was preached in southern churches. Ruby tried to live up to the Lord's expectations, most of the time.

Outside, a chorus of barking coon dogs challenged the sweet calls of a remarkably fine lot of little birds: the mockingbird, the blue jay, the woodpecker. In the sky above, a broad-winged turkey buzzard made a swooping, whistling sound. Not too far away, in a desolate swamp, a panther cried plaintively beneath the hot Florida sun. In the dense huckleberry patch beyond the palmetto jungles to the north, a small black bear ambled about in search of its mate. The day was coming to a dramatic close; now only a sleeve of orange sunlight separated the horizon from the heavens, and darkness was descending rapidly. A great hoot owl, the nocturnal lord of the South, perched anxiously atop a moss-draped tree outside Ruby's ramshackle house, a house almost hidden behind a knot of jasmine bushes. The hoot owl circled the house twice, then reluctantly returned to the moss-draped tree and waited.

The knocking at the front door was low at first. Ruby sat up on the sofa, annoyed by the noisy creatures outside. The knocking added to her irritation.

"Virgil!" she yelled.

There was no answer. Ruby waited a full minute before speaking again.

"I wonder where that simple boy of mine is," she said to herself. She swallowed the last of the beer, draining the can to make sure she didn't miss a drop of the precious beverage, and wiped her liver-colored lips with the tail of her duster. "Oomph . . . wonder where my teeth could be," she murmured, looking around the room. She carefully lifted a mayonnaise jar lid from the floor. In it, a pair of dull, pink-gummed false teeth lay upside down. Ruby examined the teeth, looking at them for a long time before clumsily inserting both plates in her mouth. She clamped down and ground rhythmically, securing the teeth in place. "Now," she said, as if proud of her accomplishment.

"Virgil!" Ruby yelled again, looking around the room. She felt her chest, where she carried a cross and a switchblade at all times.

A frail, light-skinned boy of eleven, with gray eyes and wavy black hair, appeared in the doorway between the living room and the kitchen. He was a reasonably attractive child with a small nose and thin lips. His square, angry face displayed a continent of dark brown freckles.

"What you want now, Mama Ruby? Seem like everytime I get me in a comfortable position, you start to meddle me. Virgil, get me a beer. Virgil, let the dog outside. Virgil, get me a beer. Virgil, change the channel on the TV set. Virgil, get me a beer—"

"Shet up, boy," Ruby said, slapping her thigh with her hand and stomping her foot.

"Yes, ma'am," Virgil muttered. His denim overalls were way too loose for his slender frame. He was shoeless, and his long, dusty feet were hard and reptilian, with curled toenails almost two inches long.

"Somebody at the door, sugar. Go answer it. I'm too tired to get up."

"Mama Ruby, I'm tired too. And I ain't your slave," Virgil whined. "You been pesterin me all evenin."

"Answer the door, boy."

"But, Mama Ruby—"

"It liable to be that ole bill collector from the grocery store again. Or the candy man what we owe for the peanut brittle. Could even be old man Parker comin to collect rent, which we ain't got."

"It could be just about anybody, Mama Ruby. You know how you is," Virgil said.

Ruby remained silent for a moment, thinking about what her son had said as if it were a startling revelation. She looked at him and sighed, shrugging her huge shoulders and shaking her head slowly.

"Praise the Lord." Ruby set the empty beer can on the floor and rose up from the sofa with great difficulty. Virgil ran across the room to assist her. He grabbed her arm to steady her, almost falling himself, for even with years of practice, balancing this elephantine woman was no easy feat. The boy's arms ached and he gasped.

"Have mercy on my soul," he said, cursing his strain.

"Thank you, son." Ruby smoothed her duster along the sides of her thighs. "Now, go answer the door. Tell whoever it is I'm at the church or somethin. I'm sho nuff tired and I don't want to see no more human beins this evenin." Ruby waddled swiftly across the room on into the kitchen. Virgil giggled and tiptoed to the front window. He pulled back the drapes and peeked out.

"Mama Ruby, I don't see nobody!" he shouted over his shoulder.

The knocking continued, louder.

"Who it is, Virgil?" Ruby hollered from the kitchen, peeking from behind a large white cabinet that sat next to the sink. "Ax who it is, boy!"

"Who it is?!" Virgil shouted toward the door.

"It's me, yall." It was the small, whining voice of a girl child.

"In the name of the Lord! What you want this time of evenin, Alice Mae? I just left your house a little while ago. What you lookin for now, trouble?"

"If she is, she come to the right place!" Ruby roared, walking back into the living room. She stood in the middle of the floor with her arms folded.

"My mama say to send Mama Ruby to her. She sho nuff sick. The devil done put somethin on her a doctor can't take off," the voice outside said.

"Sho nuff?" Virgil asked. He lifted the window wide enough to stick his head out.

"My mama sick as a dog. She say what she got she wouldn't wish on Judas. She need Mama Ruby. I think she fixin to up and die," Alice Mae replied.

"Come on in this house, sweetie," Virgil said. "Come on in before them mosquitoes eat you alive." He closed the window and went to open the door. A tiny, fair-skinned black girl of four with thick auburn hair stood timidly on the porch. She had her thumb in her mouth and it was obvious she had been crying. There were tear streaks on her sand-covered face and her nose was red and snotty.

"Un-ass that thumb, girl! You want your lips to end up lookin like goldfish lips?" Virgil bellowed, stomping his foot. "Do you?"

"No," the child said, removing her thumb from her mouth. She had on a soiled flower-sack smock and a pair of man's tennis shoes. She was thin, but uncommonly pretty. Her nose was aquiline and her lips narrow. She had large, light blue eyes with long thick black lashes that gave her face an angelic appearance. Her father was an Irish grocery store owner in Miami whom her mother had had problems paying on time.

"Come on in the house, and praise the Lord," Ruby said.

Alice Mae stumbled in. As soon as she was close enough, Ruby leaned down and wiped her nose with the tail of her duster. "Now, praise the Lord like I told you."

"Praise the Lord," Alice Mae sighed mechanically.

"Bless your soul. You ought to give thanks and praise every day. That way, you'll be blessed. Now, what's the matter with your mama? Her baby's fixin to come, ain't it?" Ruby said. "I knowed today was the day!"

"Yes ma'am," Alice Mae agreed, nodding her head vigorously. She stood watching with interest as Ruby ran across the floor and stepped into a pair of limp, flat brown moccasins sitting near the back of the room. The whole floor shook when Ruby moved across it. Virgil now occupied the sofa and lay with one leg tossed carelessly across the arm.

"Get your leg off the arm of my good couch, boy," Ruby growled, glaring at him. She sighed and brushed off her duster as Virgil obeyed silently. She pulled a red bandanna from the pocket of her frock and tied it neatly around her thick, knotty black hair. "Boy, find me my teeth."

"Good gracious alive, Mama Ruby! You already got your teeth in," Virgil said. Ruby felt around inside her mouth with her finger.

"Oh."

"Mama Ruby, can I play with your teeth?" Alice Mae asked.

"Say what? Girl, you must be out of your mind! My teeth ain't nothin to play with!" Ruby shouted, frightening the child.

Alice Mae turned quickly to Virgil, whose eyes darted from side to side.

"But Virgil let me play with em all the time when you get drunk and they fall out," Alice Mae said.

Ruby gasped and ran across the floor with her fist poised. She slid her knuckles across the side of Virgil's face.

"Aaaarrrggghhh!" he screamed, leaping up from the sofa.

"Don't you never mess with my teeth no more," Ruby told him, shaking her finger in his face. Tears slid down Virgil's cheeks as he whimpered softly, rubbing the side of his face.

"Yes, ma'am," he mumbled. He turned to Alice Mae and gave her a murderous look.

"And you better not tetch a hair on Alice Mae's head for tellin me. That clear?"

"Yes, Mama Ruby," came the meek reply.

"Mama Ruby, yall got any more goobers?" Alice Mae inquired.

"In the pantry, lamb. In the same bowl with the pecans and nigger toes." Ruby replied. She leaned down to pick up a broom off the floor and used it to chase a hen from the living room into the kitchen. "Virgil," she continued, on her way out the door. "You tend to my pans on the stove. Don't you let my cabbage and salt pork burn. And you might as well keep Alice Mae here with you. She'll just be in the way while I'm tendin to her mama, with all them other kids there already. You hear me, boy?" Instead of answering, Virgil waved his hand at Ruby as she rushed from the house and off the porch. Her big heavy feet ground into the sand as she lurched across her front yard to the narrow pathway leading to the other side of the bayou where Othella Johnson lived, Alice Mae's mother and Ruby's best friend.

2

Ruby, the seventh daughter of a preacher, and Othella, the illegitimate daughter of a notorious Cajun queen, had been best friends since childhood. Both had been born and raised in Shreveport, Louisiana, and had used World War II as an excuse to drop out of school, leave home at age fifteen, and latch onto servicemen.

"My mama told me to my face, when you get through with me, Othella, I'm goin to have a mess on my hands," Ruby told Othella during their train ride to New Orleans in the winter of 1941. "Mama say we ain't goin to find us no soldier-man husbands."

"We goin to live it up first," Othella said. "Then I'll find us the best husbands looks can buy."

A stout teenager, who had been carrying a switchblade since the age of eight, Ruby realized the advantages of her association with Othella. Othella was beautiful and clever, a resourceful young girl often accused of having "white folks' sense." Drawn by her beauty and brains, men and money came easily to Othella. But it was Ruby's brawn and villainy that kept Othella out of serious trouble.

"Ruby Jean Upshaw, I am fixin to show you how to live! When I get through with you, you ain't goin to know your head from your feet. I ain't got all this Cajun blood in me for nothin.

First off, I got a notion we could make a killin if we could get set up in one of them sportin houses in the District soon as we blow into New Orleans. I know this old Irish madam name Miss Mo'reen my mama use to turn tricks for. Old Miss Mo'reen could probably use a couple of brown cookies like us, huh?"

"Sho nuff!" Ruby said eagerly.

Now New Orleans was a wild town and the bordellos were booming with business. But it was Othella's exotic beauty— golden skin, large black eyes, slim body, and long black hair— that the District madams were interested in, not Ruby's plain, moon-shaped face, short knotty hair, and bell-shaped body.

"You get us a job yet?" Ruby asked, greeting Othella just re- turning to the small, dark room they had rented in a musty boardinghouse on St. Jacques Square. They had been in town four days introducing themselves around. Aware that Ruby was a handicap, but not telling her, Othella made Ruby stay in the room while she visited the madams who had not yet rejected them. Because once the madams saw Ruby, they lost interest in Othella. Finally, after a week, fifty-four-year-old Maureen O'Leary took them in. Realizing what a salable package Othella was, and recalling all the business her mother had brought in, Mau- reen gladly accepted Ruby into her house as part of the deal.

"How come you didn't come to me first, Othella?" Maureen asked, running her pale fingers through Othella's long dark hair.

"I guess I wanted to start at the bottom and work my way up, Miss Mo'reen," Othella confessed. "But it wasn't so easy, me gettin Ruby work too. . . ."

"Well . . . don't worry about her yet. Lord knows she ain't no bathin beauty . . . feet like pie pans . . . fat . . . woo!" Miss Mau- reen exclaimed, shaking her head.

But Ruby surprised them; she became popular among the male visitors. It was not long before Ruby became Maureen's fa- vorite girl.

"Ruby, you got spunk. You goin to go a long way in life. I'm so glad Othella brought you out here to me," Miss Maureen in- formed Ruby after one busy week.

After only three months, Ruby and Othella left Miss Mau- reen's place and joined a traveling carnival from Silo, Florida. Othella sold balloons and Ruby carried water.

"I declare, Othella, you is sho nuff smart. First gettin us jobs in New Orleans. Now you done got us in good with the carnival circuit. You *is* got white folks' sense!"

"Ruby Jean, I got too much good sense for my own good, true enough, but you the one with all the glory. Yep . . . you got the power and the glory."

Ruby considered what Othella said.

"Must be my Christian nature," she sighed, smiling broadly. "What we goin to do after the carnival?"

"Don't you worry none. I'll think of somethin good for us to do next."

3

"I think I'm ready to settle down with me a husband," Ruby said longingly, as she and Othella worked alongside one another in a sugar-cane field one blazing hot day after only a few months in Florida.

"OK, Ruby Jean. I'll see what I can do," Othella sighed.

Taking care of Ruby's needs had become a full-time chore. Jobs, men, places to live. Whenever Ruby had trouble with anything, Othella always came to her rescue.

"I don't know what would become of me if I didn't have you, Othella," Ruby said on her wedding day. Othella had introduced her to Roy Montgomery, a local bootlegger, and within a month he had proposed.

Ruby's happiness was short-lived. She had married a philanderer who often left her for days at a time.

Othella had married a traveling salesman and this added to Ruby's depression, as Othella had little time to spend with her anymore.

One afternoon while babysitting for a white family in their home, Ruby, who was pregnant, saw her husband driving down the street with his arm around a woman. Ruby left the children and took out after Roy. She caught up with him in a honky-tonk at the end of the street and shot him dead. She was acquitted of murdering Roy but was sentenced to a month and a day in the county jail for leaving the white kids in the house alone.

Later that year Ruby gave birth to Virgil. Othella was now without her man, as he had gone on a selling trip one week and never returned. She gave birth to her first son shortly after Ruby had had Virgil.

"Just imagine us havin babies this close to one another," Othella smiled proudly.

"It's the Lord's doin," Ruby replied.

"Ain't it so."

"Just one little thing . . ."

"What's that, Ruby Jean?"

"I kind of wanted me a little girl."

"Well, maybe your next one will be a girl."

"I sho nuff hope so."

"Remember how you use to go up side my head when we was kids and take my girl dolls?" Othella said.

"I remember."

"And I would always break down and give em to you."

"Yeah . . . every time."

"It seemed like I always had somethin you wanted, huh, Ruby Jean?"

"Sho did . . ." Ruby agreed, looking deep into Othella's eyes.

4

The years passed quickly. Before Ruby and Othella knew it, they were thirty.

"And I *still* ain't got me no daughter," Ruby lamented.

"Well it sho ain't because you ain't been tryin," Othella reminded her, adding, "Shoot, you just barely feedin you and Virgil. Your little social security check can't stand another mouth to feed."

"I don't care . . . I still want me one," Ruby said.

The women lived beggardly lives. Othella worked in the fields most of the time and did domestic work when it was available. Ruby collected a social security check.

Because of her poor eating habits, Ruby developed a gum disease and lost all her teeth within a month. The cost of a pair of false teeth sickened her.

"Satan sho like to pile a load on me," Ruby complained after receiving a threatening letter from a lawyer regarding nonpayment of her dental bill. "I need a man to live good!"

"Or a million dollars," Othella added.

There had been many men in Othella's life over the last fourteen years. She now had eight children, all with different fathers. Ruby had delivered the last six babies. Now, experiencing her most difficult pregnancy, Othella depended on Ruby more than ever.

They had been sitting on Othella's front porch drinking beer that afternoon in July when Othella's labor started.

"Mama Ruby, you reckon I'll make it through the night? My labor usually don't get real bad until after my tenth hour."

"You'll be lucky to make it through the dinner hour. We got a mess on our hands this time. You been sick every other day since you got pregnant. When the pains start to comin every ten minutes, send one of the kids to get me," Ruby said as she was about to leave.

"Don't go yet, Mama Ruby. Stay and set with me a while. I need somebody to talk to. I'm feelin right de'pressed."

"Othella, you ain't got no reason in the world to be de'pressed. You got you all these fine children. This lovely house. Men comin from every direction. And talk about pretty—girl, you sharp as a tack!"

"You know how heavy my load is? What good is a big bunch of kids to me when I work from sun up to sun down five days a week just to feed em? You think I like workin in that cane field? And them beans—woo! Stringin beans is something they can't get the chain gang to do no more! And my men friends? Where is they when I need em? Like now? Where is the one what rolled off top me and left me with this baby what now kickin my tail right and left? You tell me I ain't got nothin to be de'pressed about?"

"Well, it could be a whole lot worse. You could be struck by lightnin and paralyzed from the neck down from now on. You could get raped by a Jew, foreigner, or gypsy. You could accidental walk out in front of a bus and get both legs squashed. You could lose your religion."

"I declare," Othella said, looking Ruby over carefully. "I hadn't thought about all that. I guess you right. I ought to be on my knees right this minute praisin God."

"And another thing, as long as you got me, you got a friend. True-blue. I ain't goin to let nothin happen to you or them children of yours. Now, like I said, I'll help you with this baby when the time come," Ruby assured her.

"I know you will . . . but . . . just for a little while . . . lay your healin hands on my wretched bosom and soothe my broke heart. My man runnin off is somethin I ain't never got over."

Ruby sighed and placed her hands across Othella's chest.

"Lord, let this woman forget that scoundrel what run off and left her for dead. He's a low-down, funky black dog what ain't fit to tetch the *devil's* hem."

Othella closed her eyes and moaned as Ruby continued.

"Lord, I went up to Satan last Sunday and slapped him down where he stood with my powerful prayer. Now I ax you, will you let this woman here be in peace? Will you help us birth her baby when the time come? In Jesus' name I pray. . . . Amen."

When Ruby left Othella's house, she did so with tears in her eyes. For she felt she had delivered Othella from evil, as she left Othella with a broad smile on her face and not feeling the pain of her labor half as much.

Then, as promised, Ruby returned to assist Othella to deliver her latest child.

5

"Come on here, Othella . . . it's almost here . . . that's it . . . that's it. I can see the head. Woo wee!" Ruby exclaimed. She stood back from the bed where Othella lay, writhing in agony.

"Mama Ruby, lay your healin hands on me—help me!" Othella begged.

"You leave my healin hands out of this. This nature, what you goin through. My healin hands is for special occasions. And didn't I just lay hands on you this afternoon?" Ruby waved her hands high above her head. "You just better come on and birth this baby so I can get on back home. I got a cabbage and some pork on the stove. I leave that simple boy of mine by hisself too long, he subject to set my house afire."

"Oh, Mama Ruby, I can't stand this misery!"

"Shet up, Othella," Ruby grunted, gently slapping the side of Othella's head with her palm.

Othella gasped and trembled violently. Her legs were splayed and she clawed at the insides of her thighs.

"Oh, Mama Ruby—please do somethin! Get me a shot of gin! Call a roots woman! Do somethin!"

"Didn't I tell you to shet up!" Ruby placed her hands on her hips and glared down at the desperate woman. "Oh, Collette, bring me another beer, sweetie!" Ruby called over her shoulder. Within seconds a slender, dark brown girl of eight with nu-

merous braids came to the door of the bedroom and handed
Ruby a can of beer. Ruby snatched it and drank hungrily. The
girl disappeared as quietly and quickly as she had come.
   "Aaaarrrggghhh!" Othella screamed, arching herself off the
bed, almost folding her back in half.
   "Damn!" Ruby said. "Collette, bring me a spittoon." Again,
the dark young girl came to the door. She handed Ruby a spittoon and disappeared. Ruby cleared her throat into the spittoon, then set it on the floor and continued drinking her beer.
As soon as she finished, she set the can on the floor next to the
spittoon and five other empty beer cans. She wiped her lips with
the tail of her duster and sighed, looking at Othella with pity.
Ruby removed a limp blue towel she had draped across her
shoulder and leaned over the bed to wipe the perspiration from
Othella's face. She then wiped her own face with the towel.
   Suddenly, Othella's children entered the room and began
to move about.
   "Is Mama goin to die this time?" asked Babette, age nine.
She was the image of Othella, with the same tan skin and silky
black hair.
   "Naw," Ruby growled.
   "Mama Ruby, where you get that duster?" asked Job, age six.
He was a child with deep brown skin and catlike eyes.
   "I got it at a sidewalk sale in Tampa. Why?"
   "I ain't never seen nothin like it," the boy replied shyly. The
other children giggled.
   "Mama Ruby, what happened to your feet?" Collette asked.
"How come they so big and flat?"
   "Yall quit axin so many silly questions. You, Clyde, get me a
bowl of water," Ruby barked. Clyde was the oldest.
   "Yes, ma'am," he replied and darted from the room. He returned shortly and handed Ruby a mixing bowl almost filled to
the rim with fresh spring water. She grabbed the container and
dipped the tail of the towel in it. The children formed a line, all
staring at Ruby as she wiped her face, her neck, and her hands
with the towel. Then she quickly drank all the water from the
bowl. The children giggled.
   "Yall get out of here!" Ruby ordered. "Get out on the porch!"
   "But the mosquitoes is out! And it's fixin to rain!" one of the
children wailed.

"I said get out of this house!" Ruby shouted. She threw the bowl into the crowd and the giggling youngsters scattered, fleeing into the night. The slamming of the front door was drowned out by the screams of childbirth. The pain had become so intense that Othella passed out. Ruby shook her head, cursed under her breath, and then left the room.

"Don't tell me ain't no more beer," Ruby sighed. She was now in Othella's kitchen, frantically searching the ice box. She had drunk every can in the house. Realizing this, Ruby became alarmed. She slammed the ice box shut and ran out to the front porch. The children were catching lightning bugs in the front yard.

"Clyde, you and Collette run down the road a piece to old Mr. Hamilton and tell him I said to send me a few beers," Ruby hollered.

The children giggled again and all took off running down the dark road to the nearest bootlegger. Ruby shaded her eyes with her hand and watched until they were out of her sight; then she smiled, returned to the bedroom and sat down at the foot of Othella's bed.

It was two hours and six beers later before Othella regained consciousness. Ruby set her last empty can down next to the others. Othella looked up at Ruby, who had a scowl on her face and her arms folded.

A coal-oil lamp, burning softly, sat on a melon crate next to the lumpy bed. Under the lamp was a dog-eared confession magazine with a provocative cover. Under the magazine was a shabby Bible.

Ten minutes later the baby came; a beautiful, dimple-cheeked, brown baby girl with thick black hair, just like Ruby wanted.

"She was beautiful," Ruby informed Othella, biting her bottom lip to hold back her tears. "She was a girl."

"Was," Othella said, sitting up. "What's wrong? Where she at? How come she didn't cry none when she popped out?"

"Othella, you still got all them other kids—"

"Ruby Jean, where is my baby I just birthed?" Othella wailed, attempting to get up from the bed.

"Be still before you brain damage!" Ruby warned, gently forcing Othella back down by pushing her shoulder.

"Where my baby?"

"Othella, you just had a dead baby," Ruby announced.

The women looked at one another, each recognizing the disappointment in the other's eyes.

"Dead, huh? My baby come here dead, sho nuff?"

"Dead as a Jew's tittie."

"Mama Ruby, what you reckon happened this time? You reckon I been hexed?"

Ruby shook her head.

"This ain't nobody but the devil. That bastard been pickin on us for months. Ever since we got saved."

Othella looked at Ruby's face and frowned.

"But we get saved at least once a year. With all the backslidin we do and all. You reckon the devil got it in for us cause we been cursin him for so long?"

"Probably so. I guess I got too much glory and it's crossin Satan's wires. Like lightnin. Yeah, that's it. Satan wonderin how come he can't lay me out. He workin at me through you."

"Lord have mercy! What we goin to do?"

"Like I always do. I'm goin to beat the shit out of him. Tonight I plan to get on my knees and pray like I ain't never prayed before. When I get through, Satan'll be yellin uncle in a foreign language. Sendin us this here dead baby."

"Where is she? Where is my dead baby girl, Mama Ruby?"

"In the kitchen on the counter next to the ice box. She was a itty bitty thing. Couldn't have weighed no more than a pound or two."

"Sho nuff?"

"Sho nuff."

"Well I declare." Othella paused and closed her eyes. She rubbed her face, then looked up at Ruby again. "Mama Ruby . . . is it true what they say about you?"

"What?" Ruby asked, alarmed. She rose from her seat and moved a few feet from the bed.

"Folks say you can raise everything but hell with your healin hands. I seen you myself rub the croup out of my boy Joe," Othella whispered. "You straightened out Brother Hamilton's crooked leg what got crooked up in the war. You delivered my soul. You growed a rose bush on a bed of rocks. I seen you do it."

"I been blessed sho nuff," Ruby shrugged, faking modesty. "I don't brag about it. Much."

"Flawless. You is flawless, Mama Ruby. If anybody was ever able to help folks, it's you. Why you think I took up with you as my best friend when we was playin in sandboxes and just bein weaned?"

"You was smart, I guess. Shoot. I never denied your white folks' sense."

"Then you gotta help me. You got to do what you can about my dead—"

"I already tried it! I laid hands on the dead baby twice already and it didn't do no good. She sho nuff dead."

"You mean even *you* can't breathe life back in her? *You* is the Lord's pet nigger."

"And the devil's walkin stick! You forgettin how much stock Satan got in my soul? You know how I been battlin my tail off tryin to shake that low-down, funky black dog. Shoot. Jesus been at a tug-o-war with that baboon since the day I was born. Tryin to set me free."

"I just thought—"

"I can do anything I set my mind to . . . long as that low-down, funky black dog Satan ain't on my case. Now like I said, I tried to raise that dead baby with my healin hands but Satan say 'Hell no.'"

Othella blinked to hold back her tears.

"My poor little ole dead baby girl," she mumbled.

She closed her eyes and shook her head sadly. Suddenly she looked up again at Ruby. "Was she pretty? Was my dead baby girl pretty like all my other girls?"

"Flawless. She had your hair. She had skin that was brown like a nigger-toe nut."

"And you couldn't save her? I kind of thought you could do anything you set your mind to. You havin a hot line to heaven and all . . ."

"Well, the devil sometime disconnects my line."

"Oh."

Ruby watched Othella swing her legs across the side of the bed.

"Where you goin, Othella?"

"I'm goin in the kitchen to look at my dead baby."

"You ain't goin no place! You want to brain damage? I'll get that baby so you can look at her!" Ruby rushed from the bedroom and returned a few moments later holding the baby, which had been wrapped in a faded green towel.

"Let me see her," Othella mumbled, coughing.

"A angel if ever there was one," Ruby said, unwrapping the towel. She wiped tears from her eyes with the sleeve of her duster while Othella stared at the child's face.

"Flawless," Othella said and turned her head. "Take her away."

"Don't you want to hold her one time?"

"Naw," Othella said, returning her attention to the child. Othella was tired and anxious to be left alone. She wanted to cry. Her last child had also been stillborn. "I'd have given my soul for this child to have lived. I declare, I would have. Mama Ruby, please take care of her for me. The buryin and all. Like you done with my other dead child." Othella fell back onto the bed and breathed hard, thankful that her ordeal was over. "It just don't add up. Her comin dead. She seemed so healthy in my belly. With all that kickin and flippin and floppin and all. I even dreamed about her. A bad dream. I dreamed she was a happy little girl what got took away. Death or somethin."

"Nothin but the devil lettin you know he was sendin her here dead. I done told you Satan's a low-down, funky black dog! He the one responsible for me bein big as a Cadillac!" Ruby retorted, lifting one of her heavy legs for Othella to inspect.

Othella examined Ruby's leg and nodded.

"What about the beer?"

"What about it?" Ruby returned her leg to its place. "I wish I didn't have to drink so much of it."

"That the devil too? He the reason you drink so much?"

Ruby sighed and shook her head slowly.

"I'm a alcoholic," she admitted.

They got silent and looked at the baby again.

"Othella, let's name this one."

Othella looked from the baby to Ruby, then back to the baby.

"We didn't name that last one what come here dead. Why you want to waste up a good name on a dead baby?"

"Well . . . it's just that . . . this one different. The other one was a boy. You know yourself how bad I been wantin me a little girl. We can make out like this one was mine. You know, play like I gave birth to her." Ruby smiled crookedly, waiting for Othella's response.

"Mama Ruby, I can't do that! It ain't Christian."

"Ain't nobody but me and you got to know."

"God'll know. Satan'll know. All Satan need is us to do some more backslidin so he can go to meddlin me and you again."

Ruby let out her breath and looked up at the ceiling.

"I just want . . . I just want me a daughter," she cried.

"Have mercy," Othella whispered, watching Ruby's tears slide down the sides of her face and onto her bosom.

"Let me name her and make out like she mine," Ruby pleaded, looking in Othella's eyes. Ruby held the baby against her and swayed from side to side. "Please, Othella "

"Stop actin crazy, Ruby! Feed them kids of mine before you go back home. Hear me?"

"You goin to let me name this child. That clear?" Ruby said in a low voice, frightening Othella.

"I . . . I . . . don't know. Um . . . Mama Ruby, please go in my kitchen and hunt around for somethin for them kids of mine to sop up. Some buttermilk and cornbread. Or some molasses and tea cakes. Grits'll do."

"Othella, I ain't playin with you now . . . let me name this baby and make out like she was mine!"

"Lord, that's just what you use to say when we was kids and you wanted my girl dolls. Just before you would maul my head with your fist . . . uh . . . uh . . . if it mean that much to you, you can name her, Ruby."

Ruby's eyes got wide and she smiled.

"I'm namin her for Miss Mo'reen," Ruby said.

"I hope you happy. You write Miss Mo'reen a letter and tell her she got a dead baby named after her! Miss Mo'reen busy runnin her sportin house. You think she care about some dead baby named for her?"

"I don't care if Miss Mo'reen care or not. I don't care if nobody care. I can say I had me a baby girl I named Mo'reen," Ruby said, dancing around the room, cradling the baby.

Othella shook her head and laughed.

"OK now. Time for you to stop actin the fool you is. Feed my kids and go home so I can get me some rest. Tell that boy Clyde to get you a shoe box out the chifforobe to bury that baby in."

As soon as Ruby had set out food on the kitchen table and arranged the noisy children in an orderly fashion, she left Othella's house.

It was dark outside. Lightning bugs led the way as Ruby returned to her shack through the bayou. She stopped and looked up at the glowing moon, the shoe box containing Maureen held against her bosom. She kissed the shoe box and thanked God for letting her get this close to having her own daughter.

Outside her house, Ruby spoke to Maureen.

"You is my very own little girl. I prayed to get you and I got you."

Virgil appeared in the living room window and snatched it open.

"Mama Ruby, what you doin out there in the dark? What you mumblin about?" he asked.

Before Ruby could respond, Virgil came out on the porch holding a coal-oil lamp. Alice Mae followed behind him.

"What you got, Mama Ruby? Who you talkin to?" Virgil said, holding the lamp up high.

"Who me? Huh? Oh . . . I was talkin to these mangy coon dogs what's blockin my way! Shoo! Shoo! Get out my front yard." The two snoozing hounds ignored her.

Virgil looked at her suspiciously.

"You wasn't talkin to no coon dogs a minute ago. . . ."

"I was talkin to myself," Ruby lied, annoyed.

"Mama Ruby, Virgil went up side my head with a spoon cause I told you he let me play with your teeth," Alice Mae complained. "I got a risin on my head already."

"I'll get him, Alice Mae," Ruby said calmly, unlike her usual self. This made Virgil even more suspicious.

"Mama Ruby, what you got—aw damn!" he cursed. He held the lamp out toward Ruby and saw that she carried a shoe box. It meant only one thing. "Another dead baby I got to be up half the night diggin a grave for!"

6

"Is this here enough, Mama Ruby?" Virgil asked as he held out an armful of newspaper. They stood in Ruby's cool, dimly lit kitchen over a table cluttered with plates and pots and pans. They had eaten the cabbage Virgil had finished cooking while Ruby was with Othella. Bread crumbs, empty plates, beer cans, and assorted bones lay scattered about the table.

"Yeah. Little as this child is, she won't be needin that much paper to be wrapped up in," Ruby replied. She took the paper from Virgil and looked at him, blinking her eyes rapidly. He looked up at her and bit his bottom lip.

"What's the matter with you now? You standin here lookin at me like I'm somethin good to eat," he murmured.

"I thought I heard somethin. Like somebody cryin," Ruby replied in a whisper.

"Aw, you ain't heard nothin." Virgil waved his hand in her face. "And you hurry your slow self on here. You done had this dead baby layin around a whole hour."

"Did you walk Alice Mae all the way home?"

"I walked her to the clearin," Virgil answered.

"You was supposed to walk that child all the way home, boy! You want her to get snatched up by some maniac?"

"Mama Ruby, everybody say you the only maniac in Silo," Virgil answered seriously, with his hands on his hips.

Ruby looked away and thought about what Virgil said. She turned to face him again and quickly slapped him alongside his face with the newspaper.

"Boy, I did hear somebody cryin. You go take a look-see out on that back porch and see if that girl Alice Mae is out there. That clear?"

"Yes, ma'am."

Virgil went to the kitchen door and opened it angrily, as Ruby stood looking at him. He leaned his head out and looked around quickly. Convinced that there was no one on the back porch, he slammed the door shut and returned to Ruby.

"Ain't nobody out there. You must be hearin things, Mama Ruby."

"I know doggone well I heard somethin. Moanin and groanin."

Virgil gave Ruby a thoughtful look.

"It was probably your conscience," he suggested. Ruby slapped his face with the newspaper again. He only laughed and made a face at her as she walked over to the kitchen counter where the baby lay.

Virgil followed behind Ruby, stepping on the back of her heels. She turned to swat him with the newspaper again, but he dropped to his knees and confused her by snatching the tail of her duster.

"Get up from that floor, boy! We got work to do."

Virgil leaped up and stood next to Ruby as she bent over the counter.

"Where we goin to bury this one at, Mama Ruby?"

"Down in the bayou, I guess. Down there where we buried that ole meddlin government man what come snoopin around here last month axin questions about me and a stole income tax check. . . ."

"Oh. Mama Ruby, wonder how come nobody ever come lookin for that ole man."

"Oh they come all right. Another peckerwood with a bad attitude. Axin me them same questions. Plus axin me about that one what come before him."

"Hmmmm. I didn't know another government man had come meddlin you."

"Come tomorrow . . . I'll show you where *he's* buried. . . ."

Ruby closed her eyes and shook her head. "I'm out here in these swamps mindin my own business. Dedicatin my soul to the Lord. I don't know why folks come out here to meddle me. I don't mess with nobody . . . lest they mess with me. Nothin but the devil." Ruby opened her eyes and looked at the baby.

"How come we ain't puttin this baby where them other dead babies is buried? Othella's other dead baby. Anna Simpson's dead baby. All them other dead babies you done birthed."

"Cause I want to get this took care of tonight. These dog days. We was to let this baby set out all night she liable to bust wide open. Remember that time me and Othella forgot we had that dead rabbit in the chicken coop last summer during dog days? You remember how it swole up from the heat and busted? I know you don't want no busted baby to be cleanin up." Ruby looked at Virgil and wiggled her nose.

"Good God no! Ain't nothin worse than busted, rotted humans. Remember that time that man tried to rape Othella and we put him in the chicken coop?"

"Yeah. Just like that rabbit, we forgot he was in there. That sucker popped wide open. We couldn't get the stink out of these woods for weeks. I thank God it was the season of flowers then. Lilacs, magnolias, dandelions, and lilies perfumin the air," Ruby recalled.

". . . Mama Ruby . . . you ever . . . I mean . . . well what I'm tryin to say is, you ever think about them folks we done chastized? I mean, sometime at night I be layin in the bed thinkin about it. I use to have dreams about dead folks comin to haunt us," Virgil said.

Ruby shook her head and tapped her bare foot.

"Boy, I ain't done nothin Jesus wouldn't do."

Virgil gasped and moved back.

"But Mama Ruby—"

"But what?" Ruby said, with her eyebrows arched.

"Nothin . . ."

"What you lookin at me so funny for now, boy?"

"I guess I don't know all I need to know about Jesus, huh?"

"I guess you don't. Let me tell you somethin, boy. I carry Jesus with me everywhere I go. I always have. On account of that was how I was raised. I know I ain't perfect, wasn't nobody perfect but Jesus, but I apply myself to the Bible to a T."

"Remember that time we was comin back from. Miami and that spic gave us a ride?"

"The one what got to my house and sucked up all my beer then had a notion to rape me?"

"Rape you? I didn't know he'd a notion to rape you! Did he try to rape you, sho nuff, Mama Ruby?"

"No—but he wanted to. Why else would we carry him to the swamp? Me and you and Othella and Clyde."

"Oh. I didn't know no more than what you told me. You just made me and Clyde empty his pockets and dig a hole. Seem like we could have sent him on back to Miami. Him bein so drunk and all. I kind of liked that spic. He was all right by me. Give me a whole quarter. He give Clyde one too." Virgil dropped his head and stared at the floor. "Sometime, Mama Ruby, I go to thinkin. What if—what's wrong, sugar?" Virgil was interrupted by Ruby's frantic sobs. "What you cryin for?"

Ruby removed a handkerchief from the pocket of her duster and began to cry harder, wiping her eyes and nose vigorously.

"I've done all I could to be a Christian mama. I never dreamed my own son would question my ways. Boy, I do what the Lord tells me to do. I ain't never tetched nobody what ain't had it comin. That spic, he was better off dead. Couldn't speak no more English than a year-old baby. Now you tell me . . . what good was he to anybody?"

"Well, them other spics, they speak spic. I seen em do it. Plus the man said he had a woman and some kids somewhere. It don't seem right him gettin hisself kilt like he done. What all he do anyway?"

"He was a rapist for one thing," Ruby snapped. "What else reason did we need?"

"Oh . . . let's change the subject, Mama Ruby. I get a chill when we talk about the folks we done chastized."

Ruby returned her handkerchief to her pocket and cleared her throat.

"You know somethin, Mama Ruby, too bad we live so far from town. It would be nice to get this baby embalmed or somethin." Virgil touched the baby.

"We ain't got no time for all that red tape. You think we white folks or somethin? We fixin to bury this baby soon as I get her wrapped up. Poor little ole thing. Cutest little drink of water I ever seen."

"Sho nuff is. I noticed that right off when you opened that shoe box."

Ruby wrapped the baby as she hummed a spiritual. Once wrapped, the package resembled a small loaf of bread. As Ruby placed the package on the kitchen table, a colorful newspaper advertisement displaying kites caught Virgil's eye.

Ruby waddled across the floor to her ice box, where she removed a can of beer. She stomped and ground a roach on the floor with so much wrath the loose planks rose and fell awkwardly back into place.

"Where is my can opener, Virgil?" she bellowed.

"I don't know. You the only one what uses it; you ought to make it your business to know all the time." Virgil spoke without looking up from the newspaper. "Mama Ruby, can I have a dime so I can get me one of these here kites?" He lifted the neatly wrapped package as Ruby searched for her can opener. To read the advertisement better, Virgil began to unwrap the newspaper that contained the infant.

"What in the world is you doin, boy?!" Ruby shouted. She rushed back across the floor and thumped Virgil's head with her fingers.

"YOWWWW!" he screamed.

"What you call yourself doin to that baby?"

"I'm goin to wrap her back up! I was just tryin to see these kites better! Don't you go up side my head no more, Mama Ruby! Shoot! I got so many risins on my head from you maulin it! You do it again, I'm goin to learn you a lesson you won't forget!"

Ruby attacked the boy's head with both hands this time.

"YOWWWWW!" he cried, trembling and waving his arms about. "I declare! I ain't goin to sass you no more, Mama Ruby! Stop maulin my head!"

Ruby turned her attention from Virgil back to the baby. She quietly began rewrapping. Suddenly, she froze, her eyes bugged out, and her mouth fell open.

"What's the matter, Mama Ruby?!"

"VIRGIL, THAT BABY MOVED JUST NOW! SHE AIN'T DEAD!"

7

"Somebody comin, Mama Ruby. Somebody comin up the walkway!"

"Shet up, Virgil!" Ruby hissed.

Outside, the wind was blowing hard. The branches of the pecan tree in front of Ruby's house scraped against the side of the old building.

"Shhhhh. It's just the wind, boy." Ruby hoped it was just the wind. She sat in her living room in semidarkness, holding the pitiful infant she had wrapped in a freshly laundered flour sack. The only light in the room was provided by three large candles that sat on a crate in front of her.

"I swear to God, it sounded like somebody was comin this way, just itchin to catch us!" Virgil exclaimed, listening and looking around nervously.

"Wouldn't nobody but a stranger be foolin around my house this time of night. Or a fool. But just in case, go put your ear to the door. Let's be on the safe side. Go on now, listen at the door," Ruby instructed.

"OK, Mama Ruby." Virgil leaped from the sofa where he had been sprawling and went to the living room door. He placed his ear against it and held his breath.

"Hear anything?" Ruby asked, holding Maureen against her bosom.

"Naw." Virgil moved cautiously away from the door and stood in front of Ruby.

"You think anybody suspicion anything?" he asked.

Ruby shrugged.

"Like what? We ain't done nothin. Lately."

"We ain't opened the curtains none today. Folks been comin to the house and we ain't answered the door. And I know folks know we in here. Othella was expectin me and Clyde to catch her some crabs to make crab soup this evenin. You know how she is about crab soup right after she done birthed a baby, Mama Ruby."

"Yeah. I know how Othella is. . . ." Ruby let out her breath and gently lowered Maureen down across her lap.

"Run get me some more goat milk, boy."

"You want some more meal too?"

"Yeah."

Virgil left the room quietly and returned shortly holding a soup bowl containing goat's milk with yellow cornmeal.

"Hand it here so I can feed her some more." Ruby reached for the bowl, almost dropping it on the baby. "Boy, you make me drop this bowl on Mo'reen and kill her and the next hole we dig in the swamp'll be for you."

"Yes, ma'am."

Virgil watched as Ruby dipped the tail of her duster in the bowl, then squeezed it in the baby's mouth. The baby sucked hungrily. But after a few drops, the child slipped back into oblivion.

"She dead again and I ain't had nothin to do with it!" Virgil yelled, leaping about the floor. "Lay hands on her, Mama Ruby. You the one what raised her from dead in the first place when you fetched her with your healin hands. Lay hands on Mo'reen again!"

"Shhhhh! Somebody might walk up on us. The law come down on us, they'll be blamin everything but the last war on us!"

"But the baby dead again!"

Ruby reached up and slapped Virgil's face, then quickly returned her attention to the baby.

"Mo'reen, please don't up and die sho nuff on me. I need you. Please don't up and die," Ruby begged. She squeezed the baby's cheeks and the baby started crying. "Now," Ruby sighed triumphantly.

Someone walked up on the front porch. Loud footsteps, then heavy, frantic knocking made Virgil and Ruby gasp simultaneously. Ruby snatched the switchblade from her bosom. Popping out, the loud click that the blade made aroused the baby further and she cried louder. Virgil pulled a straight razor from his pants' pocket and turned to look toward the door. Whoever it was outside continued knocking. The baby suddenly stopped crying.

"Want me to bring em to you, Mama Ruby?" Virgil said in a low, flat voice.

She ignored him for a moment; leaning forward, she listened toward the door.

"I wonder if it's the law, sho nuff?"

"What if it is? What we goin to tell em about this baby and how come we got her?"

"We won't tell em nothin about this baby. The law ain't got nothin to do with us gettin us a baby. This ain't nobody's business but our own. Shoot. We can't help it if we been blessed with a baby. I don't question the Lord's doins." Ruby started to hum another spiritual.

The knocking ceased and the footsteps walked off the porch, back out into the darkness.

"You in here callin yourself hummin them ole hymns with folks still on the porch—you want to get us hung?"

"Boy, who you think bold enough in this part of the world'll even make like he want to hang me?"

"Oh. I'm sho nuff sorry, Mama Ruby. I should have seen your glory by now. Othella say you got glory what outshine new money."

Ruby smiled and lifted Maureen to her bosom again. Virgil looked at her with approval.

"When you goin to tell Othella bout her baby bein live and all, Mama Ruby?" His voice was firm and low. He put his blade back in his pocket.

"From now on, it's just you and me and Mo'reen. We ain't goin to associate with Othella and her kids no more."

"We ain't? We been thick as thieves from the get go. We goin to just up and act like we don't know Othella and her kids no

more? How we goin to get along without Othella? Shoot! Smart
as she is, she the one what keep the white folks off us. She the
one what help us make it in this world when we need stuff, on
account of she know how to deal with white folks. Remember
that time I needed my tonsils out and we ain't knowed what
doctor to go to? You said, 'We need somebody what would think
the way a white woman might. White folks got mucho sense.'
Anyway, you run to get Othella and she took a phone book in a
phone booth and went to callin first one doctor then another
until she got one what would cut out my tonsils on credit.
Remember that?"

"Yeah."

"Well, say I need somethin else cut out. You remember last
year how I had the pneumonia? And—"

"Othella found a doctor what would give me some medicine
on credit," Ruby finished the sentence. She tilted her head
back and rolled her eyes back in her head. "I been thinkin. I
could probably doctor as good as the next person. Me with my
healin hands and all. I could doctor if I was to put my mind to
it. We don't need Othella to find us no doctors no more." Ruby
looked at Virgil and blinked.

"Well, folks say you could do whatever you put your mind to
doin, Mama Ruby. Othella told me that one time you cussed up
a storm and it rained for six days straight."

"Yep. That was the summer of nineteen and fifty-one. We
had us somethin of a drought."

"I guess you could doctor. Still, I can't see us turnin our back
on Othella."

"I can do anything I set my mind to, boy."

"I know, Mama Ruby, cause I seen you do it."

8

It rained heavily later that night.

"Mama Ruby, did you cuss up this storm?" Virgil queried, as he got ready for bed.

"You heard me cussin around here this evenin?"

"No, ma'am."

"Well then. This rain ain't nothin but Satan's way of poutin. Poutin cause Jesus done answered my prayer and give me a baby girl."

"I wonder what Satan would do with his time if you wasn't you, Mama Ruby. Shoot! He wouldn't have nothin else to do!"

"Boy, a low-down, funky black dog like Satan can always find somethin to get into. If it hadn't been me, it might have been a weaker person. Somebody what ain't had no glory. The Lord knowed what he was doin when he fetched me. Shoot. Who else could have went up to Satan and called him a low-down, funky black dog to his face?"

"I sho couldn't have!"

"Well then."

"But it's a whole lot of other tough people in this world. I learned about em in history class. Hitler, for one. Caesar. Folks what captured slaves."

"Uh huh . . . and where is Hitler today?"

"Dead."

"Where is Caesar and them slave catchers?"

"Dead."

"I look dead to you?"

"No, ma'am."

"Well then."

"But what I meant was—"

"Boy, go to bed," Ruby ordered.

Later that night, Virgil was awakened by loud footsteps outside his cluttered bedroom. He fumbled under two flat pillows on his bed to remove his razor, and ran to the wall, where he clicked on the light. Ruby was standing in his doorway, holding Maureen. She was fully dressed and a bulging suitcase sat at her feet.

"Get ready," she ordered. "We fixin to haul ass."

Virgil packed his belongings in a shopping bag and they left Silo in the middle of the night.

Having no plan, and acting out of desperation, Ruby and Virgil and Maureen boarded the next Greyhound bus leaving Silo. An hour later, they arrived in Miami. Having just a few dollars, until her next social security check, Ruby went to the city's rescue mission.

"How long we goin to stay in this hell hole? How come we didn't go someplace excitin like Key West or the panhandle?"

"Look-a-here, boy. We is on the lam, can't you get that through your thick head? We ain't in no position to be showcasin ourself in no big city. Shoot. We got to lay low," Ruby explained. "I'm gettin too old to be dealin with folks axin me a lot of nosy questions. My blood pressure can't take it."

"I know what you mean. You ain't never been this old, Mama Ruby. Or this fat."

"I ain't *that* fat. I'm just a little on the heavy side. No matter, I am well proportioned."

"A elephant is well proportioned—"

"Shet up. We ain't goin to be here long. Matter of fact I went out to Goons to see about a furnished house this mornin before you and Mo'reen woke up."

"You got us a house already?"

"Yeah. And it's all but a palace. Two big bedrooms downstairs for me and you and a upper room upstairs for Mo'reen!"

Ruby was the only woman staying at the mission and Virgil

was the only boy his age. The others, reformed criminals with no place to go, homeless derelicts, and useless war veterans, found Ruby a pleasant addition.

"As long as we got a home, you got a home, Sister Montgomery," Brother Anderson Lee, the mission's live-in minister, said to Ruby as she prepared to leave five days after her arrival. The mission had given Ruby money to cover the first month's rent on the house in Goons.

"You is a man of God and you ain't goin to have nothin but good luck," Ruby informed the preacher, patting his frail shoulder on her way out the door.

"AND I HOPE THE GOOD LORD RETURN YOUR HUSBAND TO YOU!" The preacher had to shout as Ruby and Virgil headed for a waiting cab in front of the mission.

"AIN'T IT SO!" Ruby shouted back.

"MEN SO WEAK WHEN IT COMES TO THE FLESH!"

"THEY SHO NUFF IS, REVEREND—BYE!" Ruby slammed the cab door shut and squeezed Maureen against her bosom, cursing the fictitious husband she had told the mission people about: a dirty black dog who had mortgaged their home right out from under them, then left town with another woman.

9

Goons, a rural district on the outskirts of Miami, had less than two thousand people. The area was just a few square miles of orange groves, bean and sugarcane fields, and pecan trees. Most of the citizens were black and lived on the miserable migrant camps that provided their livelihood.

Ruby's new house sat at the bottom of a small hill off Duquennes Road, a dusty, serpentine passage that spiraled its way through Goons all the way to Miami Beach. Virgil was enrolled in a country school within walking distance while Ruby spent her first few weeks locked up in the house talking to Maureen in the upper room.

"You is *my* daughter, not Othella's. Jesus give you to me and I ain't about to give up somethin the Lord done all but handed me on a platter. Why else would he have us thinkin you was dead at first? So he could get me and you alone and glorify us. Anyway, he the one what put Othella in my path when we was babies ourself. Shoot. He knowed years later she'd give me you. So what if she the one what went through the labor to get you. It wasn't my fault. I can't help it if Jesus made her be the one to do the sufferin. . . ."

There was a cemetery not far from Ruby's house.

"Livin this close to a cemetery, we ain't got to be hidin dead folks in no swamp like we had to in Silo, huh, Mama Ruby?

That is, if we have to chastize any. What you think?" Virgil asked over a dinner of ribs and collard greens one evening.

"Boy, ain't you learned nothin bein my boy? If we have to lock horns with anybody and have to . . . you know . . . tetch em up, we'll continue to do like we been doin. I mean, it wouldn't be Christian to put folks what ain't had no funeral or nothin in the same ground with folks what is. There is all kinds of woods and swamps in back of this house, just waitin. Plus, I'd like to fertilize my backyard for me a cabbage garden. All we got to do is set back and wait on some maniac to get in our way." Ruby winked at Virgil and reached for another piece of meat. Several pies, all sweet potato, sat on the dining room table next to Ruby's plate. A can of beer sat on the other side of her plate.

"Before plantin season rolls around again, I hope," Virgil replied, scratching his chin. "Somebody fat. We could fertilize the whole backyard with just one maniac big as you," he said.

"Listen here, this ain't no time to be makin jokes. I'm talkin square business. What all you done told them folks at that schoolhouse about our business?"

"Nothin."

"My husband got carried off by a Jew woman. A rich woman from up north. His name was Booker T. Montgomery. He took off before Mo'reen was born. The funky, low-down black dog mortgaged our house right out from under us. That clear?"

"Mama Ruby, what in the hell is you talkin about?!"

"That's our story. That's what we'll be tellin folks. That's what I'll be tellin Mo'reen soon as she old enough to make some sense."

"Mama Ruby, you kilt your husband. My daddy. Othella told me the whole story. Why you makin up such a boldface lie?"

"Boy, this is square business. My man was carried off by the devil—"

"You said a Jew woman!"

"Same thing! Devil. Jew. My husband was carried off by a white Jew woman . . . with gypsy blood. Just make sure you keep the story straight. That clear?"

"I guess. I was just thinkin. I don't know if I want to be diggin more holes. . . ."

Ruby placed her silverware on the table and wiped her lips with the tablecloth.

"You mean to tell me if you was to see a man rapin me you wouldn't help me chastize him?"

"Well . . . it all depends."

"On what?"

"Mama Ruby, one time I heard a man tell another man if he seen you fightin a bear, he would help the bear. I think what I'm tryin to say is, if some maniac was to jump on you, he'd be the one more than likely needin help."

Ruby sighed with disgust and waved her hand at Virgil.

"You ain't got a lick of sense. Pass me another piece of pie."

Maureen had been fed and was now sleeping peacefully in the upper room.

Virgil lifted a butter knife off the table and reached for one of the potato pies that had not been cut. He cut the pie in half and handed it to Ruby.

"I still say we can put folks in that cemetery. That's what a cemetery for. Buryin dead folks," Virgil said, shaking his head.

"You so anxious to put somebody in that cemetery and just said you don't want to dig no more holes. How you expect to put somebody in the cemetery?"

"Mama Ruby, sometime you miss the point of what I'm tryin to say."

Ruby stuffed the rest of the pie half in her mouth and swallowed hard.

"Pass me that other piece of pie, boy."

10

The first month was the hardest. Fear kept Ruby awake nights. Seeing a woman with long black hair like Othella gave her chills.

"You need a man to take your mind off Othella, Mama Ruby," Virgil suggested. "Get out and make some friends for a change. You can't stay cooped up in the house in that upper room with Mo'reen."

Taking her son's advice, Ruby visited her nearest neighbors, Willie and Camille Boatwright. Willie was a bootlegger. He and Camille had five sons. All but an infant named Bobby were in prison. Willie worked days in the fields and Camille sat on the front porch with Ruby drinking beer and fussing over the babies.

"I declare, Ruby. I can't imagine your man runnin off leavin you and them children. What got in him?" Camille was a thin, birdlike woman with red hair streaked with gray. She was considerably older than Ruby, yet she regarded Ruby as a figure of authority. "What you reckon you ought to do about the scoundrel?"

"I done turned him over to Jesus." Ruby nodded and patted Maureen, who lay sleeping on her lap.

"And that baby girl of yours is just a livin doll. Ain't it a

shame your man didn't stick around to see what a fine job he
done makin her?"

"A doggone shame."

"And I ain't never seen no woman so devoted to her children. You don't let nobody babysit Mo'reen. Nobody but Virgil.
You wallowin in grief for losin your man, that's all. Is there anything I can do to help you pull yourself back together, Ruby? I
got a off cousin in Boca Raton."

"A off cousin? So what?"

"The best way to get over one man is to get you another. I
can call Cassius over here and turn him loose on you."

Ruby laughed and shook her head.

"Camille, you is a caution to the wind. I don't need no man.
I ain't about to leave my kids alone at night."

"Virgil ain't no baby. And I can babysit Mo'reen when you
do take a notion to get out and enjoy yourself. You keep settin
up in the house like you been doin, you liable to get house
fever. Like I said, if you want to go out and kick up your heels,
I'll keep both my eyes on them kids for you."

With Camille's urging, Ruby began attending parties on the
camps and soon men began to follow her home, making love to
her and paying her bills. Her beggardly social security check
and what Virgil earned working in the fields could not accommodate her increasing passion for beer and rich food, for she
was drinking and eating more than ever now, her weight
steadily climbing. Boatwright encouraged her to bootleg and
supplied her with watered down beer he had shipped in from
Key Largo. Ruby installed a record player in her living room
and played Bessie Smith records while her guests drank and
danced. One disgruntled visitor attacked her one night when
he discovered that the beer he had paid good money for was
mostly water. He ruined her false teeth when he slapped her
across the face with a metal object. Ruby grabbed the man and
slammed him against the wall repeatedly until he was dead, his
brains oozing onto the floor.

"Boatwright, clean up this mess," Ruby ordered. Her terrified guests shrieked in horror as she dragged the dead man out
her kitchen door to the bayou and tossed him in the swamp.
She returned to the living room. "Ain't nobody seen nothin,"

she warned. None of the people present ever mentioned the incident, not to her or among themselves. A few told Ruby where she might find a set of false teeth to replace the ones she lost.

Ruby did not buy another set of teeth right away. It was not until Virgil complained about her shabby smile and slovenly appearance.

"You with your loose mouth and gray hair, look like a old witch!"

"I like my gray hair . . . it gives me a distinguished look," Ruby said, running her thick fingers through her tangled hair.

"Well, I don't like your messed-up mouth. Specially when my friends come around and you go to kissin all over me. I know Mo'reen don't like you slobberin all over her face with them slimy gums. And how you get up enough nerve to romance a man lookin like a fat, old, no-teeth witch?"

Ruby pursed her lips and gave careful consideration to Virgil's comments.

"Uh . . . you really think I look bad? Wonder how come my friends or Camille ain't told me that."

"Cause they all seen you get loose on that drunk at the house the other night. Them folks don't want to end up out there in that swamp with him."

Some of Ruby's friends went out of their way trying to find her another set of false teeth. It was Boatwright who finally presented her with a pair he had picked up at a panhandle flea market.

"Willie Boatwright, I ought to kiss you all over!" Ruby grinned, when Boatwright handed her the teeth on a paper plate. The big, dark man with the shiny bald head moved away immediately.

"Uh . . . ain't nobody but my woman to be kissin me all over," he said defensively.

"Ha ha ha ha ha—Boatwright, you is the dickens." Ruby admired the teeth for two days before wearing them.

11

A week before Christmas, Camille had a massive stroke and died sitting next to Ruby on Ruby's front porch glider. Ruby grieved for a month and stopped going out. She went back to sitting in the house with Maureen.

"It ain't the end of the world, Ruby. Camille wouldn't have wanted you to go back to settin in the house. I want you to get you a man friend what'll carry you out and spend some serious time with you. Not another one of these hit-and-run jokers like you been latchin onto."

"But, Boatwright, I got me a man. Me and Roscoe Mattox from the Kaiser camp engaged to get married," Ruby protested.

"Roscoe is slow and lazy. He don't go nowhere but to church and down here hisself. You need a fancy man. A man what know how to go out and shake his tail feathers. Somebody like that Slim Dixon from Miami. I'm goin to put a bug in Slim's ear when I see him again. He told me to my face, you one of the finest looking women he ever seen."

"Slim told you that?" Ruby asked, eager and interested.

"Sho nuff. Matter of fact, I'm goin to drive over to his place and ax him to say it again."

Slim was a tall, middle-aged man with copper-colored skin and thin, greasy gray hair. His wife had left him twenty years earlier and he had no children. Slim was a frequent visitor to

Goons. On weekends, he bought beer from Boatwright and Ruby and danced like a teenager with some of the other drinkers. With a little encouragement from Boatwright, Slim asked Ruby to go out with him.

Virgil was glad Ruby started to go out once again. Slim took her to a saloon in West Miami that he frequently attended, a notorious place called Yocko's.

Yocko's was unusually crowded this particular Saturday night. While dancing with Slim, Ruby accidentally knocked over the table of a short, brown-skinned ex-convict named Mack Pruitt.

"You big black cow you!" Mack shouted. The attractive young woman with him covered her mouth and giggled as she and Mack leaped up from the falling table.

"What you call me?" Ruby asked calmly. She had stopped dancing and stood with her massive arms folded. A blue vein on the side of her neck wiggled as her anger rose.

"You heard me!" Mack shouted, showing out for his female companion. The bar's band, four sleepy Cubans, ceased playing. Patrons at surrounding tables moved away. Slim backed away quietly, hiding behind the bar, holding his breath. Everyone watched and waited. Nervous whispers and a loud wall clock were the only sounds that could be heard.

"That man's goin to hurt that lady," one woman whispered to another as they crouched behind a dusty, defunct jukebox.

"That ain't no regular lady—that's Mama Ruby!" the other woman gasped.

Ruby started to move toward Mack, her eyes narrowed. Her knees always knocked together when she walked and her enormous feet and legs were penguinlike.

"One other man on this planet called me a black cow. I carried him out to Squire's pasture and showed him what a black cow look like . . . that's where he at to this day," Ruby said, dropping her arms to her sides, standing in front of Mack.

"I say you is a big, black cow—and your mama one too!" Mack yelled, turning to his lady friend, who was having trouble suppressing her laughter. "I guess I told her, huh?" Mack said, winking at his lady.

"I'm fixin to beat you till you piss—then I'm goin to beat you for pissin," Ruby told him.

Mack stepped back as she reached for him. Quickly, he removed a .32 from his jacket pocket and started firing in her direction. Every woman present screamed. Every woman but Ruby.

She grabbed his arm and shook the gun from his hand. Then she tore the arm completely from his body at the socket.

Slim rushed Ruby home and insisted on staying the night to make sure she was all right.

"You sure you OK, Mama Ruby?" Slim asked repeatedly. He sat close to Ruby on her living room sofa, his arm draped lovingly around her shoulder. Blood covered the front half of her dress.

"I'm fine," she coughed. She was having difficulty speaking. Virgil hovered over the sofa breathing loudly, worried about his mother. Maureen stood in front of Ruby with a puzzled expression on her three-year-old face. Ruby looked at her and smiled. Candy and sand all but covered Maureen's pudgy brown face. Her long black hair was dotted with cockleburrs and leaves.

"I can't see how Mack missed you, close as he was when he went to shootin," Slim said, shaking his head. He scratched the back of his neck, not taking his eyes off Ruby's face. Her eyes were bloodshot and beads of perspiration covered her forehead. Slim became more alarmed when he looked down and saw that Ruby's hands were trembling.

"Ruby, I'm fixin to go up to Kaiser's camp and bring a jackleg doctor down here to see you. You ain't fine—just look how you settin here shakin! I'm goin to get a jackleg doctor."

"You better bring one for yourself too. I'm goin to coldcock you, if you come bringin a doctor down here and I ain't sick. Shoot. I'm some kind of doctor myself. Any doctorin I need these days, I can do it. Lest I need doctorin in a spot I can't reach," Ruby said in a low, weak voice.

"You do need a doctor, Mama Ruby," Virgil insisted, moving around to stand in front of her.

"Jesus is the only doctor I need," she replied with conviction. "Virgil, run get me a beer."

Virgil silently obeyed.

"I bet that gun-totin nigger won't mean mouth his maker,

which he is sho nuff on his way to meet right now," Ruby sighed.

"Shoot! Mack ain't dead! I called Yocko's and they told me Mack was hauled out of there—him on a stretcher and his messed-up arm on a tray! Shoot. That nigger ain't dead. They tell me after they got that nigger to the hospital, he set up like nothin ain't happened. Say he goin to hunt you and cut your head off, Ruby!"

"Who told you all this, Slim?"

"Old man Yocko told me. Soon as I got you back here, I run down to the camp to use the phone and called out there. I was scared the law was on the way out here."

"Ain't no law comin out here to mess with me. You know that."

"Yeah, but you never know. White folks is so unpredictable. Who knows? You kill up enough folks and they just might take a notion to come out here tryin to arrest you."

"I doubt it." Ruby coughed again and sighed heavily. "I got trouble enough without the law comin down on me. Me with the devil ridin my coattails. Shoot. My load done got so heavy I'm about to fall out." Ruby stopped talking and drank the beer Virgil had handed her.

"I'm comin back out here in a couple of days to check on you, Ruby," Slim said firmly.

When he did return, Ruby had taken to her bed with what she at first believed was just a severe case of gas.

"Virgil, get me my butcher knife. Slim, you get me a beer." Her voice had become a whisper. "Virgil, make sure you scorch the blade first," she added. Maureen lay in her arms.

"Mama Ruby, is you fixin to die?" Maureen asked with concern. She had never seen Ruby so sick that she had to be in bed. "You don't talk right . . . and your eyes lookin funny."

"I ain't goin to die. Least no time soon."

"Slim say that man tried to kill you. Why that man tried to kill you, Mama Ruby?"

"Girl, there is crazy folks all over the place. He was crazy and too blind to see my glory."

"You goin to get him, Mama Ruby?"

"Uh huh."

Virgil left the room and returned within minutes with the knife. Slim still stood over the bed looking down at Ruby.

"Slim, I told you to get me a beer," Ruby coughed.

"You ain't drinkin no more beer till we find out you ain't goin to get sho nuff sick. Shoot, Ruby. I ain't never seen you this bad off."

Virgil handed Ruby the knife and stood back to watch her sit up.

"Help me," she told Slim. He grabbed her by the arm and pulled her into a comfortable position.

Maureen climbed out of the bed and stood between Virgil and Slim as Ruby removed her gown and bra and proceeded to feel around her spacious torso.

"Look-a-there!" Virgil pointed to an unfamiliar spot on Ruby's middle. His eyes bugged out and he leaned forward to touch the dry wound.

"I declare . . . you is been hit, Ruby! You been hit sho nuff!" Slim shouted.

"Stand back," Ruby ordered, waving them away with her arm.

Maureen whimpered and Virgil quickly scooped her up in his arms and held her as they watched Ruby perform "surgery" on herself. She removed the bullet with her fingernail and the butcher knife and placed it in a mayonnaise jar lid on her nightstand. She had made no sound.

"Slim, Virgil," she began, pausing to look at Maureen, "Mo'-reen, yall, somewhere in this world is a one-armed *dead* man."

PART
TWO

PART
TWO

12

Ruby had gone to Miami to meet her cousin, Hattie Pittman, arriving from Baton Rouge on the six o'clock bus. Slim drove her to town in his pickup truck. She had ordered Virgil, who was now sixteen, to babysit Maureen, but less than five minutes after Ruby left the house, Virgil went to visit Fast Black.

Fast Black's real name was Wanda Sue Harris. She was a thin, dark-skinned eighteen-year-old who lived on the other side of Duquennes Road in a shabby little wood house with her widowed father and her five-year-old son, Yellow Jack, a child she had deliberately had by a Chinese tourist to spite her father. She was not a pretty girl; her eyes were too far apart, there were gaps between her teeth, and her nose was almost flat. She had just been released from a school for wayward colored girls where she had been sent for robbing a school teacher with a weapon she had made out of fish hooks and a bicycle chain.

When the girl was not in a reform school, her father never locked the door to his house, since when Fast Black was at home, the police visited frequently. After they had kicked down the door a few times, Fast Black's father, a humble, hardworking man named Zeus, stopped wasting money on latches.

Certain people in Goons did not allow Fast Black to visit.

"Don't let that fast girl in my house—she might get loose!" one woman told her teenagers.

"That Fast Black is forever in a mess," Virgil said to Ruby the day Fast Black was sent to jail for robbing the teacher.

Ruby had laughed long and loud.

"She ain't eatin right, that's all's wrong with her. It done drove her crazy. Shoot." Ruby laughed again.

Ruby knew that every time she left the house, Virgil went to visit Fast Black. Zeus worked as a cook in a Miami hotel nights and in the fields during the day, so he was rarely around to control his daughter, but he was a man with many good qualities. He saw that Yellow Jack was left with a responsible babysitter when Fast Black was on the loose. And since Ruby was usually the one taking care of Yellow Jack, he became Maureen's favorite playmate.

This particular day, Yellow Jack was in Miami with his grandfather helping him prepare advance meals for the springtime spate of northern tourists.

As usual, Maureen ruined Virgil's visit to Fast Black. Ten minutes after he had dashed up the hill, Maureen followed him. With her, in a meal sack full of holes, was her pet piglet, Le Pig, squealing and thrashing about madly. The pig weighed close to twenty pounds and it was a struggle for Maureen to carry him around with her, but she managed. She was rarely seen without Le Pig, either in the sack or walking along with her. He went to church in a picnic basket and was more pampered than any baby in Goons.

After Virgil arrived at Fast Black's and she had settled him in her living room, he recognized the pig's persistent squeals as Maureen stumbled up on the front porch. The front door opened and Maureen marched in boldly.

"Great balls of fire!" Fast Black yelled.

"Mo'reen, what's wrong with you, girl?" Virgil hollered, leaping up from the sofa.

"Sweet Jesus, Mo'reen! Ain't you got sense enough to knock on folks' door?" Fast Black asked angrily. She stood up and smoothed her skirt down. "And you look-a-here, girl—you get that nasty pig out my daddy's house before he footprint this clean floor! I don't go around here moppin for my health." She turned to Virgil. "You straighten out this mess!"

"Yes, ma'am," Virgil replied contritely. He shook a finger in Maureen's face. "What you got comin, I wouldn't wish on a dog!"

"Virgil, you got to come home and babysit me," Maureen whined. The struggling pig fought madly to be liberated. "Virgil, I'm fixin to—OOPS!" Maureen dropped the sack and the pig got loose, running through the house, his muddy feet leaving tracks all over the floor. Virgil and Fast Black chased after him, cursing Maureen. After Virgil caught the pig, he returned the animal to the sack and handed it to Maureen. Then he thumped her about her head with his fingers.

"Aaaarrrggghhh!" she screamed.

"Shet up!" Virgil shouted.

"I'm tellin you for the last time, Virgil, you better do somethin about Mo'reen comin here messin up everything. Otherwise I'm goin to get me a man what ain't got no baby sister!"

"Fast Black, you couldn't just quit me, like that!"

"You just watch me! You don't straighten out this girl, I'm goin to be spendin my time with another man! Shoot!"

"OK," Virgil mumbled, and backed out the front door. Maureen ran behind him, dropping the pig again on Fast Black's porch and leaving him to scramble after her.

13

Virgil stomped angrily down the hill with Maureen running to keep up with him.

"Wait on me, Virgil," she begged. Her short legs were no match for his, so much longer and determined to reach his destination. Her braids swayed in the wind. It was springtime, the smell of dandelions and lilacs filled the air. It seemed that every other day it rained. After the rain the wind, which was always mysteriously warm, would rush down their hill, lifting and scattering the sand.

"Doggone your soul, girl!" Virgil cursed, not looking back at Maureen. The wind suddenly blew sand in his face, obscuring his vision. He coughed, then stopped to rub his eyes. Maureen stopped with him, wrapping her arms around his legs.

"Virgil, carry me!" she pleaded, coughing. Sand had blown into her mouth.

"Un-ass me, Mo'reen," Virgil ordered. He removed her hands and arms from his legs and continued walking.

"You goin to get a whippin from Mama Ruby," Maureen informed Virgil, again running to keep up with him. She was a lovely child with a doll's face, dimples, large black eyes, and her mother's long, silky black hair.

"I'm goin to beat a scab on you when I get you home, Mo'reen," Virgil threatened, not slowing down as he turned

around to look at her. "I ain't got no time to be foolin around
with you and Mama Ruby. Shoot. I'm a man. I told you to stay
home in that upper room while I go pay a visit to Fast Black.
How you expect me to spend time with my woman and babysit
you at the same time? I done told you and Mama Ruby, I ain't
no babysitter. I ought to take a notion and join the army. See
how you and Mama Ruby would like that!"

Maureen blinked to hold back her tears.

"You don't like me no more, Virgil?"

"Girl, I ain't never liked you! You been trouble since the day
you was born. You is the reason Mama Ruby so crazy in the
head. We was doing all right till you come along. Mama Ruby
been nutty as a fruitcake ever since the day you was born!"

Maureen stopped in her tracks and stood looking down at
the ground. Virgil stopped and glared at her.

"What's the matter with you now, Mo'reen?"

"I wish I was dead. I wish I was dead if you don't like me," she
sobbed. "I'm goin to up and die!" She threw herself to the
ground, face down.

Virgil ran to her and forced her up, snatching her by the
arm. He brushed sand off her smock.

"Girl, Mama Ruby ain't no regular woman. She say you *can't*
die, lest she let you. She say you ain't never goin to die long as
she live. That big black woman is some kind of supernatural.
She is mucho crazy!"

"What you mean?"

"You'll find out soon enough. Mama Ruby ain't like nobody
else alive. She done changed this whole town. She do what she
want and nobody mess with her, lest they ready to die. Mama
Ruby done put a spell on Goons! Just like you done put a spell
on her."

Maureen gave Virgil a puzzled look and took a deep breath,
as confused as before.

After arriving home, Virgil swatted Maureen's legs with a
palmetto switch.

"Aaarrrggghhh!" she screamed and danced about the living
room until he sent her to the upper room.

14

Ruby's living room was large. Large enough to accommodate two big sofas, a striped easy chair, a chifforobe, and numerous other odds and ends. A large imitation oil painting of a black Jesus hung on one wall. A life-sized nude female mannequin, Maureen's favorite toy, stood against another wall. On either side of the mannequin were cheap drawings of dead presidents. A long, low dining table with six unmatching chairs sat in the middle of the floor.

It was just past seven. Ruby and her lookalike cousin Hattie had just covered the table with bowls of boiled duck eggs, a platter of fried chicken, bowls of vegetables, a slab of ribs, and several cans of beer.

"Have yourself a seat, Cousin Hattie. You been fussin around ever since you got here," Ruby said, seating herself at the table with Maureen on her lap.

Hattie sat down across from Ruby with a groan.

"That bus ride just about done wore me out," Hattie complained. She had just gotten off the bus from Baton Rouge an hour earlier and had agreed to spend a month with Ruby. "I feel like I been hit by a semi-truck," she continued, reaching for the eggs.

"Mama Ruby, don't forget to beat Virgil for whippin me," Maureen said, tapping Ruby's knees.

"I'm goin to kill him dead, sweetie," Ruby promised.

"And I'm goin to hold him while you do it," Hattie said. Maureen smiled and felt warm all over. Her smile turned into a grin as she watched Hattie toss duck eggs into her mouth and swallow them whole.

"I don't know what makes that boy's head so hard," Ruby said. She lifted a chicken leg, stuffed it in her mouth, and chewed furiously. "Got the devil in him . . . I guess." She lifted a can of beer and drank it down.

Maureen feasted quietly on a chicken wing.

Ten minutes after dinner had started, Virgil came racing down the hill. He stumbled up on the porch and fell again trying to get into the house in a hurry.

Ruby looked over at him struggling to lift himself from the floor.

"What all ail you, boy?!" Hattie asked, not looking up from the table.

"It better be the devil after him at least, for him to come tearin into my house like a wild man!" Ruby barked, rising. She gently stood Maureen on the floor and moved toward him with her fist poised.

"Don't kill me, Mama Ruby! I got some news. I got some big news! I just come back from Fast Black's house. Me and her and Yellow Jack and her cousin Loomis what just got out of prison and Moe Wilson from Kaiser's camp—we was all settin around eatin plums. The next thing we know, Moe jumped up and said I stole Fast Black from him right out from under his nose!" Virgil stopped to catch his breath again.

"Hurry up, boy!" Ruby ordered, placing her hands on her hips. Maureen and Hattie continued to eat.

"I say to Moe, me and Fast Black been sweeties a slap year! I say we even got baptized together. Which we did. I suspicioned Moe and Fast Black had a thing goin too. But I ain't started no mess on account of I know how Fast Black is. I don't want her goin up side my head with no mop handle. She done done just that once and all I had done was ax her what man that was what carried her to that party in Key Largo that time—"

"GET TO THE POINT, BOY!" Ruby roared, stomping her foot.

"Give me time, Mama Ruby. I can't never tell a story without you buttin in—"

Ruby rushed up to Virgil and thumped his head with her fingers.

"Yoww!" Virgil rubbed his head and continued. "Anyway, Moe say he goin to go up side Fast Black's head for messin around with me. Fast Black told him he better leave her in her grave cause she goin to pop her blade in him if he was to even *act* like he goin up side her head. He was drunk. He slapped Fast Black down where she stood. She jumped up and said ain't no man comin in her daddy's house and shamin her. She pulled out a pistol and shot Moe in the neck! Mama Ruby, FAST BLACK DONE SHOT MOE IN THE NECK!"

Ruby moved her tongue around inside her cheek, eyeing Virgil critically. She shrugged.

"Well . . . he shouldn't have messed with her," she said.

"The law goin to come down on Fast Black again! You got to do somethin, Mama Ruby!" Virgil waved his arms around frantically.

"Listen, I got a slab of ribs on my table right now with the meat so tender it's about to fall off the bones. I leave Hattie here with all this good food, she liable to eat my ribs, bones and all."

"I'll go down to the house to check on that shot man with you, Cousin Ruby," Hattie called out, with her mouth full of food.

Ruby looked at Hattie, then back at Virgil.

"You and Fast Black know I'm gettin too old to be straightenin out first one mess then another. You go tell that girl I'm on my way. Tell her to put that gun back where she got it and don't shoot nobody else till I get there. That clear?"

"Yes, Mama Ruby." Virgil turned and ran from the house so fast, he fell two more times before reaching the hill.

15

Hattie and Maureen accompanied Ruby to Fast Black's house. Yellow Jack answered the door, greeting them with a grin. He looked nothing like his mother or any other black person. His skin was lemon yellow. His coarse black hair was straight and his features were strictly Oriental.

"Guess what—my mama done shot Moe in the goosum-pipe and he bleedin like a stuck pig!" Yellow Jack shouted.

"So I hear," Ruby said, following the boy to the cluttered bedroom where the injured man had been placed.

Fast Black was relieved to see Ruby.

"Come on in, Mama Ruby . . . if you can get into this messy room. That boy of mine is about as organized as a train wreck. Loomis is fixin to move in and Yellow Jack mad cause he got to sleep in a chair so Loomis can have the bed. That's why he won't clean up this room," Fast Black apologized. She picked up a toy truck from the floor and sailed it across the room, where it landed in a basket of clean clothes.

"What's goin on up here?! Can't I have dinner without yall shootin up folks?!" Ruby demanded, stomping her foot.

Loomis Mitchell, Fast Black's twenty-three-year-old bull-necked, bald, dark-skinned cousin, had just been released from prison after serving five years for robbery. Having nowhere to go, as his woman had run off with another man and his parents in Key Largo wanted nothing more to do with him, he had drifted to Goons. He sat with his legs crossed at the foot of the bed where the man Fast Black had shot lay.

"Mama Ruby, this bold nigger had it comin," Loomis interjected, nodding toward Moe, who lay on his back glassy-eyed and frightened, blood trickling out from his neck.

Hattie and Virgil stood in back of Ruby. Maureen and Yellow Jack had disappeared from the house and were running and squealing in the front yard, beating one another with sticks, playing a game they had made up called grown-folks.

The bleeding man tried to speak but was only able to gurgle.

"Fast Black, you got a itchin to go back to jail?" Ruby asked angrily.

"The only way I am ever goin back to jail is if a storm was to blow me there. Another law come here to mess with me and I'm subject to—"

"Shet up, Fast Black! I fixed it with them white folks so you wouldn't have to go to jail for that commotion in Key Largo last week. You know every time you young folks go to Key Largo you get in a mess." Ruby paused and turned to Virgil. "And you— you ain't goin to Key Largo no more." Ruby looked at Loomis. "You, Loomis, you ain't allowed in Key Largo." She turned to Fast Black. "And you, Fast Black, everytime you go to Key Largo it take us a month to get you back Christian. Any of yall go back to Key Largo and I'll fix you so you'll never smile again . . . lest you smilin at me. That clear?"

"Yes, ma'am," they all said.

"What's in this Key Largo place?" Hattie asked.

"I don't know. But I'm goin to have Slim carry me there so I can find out. I been expectin trouble on account of Fast Black went there to a party last week and ain't been right since," Ruby told Hattie. "Now." Ruby looked at Loomis. "You run up to the camp to use somebody's phone and call the law. Ax for Big Red. Tell him I say come quick. Tell him I say I seen some nigger man fixin to rape a white woman and I can't stop him."

Loomis jumped up from the bed and ran from the room.

Big Red was a white Miami policeman Ruby affectionately referred to as her "connection." Generally the police avoided Goons with its confusion and bloodshed. Only a report of a white woman raped by a black man commanded the law's instant attention.

Simon "Big Red" Davies was more than a connection to Ruby. He was one of her closest friends. He was a stout man of thirty-five with flaming red hair and a passion for colored women, a commodity Ruby had supplied him with since her move to Goons.

Thirty minutes after Loomis placed the call, Big Red arrived on the scene.

"Can't I stretch out on my do-fold and enjoy the wrestlin match on the television down at the station without yall actin a fool? What kind of mess yall got goin on out here this time, Mama Ruby?" Big Red asked as he strode over to the bed containing Moe, who was now unconscious.

"We just had a little accident, that's all," Fast Black grinned.

"Shet up, girl. The man axed me," Ruby snapped. "We just had a little accident, that's all," she smiled, folding her arms.

Big Red nodded and caressed his chin.

"Who caused the 'accident' this time?" he asked, looking around the room at the puzzled faces.

"I sho didn't. Me, I just got here from Baton Rouge and ain't knowed nobody long enough to shoot em," Hattie said quickly.

Big Red looked at her, then at Ruby.

"Am I seein double or what?!"

"This is my cousin from Louisiana. Everybody say me and her look like twins," Ruby announced proudly.

"Like two nuts on the same billy goat." Big Red shook his head and whistled long and low. He turned back to Moe. "Now, who shot up this man?"

"Fast Black," Virgil volunteered.

"I might have knowed that. Girl, you been in trouble since the day you was born, huh?" Big Red glared at her.

"And I'm goin to be in trouble till the day I die!" Fast Black snapped.

"Well, what happened here? And be quick about it. I want to get back to finish seein the wrestlin match!" Big Red exclaimed, facing Ruby.

"We just had a little accident out here, that's all," Ruby explained.

"Uh huh . . . accident," Big Red said sarcastically. He removed his cap and ran his thick fingers through his hair. "That nigger dead or what?"

"Naw, Big Red. That's the problem. He just playin possum. We got to get him to a hospital sooner or later. The thing is, them white folks is bound to be axin a bunch of questions. You know how nosy them white folks in Miami is," Ruby sighed.

Big Red looked at Ruby thoughtfully.

"Let's make out like Moe here with his clumsy self dropped Fast Black's gun and it went off. Accidental," Loomis suggested.

"I say, let's make out like Yellow Jack was playin with the gun and it went off," Virgil said.

"Naw . . . now that ain't even believable. Let's make out like Mo'reen broke in the house, stole the gun, and it went off," Fast Black insisted.

"Yall tell a bare-faced lie like that on my baby and *I'm* goin to shoot somebody," Ruby said seriously.

"Loomis got the best story," Hattie muttered, tapping her toe rhythmically.

"I reckon so," Big Red sighed. He looked at Moe and shook his head impatiently. At that moment Moe came to. He looked around the room and tried to speak. Still, the only sound he was able to make was a gurgle. From that day on he was referred to as No Talk.

16

A week after being shot, No Talk resumed his relationship with Fast Black.

"You got a thing for No Talk or what?" Virgil asked her one day as they strolled down Duquennes Road. He had been hearing rumors about Fast Black dumping him entirely and devoting all her time to No Talk.

"WHY?!" she roared.

"... um ... I was just axin," Virgil replied.

Two days went by and Fast Black made herself unreachable as far as Virgil was concerned. Each time he went to her house, he was greeted by Yellow Jack or Zeus.

Everybody in Goons told Virgil to forget about her and settle down with a more stable woman. No Talk was even threatening to marry her. Since he was now eligible to collect a sizable disability check due to his neck injury, Fast Black saw him in a different light. This man who never could keep a job was now financially set for life, in addition to the fact that he would never be able to argue with her.

"My mama and No Talk went to look at a weddin ring," Yellow Jack told Virgil one time Virgil tried to see her.

"I done heard just about everything now," Virgil hissed. "The bitch!"

"He done axed her to marry him . . . he wrote it on a piece of paper," Yellow Jack continued.

"What Fast Black say?" Virgil asked. "She say she goin to marry up with No Talk?"

"She say she might and she might not," Yellow Jack giggled.

No Talk was a short, brown-skinned man of twenty-one with curly brown hair and boyish features. He lived on the Kaiser camp, also off Duquennes Road, with his uncle, Roscoe Mattox, who was Ruby's so-called fiance.

Depressed about Fast Black and No Talk, Virgil spent less and less time at home, where Fast Black was a constant visitor. And when she came, she usually brought No Talk with her.

"Where Virgil at today? I ain't seen him since he come home from school," Hattie mentioned one day.

She sat next to Ruby on the living room sofa. Both women were fanning themselves vigorously with rolled newspaper. Ruby stared at the can of beer in her hand as if she could not make up her mind whether to drink it or not.

"He went fishin with Big Red," Ruby replied. She paused to drink. "Virgil got the vapors on account of Fast Black is on the verge of givin him his walkin papers."

Hattie shook her head.

"These young folks," she complained. She turned suddenly to face Ruby. "Where is Mo'reen?"

"In the upper room. I suspect she got the measles. She broke out with itty-bitty red bumps a while ago."

Hattie continued to look at Ruby. She looked at her so long, Ruby became uneasy. She set her beer can on the coffee table and roughly wiped her lips with the back of her hand.

"What's the matter? Did a gnat light on my jaw or somethin? Why you lookin at me so strange, Cousin Hattie?"

Hattie shook her head slowly.

"I declare, Cousin Ruby. You doin so well out here in Florida. You done raised two fine children with not a penny from that scoundrel husband of yours. You reckon he'll ever get away from that Jew woman and come home?"

"If he ever come back to Florida, he better keep away from me."

"But wouldn't you want him to live close to you?"

"If that low-down, funky black dog was to move in a house close to me, he wouldn't live long."

"Oh. Don't you miss him?"

"Like I miss labor."

"Oh. What if he show up one day? What if he slide into town in a big black car?"

"It better be a hearse. With him layin in the back."

"You hate him, sho nuff, huh?"

"After the way that low-down, funky black dog took off and left me to raise two children by myself? I wouldn't exactly say he's a friend of mine," Ruby sighed, convinced that her lie was still credible. She removed a handkerchief from her duster pocket and started to cry softly.

"What's the matter, darlin?" Hattie rose up and stood in front of Ruby, gently patting her back with both hands.

"Cousin Hattie, I took a bad turn. I done run off from my daddy's house and ain't been back since. My man done done me wrong. Nothin never works out for me. I ain't got nothin but my children and Slim and Roscoe and Boatwright and Fast Black and Zeus to see after me. I'm a old woman and ain't in no shape to work. Them white folks in town, they signed me up for disability checks on account of my high blood pressure and flat feet and all this fat won't let me get a job."

"Well don't cry, Cousin. You been blessed. You got them children, this house, men friends. What more could a woman want? Gold? I should be half as lucky as you is. Me, I ain't got nothin but that little shack in Baton Rouge and my funky, two-bit job workin as a cook at the country club. I ain't got no children, no man, no nothin. Anybody need to be settin here cryin, it ought to be me."

Ruby stopped crying and looked at Hattie thoughtfully.

"And when you did leave Louisiana, you left with Othella. She was a good woman. Whatever happened to her? She come home a couple of years ago when her mama passed but ain't nobody seen her since. Where she at?"

"Uh . . . up north. Run off with a white man," Ruby lied.

Hattie looked down at the floor and shook her head vigorously.

"That Cajun blood," Hattie said, letting out her breath. "She come home with a army of children—pretty kids too and ain't

had a man since the first. I said to myself, Othella need all them
kids like I need to gain more weight. And loose as she always
been, she should have give them kids up to the home where
they could have been looked after. Women like Othella always
have a pile of children. Shoot." Hattie returned to her seat.

"I know what you mean. . . ." Ruby said in a hollow voice.

"She come paradin up and down the street in Baton Rouge
with them kids lined up like soldiers. Wench. I spoke to her and
she looked at me like I'd stole her pocketbook. I axed her
where you was."

"What she say?"

"She say, 'That's somethin that's unknown to everybody but
God.' See, she knowed ain't none of us knowed exactly where
you was till you started writin me a while back."

"What else she say about me, Cousin Hattie?"

"Somethin I couldn't make no sense out of. Say you'd listened to the wind one time too many and that the wind had
carried you off. Wonder what she meant?"

Ruby scratched her neck and gave Othella serious thought.

"Who cares."

Hattie turned to face Ruby and looked at her for a long time
again.

"What's wrong now?"

"Aunt Ida would sho nuff love hearin from you. Your papa
would too. And they would have a fit over them kids of yours,
Ruby. How come you ain't been in tetch with em?"

"I been too shame. After the way me and Othella took off. I
didn't want my sisters to pick on me about losin my husband.
You know how meddlesome they is. All six of em."

Hattie sighed and shook her head.

"Cousin Ruby, Cousin Ruby. You should have been writin
your family. Girl, you ain't got no six sisters to worry you no
more."

Ruby bit her bottom lip and looked at the door. She waited a
while before looking at Hattie again.

"What happened to my six sisters?"

"Flodell passed. Five years ago she fell off a porch in Baton
Rouge and hit her head on a cement block. Lizzie and Lola
married military men, and last I heard of them they was livin in
some foreign country. Bessie married a man from Chicago and

that's where she live these days. Just Beaulah and Carrie left in Louisiana," Hattie sighed. "They done scattered like leaves, your sisters."

"Lord, I got to go home and see my family. I want them all to see what a success I turned out to be." Ruby lifted another can of beer off the coffee table and popped the top with her teeth.

Hattie watched a blue vein on the side of Ruby's throat wiggle as she drank from the can, turning it upside down.

In the upper room, Maureen and Le Pig were performing acrobatics on Maureen's bed. Maureen was facing the window in the front of the room and spotted Reverend Tiggs sauntering down the hill toward the house.

"Come on, sugar!" Maureen said to her pet, scooping him up in her arms. She ran from the room and slid down the stairs.

Ruby was surprised to see Maureen suddenly show up in the living room.

"Where you goin with that pig and them measles, Mo'reen?" Ruby asked. She stood up and placed her hands on her hips.

"The preacher man's comin! I seen the preacher man come down the hill!" Maureen announced. "And look like he got the Bible in his hand!"

"Great balls of fire!" Ruby exclaimed. She quickly glanced around the cluttered living room. Beer cans and empty plates dominated the floor and dining room table. Old newspapers were all over the floor, the couches, and the coffee table. "This livin room look like a train wreck!"

Hattie and Maureen helped Ruby snatch up the cans and newspapers and plates. By the time the reverend reached the front porch and started to knock, the room was as neat as a pin and Hattie was spraying rose-scented room deodorizer.

"Well, look who's here!" Ruby yelled as she opened the screen door to invite Reverend Tiggs in. "What a nice surprise!" She laughed and embraced her preacher, almost squeezing the breath out of him. Hattie sat on the couch with Maureen on her lap. The pig sat quietly on the floor next to Hattie's bare feet.

"Sister Ruby, you sho nuff keep a neat, fresh-smellin house," Reverend Tiggs commented, looking around the room with his thick eyebrows raised. He looked up at the ceiling, sniffing. He was a diminutive man of sixty-five with gingerbread brown skin and hair as white as snow. His tiny body fitted nicely on the footstool that sat near the door. He crossed his short legs and placed his Bible at his feet.

"I believe in keepin a clean house," Ruby smiled, sitting down on the large sofa facing Reverend Tiggs, her eyes darting from side to side.

Reverend Tiggs coughed before speaking again, ignoring a hen that had come in with him, nibbling at his pants leg. "Look-a-here, yall. Sister Ruby, Sister Hattie, Sister Mo'reen. I come here to invite yall to the midnight revival service we fixin to have tonight."

Ruby and Hattie looked at one another.

"We got Brother No Talk on the piano this evenin. We got Brother Slim comin all the way from Miami to read the scriptures out loud. Sister Ruby, you the only grace missin. My congregation would sho nuff appreciate hearin some of your hymns. Ain't a sister in Florida can swoon like Sister Ruby, Sister Hattie," the preacher declared with a broad smile.

"Oh you go on, Reverend Tiggs," Ruby grinned, shaking her head. "I got a unfair advantage. Me bein so sanctified and all. I been walkin in God's yard all my life. Growin up a preacher's daughter and all."

"Praise the Lord," Hattie said in a loud voice.

"A man without the spirit is worse off than a Jew lost in a A'rab town," Ruby continued, shaking her head vigorously.

"Then you will join us tonight?" the preacher asked again.

"Why, Reverend Tiggs, I'll be there with bells on," Ruby promised.

"I'll be there too, Reverend," Hattie added. "Lord knows I am in need of spiritual guidance. I been in the storm too long! Wet and whiplashed by the devil's rain!"

"Amen, Sister!" Reverend Tiggs shouted, standing and leaping once into the air. Le Pig became frightened and ran out of the room.

"I had drifted away from the church back in Baton Rouge. Took up with all kinds of mens. Gamblers. Thieves. Foreigners. I suspect the Lord won't send me no husband until I cleanse my soul," Hattie said, rising. Like the preacher, she leaped once into the air, returning to the floor with a loud thud.

Maureen got off the sofa and leaped once into the air.

"Yall want me to tell Reverend Tiggs about that bill collector Mama Ruby shot at this mornin?" she said, looking from Hattie to Ruby. Ruby quickly gave her a stern look while Hattie gasped and covered her mouth with her hand. Reverend Tiggs was looking at Maureen with his mouth hanging open and his hand shading his eyes.

"Mo'reen, you mustn't tell tales in front of our preacher," Ruby gently scolded. She smiled and shook her finger at Maureen.

"But you did shoot at him. A white man. You said he was nothin but the devil. But it wasn't the devil—it was that same white man what come all the time from that store in Miami. Don't you remember? You shot at him. You let me keep the shotgun shells," Maureen insisted. "You said—"

"Mo'reen been delirious with her measles today," Hattie explained, cutting her off in midsentence. "Now what time you want us at the church this evenin?" Hattie folded her arms and tilted her head to the side, smiling at the preacher, who was still staring at Maureen.

Though he was sincere where the Lord was concerned, he was a gullible, naive man who was easily led. He heard rumors about Ruby, but he had always wholeheartedly believed her wild lies about jealous people trying to blacken her good name. Ruby, an avid churchgoer and a dependable choir member, gave Reverend Tiggs the impression that she was nothing more than a loving mother and a Christian.

"Reverend Tiggs, you don't believe I shot at no bill collector, do you? I ain't got nothin against nobody. . . ." Ruby's eyes blinked rapidly as she faced the preacher.

Reverend Tiggs turned slowly to face her. "Huh? Oh no—I don't . . . I don't believe you'd do nothin like that, Sister Ruby." He turned to Hattie. "I want yall to be at the church around ten, if it won't be no trouble. I'd like yall there early on account of I'd like to piece together some kind of agenda. With Brother Slim comin all the way from Miami and all," he said, moving toward the door. Ruby walked along with him humming a spiritual.

"Then we'll see you tonight." Ruby suddenly rushed the man on out the door so fast she caught the tail of his shirt in it.

Hattie and Maureen ran to the door and stood next to Ruby. They all waved at the preacher and watched until he was far enough up the hill that he could no longer hear them.

"Cousin Ruby, what about Zeus' fish fry tonight? Me and you been invited up there. Fast Black been in the kitchen scalin carps and cleanin catfish all day!" Hattie exclaimed.

Ruby bit her bottom lip and stared off into space. She had forgotten about the latest neighborhood gathering.

"Shoot! I had plumb forgot about Zeus and Fast Black puttin together a fish fry. And they was dependin on us to be there. I hear folks from everywhere comin!" Ruby let out her breath and shook her head. "Shoot!" She slapped her thigh and stomped her foot.

"What we goin to do? You just promised the reverend we would be at church tonight, Cousin Ruby."

Ruby had to think for a minute.

"I promised him I'd sing. I don't think he would mind so much if you didn't come. I'll tell him you couldn't come after all, on account of you had to stay home with the cramps and arthritis and whatever else I can think of." Ruby placed her hand on Maureen's head and sighed heavily.

"I want to go to the fish fry." Maureen laughed. "I want to see the grown folks fight."

"You ain't goin no place with the measles." Ruby thumped Maureen's head with her fingers. "And that's for tellin the preacher about me shootin at that bill collector this mornin!"

Maureen backed away and left quietly, returning to the upper room.

Hattie and Ruby sauntered across the room and sat back down on the sofa. Both groaned and breathed deeply.

"What we goin to do?" Hattie asked, snatching her rolled newspaper and fanning herself again. Perspiration slid down the side of her face and dropped onto her bosom.

Ruby wiped her own sweat from her face with the tail of her dress.

"You go. To the fish fry I mean. I'll go on to church. Later I might take a notion to come on over to Zeus' after church," Ruby replied.

17

L ater that evening, while Hattie prepared herself for the fish
fry, Ruby lay on the sofa eating from a bowl of pecans and
drinking beer.

"Have a good time," she called as Hattie rushed out the door
wearing a loud orange silk dress and white heels. Her thick
black hair was pulled back into a bun and pinned at the nape
of her neck.

Zeus met Hattie at the door when she arrived.

"Come on in here, Sister!" he greeted her, all but snatching
her off the front porch.

There was loud music coming from a record player in the
center of the small living room and about three dozen people
were crowded throughout the tiny house. A washtub filled with
cracked ice and cans of beer sat in a corner. Fast Black and
Yellow Jack were dancing together and causing quite a commotion.

"Come on, Hattie, let's show these folks how to dance!" Zeus
invited, grabbing Hattie by her hand. He wrestled with the big
woman as they moved toward the center of the floor, for he was
a frail man but had the agility of a teenager. His long, limp gray
hair was wet with perspiration and matted to the back and sides
of his head.

Hattie and Zeus attracted more attention than Fast Black

and Yellow Jack. The crowd clapped and roared with laughter, egging them on. People in the back of the room had a hard time seeing the lively dancers. One man, a man with one arm, managed to plow through the knot of people and get close enough to see what was getting so much attention. When he spotted Hattie, he stood stock still. A few years earlier, he had had a vicious fight with a woman in a Miami bar, something his friends would never let him live down, for he was a man with a reputation, a man who had been feared most of his life, half of which he had spent in southern prisons.

After the fight that had cost him an arm, Mack Pruitt moved to Tampa, where he lived for two years trying to adjust to his dismemberment. He was still a reasonably attractive young man with a well-cared-for body. When not in jail, he drove cabs, waited tables, and did janitorial work, anything that would please his probation officer.

Mack had recently returned to Miami, where he finally got himself another woman whom he could call his own, a plain Cuban woman old enough to be his mother. Every time Mack looked at her he remembered Ruby. Ruby was the reason he now had to settle for so much less than he deserved. Ruby was the reason he lost the woman he had loved for ten years to a whole man. She had admitted that his lack of one arm repelled her.

Mack didn't know who Ruby was, which is one of the reasons he had insulted her that night in Yocko's. The fact that the woman had literally snatched off his arm should have told him she was no ordinary woman. Now, looking at Hattie and assuming she was Ruby, Mack was determined to kill her before the night was over.

He left the fish fry and went outside, where he hid behind a pear tree in front of the house. Other guests approaching the yard paid no attention to the man sitting on the ground with his back against the tree, staring off into the night with a .32 in his hand, waiting.

18

"**O**h, Mama Ruby, where's my pig?" Maureen yelled from the upper room. It was late, almost time for Ruby to get ready for church. She was still lounging on the sofa. A pack of breath mints lay on the coffee table next to seven empty beer cans.

"Virgil carried him outside to use the bathroom, lamb," Ruby replied over her shoulder. The television was on, but Ruby was not watching it. Her mind was on the church service and Zeus' fish fry. She hoped she would be out of church in time to catch the tail end of the gathering.

"Yall know I can't get to sleep without my pig, Mama Ruby," Maureen whined.

"I know, Mo'reen. Just get back in the bed. Virgil's goin to bring the piggie to the upper room as soon as he gets through doin his business." Before Ruby could say anything else, she heard a commotion outside; muffled screams and scuffling on her front porch. Then she heard what sounded like a firecracker going off.

"Now what in the world is that boy of mine up to now?" Ruby rose up from the sofa and turned to face the front door with her fist poised. "Virgil, come on in this house and stop actin the fool you is!" Ruby was surprised when Hattie snatched open the door and fell forward onto the living room floor.

"COUSIN RUBY—I BEEN SHOT IN MY BUTT!" Hattie cried. Ruby ran to her. The door was still open, and she stopped dead in her tracks when she saw Mack standing on the porch with the gun in his hand.

Ruby was surprised to see Mack, but not nearly as surprised as he was to see her. The resemblance between Ruby and Hattie was uncanny. The man's mind went blank as he lost control of his senses and started to babble incoherently, pointing from Ruby to Hattie.

Ruby stepped over Hattie as she lay on the floor, terrified but not seriously injured. The back of her dress had a small red stain where the bullet had brushed her body.

Virgil was walking up into the yard with Le Pig in one arm and a pitchfork in the other. After the pig had relieved himself, Virgil had covered the droppings with sand. This was a nightly chore Ruby had assigned him ever since Slim had presented Maureen with the pig.

One could expect just about anything to be happening with Ruby Montgomery. To approach her house and see her chasing a one-armed man off her front porch, and the body of a three-hundred-pound woman lying in the doorway, was really not so out of the ordinary. Virgil said nothing, but continued to walk, whistling. He stepped aside as the man darted past him. Virgil saw the man had a gun in his hand. This caused Virgil to stop, looking from the man to Ruby.

"I don't know who you is, Mister, but I'd rather be in hell than where you is right now," Virgil said in a low voice. Ruby, running past, snatched the pitchfork out of Virgil's hand, knocking him to the ground. Virgil dropped the pig and it ran squealing into the woods. He stood up and watched as Ruby caught up with her prey just as he was about to run up the hill. She plunged the pitchfork into his back with so much force the prongs went completely through his body and stuck out his chest.

"Great balls of fire," Virgil mumbled. He shook his head and blinked, not knowing if what he had just witnessed was real. He sighed and shook his head again, walking swiftly over to Ruby. He put his arm around her shoulder and they both watched Mack stumble and fall on his side, landing clumsily in a lifeless heap.

Ruby cleansed Hattie's wound and covered it with witch hazel. Afterward, Hattie accompanied Ruby and Virgil deep into the woods, where Ruby made Virgil drag Mack's body by the feet, the weapon still sticking out.

Hattie stood next to Ruby. They both had their arms folded and their faces were grim. Hattie was breathing hard and every now and then she would utter a curse under her breath. Ruby hummed a spiritual. Virgil whistled as he dug a hole with a large shovel.

"Hold that lamp still, Mama Ruby. Shoot. I don't want to shovel my foot out here in this bayou," Virgil said angrily. "Shoot! I'm goin to up and join the army yet! I ain't goin to be nowhere around when the law finally come to haul you away, Mama Ruby. This here is nineteen and sixty-one. Not eighteen and sixty-one and the wild west where folks was expected to kill up one another the way you do. One day somebody bigger and badder than you goin to come along. See what you do then."

"Ain't but one bigger and badder than me . . . and he in paradise settin on a gold throne, surrounded by angels, puttin stars next to my name and blessin me by the pound," Ruby announced.

"Cousin Ruby, you is the dickens," Hattie laughed.

Virgil stopped digging and wiped sweat from his forehead with his hand. He leaned on the shovel and looked in Ruby's face.

"Cousin Hattie, don't laugh. Mama Ruby believe all that madness. Ain't no God goin to put up with nobody killin folks the way she do. Come judgment day God goin to need half his angels just to tell him all the devilment Mama Ruby done done."

"Boy, I got the strength of a nation . . . and just as much nerve!" Ruby exclaimed.

"Amen!" Hattie yelled, waving her hand in the air.

"I got A-one credit in heaven. I got a telephone in my heart with a direct line to my savior. I got the wisdom of a Jew. I got the glory of a saint. How can you stand there and fix your lips to low-rate me so, boy?" Ruby growled, waving the lamp about.

"Shet up, Mama Ruby, and just hold that lamp still. Shoot. I want to get to the church on time." Virgil started to shovel again.

Ruby gave Virgil a stern look and turned to Hattie.

"How was the fish fry, Cousin Hattie?"

"It was fine. I was just comin home to change me into a more comfortable pair of shoes when that one-arm devil got after me," Hattie sighed.

"He won't molest another woman," Ruby grunted, touching

the corpse with her bare foot. "Hurry up, Virgil! Finish diggin that hole. You know I got Fast Black comin to the house to help me clean my teeth with that Ajax Zeus picked up in Miami. I want to look my best for the Lord."

Virgil stopped and turned to Ruby again with a smile on his face.

"Fast Black comin to the house, sho nuff? She comin by herself?" he asked.

"I ain't goin to mention it, but I heard Fast Black tell Zeus she was a fool over you. She don't really care nothin for No Talk," Hattie teased.

Virgil whistled and began to dig fast and vigorously.

"Dig deeper, boy!" Ruby repeated firmly. "You remember what happened that time you dug that shallow grave for that half-breed from the panhandle what was down here in Goons causin trouble." Ruby paused and turned to Hattie. "Some half-breed bastard come down here messin around with our women and beatin up on our men. Even had Loomis scared. Yellow Jack come to get me. I crawled out my bed, on account of Fast Black told Yellow Jack she would give me some rock candy to come to the house. Now I ain't knowed about this half-breed down the camp raisin so much hell. When I got there, there was Loomis sittin on the back porch with his nose broke. There was No Talk settin in the livin room with a scab already formed on his lip. There was Boatwright cryin the blues cause the half-breed won't pay for drinkin up his liquor. And there was Fast Black with a black eye where this punk done went up side her head."

"What you do?" Hattie anxiously.

"She bit off his nose then snapped his back," Virgil said, still shoveling.

"I declare!" Hattie hollered. "And then what happened when you buried him?"

"Well, this happened when Mo'reen was a itty-bitty baby. Three. One day she come runnin in the house playin with a skull. The chickens had scratched up that half-breed's bones!" Ruby told Hattie.

"Have mercy," Hattie gasped. A chill passed through her body.

After the burial, Fast Black came to the house and scrubbed Ruby's teeth. Then she and Virgil escorted Ruby to church. They were eagerly greeted by the anxious Reverend Tiggs.

The service began. No Talk, with his bandaged neck, played the piano off-key and could not keep his eyes off Fast Black and Virgil sitting dangerously close together on a bench near the back of the small room.

"Say Mama Ruby sent another maniac to glory, huh?" Fast Black asked Virgil in a whisper. She had changed from her white party dress to a simple black smock and she had removed all traces of makeup from her face.

"Sho nuff did. I seen her do it with my own eyes. I swear to God, Fast Black, I'm gettin scared as hell livin with Mama Ruby. She my own mama and I'm scared to death of her."

"Aw, Mama Ruby is a good woman. She don't mess with nobody, lest they mess with her. You don't mess with her you'll never have nothin to worry about. Shoot. You can take my word for it, I never is goin to cross Mama Ruby. Shoot. I don't want my tongue snatched out like that gambler from Tampa—"

"What gambler? What tongue got snatched out?! What you talkin about, girl?"

"Um . . . you didn't know?"

Several annoyed church members gave the young couple stern glances, and loudly advised them to stop talking, as everyone present had come specifically to hear Ruby sing.

"You didn't know about that?!" Fast Black whispered to Virgil, loud enough for the woman sitting next to her to hear.

"Shhhhh!" the woman said. "Girl, you in the Lord's house. And stop talkin about Mama Ruby before she come down here and snatch a knot in you."

"Yes, ma'am," Fast Black muttered.

"Psst!" Virgil got Fast Black's attention.

"What?" she mouthed.

He leaned over and whispered in her ear. "Take my word for it, you better not go blabbin about what I just told you what Mama Ruby done tonight. You do, you'll never smile again, lest you smilin at her. You go to puttin bugs in folks' ear about what happened tonight the law might come down on my mama."

"Virgil, if I live to be a hundred, I ain't goin to never put the word out on Mama Ruby. She told me to my face I better not tell nobody about that man what she snatched the tongue from. . . . *I ain't told nobody yet.*"

19

The dusty police car driving along Duquennes Road slowed down as it approached Ruby and Maureen walking toward their hill. When Ruby and Maureen went out walking, which they did daily, they rarely walked side by side. Instead Ruby usually walked several feet in front of Maureen and a few feet off to the side.

Ten minutes away from Ruby's house were four migrant camps, each containing two-room houses lined up like gray children's blocks. Most of Ruby's friends lived on the camps. Ruby and Maureen were just returning from a visit with Roscoe Mattox, Ruby's fiance, who lived on one of the camps.

"I been meanin to come to the house and set with you, Ruby," Roscoe had said, walking them part of the way down Duquennes Road.

Ruby turned to face Roscoe, looking him up and down. He was a tall, stout man with bright green eyes and light brown skin. His thin gray hair was always combed back and plastered to his neck with a heavy pomade.

"I want you to come by the house to see Cousin Hattie before she leave," Ruby replied in a deep voice.

"I'll be there," Roscoe promised, stopping. The hot sun temporarily blinded him as he stood and watched Ruby and

Maureen continue their walk. Maureen leaned down, lifted a rock, and threw it at Roscoe, missing his head by inches.

"Them rocks goin to get you in a heap of trouble, Mo'reen!" Roscoe scolded, laughing.

Roscoe turned and started back to the camp and Ruby and Maureen watched until he was out of sight. Ruby became annoyed when she recognized Big Red's police car pulling up. The car stopped and Ruby folded her arms as she faced Big Red. He rolled the window down on the passenger's side and leaned toward it.

"Evenin, Mama Ruby," he said.

"Evenin," Ruby grunted. "Who done raped a white woman?"

"Nobody I know of," Big Red chuckled.

"Then why is you out here? I didn't call for you."

Maureen stood next to Ruby, kicking one of the car's front tires with her bare toe.

"I'm kind of huntin some nigger what was last seen at Zeus' house. Ain't nobody seen him since the fish fry. We got him down as a missin person. Loomis, who brought that nigger out to Goons, suspect he met with foul play. Know what I mean? . . ." Big Red said, looking up into Ruby's dilated eyes. "Um . . . what's wrong with your eyes, darlin?"

"The sun gettin to em, I guess." Ruby's voice was hoarse and deep.

"About this missin nigger . . . you ain't seen him, is you, Mama Ruby?"

"Naw." Ruby shook her head and shrugged her shoulders.

"Think hard now, Mama Ruby. Maybe you seen him and forgot. Think hard now, darlin. Is you seen this here missin spook?"

"You thinkin he might be in my back pocket or somethin?" Ruby asked, with her eyebrow raised.

"Naw."

"Then why you axin me about him? I ain't seen nothin."

"You ain't seen nothin? Well that takes care of that," Big Red grinned, slapping his forehead with the palm of his hand. "See . . . this missin nigger . . . he was a one-armed man. Fact is, he the same one you locked horns with in Yocko's some years back. Snatched his arm clean off, I hear."

"Ooooh . . . *that* man. A pitch-black nigger with a bad attitude? Lopsided head? Buck teeth?"

"That sho nuff sound like that nigger."

"Naw. I ain't seen him," Ruby repeated.

Big Red looked in Ruby's eyes and sighed with exasperation.

"Look-a-here. I'm on your side, darlin. You and me thick as
thieves. In the first place, I ain't goin to let nobody come down
here and haul you off to jail, Mama Ruby."

"Whatever gave you the notion I needed protectin?"

"What I meant was—"

"Since when was it up to you to keep them laws off my tail?"

"Mama Ruby, I didn't come out here to argue with you. I'm
just doin my job."

"Then how come you ain't doin your job? How come you
out here axin me about a dead man?"

"Whoa there! I ain't said nothin about no *dead* man!"

"I'm lookin at one," Ruby threatened.

Big Red gasped and covered his mouth with his hand.

"Mama Ruby, me and you been cut buddies since you come
here. We ain't never had a cross word between us. But I'm a
sho-nuff lawman. Folks expect me to keep some kind of order
among yall. You know how yall colored folks is. Fightin and cuttin up one another all the time. We got to keep yall in line.
Them jealous up North agitators just waitin for us to cause a
commotion down here, so they can have somethin to politic
about. We all Christians down here, that's the trouble. Them
up North folks done been took over by Jews and communists.
Now they itchin to come down here and mess with us. When
the war break out between us Christians and the rest of em, me
and you'll be on the same side. Now you take somebody like
that Loomis—or No Talk—folks will be shootin at them from
both sides, they so ornery."

"You through?" Ruby asked, impatient.

"Ma'am?"

"I axed if you was through?"

"Yeah. By the by, I got to report somethin about this here
missin man. Can you tell me anything at all?"

"I ain't seen no one-armed man. Now if you'll excuse me."
Ruby took Maureen by the hand and resumed her walk down
the hill.

The police car turned around in the middle of the road and slowly left.

"Mama Ruby, you think Big Red got my pig?" Maureen asked, turning to watch the car. Le Pig had not been seen since the night Ruby attacked Mack in the front yard.

"I doubt it, angel. Old goats and pigs don't mix. Come on now, sugar. Let's get on back to the house so we can help Cousin Hattie get packed." Ruby lifted Maureen up in her arm and descended the hill, running wildly, her other arm flapping like a wing.

Virgil sat on the front porch shelling peanuts. He ignored Maureen and Ruby as they stepped on the porch.

"Cousin Hattie!" Ruby called, leaving Maureen on the porch with Virgil as she went inside the house. Seconds later Maureen went inside, following Ruby to Virgil's bedroom where Hattie was quietly packing her clothes.

"Yall back already? You find Le Pig?" Hattie asked. She had occupied Virgil's room during her visit. Ruby had made Virgil sleep on a pallet on the kitchen floor.

"We just had a nice little walk in the woods and a nice visit with my fiance," Ruby smiled.

"And we didn't find my pig!" Maureen pouted as she climbed up on the bed next to Hattie's opened suitcase. As if on cue, Virgil entered the room with a can of beer. He handed it to Ruby and left without a word.

"I'm sho nuff goin to miss yall. I had me such a good time," Hattie said sadly. She gazed at Maureen, then turned to Ruby standing in the middle of the floor drinking from her can of beer.

Ruby cocked her head to the side and smiled. "I sho nuff wish you would consider movin to Florida. I tell you, it's the land of opportunity. Me, I been in hog heaven since I come to Florida."

"I know. I just can't up and leave Louisiana though. I'm too use to that Creole atmosphere. Least you was a young girl when you left, Cousin Ruby. A old woman like me, I ain't got no business leavin my hometown!" Hattie declared.

Ruby laughed and shook her head, then turned the can upside down to finish her beer.

"Cousin Hattie, ain't you goin to stay and help us find my

pig?" Maureen inquired, looking at Hattie with tears in her eyes.

"I wish I could, angel. But you see, your cousin got to get on back to Baton Rouge. Somebody liable to rob my house and set it afire. Them niggers is so jealous of me back there," Hattie lamented.

"Better you than me," Ruby growled.

"I declare, Cousin Ruby. You ain't never been one to take no mess. Me, I believe in a eye for a eye and all, but you do everything so *final*. Buryin devils right and left." Hattie looked at Ruby for a full minute.

Virgil entered the room again and stood quietly in the doorway with his hands in his pants pockets as he listened to Ruby.

"Papa say I been had a mean streak since I was a baby. Say I used to bite plugs out my crib mattress just to be spiteful. I come by my meanness natural. Yeah. We all got mean blood but I'm the one it come out the meanest in. Papa say his papa told him and his papa told him that his mama told him our folks come from one of the most warlike tribes in Africa. Say durin slavery couldn't nobody do nothin with us. Shoot. *I ain't scared of nothin,* "Ruby announced. "Not a snake!"

"Amen!" Hattie shouted.

"Not a gun!" Ruby added.

"Amen!" Hattie repeated.

Virgil and Maureen looked at one another and held back their laughter. Maureen ran to stand next to Virgil.

"Not a peckerwood! Not a wild bull! Not a hurricane! And not the devil!" Ruby shouted, stomping her foot.

"Glory be," Hattie sighed. "Awesome. That's what you is, Cousin Ruby. Sho nuff awesome."

"Sho nuff," Ruby agreed.

"Mama Ruby don't take *nothin* off *nobody,*" Virgil interjected.

Ruby looked at Virgil, then back to Hattie.

"The boy's right." Ruby nodded.

"Mama Ruby, will you kill whoever stole my pig?" Maureen asked.

"Probably so." Ruby shrugged.

"I'm convinced some cheapskate snatched this girl's piggie, Mama Ruby. With Memorial Day comin up and all. Everybody'll be barbecuing pork. A pig-nappin sounds a likely thing," Virgil insisted.

"Somebody goin to eat up my piggie?" Maureen sobbed.

"Don't cry, darlin. I'll make Virgil find you a better pig," Ruby soothed, walking to Maureen.

"I don't want no better pig—I want my old one!" Maureen wailed.

Ruby picked Maureen up and carried her to the bed and sat her down.

"That poor little angel," Hattie commented, looking at Maureen and shaking her head. "I ain't never seen no child so devoted to a pig."

When Slim arrived with his truck to take Hattie back to the bus station, the first thing he asked Ruby was, "What you ladies been up to? Ain't heard from yall in a week."

"We ain't been up to nothin," Ruby said, giving Hattie a peculiar look. Virgil and Fast Black lay on the living room floor shelling peanuts.

"I heard somethin about a commotion happenin out here . . ." Slim continued.

"Oh?" Ruby looked at him with her mouth open and her eyebrows raised. She then turned around in her seat on the sofa to face Virgil and Fast Black. "Yall kids know anything about a commotion out here?"

"Naw," Fast Black coughed, shaking her head.

"Naw," Virgil replied, unable to face Slim.

"You, Cousin Hattie?" Ruby asked, turning to Hattie.

"Naw," Hattie agreed, unable to face Slim.

"See. Ain't none of us know nothin about no commotion." Ruby looked at Slim and smiled broadly.

"Ain't you goin to ax me?" Maureen asked.

Ruby snatched her head around to face Maureen.

"Lamb, you know anything about a commotion out here?" Ruby cooed.

"I don't know nothin about no commotion, but I know somethin about that man yall kilt."

Virgil rose quickly and eased out the front door. Fast Black followed. Hattie snatched a newspaper from the coffee table and pretended to read. Slim looked from Ruby to Maureen.

"Slim, you ever kilt you a man?" Maureen continued.

"Naw, darlin," Slim sighed, rolling his eyes back in his head. "It take a special kind to go to killin. . . ."

Ruby sat with her face straight, her eyes staring along the wall. The room got uncomfortably quiet.

"Like Mama Ruby?" Maureen asked, moving toward Slim. "She ain't no real lady on account of Virgil say she got more nerve than a Russian. Huh, Mama Ruby?"

"Darlin, why don't you go to the upper room and look out the window. You might see somethin," Hattie suggested. She rose from the sofa and walked over to Maureen. "Come on, darlin. Let me carry you to the upper room, where you belong."

"Ruby, I know it ain't my business, this here missin, dead, one-armed man, but—"

"You said it, Slim. It *ain't* none of your business. Now, you about ready to carry my cousin to the bus station?" Ruby stood up and folded her arms.

Hattie escorted Maureen to the upper room.

"Like I said, this man what can't nobody find, his folks been down here axin questions, Ruby."

Ruby sighed and cocked her head to the side, giving Slim an exasperated look.

"Anybody got any questions, send em to me."

"Uh huh . . . and they'll meet up with a accident, Mama Ruby?"

"I ain't got nothin to do with no accidents. No murders. No nothin. Shoot. Big Red done already been out here messin with me. The last thing I need, is for my man to third degree me. I don't want to hear nothin else about that missin man. That clear?"

Slim nodded and joined Virgil and Fast Black on the front porch.

20

After Slim and Ruby left with Hattie, Virgil chased Maureen back to the upper room so he could romance Fast Black in private on the living room sofa.

Staring out the front window of her room, Maureen hoped to see her pet pig waddle down the hill. After sitting in the window for an hour, she was convinced she would never see Le Pig again. Suddenly, she leaped up and ran from the room and down the stairs. Virgil had transferred Fast Black to his bedroom and was unaware of Maureen's frenzy. She threw herself on the living room floor and sobbed frantically.

An hour later when Slim and Ruby returned, Virgil greeted them by running out on the porch with his mouth stretched open and his arms waving. Fast Black stood in the window peeking out, biting her nails.

"Mama Ruby, Mama Ruby—Mo'reen done run away from home on account of her pig got kidnapped!" Virgil shouted. Ruby took a deep breath and narrowed her eyes to see Virgil better.

"WHAT DID YOU SAY?!" she roared.

"I said, Mo'reen done run away from home cause her pig got stole!"

Ruby fainted on the front porch and the whole house shook.

21

The upper room was deathly silent as Fast Black entered to search for Maureen.

Because of the palm trees on one side of the house, the room always seemed dark. At the back window the view was obscured by a sumac tree and a jasmine bush, but there was only the bayou to be gazed at anyway.

Maureen's favorite spot was the front window. A footstool sat before it and she would sit for hours at a time looking up the hill toward Duquennes Road, hoping to see something. But the most fascinating thing to be seen from the upper room was the Blue Lake, off to the side of the hill. People came from as far away as the state's panhandle to fish in it. The lake was a popular swimming pool among Goons' youth, and in the summertime, fish fries were held on its banks. Everyone Maureen knew who had been baptized had been baptized in the Blue Lake, at least twice.

But the Blue Lake had also been a source of misery. Twenty-year-old Earl Cundiff, just back from four years in the marines, had got drunk at his welcome-home party on the bank of the lake, had fallen in, and had drowned. Two of Maisy Carter's teenage daughters stole a visiting preacher's car and drove it down by the lake. The youngsters lost control of the vehicle and it went into the water. Both girls had drowned.

Too young to understand death, Maureen had not been

bothered by the drownings. The Blue Lake was her favorite playground. Parts of it were shallow enough to wade in and she loved making mud pies with water from the lake. On a very hot day the water on the Blue Lake glistened, and gnats, crayfish, and turtles kept Maureen and her young friends from under Ruby's feet for hours.

Fast Black stared out the front window in the upper room with her eyes shaded, looking at the Blue Lake. She sighed and turned away.

"Mo'reen," she called out, looking slowly around the room. "Come out from hidin and I'll give you a kiss and a nickel." There was no response.

This was the first time Fast Black had ever been in the upper room. No man, excluding Virgil and the preacher, had ever been allowed in.

"Mama Ruby say ain't no regular man or boy allowed in the upper room on account of if one go in there, he'll take the devil with him," Virgil explained to Loomis one evening when he had come to the house looking for a place where he could hide from an irate lover. Fast Black had never been allowed to enter the upper room.

"Fast Black is too much like a man," Ruby had decided. "She get loose in the upper room and Mo'reen'll never be the same."

Fast Black was not liking what she felt, saw, or smelled. There were fresh-picked flowers in jars sitting on the floor and on all three of the window sills. Lilac, dandelion, rose, and other wild fragrances filled the air.

"Smell like a funeral parlor in here . . ." Fast Black said out loud. "Feel like one too."

The wallpaper had started to crack and curl up at the ends. Long jagged cracks had formed on the ceiling. Other than Maureen's bed—a limp roll-away with two wheels missing—a large chifforobe backed up into the corner next to the back window, and a lopsided easy chair at the foot of the bed, there was little else in the room. The cardboard box with a pillow in it where Le Pig had slept sat at the head of Maureen's bed.

After looking under the bed and in the chifforobe, Fast Black left quietly and returned to the living room to join the others.

"Yall, I bet that girl's halfway to Mexico by now!" she hollered.

22

Maureen, blinded by her tears, stumbled along the bank of the Blue Lake.

"What's your name, girl?" she heard a masculine voice, unfamiliar to her, ask.

She stopped crying and looked up.

"My name Mo'reen," she replied to the fisherman, an elderly white man holding a bait can in one hand and a fishing reel in his other.

"What's the matter with you?"

"Nothin. I'm just runnin away from home," Maureen wailed. "I had me a pig, and some crook stole him and ate him up!"

The man looked Maureen over thoroughly.

"Whose little ole girl is you?"

"I'm Mama Ruby's little ole girl."

The man looked at her hard.

"You drag your tail on back home, girl. Somethin was to happen to you and Mama Ruby'll raise everything but the *Titanic!*"

Back at the house, Virgil fussed and fought with Slim. Reverend Tiggs had just arrived and was standing over Ruby, who lay in a deathlike state in the middle of the floor, her eyes rolled back in her head, her mouth wide open. Fast Black stood over Ruby and fanned her face. Suddenly, she removed Ruby's teeth and backed over to the coffee table to place them in an ashtray. Then she returned to Ruby and resumed fanning.

"You ain't had no business lettin Mo'reen out your sight, boy!" Slim shouted at Virgil.

"Shet up, Slim, and let me finish explainin! I am tellin you, I had just run outside to get me a breath of fresh air. You can ax Fast Black."

"He ain't lyin, Slim! He had just run outside to get a fresh breath of air. I seen him do it!" Fast Black agreed.

"How Mo'reen get out this house without you or Fast Black seein her?" Reverend Tiggs asked Virgil.

"Huh? Well—we was in the kitchen at first. Me and Fast Black. I was cleanin a catfish!" Virgil lied.

"He sho nuff was, yall—I seen him do it!" Fast Black said. Slim looked from her to Virgil.

"Where the catfish at now?" Slim folded his arms and waited for a response. "I just come from the kitchen and I ain't seen no catfish."

"I cooked and ate it?" Virgil suggested.

"Sho nuff—I seen him do it!" Fast Black nodded.

"Listen, I want the true story from yall." Slim walked up close to Virgil and shook his finger in Virgil's frightened face.

"Tell the truth, Slim . . . me and Fast Black was in the bedroom," Virgil admitted.

"Doin what?" Slim demanded.

"See—see Fast Black told me to carry her to the bedroom on account of she had a notion between her legs that was hot as a stole car!" Virgil moved back from Slim and leaned against the wall.

"You lyin baboon!" Fast Black ran across the room and slapped Virgil's arm.

"STOP THAT!" the preacher ordered. "Yall in enough trouble already! Virgil, I'm ashamed of you, corruptin this young girl!"

"Let's try to get to the bottom of this mess. We ought to be tryin to get Ruby back to normal." Slim clapped his hands as he spoke, moving over to Ruby.

"Mama Ruby ain't dead, is she, Slim?" Fast Black returned to Ruby as well.

"Ain't moved a muscle since I been here," the preacher complained. "If she ain't dead, she sho nuff playin possum."

"Poor Mama Ruby. Just look at her layin there. You could buy her for a nickel the shape she in." Fast Black dropped to her knees and touched Ruby's cold face. "Lord, her face hard as Chinese 'rithmetic." Fast Black began to cry.

"All this on account of Mo'reen runnin away," Virgil said hoarsely. "Mama Ruby is sho nuff crazy when it come to Mo'reen. I can't believe that girl done run away."

"Virgil, what make you so certain the girl is done run off? We all standin here assumin. She ain't left no note or nothin," Slim said suddenly. "Shoot. This just might be a fake alarm."

"Slim, I looked everywhere for Mo'reen. I checked her chifforobe. I checked under the tables and beds. I searched this house from asshole to appetite and the girl ain't in it. The girl done run off. Even stole my suitcase!"

The screen door slammed.

"This girl live here, sho nuff?" It was the white fisherman talking.

Maureen set down the suitcase and ran to Ruby and gasped.

"Who done kilt my mama?" she cried out. She leaned over Ruby and placed her hands on Ruby's shoulders and shook her violently. "Mama Ruby, Mama Ruby, don't be dead."

The pupils in Ruby's eyes returned to their proper place, her mouth closed and she sat up, coughing. She ignored the others, and rose from the floor with Maureen in her arms and they went to the upper room.

Slim and Reverend Tiggs looked at one another. Virgil looked at the fisherman and shrugged.

"I declare, yall. Somethin was to ever happen to Mo'reen, we just as well give Mama Ruby up for dead," Slim muttered.

23

Across from Ruby, at her living room table, Zeus shuffled a tattered deck of playing cards. To Ruby's left was Irene Flatt, a woman who lived near the camps. Irene was a florid, gap-toothed woman of forty, with limp greasy hair and dull brown skin. The sleeves of her red shirtwaist dress were rolled way up her arms, revealing developed muscles. Facing Irene was her plain brown husband Bishop, a retired janitor. Of Ruby's vast circle of friends, the Flatts were the only married couple. Catherine, the Flatts' eight-year-old daughter, was Maureen's schoolmate and best girlfriend.

"You goin to read them cards or eat em?" Ruby asked Zeus.

Zeus read fortunes with playing cards, sometimes with startling accuracy.

"Give me time, Ruby," he coughed. "You just give me time to read these damn cards."

Irene and Bishop sat completely still, sphinxlike, afraid Zeus might rearrange their future. Four beer cans sat on the table, emptied, and a platter of rib bones sat on the floor next to Ruby's feet. Both windows in the room were propped open, for even though it was December it was uncomfortably warm.

A scratched Ray Charles record had been playing over and over for two hours straight.

Zeus flipped a card.

"Ace of spades," Bishop said with alarm. He shuffled around in his chair, straightening his suspenders and rearranging his too-small shirt.

Irene turned to Ruby.

"What is it, Zeus?" Ruby asked in a weak voice. "I know that's the bad-news card. . . . My boy . . . my boy . . . my boy over there in that V-Eight Nam . . . is he?" Ruby stopped speaking and rose slowly. "Virgil ain't been in that army but a few months. Don't you tell me somethin done happened to him already!" she shouted angrily. Irene reached up and took Ruby's hand, gently pulling her back down in her seat.

"These cards don't lie. Somebody in this room, at this table, got a dark cloud over em . . . could even be me," Zeus announced tiredly. He reached in his shirt pocket and removed a container of eyedrops. "Yall all know how wild Fast Black is. Yellow Jack ain't got a lick of sense. My nephew Loomis is just as wild as Fast Black. Always runnin over to that Key Largo or into Miami and them honky-tonk bars." Zeus shook his head. "Poor Fast Black is bound to get herself raped or kilt or somethin." Zeus applied the eyedrops in his fishlike eyes. The others stared at him quietly as he returned the eyedrops to his pocket, then flipped over another card: the queen of spades. Irene covered her mouth with her hand.

"The dark cloud hangin over one of yall women," Zeus said, relieved.

Ruby snatched her handkerchief from inside her bra and sobbed quietly.

"Zeus, you put them cards away," Irene ordered gently.

Zeus sighed and stuffed the deck of cards back into his pants pocket.

"Hush up, Ruby," Bishop shouted. "You is some crazy if you think Virgil stupid enough to let them Japs in V-Eight Nam get the best of him. Shoot."

"Somethin awful is fixin to happen to me," Ruby mumbled. "My children—Mo'reen!" She leaped up from the table and ran out onto the front porch.

Maureen was at the side of the house playing grown-folks with Catherine and Yellow Jack. All three children, bloody and scratched, threw down their sticks when they heard Ruby's voice.

"What?" Maureen asked.

"Is you OK?" Ruby asked, running around the side of the house.

"Yeah," Maureen shrugged, wiping blood from her forehead. "I beat Yellow Jack and Catty the most," she said proudly.

Yellow Jack and Catherine, whose nickname was Catty, sat on the ground with blood and tears streaming down the sides of their cheeks, but they were grinning.

Ruby grabbed Maureen's hand.

"You come on in the house with me . . . I'll feel better with you bein somewhere where I can see you." Ruby's voice shook as she spoke.

"Mama Ruby, I want to stay out here and play! I ain't no baby no more! I'm eight! Why I got to be somewhere for you to see me?!" Maureen stomped her foot, then kicked at the sand.

Catty stood up. Like Maureen, she was a tiny, dark, cherubic youngster with long jagged braids.

"Mama Ruby, Mo'reen chased Bobby Boatwright home with a rock up side his head," Catty informed Ruby.

Ruby glared at Maureen.

"You have to come in the house cause you fight too much," Ruby explained. "Chasin Bobby Boatwright with rocks up side his head. You want old man Boatwright to come whip you? And look at all the blood on Yellow Jack and Catty and yourself! Yall will wake up with scabs in the mornin. You out for school Christmas vacation. Don't you children want to do somethin different for a change? Yall kept on playin grown-folks, one of yall liable to end up dead!"

"We like playin grown-folks!" Yellow Jack said truthfully. "I want to bust me somebody's head open one day, like you do."

"We fight like this all the time. It's sho nuff fun, Mama Ruby! Me, I want to choke folks' tongues out like Yellow Jack say Fast Black told him you done!" Catty shouted.

"When that girl tell you that?" Ruby gasped, facing Yellow Jack.

"When I was a little bitty boy. She ax me if I wanted her to get you to take my tongue and feed it to the gators! Shoot naw, I told her! But I want to snatch out somebody's tongue myself. Will you show us how?"

"Uh . . . uh . . . you kids shouldn't try to grow up too fast.
Grown folks is serious business. See, I be settin in the house all
the time worryin on account of I'm grown and that's what
grown ladies have to do. Worry. Like now. I'm worryin about
Mo'reen out here. I want her to come in the house and let me
keep my eye on her."

Catty tugged at Ruby's dress tail.

"We fixin to shoot marbles." Catty removed a fistful of marbles from her pants pocket. "Please let Mo'reen play with us."

"Well . . . I guess it's OK. But no more playin grown-folks
today. Catty, you run down to Roscoe's and tell him I said to
send me some beers," Ruby commanded. Catty darted off toward the hill.

"Don't yall leave the yard," Ruby called to the other children, as she turned and went back inside.

Yellow Jack removed a fistful of marbles from his pants'
pocket and Maureen lifted a coffee can containing her marbles
off the ground. Within ten minutes, Yellow Jack had won all of
Maureen's marbles.

"I declare. I ain't playin with you no more. I'm goin to go
back in the house and play with my mannequin if you don't
give me back my marbles," Maureen threatened.

"You ain't no fun, girl. I'm goin to stop walkin to school with
you." Yellow Jack stabbed Maureen in the chest with his finger.
"And I ain't goin to eat lunch with you no more neither. I
might take a notion and beat you up side the head with a stick
and bust your goddamn brains out."

"Sho nuff, Yellow Jack?"

"Sho nuff."

Maureen sighed and shrugged.

"OK. Give me back some of my marbles so we can play some
more, Yellow Jack. I don't really want to go in the house and
play with that ole mannequin no how."

Yellow Jack looked around and moved closer to Maureen.

"Mo'reen, you want your marbles back?" he asked in a low,
deep voice that did not sound like an eight-year-old boy. He
placed his arm around Maureen's waist.

"Yeah," she replied, bug-eyed and anxious.

"You give me some pussy and I'll give you back all your marbles."

Maureen jerked her head back and looked Yellow Jack in the eyes.

"What's pussy?" she asked.

Instead of speaking, he lightly touched her crotch.

"What you goin to do with it?" Maureen giggled.

"See, grown folks do this thing. I seen my mama do it with No Talk and I seen her do it with Virgil. One time I peeped in Mama Ruby's room and I seen her do it with Slim. I have to lay on top of you—"

"Oh yeah—*that!* I seen Fast Black and Virgil doin that in Virgil's bed that night before he went to V-Eight Nam. You want to lay on top of me and shake?"

"Well . . . there's more to it than that. From what I seen No Talk do, I have to put my thing inside you. Then we shake."

"Oh." Maureen thought for a moment, then frowned. "That don't sound like much fun. And it'll make us talk crazy. Virgil and Fast Black was sayin, 'oh baby baby baby' and 'oooh oooh oooh.' I don't want to talk crazy," Maureen giggled, turning up her nose and frowning.

"Listen here, girl. You ain't got to talk crazy. All you got to do is shake."

"That all?"

"I swear to God that's all you got to do."

"OK—first let me ax Mama Ruby!" Maureen said, running up the stairs.

"WAIT A MINUTE!" Yellow Jack yelled after her, but he was not quick enough. As soon as he heard the screen door slam, he fled into the bayou.

Maureen entered the house and ran across the room to Ruby.

"Mama Ruby, can I give Yellow Jack some pussy? Can I, Mama Ruby?" she asked excitedly.

"Say what—get thee behind me, Satan!" Ruby shouted. She jumped up so fast she knocked her chair over. Irene, Bishop, and Zeus roared with laughter.

"Yellow Jack axed me to give him some pussy and I told him I had to come ax you first. Can I, Mama Ruby?" Maureen begged.

Ruby ran outside, calling Yellow Jack. Irene grabbed Maureen by her hand and pulled her close.

"That's a bad word," she scolded, shaking a finger in Maureen's face.

"How come?"

"That's somethin just grown folks do," Bishop explained. "Kids can't do what grown folks do."

"We fight like grown folks. Catty say next time we play grown-folks, we goin to kill somebody. Maybe Yellow Jack or Bobby Boatwright. We goin to kill Bobby Boatwright next time we play grown-folks," Maureen smiled.

"Mo'reen, child. Just cause grown folks do certain things don't mean they right," Zeus informed Maureen.

Confused, Maureen pulled away from Irene and retreated to the upper room.

Twenty minutes later, from her footstool at the upper room's front window, Maureen watched Catty moving down the hill hugging a large brown bag with the beer Ruby had sent her for. Before Catty made it to the porch, Maureen spotted an unfamiliar car coming down the hill.

"White folks!" she gasped. She leaped up from her stool and ran downstairs. "Mama Ruby, here come the white folks drivin down the hill! *Real* white folks—not the kind like Big Red! They in a po'lice car!"

Irene and Bishop ran to the door. Catty rushed in and handed the beer to Ruby, who quickly set it on the floor, then ran to the window.

"Who is that, Irene?" Ruby asked. "Who is them white folks comin here?"

Zeus ran to the door.

"That a po'lice car or what?" Ruby asked.

"Yeah," Zeus said. "Look like they might be some of J. Edgar Hoover's mens. . . ."

"Lord . . . no it ain't. Them ain't no J. Edgar Hoover mens. That's a government car. The same kind what came when Lottie's boy got hisself shot up in V-Eight Nam." Bishop's voice trailed off.

Ruby started to tremble as she watched the car come to a stop in her front yard. Dust rose up and drifted slowly back to the ground, like sheets of sepia. Two tall white men in military uniforms got out. They coughed and fanned the dust as they walked toward the house, their colorless faces grim and stone-like.

"I seen them mens before. Last year. Ooooh, yall, them *is* the same two what come to tell Lottie about her boy gettin hisself shot up in that V-Eight Nam!" Bishop said again. "Wonder *who* they got bad news for?"

"Shet up, Bishop!" Irene hollered. "We all know Ruby the only one live in this house what got a boy in V-Eight Nam. Ruby, I—" Irene stopped. Ruby stumbled backwards, sideways, and finally forward. When she hit the floor she fell on Irene, almost squashing the life out of her.

24

Roscoe and No Talk carried a huge, heavy footlocker out of Ruby's house and set it on the back of Roscoe's old pickup truck. Ruby sat on her front porch glider next to Loomis. The temperature had dropped considerably the last few days, and it was now cool enough for sweaters. Ruby and the three men wore long-sleeved shirts with thick linings. There was a snug-fitting black cap on Ruby's head pulled down over her ears, giving her face a severe look. A thick bandanna was tied around the cap to keep it in place.

"Don't you worry none, Mama Ruby. I intend to take real good care of your house while you and Mo'reen in Louisiana," Loomis said. He placed his arm around Ruby's shoulder and moved closer to her.

"Just make certain you don't go in the upper room," she said firmly. "And you better not let nobody else in it neither."

"Honest to God, the door to the upper room'll stay shet till yall come back home," Loomis promised, crossing his heart with his finger.

Irene came out on the porch just as Roscoe and No Talk were walking back up the steps.

"How long yall goin to be gone?" she asked Ruby, stepping aside so Roscoe could pass and go back inside.

"Huh?" Loomis asked, turning to face Irene. She frowned at him and shook her head in exasperation.

"Loomis, I ain't talkin to you. I was talkin to Mama Ruby. I axed her how long her and Mo'reen was goin to be gone?"

Loomis turned back to Ruby.

"Mama Ruby, how long you and Mo'reen goin to be gone?" he asked.

Ruby sighed and turned her head mechanically to face him.

"Just a couple weeks. Mo'reen got to get back here for school. I . . . I don't want her to grow up to be a fool or nothin . . . she . . . she need her book learnin." Ruby's voice was weak and barely audible and had been for three days, since the word had come that Virgil had disappeared in the jungles of Viet Nam and was feared dead.

No Talk, standing at the side of the glider, reached out and touched the top of Ruby's head and she started sobbing.

"Mama Ruby, don't worry about nothin," Loomis sniffed. Seconds later he was sobbing as hard as Ruby. No Talk touched his back and patted him gently. "I'm OK, No Talk," Loomis mumbled. "Now, Mama Ruby, like I just said, you stop cryin. . . . Me . . . Me and No Talk and Fast Black and Big Red ain't goin to let no maniac mess up your house. . . . I . . . I . . . I declare we ain't."

Ruby wiped her eyes with the tail of her duster and laid her head on Loomis' shoulder.

"Yall so good to me. You'll be blessed, Loomis, on account of you is a righteous man to the end. I never thought I would be took to the bosom like I been with yall. Me bein from Louisiana and not Florida and all. Yall folks treat me good as my mama. I declare, I got some true-blue friends." Ruby forced herself to smile.

"And I intend to see that No Talk feed your hens. I'm goin to keep them kids out your yard scatterin rib bones and other mess," Loomis said.

"Thank you, Loomis," Ruby sighed, rising.

Roscoe came to the door and leaned his head out.

"Mama Ruby, you about ready for me to carry you and Mo'reen to the train station?" he asked.

"Yeah. Let me get Mo'reen from the upper room."

Ruby eased past Roscoe and stepped into her living room, where Fast Black, Bishop, Reverend Tiggs, Zeus, Big Red, and a knot of children moved about noiselessly. Suddenly Fast Black ran to Ruby and threw her arms around her waist.

"Lord in heaven—I got a feelin we ain't never goin to see you again, Mama Ruby! I got a feelin you goin off and ain't never comin back!"

"Fast Black, you stop that nonsense! I ain't never leavin Goons. I wouldn't leave Goons to go to heaven . . . lest the Big Boss call me. And the way I been servin Him, he liable to let me live forever!" Ruby shouted.

"Ain't it so," Bishop interjected. "Fast Black, ain't nothin goin to stop Ruby from comin on back here where she belong. She was sent here to us for a reason."

Fast Black removed her arms from Ruby's waist and leaned back to admire her face. Ruby smiled at her.

"You sho nuff belong to us, Mama Ruby? What about your folks in Louisiana? What if they take a notion not to let you come back?"

"Girl, ain't nothin can hold me down. Not a rope. Not a slab of concrete settin on my bosom. Not a court order. I'm comin back here like I said. This is my home," Ruby declared.

Zeus started to cry. He snatched a large, dingy white rag from his pants' pocket and blew his nose.

"Oh Lord!" Catty wailed. "I want to go to Louisiana with you and Mo'reen!" She stomped her foot and put her thumb in her mouth.

"Mama Ruby, how come you got to go anyway?" Yellow Jack asked.

Ruby walked to the center of the floor and stopped.

"Yall listen. Yall all know I ain't been out of this state since I come here. Eight years ago. I ain't seen my mama and daddy and sisters in a coon's age. It's time for me to go home. I need em right now. I'm goin to need all the help I can get in my hour of need. We all got to pray. And the more of us knockin on the Lord's front door, the easier it'll be for Him to hear. We got to get Him to find Virgil and send him back home! I been a child of God all my life!" Ruby shouted.

"Amen!" someone said.

"On account of the Lord, I had a choice to eat from either a picnic table or a hog trough—I been picnickin like a hog! One reason yall all livin so well since I come here is on account of my good credit on God's bill. Don't worry none about me. Can't nothin harm me, cept lightnin—even then it's got to strike me ten times!"

"Sister Ruby, you is a saint to the bone," Reverend Tiggs said with a wide-mouthed grin.

"Can't you leave Mo'reen here to keep me company, Mama Ruby?" Catty asked, tugging at Ruby's arm.

"Have mercy on your soul, Catty! Mo'reen is the Lord's gift to me and she must accompany me everywhere I go. Just like I carry the Lord with me everywhere I go, I must carry Mo'reen." Ruby moved across the room to the steps leading upstairs.

"Mo'reen, come say good-bye to everybody, darlin. Yoo-hooo—come on down, sweetie. We fixin to haul ass," Ruby yelled, fighting back more tears.

Within seconds Maureen stomped down the stairs hugging a shopping bag.

"Lord, Mama Ruby, I hope I don't have to come back to that ole scarey upper room," Maureen said seriously.

Ruby gasped and had to be held up by four of her friends to keep from falling to the floor.

25

"Mama Ruby, how come you lookin so sad? You ain't no fun no more," Maureen complained.

"I'm tired. My blood pressure done run up hog high. And I got a lot of things on my mind," Ruby replied weakly. She lay half sprawled across a bench in the Shreveport, Louisiana, Southern Railways train station with one hand on her chest, breathing with some difficulty.

Maureen stood in front of her looking into her eyes.

"What's wrong, Mama Ruby? You just keep on cryin."

"Mo'reen." Ruby stopped and attempted to smile. "I tried to tell that hardheaded boy of mine not to run off to that army. He just done it to spite Fast Black."

"Virgil said he was joinin the army to get away from you, Mama Ruby. He told Loomis that," Maureen revealed.

Ruby looked at her for a long time. More tears flowed.

"*Why* would anybody want to get away from me?" Ruby whispered.

"Cause you crazy, I guess," Maureen shrugged. "Virgil said he wanted to get away from you so you wouldn't drive him crazy. Mama Ruby, is you goin to drive me crazy?"

Ruby removed her handkerchief from her bosom and wiped her eyes and nose.

"Stop cryin, Mama Ruby."

"Mo'reen, as much as I've done for you and Virgil, why would yall think I'm crazy?"

Maureen shrugged.

"Everybody say you is. Loomis. Zeus. Bishop. Yellow Jack. Big Red. Catty. Bobby Boatwright. Bobby Boatwright's daddy. Everybody."

Ruby considered what Maureen told her.

"Is there anybody what ain't said I'm crazy?"

"No Talk. And I guess that's on account of he can't say *nothin.* But I bet he *think* you crazy too."

"I'm different."

"I know," Maureen said. "Loomis said if God made another one like you, she up there raisin sand in heaven cause this planet wasn't big enough for two of you."

"Ain't nothin wrong with me. I ain't crazy. I'm just a little tetched cause my boy gone. He ain't had no business joinin no army."

"Virgil was a growed-up man," Maureen reminded Ruby.

"That ain't had nothin to do with him leavin home. I didn't want him to go."

"You don't never want me to go neither? Nowhere?"

"Girl, Virgil runnin off is one thing, but you ain't never ever goin nowhere, lest you goin with me. You is my gift from the Lord above."

Maureen gave Ruby a critical look.

"I don't want to stay with you forever, Mama Ruby."

"Why not?"

"Well, I want to be like other girls. I want to move in a house in Miami or somethin. Fast Black say if I ever was to want to have me a good time, I should go live in San Francisco. She went there when she was fifteen and stayed for a whole year. She say ain't no place in this world like San Francisco."

"San Francisco is the most wicked city since Sodom and Gomorrah. A girl with your upbringin ain't got no business in no San Francisco. Don't you never let me hear you mention that place no more. Only way you'll go to San Francisco, is if I was to die. And I ain't got no plans to die."

"OK," Maureen mumbled, moving back a few steps. She was close enough to see out the window. "I see a cab. I think it's ours, on account of we the only ones left in here."

Outside, a young black cabdriver groaned when he saw the gigantic black woman emerge from the train station. The large footlocker she carried was one thing. That would take up enough space. He would probably have to put it in the trunk. But the woman herself had to weigh at least three hundred and fifty pounds. He wondered if the springs in the backseat of the old taxi would survive the long ride from the train station all the way out to Thelma City, a black residential area in Shreveport. Ruby slid the footlocker down on the ground next to the cab and the driver quickly got out and put it in the trunk. She smiled at him, then snatched open the back door and fell into the vehicle. Her flesh, now loose and saggy, seemed to spread over the entire length of the seat.

"Where I'm goin to sit?" Maureen whined. "You so big and fat you take up all the room, Mama Ruby." Ruby had left the back door open for Maureen to get in, but there was no place left for her to sit.

"Let me try and scoot over," Ruby offered. She tried to move but there was very little room for Ruby to arrange herself in such a limited space. She struggled as she continued to try to move over. "I declare . . . I can't barely move. Must be all this heat."

"Must be all your fat," Maureen declared.

"You can sit up in the front with me, lamb," the driver said to Maureen. He smiled and tickled her chin. She climbed in and immediately started to meddle with the cab's radio. "Now you behave, darlin. You might lose me my job," he said as he took the mouthpiece from Maureen and called in his destination.

"Wasn't that a mess, President Kennedy gettin hisself shot last month?" he said, making conversation.

"Devil's work. Satan's got a toe-hold on half the folks in the world. Me, I been holdin him back the best I could." Ruby sighed and shook her head. "But he's a low-down, funky black dog with the strength of ten bulls. You a Christian?"

"I was raised in the church."

"Just think what a mess we would have on our hands without the Lord," Ruby moaned, shaking her head.

"Don't I know it, ma'am." The cabdriver shook his head too and sighed. "Yall just get off the ten twenty-eight in from Jacksonville?" he asked, as the taxi pulled out into traffic.

"We just come in from Goons in Miami," Ruby replied.

"I got a off cousin in Miami. Ain't seen him in three years. I been meanin to drag my tail to Florida to see him someday. I don't know though, them niggers out in Florida is sho nuff mean! Wooo weee! Every time I talk to my cousin on the phone, he just gettin out either the hospital where some maniac done cut him up or shot him up, or he just gettin out of jail for cuttin up or shootin somebody. What's wrong with them folks in Florida? Them white folks must put somethin in the water, huh?"

"See, Satan workin his way from the bottom up. Meanin, he started actin a fool in Florida. The thing is, he done got there and took up residence."

"I declare, you got more religion than a little bit. I feel shame to be settin here amongst all your glory, miss," the cabdriver said with embarrassment.

"My prayers is with you, son. I got a boy round your age. Went and got hisself caught by them Japs in V-Eight Nam and they done hid him somewhere where the U.S. Army can't find him."

The driver looked at Ruby through his rearview mirror and bit his lip, feeling sorry for her.

"Ma'am, two of my brothers got kilt over there. I tried to join up but they wouldn't take me on account of I got flat feet and a nervous condition on account of I seen my own mama get kilt. She involved herself with a sailor and he shot her down like a dog when she tried to break off with him."

"Devil's work. I see I'm goin to have to go up to that lowdown, funky black dog again. Devil."

"I prayed till I was blue in the face. Seem like God done fell asleep on me," the driver said sadly.

"I will include you in my prayers, boy," Ruby promised.

"You know, I feel better just from talkin to you, ma'am. You seem different. I can't put my finger on it, but you ain't no regular lady. There's somethin about you."

Maureen turned to face Ruby, looking her over thoroughly. A stern look from Ruby discouraged Maureen from speaking.

"What brings yall to this part of the South?"

"I'm visitin my family. I'm originally from Shreveport and I ain't seen my family since nineteen and forty-one," Ruby explained.

"Woo wee! That's a coon's age! That's more than twenty years ago. You been away all this time, what possessed you to come home, if you don't mind me axin?"

Ruby sighed and shook her head slowly, looking off to the side.

"The devil separated me from my family. The devil chased me out my daddy's house. But with God, I done found my way back home!" Ruby exclaimed, waving her hands high above her head.

"I see," the driver replied, looking at her again through the rearview mirror. "You reckon your folks ain't done forgot you? You been gone a long time."

"I ain't no easy person to forget," Ruby replied.

The cabdriver bit his bottom lip, not knowing how to interpret the smile that suddenly appeared on Ruby's face.

As they rode through downtown Shreveport, Ruby noticed how much the old city had changed. On the corner of Main and Reed streets, Murphy's five and dime had become Archie's Soul Food Kitchen. A block farther, Doctor Mason's Ear, Nose, and Eye Clinic had become Leroy's Poolroom. A crowd of shabbily dressed black men, their ages ranging from eight to eighty-eight, wandered about, looking lost. Some had blank, bored expressions on their faces. Some looked bitter and suspicious. Young boys, wearing thin T-shirts and with bare feet, threw dice on the sidewalk in front of Leroy's Poolroom.

As the cab passed a rib joint with a long line of hungry people standing outside, Ruby stared out the window with interest.

"That rib joint use to be a Baptist church," she said.

"I know, on account of I use to go to it. My mama use to scrub me with lye soap and rub my whole face with vaseline till I shined like new money, then she would drag me off to that Baptist church," the driver laughed.

They passed a crowd of buxom black ladies wearing chiffon dresses, cursing at the men wandering about the streets.

"Black folks sho nuff like to fuss with one another," the driver lamented. "I guess that's why we always got some kind of mess on our hands."

"We Ham's children. That's why we always got a mess on our hands. Not only that, we bear the mark of Cain," Ruby explained.

The driver looked at her again, wondering what the smile on her face meant this time.

The cab finally stopped in front of a large, dusty, red-shingled house located at 123 North Easly Street.

"That'll be five dollars and a dime," the driver informed Ruby.

She searched the contents of her flimsy purse, shaking it first, then turning it upside down. Two coins, a penny and a nickel, fell out on her lap.

"Wonder what happened to all my money," Ruby mumbled. "Mo'reen, you got any money?" she said, without looking up from her purse.

"Naw," Maureen shrugged. "Where would I have got any money from? You took back that dime you give me before we left home."

"Just a minute, sir." Ruby reached down inside the front of her dress and pulled a knotted handkerchief from her bosom. Fussing, she undid the knot with her teeth. Unwrapping the handkerchief, she revealed a crumpled one-dollar bill, four more pennies, and a stick of bubble gum. "I guess I was pick-pocketed on that train," she mumbled, looking up to face the driver as her eyes filled with fresh tears. "There's so much dis-honesty among us. It's gettin so a Christian can't go nowhere without gettin molested. I guess I'm lucky I wasn't raped on that train too. . . ."

"What about the money you took from Roscoe's wallet be-fore we left home? Remember how we broke in his house when he was asleep? Me and you and Fast Black and Loomis. His wal-let was on the coffee table," Maureen said, rising up from the seat and pointing at Ruby's leg. "You stuck it in your sock."

Ruby glared at her before responding.

". . . Oh . . . I had plumb forgot about my sock money," she grinned sheepishly. The embarrassed driver scratched his head and looked out the window.

After Ruby paid the man, he unloaded the footlocker from the trunk, set it upright on the sidewalk in front of Ruby's par-ents' house, and quickly got into his taxi and sped off.

Ruby immediately turned to Maureen, anger in her eyes.

"You ain't had no business tattlin on me in front of no rank stranger! Come on, girl!" Ruby shouted. She lifted the foot-locker with one hand as if it weighed nothing, and Maureen fell in behind her as Ruby stomped up onto her parents' front porch, pushed open the door, and walked in.

"Mama, Papa! Yoo-hooooo! It's me, Ruby Jean! I done come home," Ruby called out as she stopped in the middle of the living room floor. Maureen hid behind her.

An obese, dark-skinned man of about sixty with a pie-round face entered, carrying a spittoon and a package of chewing tobacco.

"Close that door before you let them flies in this house, Ruby Jean," Ruby's father said. He was wearing a red-and-white-checked flannel shirt and green corduroy pants. He sat down hard on a footstool backed up next to the wall near the staircase.

"Papa, I'm so happy to be home! I'm so happy I could wrap it in egg shells!" Ruby exclaimed. She ran over and embraced her father, kissing him on his cheeks and burying her nose in his thick white hair. Maureen stood timidly in the middle of the floor.

"Where is Mama at, Papa? How has everybody been? Cousin Hattie told me Beaulah and Carrie the only two of my dear sisters left here what still livin."

"Girl, where you been all this time? And what you been doin to get so fat? Look like you been swallowin watermelons whole!"

"Papa, you know heaviness run in our family! Look at you! We all fat!"

"Where you been, girl?" the reverend asked again, pulling away from Ruby's kisses long enough to stuff a wad of chewing tobacco in his jaw. He folded the tobacco bag and squeezed it before putting it in his shirt pocket.

"I been some of everywhere, Papa. New Orleans. Miami. Silo. You know I always had a itchin to travel." Just then, a short, stout, light-skinned woman of sixty with long white braids came into the room from a back entrance. She was carrying an armload of clothes and a sack filled with clothespins.

"Ruby Jean! The good Lord done sent me my baby girl on back home!" Ruby's mother, Ida, dropped the clean clothes and the pins on the floor and rushed toward her daughter. Maureen was still standing in the middle of the floor watching as Ida kissed and cried and hugged Ruby. On the wall a large picture of seven plump young girls smiled at Maureen. The girls resembled one another and it was obvious that the youngest one, a pear-shaped toddler with a moon-shaped face, was Ruby. Two limp hound dogs lay sprawled across the floor, refusing to acknowledge the presence of the visitors. A whatnot stand stood backed up in a corner, every shelf filled with miniature ornaments: little ceramic horses, plastic Oriental people, tiny glass kittens, and dime-store pictures of various movie stars. Ida whirled around and looked at Maureen.

"Whose little ole girl is this here, Ruby Jean?" she demanded.

"Mine. Ain't she pretty, Mama? You ever seen such a angel?"

"What your name is, girl?" Ida asked Maureen, shaking a finger in her face and leaning forward with one hand on her knee.

Maureen looked at Ida and blinked.

"What's the matter? Cat got your tongue?" Ida asked, looking at Maureen out of the corner of her eye.

Maureen opened her mouth wide and pointed inside.

"Ain't no cats in my mouth," she said.

Ida laughed and looked at her husband, who had fallen asleep, his thick arms folded across his chest.

"Wake up, old man!" she shouted, receiving no response. "That old goat ain't worth a nickel no more," Ida said to Ruby.

Ruby turned to look at her aging father.

"Ruby Jean, how come you didn't come back with Othella for her mama's funeral?"

Instead of answering right away, Ruby removed her handkerchief from her bosom and wiped tears from her eyes.

"Othella got on a high horse and acted like she ain't knowed me. I ain't knowed nothin about her mama passin till Cousin Hattie told me when she come to visit with me that time."

"Well, you couldn't expect nobody with Cajun blood to act like regular folks. I always said Othella was crazy. I guess I been proved right."

"I pray for her every night," Ruby said, returning her handkerchief to her bra.

Ida caressed her chin and nodded.

"Uh huh. Now how come you ain't been in tetch?"

"Oh, Mama—it was awful! I got myself mixed up with the devil and he led me to the ruins. I'm in worse shape than a foreigner with nowhere to go!"

The reverend looked up and faced Ruby. He and Ida looked at one another.

"I raised you to dispute the devil. You is the seventh daughter of a seventh daughter. You supposed to set a example, Ruby Jean!" the reverend shouted.

"I know, Papa. And that's what I been doin. Why so many folks in Florida done got on the right track on account of me! It's a wonder they ain't renamed that state the Holy Land, we got so much connection with the Lord!"

"I declare, Ruby Jean. You ain't forgot your upbringing. Most kids what leave home go to livin like fools soon as they out of sight. I bet ain't a soul in Florida regret you come there, huh?" Ida said proudly, smiling.

"Them folks would be lost without me."

Ruby smiled and blinked her eyes as her parents took their time looking her over. Reverend Upshaw looked at Ida again and shook his head.

"Don't your little girl talk?" Ida asked, turning to Maureen, brushing the tail of her dress, then inspecting her hair.

"Mo'reen, talk to your grandmama and grandpapa," Ruby ordered.

"Mama Ruby, you want me to tell em about—" Maureen began but was abruptly cut off by Ruby.

"I got me a boy too!" Ruby said.

"Where he at?" Reverend Upshaw asked.

". . . I don't know," Ruby replied, with her head lowered. She moved slowly across the room and sat down hard on the sofa facing her father. Ida looked at her suspiciously.

"What you mean, you don't know?" she asked.

"He run off and joined the army cause he was mad at some ole fast-tail girl named Fast Black and went and got hisself lost or captured or somethin in that V-Eight Nam," Ruby said in a low voice.

"Praise be." Ida spoke under her breath. "That poor boy."

"Mama, he looked just like you," Ruby muttered.

Ida nodded.

"Where your man?" she asked, locking eyes with Ruby.

"Don't tell us you still single, runnin around loose as a goose like your cousin Hattie," the reverend hollered.

"Shoot! I married me a sho nuff sport!" Ruby shouted back. "A man what use to wear socks that matched the color of his underwear. A sport if ever there was one!"

"Where is he?" Ida demanded. "With another woman?"

"I bet he left you for another woman!" The reverend said to Ruby. "Stubborn as you is, Ruby Jean."

"Well, the first year it was wine what come between us. The second year it was wine *and* women. I took all I could, then the Lord run him off. I been in Goons by myself tryin to raise my children and continue to live like a Christian should."

"When your husband leave you? How old was your kids?" Ida asked.

"Well, Virgil was eleven. I was still carryin Mo'reen."

"That ain't what Othella told folks when she come for her mama's funeral," Reverend Upshaw informed Ruby.

"It ain't?" Ruby gasped.

"Othella said you shot your husband down like a dog when Virgil was a baby." Ida folded her arms and glared at Ruby.

"I . . . I . . . was too shame to tell yall. It was a accident. My husband got involved with this woman and run me crazy. I didn't mean to kill him. Oh, Papa, Mama, he axed for it!"

"If you kilt your husband, where you get Mo'reen from? You been married twice or what? Othella ain't said nothin about you havin no two children. And what Othella do that was so bad you skipped town?"

Ruby removed her handkerchief from her bosom and wiped away her tears again. She staggered to the sofa and sat down. Maureen giggled and joined her, placing her arm around Ruby's shoulder.

"I declare, yall. Othella wasn't no true friend of mine. She just wanted somebody to leave home with her. She tricked me into goin from New Orleans on to Florida. I wanted to come home and take up ministry. She went to drinkin home brew and listenin to ex-convicts. She wanted to live like a gypsy. I told her I was a Christian to the bone and wanted nothin to do with her wicked ways. So I left Silo. Scared to death on account of her havin all that heathen Cajun blood. I knowed if she found me, she'd take a plank and go up side my head and bust my brains out. She was that kind of woman. She'd bust your brains out in a minute. I know, cause I seen her do it. She was a terrible liar. Virgil *was* eleven when my man left and I was pregnant with Mo'reen when I had to chastize him. Othella had me so scared of her. She had white folks' sense, yall know. She knowed how to talk to them white folks about keepin us dumb niggers in line. She held her smarts over me like a lamp! She was evil! She was violent!"

"I declare," Ida sighed. "And she was such a tiny little thing. To think she claimed Christian blood."

"Oh, the devil come in many disguises. Poor Ruby Jean." The reverend went to Ruby and patted her shoulder.

"Well, I finally put Satan where he belong—behind me. I felt him sneakin up on me the other day, tryin to make me not come home to see yall. I slapped him up side his head, bent his horns back and he hauled ass. I ain't seen him since," Ruby said, waving her hand. Her smiling parents looked at her with pride.

Ida went to Maureen and wrapped her arms around her and kissed the side of her face.

"Girl, you don't know how blessed you is to have Ruby Jean for your mama."

26

The next morning Reverend Upshaw and Maureen sat next to one another on the living room sofa watching cartoons while Ruby and Ida prepared a late breakfast.

"How come yall so quiet in there, Papa and Mo'reen?" Ruby called from the kitchen.

Maureen looked at the old man, who had dozed off, and shook his arm.

"Huh?" he replied, disoriented.

Ruby came to the door holding a spatula and a mixing bowl.

"Why come yall so quiet in here?" Ruby asked again.

"This baby is mad cause she want some pretzels," the reverend told Ruby, pointing at Maureen. "You reckon she can run down to that corner store by herself, Ruby Jean? She ain't so big a fool she'll walk out in front of a bus, is she?"

"Mo'reen ain't that simple-minded. She got white folks' sense," Ruby replied. She removed a dime from her bosom and tossed it in Maureen's lap. "Run get you some pretzels and come straight on back here," Ruby instructed her. "Papa, you don't reckon nobody'll kidnap her?"

"Who other than a gypsy would kidnap a colored kid, Ruby Jean?" Ida asked, walking in with her hands on her hips.

"Mo'reen ain't no regular colored kid," Ruby explained. "And anyway, folks *do* kidnap colored kids."

"Ain't nobody goin to snatch up Mo'reen and run off with her, takin her away from her own flesh and blood mama!" Ida declared.

Ruby's breath caught in her throat.

"What's wrong, Ruby Jean? You look like you just seen a ghost."

"Ain't nothin wrong, Mama. I just . . . Mo'reen." Ruby turned from her mother and looked at Maureen. "Go on to the store and get you some pretzels, angel."

Maureen grinned and ran from the house with the dime in her mouth.

Having purchased her pretzels, she rushed back to the house and ate them while watching the cartoons. Ruby came and sat next to her.

"Mama Ruby, some kids was messin with me when I went to the store. They said you and Grandma and Grandpa and everybody in the family was big and fat and sloppy. Am I goin to be big and fat and sloppy like you when I grow up?" Maureen asked with concern.

"You took after your daddy's family. All the women and men in his family was small. You ain't got nothin to worry about."

"My daddy was skinny?"

"Yeah . . . he was thin as a rail. Look, darlin, run get me another beer while Papa is sleepin and your grandmama is next door."

"Then can I go outside and play?"

"Sho nuff, darlin. Just get me the beer first before your grandma come back. Make sure you sneak it to me," Ruby whispered. "And don't forget me a straw."

Maureen returned minutes later with a Pepsi-Cola bottle filled with beer. This was Ruby's way of concealing her passion for beer while she was home. Moments after Maureen left to play outside, Ida returned and joined Ruby on the sofa.

"Ruby Jean, you sho nuff drink a lot of Pepsi. You was sippin on one when I left. Seem like you always got one in your hand. And how come you don't use a glass? Seem to me that straw ought to be gettin a bit frayed."

"It's easier for me to use a straw with my uppers and lowers bein so loose. I drink a lot of Pepsi cause my doctor back in

Miami, a respectable Jew, told me it was good for my blood pressure."

"Oh. Well, one thing about it, you can't argue with no Jew. They is some smart. Doctors. Lawyers. Businessfolk. Give me a Jew everytime. Wonder how come Jews got so much sense, Ruby Jean?"

Ruby scratched her chin and considered her mother's question.

"Blessed."

"Blessed?"

"Jews was persecuted all through the Bible. Bein so smart is the blessin they received from the Lord for all the sufferin they done," Ruby explained.

Ida looked at Ruby for a moment before responding.

"Us colored folks done suffered a lot. During slave days, when one of us went rotten, we stayed rotten. Back then, when a nigger got the devil, he kept the devil," Ida said with pity.

Ruby nodded sadly.

"And that's still true today," she sighed.

27

"**B**less this girl, Lord. For she know not her sins! Shake that devil out of poor Ruby Jean's life for once and for all. She done kilt her husband. She is guilty of just about some of everything. Runnin with a Cajun wild woman. Takin up with a carnival. Not communicatin with her family in a coon's age. And"—Ruby's father began his sermon with vigor—"what all else, daughter?" he asked. Ruby sat on a footstool in front of the whole congregation of the Reed Street Church of God in Christ, surrounded by flowers and crucifixes. "What else that devil had you doin, girl?"

Ruby shrugged before speaking.

"Gluttony . . . bad credit . . . tellin lies." She paused to think, rolling her eyes off to the side, as the silent audience waited in a fever of anticipation to hear her story. "Let me see now . . . name-callin and associatin with foreigners, all the usual backslidin activities."

Her father turned to face her with his hands on his hips. He was a big man, even more rotund than Ruby. He wore a long black robe that was noticeably shorter in the back than it was in the front and in his hand he clutched a thick white cloth he used to wipe his brow during his foot-stomping sermons.

"I ax yall," he continued, turning back to the audience. "I ax yall if you ever knowed of a sister with so much of the devil in her as Ruby Jean? My child done spent the last half of her life ridin Satan's coattails!"

"AMEN!" the congregation shouted.

"She been lost!" the preacher yelled.

"LOST!" the congregation agreed.

"But now she done found her way back home!" the preacher grinned. "Now, brethren . . . we got to get her boy Virgil back home. Lord, the boy done slid from the embrace of his mama's bosom into a heathen country. A country that don't even recognize the Holy Ghost! A country where the folks don't even believe in eatin meat! Can yall imagine not bein allowed to eat *ribs?*"

"NO!" the congregation hollered.

"A country where they worship *cows* when Jesus done told em he was the *only* way! A *cow*, all!"

"COWS!" came the response.

Some of the younger members of the congregation looked at one another with puzzled expressions on their faces.

"Hey—he don't know what he talkin about! That's India where they worship and don't eat cows, not V-Eight Nam!" a young boy said, snickering. He received sharp looks from his elders.

"What's the difference?!" a woman asked the boy. The boy quickly returned his attention to the preacher.

"And the girl's been misled and raped and—and robbed and beat up and, and—what else, Ruby Jean?" the preacher asked, turning to Ruby again.

She looked out into the audience at Maureen sitting in the front row of benches, an incredulous look on her face.

". . . Um . . . my husband got involved with another woman," she said.

The preacher turned to his congregation with his mouth open and his hands held up high in the air.

"As if the girl ain't got troubles enough, the devil walked into her house and carried her man off, before she kilt him. Came in the guise of a hussy!"

"A *white* woman at that!" Ruby added.

The congregation went wild.

"THE WHITE MAN IS THE DEVIL!" they shrieked.

Maureen's heart was beating fast. She was terribly frightened. The reverend started to dance about the stage and speak in tongues and Ida began to hit random keys on the red piano sitting in a corner near the stage. Women, men, and children joined in the confusion, dancing. Some started to sing, no two people singing the same song, and they all shouted and spoke in tongues. Some fell to the floor writhing. A woman sitting next to Maureen lost her wig and some young boys grabbed it up from the floor and started tossing it back and forth across the room.

Maureen rose from her seat, eased out of the church, and ran down the street back to her grandparents' house two blocks away.

When Ruby and the others returned home Maureen was sitting on the bed in Ruby's old room staring off into space. Ruby stood in the doorway for a moment looking at Maureen lovingly before making her presence known.

"What's the matter, Mo'reen?" Ruby gently closed the door. She moved to the bed and sat next to Maureen.

Ruby's former room looked a lot like it had during the days she occupied it. Neat and homey, with bright-colored curtains, bedspread, and throw rugs. A large cloth illustration of the Last Supper almost covered half of one wall.

"I want to go home," Maureen answered.

"Don't you like it here?"

"Naw. Do you?"

"Of course I like it here! This is where I come from," Ruby said. She made a sweeping gesture with her hand and glanced around the room.

"Then how come you left and stayed away so long, Mama Ruby? How can you leave somethin you like? . . . I'd never do that."

Ruby looked at Maureen's lips as she spoke, then looked up alongside her head.

"Do you like me, Mo'reen?"

"Ma'am?"

"I ax you if you like me?"

"Yes, ma'am."

"Then you'll never leave me?"

"I don't know."

"You just said you'd never leave nothin you like."

"I wouldn't . . . I guess . . . I ain't never leavin you then," Maureen smiled. "Unless . . ." her voice trailed off.

"Unless what?" Ruby asked with alarm.

"Unless I . . . unless I get carried off by the devil, like you say my daddy was."

Ruby turned away and considered Maureen's words.

"I won't let the devil get near you. I'm tough," Ruby whispered, looking toward the door.

"Then how come he carried off my daddy? You couldn't stop the devil from carryin off my daddy, how you goin to stop him from carryin me off?"

"Remember that day me and you was sittin on the porch and you axed me if I was the devil?"

"Yeah. You said. . . ."

Ruby looked toward the door again, then leaned closer to Maureen, glancing about the room nervously. "I ain't goin to mention it, but I am. Don't you never tell nobody I told you this. Don't tell Cousin Hattie. Don't tell nobody back in Florida. They wouldn't be able to handle havin the devil so close to em. How you think Roscoe would feel knowin he was engaged to marry the devil? What you think Irene and Bishop would say if they knowed they best friend was the devil? And what would my daddy say?"

"If you is the devil, how can you be a Christian too?" Maureen asked, cocking her head to the side and looking at Ruby out of the corner of her eye.

"The devil is the master of disguises! He the only one, cept the Lord, what can be more than one thing at the same time. Though I am filled with the Holy Ghost, I also am the doorway to darkness."

Maureen covered her mouth with her hand to suppress a giggle. "Mama Ruby, you so funny. You ain't the devil. The devil was a man."

Ruby sighed and moved to the window. She started talking with her back to Maureen.

"Virgil's dead. I just know it. He done died in that foreign country. He took secrets with him," Ruby said. "Secrets I will carry with me to my grave."

"About what?"

"You for one. Me. Him. Things I can never tell nobody. Not even you." Ruby turned slightly to see Maureen's reaction.

"Bad things?"

Ruby looked at Maureen thoughtfully and nodded.

"Don't never tell me what they is," Maureen said softly.

"I hadn't planned to," Ruby said firmly.

Maureen leaped up from the bed, ran to Ruby, and grabbed her hand.

"Mama Ruby, let's stop talkin sad talk. Tell me again about that ole white lady we goin to visit this week."

Ruby lifted Maureen up, returned to the bed with her, and sat down, putting Maureen on her lap.

"Her name is Miss Mo'reen."

"That's my name!"

"It was Miss Mo'reen's name first. She the one I named you after. She live in New Orleans and got two plum trees in her front yard."

"She got any kids I can play with?" Maureen asked, her eyes wide and her heart thumping madly.

"She got kids but they all growed up and livin in a foreign country called Ireland. That's where Miss Mo'reen come from."

"You said foreigners was the devil's relations."

"Not all foreigners. See, Miss Mo'reen been in America most of her life. She don't even talk like no foreigner. She talk regular English like me and you. None of them crazy accents or nothin."

"She a nice lady?"

"If God made anything better than Miss Mo'reen, he kept it for hisself. She made me what I am today," Ruby said proudly. "Girl, I am some successful!"

Maureen looked at Ruby carefully, from her feet up to her face.

"What she make you into, Mama Ruby?"

Ruby looked at Maureen with surprise on her face.

"What Miss Mo'reen make you into?"

"A Christian. In spite of Satan's toehold," Ruby answered. She lightly touched her bosom, confirming the presence of her cross and her switchblade.

28

"You sure you don't want me to drive you and Mo'reen to New Orleans, Ruby Jean? Them buses is goin to sho nuff be crowded with Christmas travelers."

"Don't bother, Papa. Mo'reen ain't never been on no Greyhound bus. She lookin forward to this little ride," Ruby smiled.

"When yall comin back?" Ida asked.

Ruby sat with her parents and her two sisters, Carrie and Beaulah, on her father's patio. They all occupied lounge chairs. A breeze caused goose pimples to rise on Ruby's bare arms. The others had sweaters on.

"I'll just be gone a couple of days. Then we'll spend our last days here. Mo'reen gettin antsy and want to get on back to Florida," Ruby explained. "I got to get her back to school. She can't miss too much. Lord knows I don't want her to grow up to be a fool."

"Too bad you didn't apply that same principle to yourself," Carrie said.

Ruby glared at her sister. Carrie returned the gaze, leaning forward. "You act like you don't like what I just said!"

"I see you ain't changed none. Always pickin on me," Ruby said. "Ain't you got eyes? Can't you see I'm a successful woman?" Ruby demanded.

Carrie and Beaulah were as large as Ruby and had the same fiery temper, though her sisters resembled their father rather than their mother, as Ruby did.

"No husband. You just like that Cousin Hattie," Beaulah said, disappointment in her voice. "Now, why don't you drag your tail on back to Shreveport and find you another husband? You ain't got no business bein in Florida in the first place."

"I told yall how I been wrestlin with the devil for so many years," Ruby said.

"Yall leave Ruby Jean alone. Can't you see she is trying to get back on the right track?" Reverend Upshaw said, giving Carrie and Beaulah stern looks.

"Least I got Jesus to fall back on," Ruby said.

"We all got Jesus to fall back on," Ida said. "What's keepin you in Florida anyway, girl?"

"My lovely home for one. I got a house fit for a king. Why, compared to what yall got—my house is heaven!" Ruby shouted. "I got me a house out in the country away from all the mess that go on in a city."

"Ruby Jean, Mo'reen say yall live damn near in the Everglades!" Carrie said, rising, facing Ruby with anger in her voice. "She told me hens lay eggs on your living room sofa!"

"And say every kind of bug you can name get loose in the house durin bug season," Beaulah added.

Carrie returned to her seat after Ruby's glare got the better of her.

"Ruby Jean, what's so special about your house?" Ida asked quietly, touching Ruby's knee.

"It's Mo'reen's room," Ruby said in a low voice.

Each member of her family turned to look in her face.

"What about Mo'reen's room?" Reverend Upshaw asked.

"It's sanctified," Ruby said. "If I remove her from it, she'll surely die."

"That Florida sun done baked what little bit of a brain you had," Beaulah said nastily. "A bedroom is a bedroom!"

"Yall don't understand. Mo'reen ain't no regular child. She a gift from the Lord. Her presence make the upper room so special," Ruby wailed.

"THE UPPER ROOM?!" Beaulah shouted, laughing so hard her sides hurt and she cried. She laughed until she started to choke on her own tongue. Ida leaped up from her seat to pound on Beaulah's back.

"You see why I can't stay around yall?" Ruby said, rising. "Papa, you know I never liked bein laughed at," Ruby pouted. She went to her father and threw herself down on the ground, placing her hands on his lap. "Papa, I love yall, but I'm important in Florida. Them folks in Goons, they need me. They'd be lost without me. I can't turn my back on em."

"We need you too, daughter," the preacher said.

Ruby looked at Beaulah, who was holding her sides and trying desperately not to laugh again.

"I see now why you run off with that carnival woman. You is sho nuff a clown, Ruby Jean," Carrie said.

Carrie and Beaulah were both married to preachers and lived in comfortable houses not far from their parents.

"My husband always said Ruby was a fool," Carrie laughed. "Even if she is a seventh daughter of a seventh daughter."

"Ruby Jean never had a lick of sense no how," Beaulah added.

Ruby remained at her father's knee, looking up in his face for consolation.

"Carrie Mae, where is your husband today?" the reverend asked.

"Huh? I don't really know," she replied.

"Where your husband at today, Beaulah Lou?" he asked.

"I ain't seen him since this mornin," she said nervously.

"Neither one of em was in church this mornin," the reverend pointed out. "And their whereabouts at this moment is unknown."

He looked down at Ruby.

"Where your husband, girl?" he asked.

"Dead. I suspect his soul is poppin like popcorn in the lake of fire."

"The devil he was, that's where he should be."

"I know it, Papa. Him with his white woman and his drinkin and all . . ." Ruby sobbed.

The reverend looked from Beaulah to Carrie.

"Least Ruby Jean know *where* her man is," he said.

Carrie and Beaulah sighed and gave Ruby dirty looks.

"Carrie, didn't your man go up side your head last month

with a pop bottle?" Ida asked. "And you, Beaulah, didn't your man get caught with his hands in the church treasury? With all that commotion in yall's own backyard, you ain't got no right to be low ratin Ruby Jean, is you?"

"No, ma'am," Beaulah mumbled.

"No, ma'am," Carrie said, lowering her head and coughing to conceal her embarrassment. "No, ma'am," she repeated contritely.

"Long as Ruby Jean here, don't let me hear yall messin with her no more. Is that clear?" the preacher said.

The two sisters nodded.

"Now, Ruby Jean, what time your bus leavin for New Orleans?" Reverend Upshaw asked, stroking Ruby's face.

"First thing tomorrow mornin," she said. "My bus leave here first thing tomorrow mornin."

Maureen suddenly came running out on the patio before the conversation could continue.

"Mama Ruby, carry me on back to Florida—I can't stand it here! I'm fixin to go out of my head!" she wailed, throwing herself to the floor on her knees next to Ruby.

"Yall see what I mean? This girl would have to be weaned before she could give up Florida," Ruby said.

The visit had done nothing but depress Maureen. None of the kids in the neighborhood had ever heard of the game grown-folks and none had ever seen a murder. Only a few of them would admit to drinking pot liquor! And being surrounded by so much obesity annoyed Maureen. Both of Carrie's daughters were stout and made bad playmates. They couldn't even run fast. The most walking they did was to and from the kitchen and the candy store. They only talked about food. Beaulah's only child, a homely thirteen-year-old named Lee Humphrey, was even worse than Carrie's girls as far as Maureen was concerned. He was tall and had a slablike face with pimples. On three separate occasions, he had enticed Maureen upstairs to a vacant bedroom in her grandparents' house and exposed himself to her.

"Mo'reen, tetch my thing," he'd said the last time.

"How come?" Maureen asked, frowning at her cousin's limp penis. "Yeck!" she said, shaking her shoulders, not taking her eyes off the boy's organ.

"Just tetch it like I said, girl!"

"What's wrong with it?" she asked. She looked up at Lee's face for a long time, before lightly touching his penis.

"That's it . . . that's it," he sighed. "One day we'll do somethin different," he promised.

"The shake?" Maureen asked.

"The what?"

"I seen Virgil do what I think you want to do to me with a lady back home. The shake," she said quietly.

"Oh we'll do some shakin all right," Lee promised with an obscene grin.

"Mama Ruby say if I was to ever let a boy get in my step-ins he'd bring the devil with him and I'd have the devil in me for the rest of my life."

"Listen here, girl, you keep listenin to Mama Ruby and you goin to end up believin everything she say."

"What you mean?"

"Grown folks don't want kids to have no fun."

"How come?"

"Cause they want to have it all. Long as Mama Ruby don't know you havin fun, she'll be happy. You remember that. Do you hear me?"

". . . Yeah," Maureen said thoughtfully, promising herself to remember.

29

Maureen kept thinking about what Lee had said to her during the bus ride from Shreveport to New Orleans. She sat next to Ruby, resting her head on Ruby's chest. Maureen could feel Ruby's bosom rise and fall with each breath. Ruby leaned her head against the window.

Surely she could have a good time and keep it from Ruby so Ruby would still believe she was totally devoted to her. She could remain with Ruby until Ruby died. That thought frightened Maureen. Where would she be without Mama Ruby? What kind of life would she have without Mama Ruby? What would she be prepared for? If Ruby suddenly died, she would have nobody. And she'd be lonely. Maureen lifted her head and looked at Ruby.

"What would I do if you was to die, Mama Ruby? Who would take care of me? Who would keep the house clean? Who would iron my clothes? Who would cook for me and whip me when I needed it?"

Ruby turned her head mechanically and faced Maureen, her lips quivering.

"What?" Ruby mouthed.

"I ax what would I do if you was to die?"

"I don't plan on dyin no time soon."

"Oh," Maureen said. She returned her head to Ruby's chest. A minute later she lifted it again.

"But what if you die in a accident or get cancer or somethin? What would I do? I wouldn't have nobody to take care of me."

"You got Jesus," Ruby said with conviction.

"Oh," Maureen said again. "You don't never want me to leave the upper room. You don't want no man in the upper room. Then I can't never get married, right?"

"Right."

"No husband. No kids. I won't have nobody in this world if you was to die. I'd rather die myself than get adopted by Grandma Ida and have to live in Shreveport. I wouldn't want to be Fast Black's little girl or Irene's little girl. What would happen to me?"

"Didn't I just tell you you had Jesus? What more do you want? Gold?"

"I can't *see* Jesus. He can't talk to me. I'll be lonesome. Mama Ruby, do you want me to have fun?"

"Is what you call fun in the Bible?"

"I don't know."

"If it ain't in the Bible, I don't want you to have nothin to do with it. I done already locked horns with the devil enough over you."

"And if you is the devil, how come you keep talkin about how you been wrestlin with him and lockin horns with him, if you is him?"

"How many times do I have to tell you Satan is capable of bein more than one person?"

"What you mean by that?"

Ruby lowered her eyelids and took several long, deep breaths before talking again. Maureen waited anxiously.

"What you mean, Mama Ruby?"

". . . 'And he asked him, what is thy name? And he answered, saying, my name is Legion: for we are many,'" Ruby whispered just loud enough for Maureen to hear.

"Reverend Tiggs talked about that from the Bible one Sunday . . . the man with the unclean spirit what couldn't be tied down with chains," Maureen said.

"Couldn't be tamed . . . for we are many," Ruby said, turning to face Maureen. "Did I answer your question?"

". . . St. Mark . . . chapter five . . . verse nine?"

"Hallelujah," Ruby replied. "You understand how I can be the Lord's fold and the devil's walkin stick?"

"Yeah . . . I think I do," Maureen responded, still confused. "Mama Ruby, how in the world did you get in such a mess? Is you the only person in the world what tangle with the devil so much? How come you can get away with so much and still get to go to heaven?"

"I been to hell and back. I seen the Lord's throne. I seen a serpent rare back and spit oppression in the face of man. I seen it all. I seen em string up a man by his neck. I seen em set a fire to a house with a old man confined to a wheelchair in it. I seen it all. These old eyes done seen it all. I can't explain it all to you now, how I ended up in such a mess. You too young to understand. I'll tell you one day after you get growed up. But believe, I done seen some of everything."

"You seen God?"

"Stared in his face."

"You seen the devil?"

"Looked him eyeball to eyeball."

"Oh. Well, can you beat up God?"

"I done cussed out the devil. That's bigger than beatin up God. What you got to say about that?"

Maureen nodded and reached up to brush Ruby's hair back from her forehead.

"Mama Ruby, you is tough, sho nuff. I heard Fast Black do a brag on you. She say you could bite a nail in half."

"With my *gums.*"

"Fast Black say you can beat up Cassius Clay."

"With one hand tied behind my back."

"What about Fi'del Castro?"

"What about him?"

"Can you beat him up?"

"Him and the horse he ride."

"Oh."

The bus pulled into the town of Scheny and parked in front of Sam's Grill, where all the passengers got off and went inside to order beverages and snacks. Ruby and Maureen devoured their french fries and sloppy joes quickly and carried their drinks back to the bus with them.

Minutes later, after all the other passengers had returned to their seats, Maureen started to whine.

"I left my doll back at that restaurant."

"What doll? Where you get a doll from?"

"I got it outta gum machine in the bus station in Shreveport. It was a itty-bitty doll I had in my pocket. I left her layin on the seat and forgot to pick her up when we left," Maureen pouted.

"We'll get you another one when we get to New Orleans," Ruby promised.

"But I don't want another one—I want the old one," Maureen wailed, starting to cry.

Ruby became embarrassed. The other passengers were turning around, giving her annoyed looks.

"Shhh, Mo'reen. I swear to God I'll buy you not one but two new dolls, just as soon as we get to New Orleans. Hear me?"

"Aaarrggghhh," Maureen wailed, her eyes closed and her mouth stretched wide open.

"Shet up, girl, before these folks think I'm treatin you like a stepchild," Ruby begged. She reached inside her bra and removed her handkerchief and wiped Maureen's eyes and nose, but Maureen continued to cry. The bus had not started again yet. Ruby cursed under her breath as she got up from her seat, climbed over Maureen, and hurriedly left the bus.

It took her two minutes to retrieve the doll and return. When she did, the bus was gone.

"MO'REEEEN!" Ruby screamed, running down the middle of the street after the bus. But the bus was too far away already.

Somehow Ruby managed to retain enough control to go back inside the restaurant and call the local police. But she left before they arrived. She had got a ride to New Orleans on the back of a pickup truck driven by a Cajun man who had been sitting in the restaurant. Ruby had put her switchblade to the man's throat, giving him no chance to refuse her request. They arrived in New Orleans twenty minutes ahead of the bus Maureen was on.

As soon as the bus door opened, Maureen ran to Ruby.

"Mama Ruby, I thought I'd never see you again! That ole nasty bus driver wouldn't wait on you to get back!"

"Where is that hound of hell?!" Ruby thundered, "I ought to de-ball him!"

"Don't kill him, Mama Ruby . . . let's just get our stuff and get on to Miss Mo'reen's house," Maureen begged.

30

After two light strokes left one of her arms partially paralyzed, Maureen O'Leary had curtailed her activities considerably. Some of her best girls had been lured away from the old madam, now in her seventies, by smooth-talking local pimps. Her youngest girls had run off to such faraway places as New York and Chicago. The smart ones had been attracted to the western cities, where life was more relaxed and folks more liberal about prostitution. The brothel, a sprawling old plantation house with four white columns and two swings on the front porch, was painted off-white. It had been an icy blue during the months Ruby and Othella lived there.

"Most of my girls done up and left me. Ain't nothin been right since you and Othella left us, Ruby. Every now and then a fancy man come by and drop dollar bills on us," Old Maureen said sadly. She sat next to Ruby on one of the front porch swings. A large pitcher of iced tea and a tray of coasters and napkins sat on a cart next to the swing. A thick tapestry shawl lay across Old Maureen's shoulders. Her hair, once black, was now snow white, her narrow face profusely lined, her loose, liver-spotted skin sagging like the jowls of a turkey.

"I been thinkin about comin out of retirement and takin over my old room here, on a off-and-on basis. I'd never really leave Florida. I love Florida and my friends, but many a day I wish I'd never left New Orleans and this house, Miss Mo'reen."

"Why you run off, Ruby Jean? Why you let Othella carry you off? We lost so much business when you took off like you done. Word come to me about yall joinin a carnival and I like to died on the spot. What Othella give you that you couldn't get from me?"

Ruby swallowed hard and looked out into the street.

"She give me a new life . . ." she replied.

"Pardon?"

Ruby turned to face the old woman.

"After I got to Florida, the Lord made known his presence in my path. He blessed me with a husband, a son, and a livin doll for a daughter."

"Where is your man?"

". . . Um . . . he had a little accident."

Old Maureen looked at Ruby, studying her features. Ruby sat staring down at her lap, rubbing the tips of her fingers together.

"Did you kill him, Ruby? Tell me the truth now; I know how you is. You was always struttin around talkin about killin this trick and that trick for one reason or another."

Ruby nodded and cleared her throat.

"Who told you?"

"Nobody. I just had you pegged right. Since the day Othella brought you to me, I knowed you wasn't no ordinary girl. Folks can look at you and see you ain't like most folks. By the way, seem like you done put on a bit more weight since you left."

"A pound or two."

The old madam looked at Ruby's gigantic arms and touched one.

"How's your health, Ruby Jean? You was wheezin a awful lot this mornin."

"My blood pressure done gone wild. Other than that, I'm in pretty good health. Why?"

"A woman your size can fall victim to just about some of everything. Heart attack. Stroke. You name it. Look what happened to me and I ain't half as big as you."

"Long as I got Jesus, I don't need nothin else. He is my mama,

my daddy, and my doctor. That's why I ain't spent nary a day in
jail for killin that low-down, funky black dog I married."

"Why'd you kill him? And how you get out of goin to jail?
They tell me the state of Florida is one of the worse states in the
world to commit a crime. They got more folks on death row
than the rest of the southern states put together."

"Well, my man had shamed me beyond redemption and
everybody knowed. I was scandalized before my friends and
made to look like a fool in front of white folks. That nigger was
better off dead anyway. I done it for his own good. He had
women comin out his ear. I killed him for that reason."

"And the laws ain't fetched you?"

"Well, not exactly. They give me a month and a day on account of when I went to kill that thing I married, I run off and
left some white kids alone I was babysittin. *That's* what I went to
jail for," Ruby explained.

Old Maureen nodded and shivered. Ruby rose and rearranged the shawl on the old woman's shoulders.

"Well, Ruby, what else you been up to?"

Ruby smiled mysteriously.

"I got me a fiance and a truckload of Christian friends. And
a house—let me tell you about my house!"

While Ruby was giving Old Maureen a detailed report about
her house with its sanctified upper room, Maureen and two
young girls came skipping from around the side of the house,
where there was a wading pool and a sandbox behind a large
chicken shed. In season, large plums fell from the two trees
that shaded the pool. Debbie Starr was the twelve-year-old
daughter of Old Maureen's black "boarder," Rosalie. And Lola
was the nine-year-old daughter of blond, Mississippi-born Bonnie
Henderson, Old Maureen's current favorite girl. Maureen and
her two companions stopped and carefully situated themselves
on the steps leading up to the front porch. Debbie had a catalogue she placed on the steps and began leafing through. Lola
produced a pair of scissors and they started cutting "paperdolls" from the catalogue. Maureen, carrying a handful of plastic daisies in one hand and big rocks in the other, walked up
the steps to Old Maureen and climbed on her lap.

"I brought you some flowers, Miss Old Mo'reen," she said.

"Mo'reen, girl, climb down off Miss Mo'reen's lap before

you cause her another stroke," Ruby said, clapping her hands together once. "Go on and play paperdolls with the girls."

"You leave her alone, Ruby. Can't you see she done brought me some flowers." Old Maureen hugged the girl with her one good arm, squeezing her until she squirmed.

Bonnie and Rosalie sauntered through the front door onto the porch, taking over the other swing. Both carried fans and glasses of Pepsi. Bonnie, an occasional snuff dipper, carried an empty coffee can in her other hand that she kept spitting into. Both wore bandannas to conceal their uncombed hair. Their clothes were plain and wrinkled, gray housecoats that were too small and soiled with barbecue sauce and pork drippings.

Rosalie sighed and took a sip of her drink. She toyed with the ice cubes with her long nails, and began talking quietly.

"Ruby, was Santa Claus good to you this Christmas?"

"I ain't had much of a Christmas this year. See, a couple of weeks ago my boy got lost in that V-Eight Nam. I come to visit my family cause I needed some extra prayer assistance. I ain't thought much about no Christmas. Otherwise, I'm enjoyin the season. How was Santa Claus to you?"

"Oh, he just by-passed all of us this year," Rosalie said.

"And everybody else been by-passin us the rest of the year," Bonnie added. "Ain't been a sport or a fancy man by here today. Things keep up like they been and I'm subject to drag my tail off to New York somewhere," she drawled.

"I got a itchin to do the same thing," Rosalie said, looking directly at the madam. Old Maureen's eyes filled with tears and she released young Maureen and stood up. Still clutching the fake daisies, the old woman hobbled off the porch, walked softly across the front yard and seated herself on a padded settee inside a white gazebo.

"What's wrong with her?" Maureen asked Ruby. "What's wrong with Miss Old Mo'reen?"

Ruby shaded her eyes to look at the old woman, then slowly turned to face Maureen.

"Look like the devil done dragged his tail into Miss Mo'reen's life . . . just like he done with me." Ruby took Maureen's hand in hers and squeezed it.

31

The sun glistened on New Orleans in the early morning as white-hooded figures, with their white faces showing, paraded boldly down Seneca Street on horseback. The earliness of the hour accounted for the lack of curious spectators usually drawn to public Ku Klux Klan rallies. The Klansmen halted and dismounted in a plaza less than a hundred feet away from the cobblestone walk that led to the entrance of Jimmy's Confectionery Store. Some of the men carried large Confederate flags held high on long poles. Some displayed crudely printed signs with logos:

DOWN WITH MARTIN LUTHOR COON
and
NIGGERS GO BACK TO AFRICA

Some of the signs were more malicious.

Maureen and Debbie were skipping rope in front of the store while waiting for Ruby to come out. Ruby planned to return to Shreveport with Maureen the following morning, and Old Maureen was throwing a pre-Mardi Gras party in their honor. Ruby and the girls had come to the store to pick up some last minute items needed for the party.

"Look, Debbie, a parade," Maureen exclaimed as she dropped

the rope and leaped into the air, clapping her hands and waving at the Klansmen.

"Girl, that ain't no parade," Debbie informed her. "That's the Klan."

Maureen looked at her with a puzzled expression and started to walk toward the rally, but Debbie grabbed the tail of Maureen's dress and held her back.

"Let me go! I'm goin to look at the parade. I like horses," Maureen said, pulling away.

"You ain't goin noplace! Them folks'll kill you dead! They kilt a boy from my school," Debbie said, placing her hand on Maureen's arm. "That's the Klan."

"The what?"

"The Klan. Look at them signs they carryin. They hate black folks like us. Here it is almost nineteen and sixty-four and they still actin like fools!"

Maureen looked at her hands, turning them over for inspection. Then she looked at Debbie's hands.

"We ain't black, we brown. Who they kilt and why?"

"Mo'reen, the Klan law say they hate people like us. The boy they kilt was a boy what messed with some nasty ole white girl. I'm tellin you, girl. They hate us!"

Maureen gasped and covered her mouth with her hand. Debbie roughly removed Maureen's hand and forced her to speak.

"Don't be mumblin under your breath. You got somethin to say, say it, Mo'reen."

"I don't believe what you just said about them Klans, Debbie. You just don't want me to go to the parade. I'm fixin to go—"

"Mo'reen, them folks kilt my brother too," Debbie said, her voice wobbling on her words.

Maureen looked at the Klansmen, then quickly back to Debbie.

"What your brother do?"

"Nothin. He just happened to be in the wrong place at the wrong time."

"Like my brother. Mama Ruby say he was just in the wrong place at the wrong time." Maureen turned to look at the Klansmen again, this time with anger. Before Debbie realized what was happening, Maureen picked up a huge rock and hurled it into

the crowd of Klansmen. One of the men—there were at least
twenty—screamed and stumbled off his horse. The rock had
hit him on his forehead. His comrades helped him up, and as
soon as he steadied himself, he grabbed his flag and ran in the
children's direction.

Debbie grabbed Maureen by the hand and they disappeared
around the corner leading to the back of the confectionery
store.

"Come on, Mo'reen! Somethin was to happen to you, Mama
Ruby said she kill everybody in New Orleans!" Debbie screamed,
and she and Maureen ran as if the devil himself were in pursuit.

Egged on by his companions, the Klansman chased the girls
into an alley in back of the store. Maureen ran up the back
porch steps to the store but fell down on her face. Debbie fell
over her to shield Maureen's body as the Klansman brought his
flagpole down across Debbie's back. Moaning and pretending
to be hurt, Debbie lay motionless as the vengeful man turned
and began to walk back to rejoin his party.

A well-aimed switchblade thrown with the fury of the devil
caught the Klansman at the base of his neck, and a small red
stain soiled the white hood. The man staggered, then fell to the
ground, dead. Ruby stood on the top step of the store's back
porch. She calmly retrieved her knife, then lifted Maureen
from the steps, and with Debbie close behind they made it back
to the brothel, long before anyone discovered what had happened in the back alley.

Old Maureen stood in the doorway of the bedroom Ruby
and Maureen had been staying in, breathing with great difficulty and leaning on a cane, tears streaming down the sides of
her face.

"Ruby, stay here and let me help you. I got a lot of friends in
this town what owe me big favors. You won't spend much time
in prison," Old Maureen cried.

"I got news for you, I ain't spendin *no* time in prison," Ruby
replied, moving about the room quickly, collecting her belongings.

"How far you think you'll get runnin off like this? You done
kilt another man. You got a record back in Florida. Runnin off
like this will only make matters worse! That's the law!"

"Law shmaw. Law ain't got nothin to do with me," Ruby muttered.

Only minutes had passed since Ruby and the children returned to the brothel. Debbie hid in her room. Lola stood in the window to see if the authorities knew where to start looking.

Rosalie and Bonnie had hurriedly left the house.

"We'll go spread the word we seen a foreigner runnin from where the Klansman was kilt!" Bonnie had assured Ruby.

"And I'll swear on a stack of Bibles, I seen the foreigner throw the knife myself!" Rosalie said, dashing out the door behind Bonnie.

Ruby thanked her friends for their help and rushed to start packing.

"We goin home now, Mama Ruby?" Maureen asked eagerly, as soon as Ruby brought out the shopping bag they had packed their belongings in. The footlocker remained at Ruby's parents' house with most of their clothes and their train tickets back to Florida.

"Yeah, we goin back home! I'll write Mama and Papa a letter and tell em we had to rush back cause somebody broke in my house! I can't hang around this state a minute too long!" Ruby said, throwing clothes in the bag.

"You ain't got no money. You ain't got no tickets. How you goin to get back to Florida runnin off like this? Anyway, the law'll be lookin for suspicious people at the bus station, the train station, and the airport. Ain't no way you can get out of this state alive, Ruby!" Old Maureen wailed. She struggled to move across the floor to the bed where Ruby stood. Maureen stood near the window, peeking out from behind the drapes.

"I'ma worry about that bridge when I come to it," Ruby said, almost out of breath.

Old Maureen grabbed Ruby's wrist.

"You can't keep livin the way you been. Your luck is bound to run out one day. Stay here . . . let me get us a Jew lawyer to straighten out this mess! We don't know the whole story. Them kids leavin somethin out. I don't believe that Klansman just lit out after them for no reason at all." Old Maureen looked over at Maureen, who looked at her and blinked her eyes rapidly.

"Miss Old Mo'reen, see, I hit the man up side his head with a rock," Maureen confessed.

Ruby stopped for only a moment, then continued packing.

"You heard her. You heard the child admit she give the man good cause to come after her and Debbie, Ruby. Oh, you in a heap of trouble this time! The Klan ain't nothin to play with!" Old Maureen hollered, following Ruby around. "You hear me—the Klan ain't nothin to play with!"

"T'ain't neither!" Ruby replied as she folded the top of the bag over. "Mo'reen, let's go. We fixin to haul ass again," she yelled. "Get your shoes, darlin."

"I can't let you go, Ruby," Old Maureen cried, grabbing Ruby's wrist again. "You can plead insanity—anything!"

Ruby pulled away from the madam and stepped back.

"Miss Mo'reen, I can't let nobody mess with Mo'reen and live to tell about it. I wish that white-sheeted devil was alive again so I could kill him again! If it wasn't for me, Mo'reen would have been dead a long time ago."

"Mama Ruby, come on. Let's get out of here," Maureen pleaded, tugging at Ruby's dress.

Ruby held out her hand to Maureen and they left. Old Maureen, sobbing softly, watched from a back window as Ruby and Maureen disappeared into the bayou behind the brothel.

The old woman was still in the window when Bonnie and Rosalie returned more than a half hour later.

"Ruby and Baby Mo'reen get away?" Bonnie asked with concern. She stood behind Old Maureen with her hands on the old woman's shoulders.

Old Maureen reached back and touched Bonnie's hand affectionately.

"Yeah. They got away . . . this time," the madam sighed.

32

Cousin Hattie had just turned in for the night, but before she could get comfortable someone knocked hard on her front door.

"Now who in the world is that?!" Hattie asked, hurrying through her dark little congested house on Market Street in Baton Rouge. She held a coal-oil lamp in one hand and a rolling pin in the other. "Who is that knockin on my door this time of night?" Hattie shouted toward the door.

Hattie led a regulated life. She restricted herself to a handful of friends and rarely had unexpected visitors.

"OPEN THIS DOOR BEFORE I COME THROUGH IT!" Ruby shouted from outside.

Hattie dropped her rolling pin and snatched open the door. She was not prepared for what she saw. Ruby stood before her cradling Maureen, who was asleep in her arms. Both were stained with mud and sand. Leeches had attached themselves to Ruby's legs. Her torn dress had blood on it and both she and Maureen had lost a shoe along the way.

Hattie gasped and held her lamp up to Ruby's face and saw that her eyes were bloodshot and had deep dark circles that were so distinct they looked as if they had been drawn on. Hattie let out a scream.

"I got a mess on my hands!" Ruby said, talking in a low voice, glancing nervously over her shoulder. A light went on in the house next door and there was the sound of a noisy window going up.

"Come on in the house," Hattie whispered, grabbing Ruby's arm and pulling her in. Ruby hurried in, carried Maureen to the sofa and put her down, then ran back to the porch to get the shopping bag she had left sitting outside.

"What done happened this time?!" Hattie demanded, locking her door. "Tell me, Cousin Ruby, what you done done now?"

Ruby made sure Maureen was comfortable; then she sat down on the sofa herself and started to fan her face with her hand.

"Cousin Hattie, I ain't shook the devil loose yet," Ruby gasped, almost losing her teeth.

Hattie listened with interest as Ruby told her what had happened in New Orleans, revising the story to suit her needs.

"A Klansman tried to rape you, huh?" Hattie said. "That bastard! Killin was too good for him. You done the right thing, Cousin Ruby."

"Me and Mo'reen come through the woods till the coast was clear. Then we flagged down a preacher comin this way . . . and here we is," Ruby sighed, making a sweeping gesture with her hand.

"I declare, Cousin Ruby. You have more run-ins than the man in the moon. The devil been had it in for you all your life, huh?"

"Sho nuff. He done stole my boy and now this. Got me on the run like a regular criminal. Cousin Hattie, please tell me you got a friend with a car or a truck what can carry me and my baby back to Florida. We ain't got no money and even if we did have some, we can't take no chance on the bus or nothin. Can you get us a ride back to Florida?" Ruby pleaded.

"I got friends with cars and trucks, but I don't know how eager one of em'll be to drive all the way to Florida," Hattie admitted. She moved across the floor to a stand next to the sofa. "I'll start makin calls right now."

"See if you can get em to come over here; don't tell em what for. When they get here, let me ax em. Ain't too many people can say no to me to my face." Ruby nodded as she finished speaking.

PART THREE

33

Maureen spent her eighteenth birthday picking string beans in one of the many fields owned by the directors of the Gressenger Brothers migrant camp. Her occasional boyfriend, Willie Boatwright's eighteen-year-old son Bobby, a tall, rust-colored boy with thick brown hair, wicked black eyes, and a seductive grin, squatted between the two rows to her left. Catty and Yellow Jack were to her right, sharing a row. Catty and Yellow Jack had been lovers for the past three years and spent little time apart.

"Mo'reen, I want to carry you to the movies tonight for your birthday," Bobby hollered without looking up.

"I can't go. I got to mop the upper room," Maureen replied. It was too hot to pay attention to anything other than her job. Picking beans was piecework. At a dollar per peck, Maureen found it worth her while to try for twenty pecks a day.

She had graduated from school with a C average and she was now a young woman, the most beautiful woman in Goons. Her figure was slim and well proportioned. Long, straight black hair framed her high cheekbones, large eyes, and full lips. She was the image of Othella.

"Girl, you just mopped the upper room yestiddy. And anyway, wood floors don't even need no moppin!" Bobby shouted angrily. He stood up and faced Maureen with his arms folded.

He rolled up his shirt sleeves and wiped perspiration from his face with his arm. "Is you messin with some fancy man or somethin?"

"I ain't got me no fancy man, Bobby Boatwright!" Maureen retorted. "You keep accusin me of havin a fancy man, I'm liable to get me one."

"You do and I'll . . . I'll—"

"You mess with Mo'reen and Mama Ruby'll cut your head off," Catty warned seriously. "And don't think she won't do it. I seen her do it. . . ."

There was silence for a full minute as they looked at Catty. She had stopped growing at four feet eleven. Her thick wavy black hair was in two braids. She grabbed a handful of sand and tossed it at Maureen.

"What you do that for?" Maureen asked, brushing sand from her hair.

"I'm tryin to get your mind off Bobby Boatwright. Don't you go to no movies with him. Me and you got somethin to do tonight. Remember?"

"Oh." Maureen gave Bobby a dry look.

"Go on off with Catty. See if I care. Me and Yellow Jack goin night fishin in the Blue Lake anyway. Ain't we, Yellow Jack?" Bobby said.

"Sho nuff is. We done already dug the bait. A couple of white boys goin with us," Yellow Jack responded.

"Yall shet up and get back to work! Stop disturbin the rest of the bean pickers!" Willie Boatwright ordered. He squatted over the row on the other side of Catty and Yellow Jack. "Yellow Jack, you and Catty ain't filled but three pecks today. With all that stoppin to smooch and carry on. And you, Bobby, you better not bring your nasty tail home this evenin with less than twenty dollars. You do and I'll bust your head wide open."

"OK, Daddy," Bobby mumbled, returning to his work.

"Oh, *you* shet up, Boatwright. You can't boss me and Mo'reen and Yellow Jack around no more. We all eighteen now," Catty reminded Boatwright.

"Girl, don't you be sassin my daddy!" Bobby warned, tossing a handful of sand at Catty.

"OK, the party is over!" Loomis said, walking up. "Yall teenagers better behave, lest you want me to put the Gressengers on

you. They done told me to tell em which ones act a fool and
they wouldn't pay em. Yellow Jack, you know I'll slap you up side
the head in a minute and make Fast Black do the same thing
after I'm through with you."

"I know," Yellow Jack muttered.

"And you, Catty, I'll beat the shit out of you—"

"You low-down, funky black dog! You tetch me and I'll get
one of my fancy men from Boca Raton to come out here and
do a Mama Ruby on you!" Catty threatened. This outburst
caused everyone within hearing distance to laugh long and
loud.

"What fancy men from Boca Raton?" Yellow Jack asked. He
was the only one not laughing.

"She ain't got no fancy men from Boca Raton, Yellow Jack,"
Maureen said low enough for only Yellow Jack to hear. He
smiled when she winked at him.

Loomis lowered his eyes and returned to his row. He had recently left Zeus' house and moved into one of the newly va-
cated houses near the camps. No Talk lived with Fast Black
now, sharing her bedroom. With Loomis gone, Yellow Jack had
his old room back and was glad to be sleeping in a bed again,
rather than in a living room chair.

Yellow Jack had skipped a grade and graduated a year ahead
of Maureen and the others. He had been working in the fields
full time for a year and doing other odd jobs in Miami. With his
first month's pay, he had purchased a car, a five-year-old
Cadillac convertible, which was one of the reasons Catty's parents agreed to let her get engaged to him. Yellow Jack had
bought the car from an aging Miami pimp, so it had low
mileage and was in pretty good shape. The same day he bought
it, Bobby played with the convertible activator so much that he
had broken it, so Yellow Jack could never put the top up again.
Then a week later Fast Black borrowed it to drag race with
Bobby. Mr. Boatwright had bought Bobby a rusty old Mustang
to compete with the overly proud Yellow Jack. During the race,
Fast Black had slammed into a chinaberry tree and damaged
the left headlight. From that day on, Yellow Jack's topless
Cadillac had only one headlight.

"Mo'reen, can you go to the movie with me tomorrow night
then?" Bobby begged.

Maureen pursed her lips and looked at him with annoyance, recognizing a familiar gleam in his dark eyes, a gleam she had noticed many times before. A year earlier, she had succumbed to that gleam and allowed Bobby to talk her into surrendering her virginity on the bank of the Blue Lake one hot evening in June.

"I declare, I can't do what you axin me to do, Bobby Boatwright," she had said. "I done told you a thousand times, Mama Ruby say I got to live by the Bible." She glanced over Bobby's shoulder at Catty and Yellow Jack rolling about frantically on the ground, half-naked and oblivious.

"Catty let Yellow Jack do it to her," Bobby pouted.

"Yeah, but they engaged."

"Mo'reen, you say Mama Ruby told you if what you wanted to do wasn't in the Bible, don't do it, right?"

Maureen nodded, looking at Bobby with a puzzled expression on her face.

"Remember how Reverend Tiggs told us about how in the Bible Adam 'knowed' his wife? And all them other mens in the Bible 'knowed' they wives. Remember all that? We had to learn it all in Sunday school."

"Yeah. And they all begat a bunch of kids."

"Well, to 'begat' all them kids, them men had to 'know' them women in the Bible," Bobby explained. He paused and slid his hand under Maureen's skirt. "'Know' is just another word for 'fuck'," he informed her.

"I don't want to begat no kids till I get married."

"Girl, I ain't about to get you pregnant. I just want to have a good time."

Maureen grabbed Bobby's hand and held it while she considered his comment.

"I declare," she said with a soft chuckle, looking at Catty and Yellow Jack again.

"You won't tell nobody, so it'll get back to Mama Ruby. If I was to do it?"

"I swear to God I won't," Bobby promised. He crossed his heart with his finger. "Cross my heart and hope to die." He kissed her cheek.

". . . Well," Maureen said with hesitation, toying with Bobby's fingernails.

"Come on, girl. Just this one time and I won't pester you no more."

". . . OK," Maureen giggled.

But the one time was not enough. She and Bobby became lovers and surrendered to passion regularly, in the backseat of Bobby's Mustang, on the bank of the Blue Lake, and in Bobby's bedroom when Willie was away.

"Wake up over there, Mo'reen! Quit dreamin and answer me," Bobby ordered. He tossed a fistful of sand at her.

"Later on tonight, come set on the porch with us and we'll talk and eat ribs, Bobby Boatwright," she smiled.

34

Bobby arrived just before midnight. Catty and Yellow Jack were already on the porch with coal-oil lamps at their feet and barbecued ribs on their laps. Ruby, who usually stood in the doorway whenever Maureen sat on the porch in the dark with Bobby, so she could make sure the devil didn't show up and "make something happen," was standing in the doorway now.

"Mo'reen . . . what's that yall eatin out there?" Ruby asked softly. Yellow Jack had smuggled the ribs to the house without telling Ruby, knowing her appetite. Ruby's obesity was a major concern among her friends. But rather than discourage her gluttony, they appeased her with beer and rich food. Ruby was now close to fifty and in some ways disabled. Her huge, flat feet troubled her constantly. The flab between her thighs caused painful friction when she walked. And her neck, which had always been short, seemed to have disappeared into her shoulders.

"I axed what yall had out there. I hear wax paper rattlin," Ruby said, her voice loud.

"Some ribs," Maureen answered. The others groaned.

It was hot that night. Ruby came out on the porch wearing only her slip. She snatched some ribs off Yellow Jack's lap and started to devour them.

"I knowed I smelled somethin good out here," Ruby said between swallows. "Catty . . . let me . . . have . . . one of yours too."

Annoyed, the boys went home earlier than they had intended, leaving Maureen and Catty with a pile of bones and empty pop bottles. Seeing that Maureen was in no more danger of being molested, Ruby excused herself and turned in for the night.

When the screen door slammed, Maureen and Catty breathed a sigh of relief as they sat together on the glider.

"Mama Ruby sho nuff careful not to let nothin bad happen to you, Mo'reen."

"I know. It's a wonder she let me out of her sight with Bobby Boatwright. She say the devil done slid into his pants. . . ."

"Bobby Boatwright have got too big for his britches since he got him a car, if you ax me. He just a copycat. Cause Yellow Jack got him a car, Bobby Boatwright had to get him one," Catty complained.

"You don't like Bobby Boatwright, do you?"

"Not really. I know he is your man and all, but he is a little too uptown for me. With creases ironed in his pants legs and wearin cologne like a regular man—how you stand him?"

"I don't know," Maureen admitted. "I guess cause I ain't got nobody else. Is you jealous cause Yellow Jack ain't as big a sport as Bobby Boatwright? Bobby Boatwright is a sho-nuff sport, you know. He the first black boy we ever knowed got his toenails clipped in a salon."

"I ain't jealous. I just don't trust him for some reason. He kind of remind me of Loomis, with his bad self. See, Loomis is what you call a natural born sport. A *fancy* fancy man. Me, I don't think I could never love such a man. He got a different woman every week. I suspect Bobby Boatwright is goin to change women like he change socks, new ones every other week."

Maureen looked at Catty angrily.

"How in the world can you set here and talk to me like that about my man. You know somethin, girl, I'm sho nuff sick of you. I'm sick of Bobby Boatwright. I'm sick of Goons. I'm sick of everything!" Maureen cried. "I'm sick of my half-assed job! I'm sick of bein hemmed up in that ole upper room like a convict. Oh—one day I'm goin to haul ass!"

Catty gasped and looked at Maureen, whose mouth was stretched open, her arms raised high above her head.

"Mo'reen . . . what done come over you?" Catty asked in a nervous whisper. Catty was alarmed. Such an outburst was unlike Maureen. "Where would you go? You ain't never lived in no town but Goons! Shoot. You move to a big city, with your dumb self you liable to walk out in front of a bus and get your brains knocked out. Where would you go, *if* Mama Ruby was to let you leave?"

"I don't know! Somewhere far off! I—I—*San Francisco!* Yeah . . . that's where I'd go! I'd run off to San Francisco."

"Of all the crazy things I ever heard in my life. Don't you know that's the most dangerous city in the world? They got men out there you can't tell from women. They have earthquakes. They do more cuttin up and shootin up out there in a day than we do in Goons in a year. What would you do in San Francisco, before you get kilt I mean? Lord knows, you wouldn't live a day. You just wait till I tell Mama Ruby—"

"Don't you tell her what I said about runnin off to San Francisco! She already crazy enough. Just make out like I didn't say what I just said . . . *please.*"

"I won't. I won't if you promise you won't bring it up no more."

"I won't. . . ."

Catty looked in Maureen's eyes, making Maureen uncomfortable.

"What's the matter now?" Maureen asked.

"Loomis was right about you."

"What you mean? When was Loomis talkin about me?"

"He talk about you all the time."

"Why? What he say?"

"Loomis told me to my face, you didn't know what to do with yourself. He say you ain't got no future. You is goin to stay in the upper room till the day you die. He say if you had any brains, you'd have left right out of school and moved to one of the camps and latched onto you a man like him. Loomis say you is Mama Ruby's puppet and he'd pay a month's pay in a bet that you ain't never goin to take a stand against Mama Ruby. She is goin to dangle you on a string till times get better. You ain't never goin to be like me and Fast Black. We is independent. Don't nobody boss us. Shoot. My own daddy and mama don't boss me. I'm grown. You, you will be Mama Ruby's play pretty forever. I *dare* you to take a stand against Mama Ruby."

Maureen was thankful that there was so little light coming from the lamps. Catty could not see the anger and misery in her eyes.

"I ain't got the strength to argue with you, Catty. I'm just that tired. I'm tired of you. Mama Ruby and everything here. I'm just like you and Fast Black. I want the same things, I mean. A husband. Kids. My own house. I don't want Mama Ruby actin like my shadow for the rest of my life."

"Girl, don't you never holler at me again and talk down at me like I'm a in-law like you just did. I'm subject to bust your brains out and hand em to you."

"I'm sho nuff sorry, Catty. I didn't mean to show out like that. It's just that . . . I'm so tired of this same old routine." Maureen paused and clasped her hands. "I don't know what I'll do with myself, with you and Yellow Jack gettin married and all."

"Marry Bobby Boatwright. He ain't much, but he'll do until somebody better come along." Catty placed her arm around Maureen's shoulders.

Maureen frowned and shook her head slowly.

"You ever seen Bobby Boatwright buck naked?"

"Have mercy, girl—he your man, not mine! What make you think I seen him buck naked?" Catty asked, looking at Maureen with an incredulous expression on her face.

"Oh. Anyway, he got birthmarks on his butt and my mama told me that was the mark of the devil. Havin birthmarks on the butt, I mean. I don't need to start off married life with that against me."

"What else he got?"

"Well . . . he got this string," Maureen whispered.

"Say what?" Catty gasped, moving closer to Maureen. "Where?"

Maureen lowered her head.

"Down there."

"Lord . . . what is it?"

Maureen shrugged.

"I don't know. I been wantin to ax him but I don't know how."

"All you got to say is 'Bobby Boatwright, how come you got a string on your thing?' That's all you got to say, Mo'reen."

Maureen giggled and removed Catty's arm from her shoulder.

"Stop bein so nosy, Catty," she laughed. "I wish I hadn't told you about Bobby Boatwright's string."

Catty took a deep breath and stood up to smooth her skirt down. She quickly returned to her seat and turned to face Maureen, looking at her with renewed interest.

"I feel so sorry for you, Mo'reen. Too bad you ain't the one marryin Yellow Jack like me, huh?"

"I wouldn't marry Yellow Jack. I want somebody with excitement in his background. Somebody that's been around," Maureen said.

"You better not let Mama Ruby hear you talk like this," Catty warned, glancing back at the screen door.

Maureen gave her a hard look.

"I *will* get married one day. Mama Ruby can't run my life forever," Maureen insisted. "I'll have to leave her sooner or later; I don't care what she say."

"You ain't goin no place," Catty informed Maureen, shaking her head vigorously. "Mama Ruby say you ain't never goin to leave the upper room. Not as long as you live."

Maureen remained silent for a full minute before speaking again.

"Let's talk about somethin else," she suggested.

"OK. Now, what you goin to get me for my weddin gift?"

"Catty, I wonder what would happen if I was to marry that albino what always after me."

"I thought you wanted to change the subject?" Catty slapped Maureen's shoulder roughly.

"I do. We talkin about me and that albino."

"What albino?"

"The one we call Snowball. The one from the panhandle."

"What about him?"

"He could marry me and carry me off to the panhandle, huh?"

"Naw . . . I don't think Mama Ruby would like livin in the panhandle," Catty concluded.

Catty left and walked up the hill to her house. Maureen lay awake long after turning in, thinking of her future with increasing dread.

* * *

Before daylight the next morning, Maureen heard Ruby stomping up the stairs to the upper room. Ruby entered noisily. She snatched open the door, singing "Swing Low Sweet Chariot" at the top of her voice. Maureen pretended to be asleep when Ruby came and stood over her.

"Oh, Mo'reen, you sleep?" Ruby whispered. Maureen said nothing. Ruby leaned over and started to shake Maureen's shoulder. "Oh, Mo'reen . . . you sleep?"

"Let me alone, I'm tired," Maureen replied.

"I need to talk to you about somethin real important, darlin. Set up."

"I know what you want . . . let me alone, Mama Ruby."

"I do need to talk to you about somethin, Mo'reen."

"What is it, Mama Ruby?" Maureen opened her eyes wide and sat up.

"Darlin, is Bobby Boatwright comin to the house today?" Ruby asked in a near whisper.

"I don't know. He was just down here last night."

"I know. What about that little albino boy that is so crazy about you?"

"What about him?"

"You think he might be comin this way today?"

"I ain't see him in a long time. You know that."

"Hmmmm. I wonder why he stopped comin over here?"

"It's probably because you pulled a gun on him the last time he was here," Maureen reminded Ruby.

"Oh."

Ruby sighed and bit her bottom lip.

"When you see him, tell him I ain't goin to mess with him. Also, ax him to bring me a few beers. If you see Bobby Boatwright first, ax him to get some of his daddy's beers and bring em to me."

"Boatwright say he ain't sendin no more beer to you on credit on account of you never paid him the last time. Snowball scared to come here."

The albino, Tommy "Snowball" Hutchins, was a twenty-one-year-old who lived on the Belknap migrant camp. He was the only person Maureen knew who was involved with drugs. He had a heroin habit and it was common knowledge that whenever he was coherent, he pursued Maureen. But Bobby was her man and she had only a vague interest in Snowball.

"I don't want him comin to see me on account of I don't want to see him," Maureen said tiredly.

Ruby looked hurt and turned away from Maureen with tears starting to form in her eyes.

"Well . . . if he do come here today, ax him to go get me a few beers. I ain't goin to mention it, but you can run up to his camp and ax him if he plans to come to see you today. That way, you can put in a bid for them beers in advance."

Maureen let out her breath and gritted her teeth.

"OK, Mama Ruby, you win again. I'll go see if I can find you some beer. When I get up. It's too early to be peckin on somebody's door." She turned over, turning her back to Ruby.

"Oh horsefeathers!" Ruby pouted. She sighed heavily and started to ramble around in the upper room, humming another one of her spirituals. Maureen turned back over and sat up to find that Ruby was on her knees on the floor looking under the bed.

"What you lookin for, Mama Ruby?"

". . . Um . . . you got any peanut brittle?"

"Since when did I start keepin peanut brittle under my bed?" Maureen hissed. She leaped from the bed and grabbed a wrap-around housecoat from her footstool and put it on. Ruby followed behind as Maureen left the house, trotting down Duquennes Road to Catty's house.

"Catty, Irene, Bishop—yall come to the door!" Maureen called. She stood in front of the house with her hand shading her eyes. Irene quickly leaned her head out her bedrooom window and frowned.

"What you want this time of mornin, girl?"

"Irene, yall got any beers layin around in there?" Maureen asked.

"Naw. Why don't you go ax Boatwright to lay some beers on you. You must be some crazy to be comin up here gettin folks out the bed axin for beer!" Irene retorted.

"Mama Ruby havin one of her beer fits. Have mercy," Maureen begged.

Ruby stood next to Maureen with a blank expression on her face, leaning forward anxiously, hoping for a positive response from Irene. Irene shook her head as Ruby whispered in Maureen's ear.

"Irene, Mama Ruby say get Bishop out the bed so he can go to Miami and get her some beer. Ain't nobody out here that'll give her credit anymore."

"Mo'reen, you tell Ruby this old man of mine ain't worth salt. I was to drag his tail out this bed he liable to beat a scab on me," Irene said seriously.

"Irene, please lend us some beer if you got any," Maureen pleaded.

Irene left the window and Catty suddenly appeared, wearing a stocking cap on her head.

"I got a few beers stashed away for emergencies like this. Hold on, Mama Ruby," Catty said, leaving the window.

"Know what, I'm goin to make Catty's weddin dress for her." Ruby grinned. "With my own hands."

35

"Mama Ruby, that sho nuff is some pretty material you makin Catty's weddin dress out of. So nice and white and everything," Fast Black commented. She stood in front of Ruby as Ruby sat on her front porch glider working on the dress. Maureen sat on the bannister watching quietly.

"Mo'reen, ain't this some pretty material? Lacy. Snow white. All girls should wear such a pretty thing when they get married," Fast Black said longingly. "I declare, I wish I'd have had me a real weddin. To this day I ain't never walked down the aisle. I thought for so long me and Virgil would cut the cake," she sighed sadly. "But he up and got hisself lost in that foreign country." Fast Black quickly turned to face Maureen. "Mo'reen, when you get married, get Mama Ruby to make you the same kind of pretty dress. Hear?"

"Mo'reen's already married," Ruby said without looking up from her sewing.

Fast Black's breath caught in her throat as she turned back to Ruby.

"When Mo'reen get married? And who?!" she asked.

"Mo'reen married to the Lord . . . just like me," Ruby answered calmly.

Fast Black looked at Ruby and blinked.

"Yall is the most sanctified women I ever seen in all the days of my life. I was to get so sanctified, No Talk will be fit to be tied. Flawless, yall is. Not a rotten bone in your body." Fast Black looked at Maureen, who was annoyed. Maureen excused herself to the living room.

Ruby came in an hour later and found her lying on the sofa watching a comedy on the television. After putting her sewing materials away, Ruby sat next to Maureen.

"Where is Fast Black?" Maureen asked, not really caring.

"She went on back home. She been tryin to brighten up Yellow Jack's bedroom. She got to make it fit for him to be bringin a wife. Shoot. Catty's a 'phisticated gal. She likes nice things." Ruby sighed and shook her head. "Lord, I remember when Catty was a baby and now here she is fixin to get married. Seems like just yestiddy her and Yellow Jack was in diapers and cuttin teeth."

"So was I," Maureen reminded.

Ruby touched Maureen's face.

"I'm so happy I got you all to myself. I ain't got to worry about no nasty man carryin you off, huh?"

". . . No," Maureen replied, rising. She was surprised when Ruby took her arm and gently pulled her back down.

"What is the real reason you won't let me go, Mama Ruby? How come you don't want me to be like other folks?"

"'Cause you *ain't* like other folks. I ain't neither. Why, you heard Fast Black. Me and you is some sanctified. Ain't a woman in this whole wide world as good off as you or me. We got it made, girl."

Maureen looked at Ruby and folded her arms.

"Mama Ruby, tell me *what* it is about me and you that makes us so different. You keep tellin me about how much glory we got and all this other stuff. What we got?" Maureen asked, making a sweeping gesture with her hand.

"Girl, long as you got Jesus, you don't need nothin else."

"Everybody we know got religion."

"Yeah, but we got a little bit more. I bet I got more religion in my baby toe than Boatwright got in his whole body. I been blessed with healin hands. You been blessed with so much beauty—girl, you is sharp as a tack. Everbody say you is. You could get you any man in the world, if you wanted him."

"What good would it do me to want any man in the world? I can't get married and lead no normal life."

"Why would you want to lead a normal life? Don't you like livin like a queen?"

Maureen sighed heavily and threw up her hands.

"I don't know what you call livin like a queen. But I don't think I am right now. I ain't got nothin goin for me."

"Here you is with a whole upstairs to yourself—"

"A *whole* upstairs? Mama Ruby, ain't but one room up there. That upper room."

"That alone is more than any queen got. I bet Queen of England would give anything to have the upper room to come home to."

"Mama Ruby, if you believe a mess like that, you'd believe anything. I ain't never seen or heard of nobody like you. Cousin Hattie. None of your family. They is crazy a little bit, but nothin like you. You is some nutty. I just want some good reason why you is so crazy about me stayin with you forever."

"I'm through talkin. My head hurt when I get upset. Stop talkin crazy to me. That clear?"

Maureen slapped Ruby's hand.

"If I make you mad enough, what would you do? Would you kill me, Mama Ruby?"

"What?" Ruby gasped.

"I really want to know what I'm up against."

"You ain't up against nothin but the devil. I wouldn't harm a hair on your head, girl. Don't you know you is my life. I was to kill you, I'd be killin myself."

"Why you don't never want me to go, Mama Ruby? Give me a straight answer. Don't give me no more of them crazy explanations like you use to give Virgil when he would ax you somethin about how come you the way you is. I'm sick of you tellin me first Satan got me this way, then Jesus got me this way. I want to hear about *you*. I want to hear about *why* you have to hold on to me. Shoot. You act like I'm a dollar bill or somethin."

Ruby started to cry. She slowly removed her handkerchief from her bosom and wiped her eyes and nose.

"Don't you . . . don't you know?" Ruby choked.

"I only know what you tell me. I got a feelin you leavin something out." Maureen looked into Ruby's tear-filled eyes. For years Maureen had suspected Ruby was hiding something important from her. During their visit to Louisiana, Ruby had admitted there were secrets she wouldn't share with her. Maureen was convinced it had to do with her birth. Had she really had a lame, deformed daddy? Or perhaps he had been a foreigner, or a Jew? Perhaps the man who had fathered her had been a villain of some sort, some ungodly rogue on the loose who had been unable to fulfill his role as a husband and a father. "Tell me everything I need to know about myself, Mama Ruby, and you tell me right now!"

Ruby jumped and cried harder.

"Stop cryin and tell me!" Maureen ordered.

"After all . . . after all I had to go through for you . . . lost me my boy . . . my man . . . the devil is still on my case . . . now . . . now you treatin me like a stepmama," Ruby wailed. She started to choke on her teeth. Maureen slapped her hard on the back.

"Don't set here and choke to death. Not till I get the whole story out of you. What is the real reason you so crazy about me?"

Ruby stopped crying and returned her handkerchief to her bosom. She took a deep breath and cleared her throat.

"All you care about is Bobby Boatwright and that albino. You just itchin to run off with one of em so you can spite me."

"If I was goin to do somethin like run off, why would I run off with Bobby Boatwright or Snowball? They some of the things I'd be runnin off from. Shoot! You talk about San Francisco bein such a sordid place. I bet ain't nothin bad as what go on here goin on in San Francisco."

"Girl, you go to San Francisco and you ain't never comin back. I told you the truth. That's Babylon. You subject to turn into a pillar of salt if you was to go there. It happened in the Bible when they was runnin to get out of Sodom and Gomorrah."

"You done said so many bad things about that place, I want to see it all the more. I just might—"

Ruby held her breath and her body stiffened. Maureen gasped as she watched Ruby's eyes dilate.

"Lord—what's the matter, Mama Ruby?"

"Eeeeeeeeeeeee," Ruby babbled, saliva sliding out the sides of her mouth. "Eeeeeeeeeeeeee."

Maureen stood up and slapped Ruby on the back.

"I ain't goin no place, Mama Ruby! I declare I ain't! Don't set here and die on me!"

Ruby started to cough and gasp for air. A sudden knock on the door startled her.

"Who is that now?" she asked, talking in a normal voice, looking toward the door. "Go see, Mo'reen. It liable to be that ole bill collector from Krogers." Ruby stood up and waved her arms toward the door.

"I thought you was sick. The way you was just now talkin—"

"Girl, don't stand there runnin off at the head. See who at the door."

Maureen composed herself, dismissing Ruby's odd behavior.

"Well—want me to get you your thing, Mama Ruby?"

"Yeah. And make certain it's loaded."

Maureen went to Ruby's bedroom off to the side and returned a minute later with a shotgun.

36

Fast Black and Irene had helped Ruby and Maureen get Ruby's house in order for Catty's marriage to Yellow Jack. Irene mopped. Fast Black washed and starched the drapes, and Ruby and Maureen dusted and rearranged the furniture.

It seemed like everybody in Goons showed up for the event hours before the ceremony began. The house was filled to capacity and dozens of people stood on the front porch and in the yard.

Catty was as proud as any other bride-to-be. Loomis had donated the money to pay for Catty to have her hair done by a fancy beautician in Miami and Willie Boatwright had stood for the wedding fee, which he paid Reverend Tiggs with a post-dated check. Ruby had cooked for two days and Big Red had put on a suit for the first time in seventeen years.

The ceremony got under way an hour late, since Catty insisted on opening her gifts first to make sure a Ray Charles album was among them. To her surprise she found not one but three, and was suddenly more enthusiastic than ever.

A mob of disorderly children had to be exiled to the backyard in order for the exchange of vows to be heard. As the children were being hustled out, a speckled hen slipped in the house and headed straight to Reverend Tiggs' pants leg and started pecking frantically.

"Do you, Jack 'Yellow Jack' Wong Harris . . . take this woman to—somebody get this chicken!" Reverend Tiggs shouted. He stopped to scold and dismiss the disrespectful hen.

A muffled roar of laughter from the spectators followed.

"Hurry up, Reverend Tiggs, so I can go get myself drunk," Fast Black said impatiently.

A few minutes later, Yellow Jack kissed his bride.

The wedding party was still going on four hours after the wedding, but the crowd had thinned out considerably.

"I don't care what Yellow Jack do to Catty—she better stay with him!" Irene laughed.

"Wouldn't nobody *but* Yellow Jack have Catty and wouldn't nobody *but* Catty have Yellow Jack!" Loomis said.

"Shet up, you drunk, *unmarried*, middle-aged son-of-a-bitch!" Irene replied.

"Shhhhh! Don't be cussin with this preacher still here!" Ruby hissed. "Irene, you go in the kitchen and bring out some more beer. Loomis, you keep your eyes on these folks. Make certain nobody wander to the upper room."

Catty and Maureen moved back so Irene could pass. Loomis moved to the bottom of the stairs leading to the upper room. He removed his switchblade from his back pocket and stuck it in his shirt pocket so that it was visible.

"Just look at ole Loomis flashin his blade. He just want to get attention! Devil! And it's *my* weddin. He show out on my weddin day I'm goin to have Mama Ruby beat the shit out of him, Mo'reen!" Catty whispered. "Shoot. This is the happiest day of my life."

"Catty, do you really love Yellow Jack?" Maureen asked, eyeing her friend suspiciously.

"*Love* him? Shoot, girl. I don't even *like* him. What's the matter with you, Mo'reen?"

"Why you marry him then?"

"How else was I goin to get them weddin gifts? You think I'd have got me three Ray Charles albums just to be gettin em? I don't know though. Ole Yellow Jack just might make me a good husband for the time bein. I declare, I wanted them gifts. You know I got me a tea-pot . . . and a hangin lamp . . . some linen . . . a iron . . . all kinds of things."

"I seen em."

"Shoot. I been waitin to get married all my life."

"Just to get a bunch of gifts? You married Yellow Jack just to get a bunch of gifts?"

Catty gasped and looked at Maureen incredulously.

"Why else would I marry that snake-eyed baboon? Shoot! To get this many gifts I'd have even married Bobby Boatwright, cept he your man. Lord. I just think of all the gifts you goin to miss out on, on account of Mama Ruby ain't never lettin you go. . . ."

Maureen gave Catty an exasperated look and turned and walked away. She stood in a corner, depressed, watching everyone else fuss over Catty and Yellow Jack.

On her way to the upper room, Maureen brushed past Ruby and Ruby turned around and grabbed her by the arm.

"Where you goin, darlin?" Ruby asked.

"I'm fixin to go to bed, I'm sho nuff tired," Maureen said sadly. "We got a big mess to clean up here tomorrow and I want to be well rested."

Ruby drank from a can of beer before responding.

"Fast Black say she comin over first thing in the morning to help us clean up," Ruby said, releasing Maureen's arm. Before Maureen could say anything else, Bobby came rushing over and grabbed Ruby.

"Mama Ruby, my daddy done fell out dead on the floor! He drunk as a skunk and loose as a goose! He done hit his head on the coffee table—I think he done busted his brains out! Come lay healin hands on him!" Bobby shouted.

The remaining guests ran to Willie Boatwright, who lay stretched out on the floor in a drunken stupor. Maureen stood in back of the crowd watching Ruby perform one of her "miracles."

"Boatwright, I say, oh, Boatwright, I'm fixin to haul you up off this floor. With the help of the Lord I am fixin to bring you back to life! Lord"—Ruby stopped and got on her knees and rubbed Boatwright's shoulders— "RAISE THIS MAN! LOOK-A-HERE, LORD, YOU RAISE BOATWRIGHT LIKE I JUST SAID! HE'S A CHRISTIAN FROM HIS HEART AND YOUR FAITHFUL SERVANT TO THE END. WALKIN IN YOUR LIGHT! HE JUST HAD A LITTLE TOO MUCH TO DRINK,

LORD—BUT YOU CHASTIZE HIM FOR THAT LATER ON . . .
PUT IT ON THE REGISTRAR. GET UP, BOATWRIGHT!"

Boatwright sat bolt upright, opening his eyes wide, and the
crowd cheered. Two men rushed to help Ruby off the floor and
Fast Black went to help Willie Boatwright up.

Maureen slipped into her room and lowered herself onto
the bed.

Another hour passed and Ruby came to the upper room.
She seemed surprised to find Maureen lying on her back looking up at the ceiling.

"What's the matter, Mo'reen?" Ruby asked. She stood in the
doorway with her hand still on the knob of the half closed
door.

"Nothin . . ." Maureen groaned, turning over on her side to
face Ruby. "I just wish . . . I just wish . . . oh, Mama Ruby . . . I'm
so de'pressed. . . ."

Ruby's eyes got big and she shut the door and came to stand
over Maureen.

"De'pressed about what?"

"Cause I want somethin good to happen to me for a
change," Maureen answered.

"Somethin good is happenin to you right this minute."

"I want to get married!" Maureen blurted.

"What—why? Girl, don't you listen when I talk to you? I
done explained till I'm blue in the face why you don't need no
husband. A man ain't what you need!"

"You better look at me real hard, Mama Ruby. I'm eighteen
years old."

"I know that! What's that got to do with a man? What you got
men on your mind for? Shoot."

"Don't you know?"

"Don't I know—why you nasty puppy! It's that television put
this mess on your mind. I'm gettin rid of that television. It's
that television what got you believin that wretched San
Francisco is the land of gold! I'm goin to take a stick and bust
that television wide open."

"You ain't doin nothin! You just mad cause I'm growin up."

"What is you growin up got to do with you wantin to get married?"

"Don't you know? I'm human. I want to—"

"Don't you say it! You want to lay up with some nasty man and forget all about me. Me who done got old and sufferin with every kind of pain there is. Me who got high blood pressure and should not be livin on my own. Me who could get raped if these men around here knowed I was livin by myself, if you was to haul ass."

"Mama Ruby, you got to understand why I'm feelin this way. I'm a woman now."

"Is it Bobby Boatwright puttin these notions in your head? If it is, I'm goin to stop lettin him carry you to the movies and stuff. I'm goin to stop him from comin to see you. I might even kill him. Take a brick and bust his brains out."

"Don't you mess with Bobby Boatwright."

"He carried you off to that party last week and kept you out till nine o'clock at night—"

"Leave me alone, Mama Ruby! I can't stand this no more!" Maureen turned her back to Ruby.

"One day you goin to thank me and kiss me all over for lovin you so much, Mo'reen." Ruby gently closed the door and left the room.

The next morning Ruby and Maureen started to clean up the mess from the party, cursing because Fast Black did not show up at eight A.M. to help like she promised. It was past nine when Maureen finally went out on the porch.

She shaded her eyes and looked up, startled to see Fast Black running down the hill, her arms waving and her eyes bugged out. "Mama Ruby, come look at the way Fast Black runnin down the hill. Like the devil after her!"

Ruby rushed out on the porch and stood next to Maureen.

"Somethin is sho nuff the matter with Fast Black!" Ruby said. She stepped down on the ground and started walking toward Fast Black. Maureen jumped from the porch and followed her. Fast Black fell twice before reaching them.

"What done happened?!" Ruby shouted, holding out her hand to the hysterical woman.

"I declare, yall—aarrgghhh—CATTY DONE LEFT YEL-LOW JACK FOR ANOTHER MAN!" Fast Black screamed.

37

"Mo'reen, tell me, darlin. Who is this nigger my daughter Catty done run off with?" Bishop demanded. He stood over Maureen as she lay on the sofa licking an orange-flavored Popsicle. "Ain't been a whole day and the girl done already left her husband," Bishop lamented. "A man with his own Cadillac!"

"Catty got her gifts. She ain't had no reason in the world to stay with Yellow Jack," Maureen said seriously. She looked from Bishop to Ruby and Fast Black standing near the window. Every few seconds one of them would look out and gaze up the hill.

"Catty's a Christian," Ruby offered.

"What's that got to do with her runnin off with another man? My goodness, Mama Ruby, would YOU want to be married to Yellow Jack? You ever smelled his breath first thing in the mornin? Whew! Smell like Tampa Bay!" Maureen said, looking at her incredulously.

"I believe that nigger Catty left with this mornin kidnapped her. This ain't like Catty to run off and not tell nobody." Bishop sighed and scratched his head thoughtfully before continuing. "Her mama home now prostrate with grief. Couldn't get out the bed if the house was on fire. Yeah. Catty was kidnapped."

"Kidnapped my tail! That bold hussy packed some of her glad rags right in my face! Whoever that nigger is what took her, he was drivin a big black car and wouldn't let none of us see his face," Fast Black said angrily.

"I tell yall one thing, whoever the home wrecker is, he livin on borrowed time," Ruby said with a nod. Maureen and Bishop watched as Ruby leaned over and whispered in Fast Black's ear. Fast Black's eyes rolled from side to side twice; then she nodded.

No Talk and Loomis entered the house through the kitchen, grim expressions on their faces.

"Mama Ruby, remember that pitch-black nigger from the weddin reception yestiddy what had on them plastic white shoes?" Loomis asked. He and No Talk strode across the floor and stopped in front of Ruby and Fast Black. "The one what was doin so much talkin?"

"The way that duck was suckin up my beer, I never is to forget him. What about that loose-lipped spook?" Ruby asked, looking from No Talk to Loomis. She placed her hands on her hips. "What yall find out?"

"That's the nigger what stole Catty right out from under Yellow Jack's nose. I suspect they fell in love last night and planned to haul ass while the rest of us was drinkin home brew and not payin em no attention. Poor Yellow Jack ain't got the strength to be out huntin Catty. He got up and seen that she had took them albums and like to had a stroke! He told me he had been thinkin about them albums in his sleep. He went to cussin on account of she took all three of em. She could have left that boy one of them albums to listen to. Shoot. Them weddin gifts was as much his as they was hers. That's why I ain't never married. I marry some bitch and she run off with my weddin gifts I'm liable to end up back on the chain gang for bustin her brains out."

"I just can't believe Catty run off with all three of them albums!" Fast Black yelled, shaking her head.

"Albums is expensive," Bishop interjected, defending his daughter. "Yall got to realize, ain't none of us can go around buyin three albums at a time. Catty always was lookin for bargains. Yall got to give the girl credit for thinkin about dollars and cents."

"Catty ain't had sense enough to just up and run off. That nigger put this mess in her head. That girl is generous. She was tricked into leavin Yellow Jack," Ruby said.

"And takin them three albums," Loomis added.

"Tell me, whereabout do this hound of hell live what stole Catty?" Ruby asked Loomis.

"Believe it or not, Mama Ruby, he some kind of business-man. He got him one of them Mickey Mouse rib joints in West Miami and got the nerve to live in a big white house on Crawford Street, tryin to pass hisself off as a sport." There was envy in Loomis' voice.

"This wife stealer, who is his people, Loomis?" Ruby asked.

"I heard Boatwright tell Roscoe the dog come from a old family in New Orleans. Some uppity Creoles at that!" Loomis said.

Ruby shook her head sadly and let out her breath.

"You just can't trust them Creoles . . . stealin wives and takin folks' money. I suspect they all got Jew blood. Well, when we find this home wrecker, I'm goin to treat him like he stole my pocketbook. Fast Black, when we get to Miami, you call Big Red and tell him to stand by. Loomis, you and No Talk go get Yellow Jack's Cadillac. We got a job to do," Ruby said.

No Talk took a step back and Loomis looked at Ruby with admiration.

"Mama Ruby, you ain't nobody to fool with. They couldn't pay me to cross you," Loomis said.

Ruby nodded and reached out to touch Loomis' shoulder and she patted him affectionately.

"Tell me more about the wife stealer, Loomis."

"OK, Mama Ruby. The baboon followed me and Slim to the weddin. We had been rollin dice with him at Slim's house and he overheard me and Slim talkin about the weddin and all. Slim had told me to my face, that nigger was a crook of some kind. Him with his own rib joint and ain't no more than twenty-five. He's up to somethin illegal," Loomis insisted, winking.

Maureen's heart was beating fast and she held her breath. She could already smell the blood in the air. The last time Ruby, Fast Black, Loomis, and No Talk had conferred the way they were doing now, a gambler from Atlanta working on the Kaiser camp had suddenly disappeared. The night of the disappearance, Maureen had been looking out the front window in the upper room. It had been late as she watched the foursome, along with Big Red, move slowly down the hill. No Talk, Loomis,

Fast Black, and Big Red were carrying something wrapped in what looked like a blanket. Maureen had run downstairs and watched them disappear into the bayou in back of the house. The next morning, she found a man's shoe on the ground in front of the house. Later that day she found its mate in the backyard. She never mentioned it to Ruby and nothing was ever said. Other than that a gambler caught cheating at dice at Zeus' house had mysteriously disappeared.

"Mo'reen, I'll be back in a hour," Ruby said. She removed a red bandanna from her housecoat pocket and tied it carefully around her head, concealing her uncombed hair. "Bishop, stay here with Mo'reen. She a little nervous right now and I don't want her by herself. No Talk, Loomis, Fast Black . . . let's go on and get this over with."

Maureen and Bishop stood on the porch watching as the four of them hurried up the hill.

"There they go . . . my mama and her death squad. Bishop, when is all this mess goin to end? I'm gettin so sick of it. Mama Ruby, Fast Black, Loomis, and No Talk and Big Red. Ain't there somethin somebody could do to straighten em out? They act like wild folks."

"Girl, Mama Ruby could part the Red Sea if she put her mind to it. She got that much glory. What fool you think goin to go up against a woman big as Ruby is? Shoot. She could stomp my brains out like she was stompin grapes. You don't see me tryin to get in that woman's way. I'd rather lock horns with a bull than Ruby."

"Fast Black, Loomis, and No Talk wouldn't be the way they is if it wasn't for Mama Ruby eggin em on."

"Yeah, but Mama Ruby just like a mama to them folks. She just like a mama to everybody. Why you think we all call Mama Ruby *Mama* Ruby. Shoot. I'd have to be weaned if Ruby—MAMA Ruby was to ever leave Goons. Mama Ruby done opened all our eyes out here in these swamps. She was sent to us by the Lord, I sho nuff believe. Healin hands and all."

"You tellin me yall would die without my mama?"

"Ruby ain't no regular woman, Mo'reen. She got a answer for everything. Ain't nothin you can't ax her, she can't answer."

"Her answers don't make no sense, Bishop. You ought to hear some of the things she done told me."

Bishop shook his head.

"All I know is, Mama Ruby is a good woman. I never is to argue with her. She liable to feed me to them gaters out there in them swamps like she done—"

"I don't want hear any more . . . please. If I hear about another person Mama Ruby done . . . I . . . just don't talk about nobody bein fed to the gators . . . I'm sick enough."

38

Just as she promised, Ruby returned home after being gone one hour. Maureen, in the kitchen stirring collard greens in a pan on the stove, watched Ruby stand at the sink and wash blood from her switchblade.

"Them greens done yet?" Ruby asked, without looking up.

"No, ma'am," Maureen mumbled.

Ruby started humming one of the spirituals she loved.

"I got to have Roscoe get me a new knife . . . this one don't cut like it use to," Ruby said.

". . . Maybe you been usin it too much," Maureen said in a low voice.

"Hmmmm. You might have a point there. I guess I ought to be usin my shotgun more, huh?"

"Why you got to use either one of em?"

"What else would I use? My fists? You have a hard time re-memberin I'm a lady, Mo'reen. It ain't ladylike to go around fist fightin. A lady needs a blade and a shotgun. My switchblade and my shotgun and Jesus done settled a lot of disputes around here." Ruby stopped talking and resumed humming and Maureen watched her huge body shake as she scrubbed the switchblade more than was necessary.

"Did yall get Catty, Mama Ruby?"

Ruby finished humming the chorus of her spiritual, dried

her weapon with a dishcloth, and returned the knife inside her bra before answering.

"We dropped her off to see a lawyer at the free legal aid place so she could get her a divorce. She'll be back at her daddy's as soon as Slim can haul the rest of her things from Zeus' house," Ruby said casually. "You should have seen how her and that rib-joint-ownin nigger was all laid back on lounge chairs on his front porch when we pulled up. Well, we put a stop to it. Catty was glad to see us and glad to be comin home. That Flatt family done let the devil in the house I suspect. Catty ain't been herself lately," Ruby said with concern.

"What about Yellow Jack?"

"What about him?"

"What he goin to do about all this?"

"He say he wouldn't have Catty back on a platter, on account of the way she run off with them albums."

"Didn't she bring the albums back with her?"

"Goodness gracious, Mo'reen, them albums all got broke up durin the commotion on that rib-joint-ownin nigger's front porch. And it's a doggone shame. Now Catty right back where she started. Ain't got a album to her name."

"I bet she mad as a Russian, huh?"

"Sho nuff is. And Yellow Jack hot as a six-shooter hisself about them albums gettin broke. He say he'll help Catty finish packin and that's all he'll ever do for her as long as she live. Say she ever come up in his face again talkin about lovin him, he goin to take a brick and bust her brains out. And Lord knows poor Catty ain't got too many brains."

Maureen chuckled as Ruby started to hum another song and left the kitchen with a can of beer in her hand.

Fifteen minutes later, Maureen joined her on the living room sofa and Ruby's arm went around Maureen's shoulders.

"What you do while I was gone?" Ruby asked.

"Nothin but fuss with them greens."

"Didn't no maniac come by here and mess with you, did he?"

Maureen looked at Ruby for almost a minute before answering.

"Mama Ruby, ain't nobody been here messin with me," she said evenly.

Ruby drank from her can, not taking her eyes off Maureen.

"Sho nuff?" Ruby asked. She removed her arm from Maureen's shoulders and wiped her wet lips.

"Lord," Maureen sighed, looking away.

A knock on the door interrupted the conversation. Ruby and Maureen looked at one another and shrugged.

"Reach me my thing," Ruby ordered, placing her beer can on the coffee table.

Maureen leaned over the side of the sofa and lifted Ruby's shotgun from the floor.

"Mama Ruby, if it's another bill collector or a maniac, don't kill em."

"How come?"

"Well . . . it's such a nice day. I don't want you to make no mess in the front yard."

Ruby looked at the gun, then toward the door.

"Oh well . . ." Ruby sighed. "Run to the door and see who it is, Mo'reen."

Maureen leaped up and darted to the front window, where she snatched back the drapes and looked out.

"Have mercy. It ain't nobody but ole John French. White devil," Maureen said, stomping her foot.

Ruby set the gun down on the floor and Maureen opened the door.

John was the teenage son of Ruby's landlord. A handsome youth with dark brown hair and green eyes, the boy had spent several years off and on in detention homes. Though he was a delinquent, he was well liked and had many black friends. Yellow Jack and Bobby Boatwright often invited him to go night fishing in the Blue Lake. During his earlier years, John and his younger sisters had often been left in Ruby's care, playing in the sandpile with Maureen. John considered Ruby something of a mammy to his family.

"What do you want?" Maureen asked John, gently kicking his shin as he entered the house.

"Mama Ruby, tell Mo'reen to quit pickin at me," John pouted. "Every time I come here she go to joogin at me."

"John." Ruby laughed. "Mo'reen just loves to meddle with boys. She don't mean no harm."

"No matter. She ain't got to be kickin me. Shoot. I got a risin on my knee from the last time I come over here and she kicked me. She upset on account of every time she want to go off to the movies with Bobby Boatwright, he done already made plans to go fishin in the Blue Lake with me and Yellow Jack," John whined, giving Maureen a dirty look. She stuck out her tongue at him.

"Mo'reen, you behave. You gettin too old to be carryin on that way," Ruby hollered.

John gave Maureen a smug look and strode over to Ruby. He kissed her forehead and sat down next to her.

"Mama Ruby, my mama want to know if you can send her a jar of your canned plum preserves," John said.

"Sho nuff can," Ruby replied, rising. John leaped up to help her.

"Whose ole sway-backed mule you rode up on, John?" Maureen asked, looking out the window.

"Mine. My daddy give it to me for my nineteenth birthday. Want to go for a ride, Mo'reen?"

Instead of answering, Maureen looked at Ruby.

"Yeah, she can go for a ride," Ruby said with a smile.

"I seen Zeus. He told me about Catty runnin off with some dressed-up fancy man from the city. I declare, yall, them Flatts sho nuff have troubles. My daddy just loaned Irene ten dollars to get her some nerve medicine," John said.

"I know the Flatts havin troubles. But it ain't they fault. The devil done got loose in the house," Ruby said, leaving the room.

Maureen had her back to John and was looking out the window at his mule, whose belly almost touched the ground.

"Whoever sold your daddy that messed up mule must have been mad at him!" Maureen laughed.

"Daddy got him for little or nothin," John said dryly, standing close to Maureen. She moved back a little and they touched. John lifted his hand and stroked her thick hair. Maureen turned and looked at him and their eyes locked. Without a word, John moved over to the side.

"You seen Bobby Boatwright? My fiance . . ." Maureen said, returning her gaze to the mule.

"Not since the weddin last night. He left out of here with that gal Jolene. . . ."

"Oh?" Maureen said, not surprised. Bobby was hardly discreet. She had seen him with many other girls, all the while claiming to be her man.

"Mo'reen, after I carry you for a ride on my sway back mule . . . want to go swimmin in the Blue Lake with me?"

Maureen gasped and turned to face John with her mouth open and her eyes wide.

"Bobby Boatwright would have a cow if I was to go off swimmin with another man. And a *white* man? John, what's the matter with you? The sun gettin to you or somethin?"

"Mo'reen, me and you growed up together. I'm just as much your friend as Yellow Jack. You go swimmin with him."

"He more like family . . . I think. I can trust him."

"What do you mean by trust?"

"Well . . . won't nothin happen."

John looked in Maureen's eyes.

"You *do* care about me, don't you?" he whispered, glancing over his shoulder nervously.

"Whatever gave you that idea?" Maureen whispered back. She looked over John's shoulder toward the kitchen.

"I swear to God, girl, you must be the cutest little colored girl I ever seen in my life. If you was to step on a nickel, when you lift your foot you'd leave a dollar bill behind. You sharp as a tack, Mo'reen." John's voice was low and level. He squinted his eyes as he looked at Maureen.

Alarmed, Maureen quickly opened the screen door and went outside to the porch.

When John emerged with the jar of plums, Maureen was already sitting on the mule's back.

"Hurry up so I can get on back home," she said.

John climbed up on the mule and secured himself in back of Maureen, handing her the jar. Her stomach muscles tightened when his body touched hers in a way much too intimate.

Ruby stood on the porch waving until Maureen and John rode out of sight up the hill onto Duquennes Road.

"Where you takin me?" Maureen asked.

"Girl, I am fixin to carry you on the ride of your life!"

The mule started to move slightly faster when John dug his feet into the animal's sides. They rode down Duquennes Road and passed Bobby driving toward the hill to Ruby's house.

"Whistle at him, John. I want to make sure Bobby Boatwright see me!" Maureen giggled.

John obeyed and Bobby stopped and climbed out of his car. Recognizing Maureen, he stomped his foot and shook his fist in her direction. A sudden, strong wind blew Bobby's wide-brimmed hat from his head. Maureen and John laughed and continued riding.

Maureen stopped laughing when she felt John's hands tighten around her waist. He leaned forward and placed his face against her hair.

"Girl, girl, girl," he swooned.

"You stop that!" Maureen ordered, frightened.

"I declare, Mo'reen. I meant every word I said back at the house. You is sharp as a tack. Sometimes I see you struttin down Duquennes Road wearin cut-off jeans and a T-shirt—"

"Let me off this mule," Maureen said suddenly, squirming.

"How come? I was goin to carry you all the way to my house and let you see what else I got for my birthday!"

"I'll see your birthday gifts some other time. Now let me down so I can go back home." Maureen handed John the jar of preserves. He looked in her eyes as she turned around to face him. "Un-ass me. Your hands is way too tight around me anyway. I can just barely breathe, John."

Before she knew what was happening, his lips came down on hers and to her surprise, she did not protest. John's hands moved down the sides of her thighs and he whimpered. Realizing they were sitting out in the open, in broad daylight where anyone could see them, Maureen pulled away.

"Don't you never do that again," she hissed.

John kissed her again, longer and much harder this time.

Maureen moaned and pulled away with hesitation.

"Didn't I just tell you not to do that no more?" Maureen was angry and aroused at the same time.

"You didn't like it?" John asked.

". . . Naw, I didn't like it. Here I am all but a married woman and you slobberin all over me." Maureen leaped from the mule and glared up at John, who was grinning and staring at her.

"Listen, uh . . . John, don't you tell nobody what we just done. You hear me? Ain't no tellin what might happen."

"I bet that Bobby Boatwright ain't never kissed you like that, huh?"

"That's for me to know!" Maureen spat.

John winked at her and turned to leave. Maureen was left standing on the road angry with herself for the ache in her loins, something she believed only Bobby could cause. She looked around quickly to make sure no one had witnessed her act of indecency. There was only the blazing sun over her head, watching.

39

Maureen took her time returning home. Strolling down Duquennes Road, she passed a truck going in the opposite
direction containing about a dozen bean pickers, all black and
Spanish men around her age. One of the workers had a radio
and a lively tune was blaring away as Maureen waved and leaped
up in the air. The radio was turned up louder and Maureen
teased the men by lifting her skirt with one hand and doing a
sexy grind to the music. She laughed and danced until the
truck, with the workers cheering and whistling, was out of sight.
On her descent down her hill, she recalled John's hands and
lips and stopped in her tracks. She remembered a conversation
about romance she had had with Catty the night before her
wedding.

"You reckon you'll marry you a sport, if you ever marry,
Mo'reen?"

"I declare, Catty, I'd like to. But I been thinkin. I been seein
some pretty sporty men in Miami lately. Cept one thing. Most
of em was white," Maureen sighed.

"Oh, I ain't got nothin against white men. I just might marry
me one of em once to see what all the commotion about white
folks is about," Catty replied.

"I axed Fast Black one time. She been around. She been

with Chinks. White mens. Spanish mens. She told me to my face a pecker is a pecker."

Catty laughed at Maureen's words.

"I don't know about all that. I got this theery about Chinks—which I guess is the main reason I laid up with Yellow Jack."

"What is this here theery, Catty?"

"I suspect Chinese men is the best in the bunch when it come to hanky-panky."

"How you figure that?"

"You know how in them movies them Chinese women be tiptoein around and smilin and bein so quiet?"

"Yeah. Ole Mai Ling Ching what live in Miami is the same way."

"Who is she?"

"Oh, a woman Mama Ruby use to visit now and then."

"Anyway, the reason Chinese women so content is cause Chinese men is fuckin the hell out of em!"

"Sho nuff?"

"Girl, I ain't as dumb as folks think I is. Why you think I latched onto Yellow Jack instead of one of these full-blooded nigger men. Shoot! Yellow Jack is a humdinger."

"Oh?" Maureen said.

"And let me tell you—he is what you call a sho-nuff lover—woo!"

Maureen laughed and gently slapped Catty's head.

"I don't know about Chinese men for marryin. Anyway, ain't but a handful in Florida. That's why I been thinkin about white men a lot lately. Say I was to get married. To a white man. Not your everyday white man now. Oh, I think I could probably stand bein married to Al Pacino." Maureen paused and scratched the back of her neck. "Course if I hook up with him, he'd probably want to carry me off to live in Hollywood or somewhere."

"You think Al Pacino too good to live in Florida?"

"Naw. But he's a city man—"

"Miami is a city!"

"He's 'phisticated. He the kind of man you'd expect to live in New York or San Francisco."

"There you go talkin about that San Francisco again. Lamb, I bet you one thing. That dago movie star was to come to Goons—"

"Let's change the subject." Maureen had become uneasy and frightened.

"Mo'reen, I seen John French eyeballin you real hard the other day. Speakin of white men," Catty purred.

"Hmmmm. John ain't half bad, but he is much too country. And I know for a fact, he don't like nothin but blondes." Maureen shook her head to get thoughts of John off her mind and she continued walking down the hill.

Roscoe and Snowball, the albino, were sitting at the table with Ruby drinking beer when Maureen reached the house. Before she could close the screen door, Zeus walked out of the kitchen carrying a tray with four beers and his tattered deck of cards.

"Hi, Zeus. Hi, Roscoe," Maureen said. She deliberately ignored the albino.

"Ain't you goin to say hi to Snowball, Mo'reen?" Ruby asked. Her eyes followed Maureen as she glided over to the sofa and sat down hard.

"Hi, Snowball," she said over her shoulder.

"Hey, Mo'reen, I just got out the halfway house in Miami. They almost cured me from my heroin, you know," Snowball said. He stood up and moved over to Maureen.

"I don't care, Snowball. You always just gettin out a halfway house from messin with heroin. You ought to be shame of yourself. Messin with dope. If you had any sense, you'd be in a school somewhere learnin a trade."

"Don't be too hard on Snowball, Mo'reen. He can't help it if he ain't been as blessed as you," Ruby scolded.

Zeus started to shuffle the cards and Ruby and Roscoe watched as he flipped over the ace of spades.

"Lord no!" Ruby gasped.

Maureen and Snowball turned toward the table.

"What is it, Mama Ruby?" Snowball asked, moving over to her. He looked on the table at the ace of spades staring boldly up at him. "Aiyeeee!" he cried.

Maureen rose and rushed to the table and stood next to Snowball, her hand on his trembling shoulder.

"Mama Ruby, somethin bad fixin to happen?" Snowball asked.

"Sho nuff," Ruby said in a nervous whisper.

"Ruby, I want you to walk a chalk line these next few weeks,"
Zeus warned. "And before you go runnin to Miami to any of
them honky-tonks, you come to see me first so I can throw the
cards to make sure the coast is clear."

"Zeus, you stop comin down here causin a commotion with
them cards. You ain't nothin but a witch doctor and a sorcerer!
Them cards is evil!"

"Shet up, Mo'reen! This is serious business. I been readin
cards since I was nineteen. I know my business. This ace of
spades mean death," Zeus said.

"Who is this ace of spades for?" Maureen asked quietly. She
moved closer to the table and faced Zeus, staring him straight
in the eyes.

"Somebody in this room," Zeus answered, looking from one
face to another.

"I'm sho nuff scared . . . maybe I'll stay here for the night,"
Snowball announced. "I'm stayin here so Mama Ruby can pro-
tect me. Ain't nothin'll get me if I'm with Mama Ruby."

"I might take a notion and stay here myself," Zeus said in a
shaky voice. The others had not been aware that Zeus had
flipped over another card, the king of spades. "The doom is
comin to one of us menfolk in this room."

Ruby breathed a sigh of relief.

Maureen eased quietly away and went to the upper room.
She went to bed without dinner, with many thoughts on her
mind. Catty and Yellow Jack. Chinese men. Bobby Boatwright.
Snowball. And John French's hands and lips.

At dawn, Maureen went to the upper room's front window
and saw Roscoe walking up the hill. Apparently he had spent
the night with Ruby too.

In Ruby's room, Maureen discovered Zeus and Snowball in
the same bed with Ruby. Ruby was the only one under the
sheets and the men lay sideways across her legs. Beer cans were
everywhere.

"Yall wake up!" Maureen ordered, clapping her hands.

Ruby sat up quickly, looking from Maureen to the two snoozing men.

"What in the world—yall menfolks get out my bed!" she
shouted, reaching for her teeth on the nightstand.

The men staggered awake and rose quickly. Snowball's shirt was unbuttoned and Zeus' pants were missing. Noticing this, Ruby became alarmed.

"Yall drunks got in bed with me? Why, this is a shame! I could have been took advantage of!" she shouted.

Snowball and Zeus looked at one another, at Maureen, and then at Ruby.

"BY WHO?!" Zeus asked.

Maureen started to giggle and clap her hands together.

"Mo'reen, you get these might-be rapists out my bedroom!" Ruby ordered.

"Now, Ruby, do you mean to set there and tell me you think one of us might have raped you!" Zeus asked, hurt.

"You's a man, ain't you?" Ruby cried.

Zeus grabbed his pants from the foot of the bed and trotted out behind Maureen and Snowball into the living room.

"Yall better go on home. Give Mama Ruby time to wear her beer off," Maureen suggested.

"We didn't mess with Mama Ruby," Snowball told Maureen. "Honest to God, we didn't. At least I didn't," he said, turning to Zeus.

"Zeus, did you take advantage of Mama Ruby?" Maureen asked. "Did you rape her?"

"Mo'reen, ain't a man alive that crazy. Anyway, me and Mama Ruby like brother and sister," Zeus answered fumbling with his pants.

"I know, Zeus. Yall go on now. Come back later after Mama Ruby done come to her senses." Maureen ushered the man on out the door.

"Mo'reen, can I come back to see you later today?" Snowball asked, buttoning his shirt.

"Write me a letter or somethin. We'll talk about it some other time . . . go on now," she insisted, closing the screen door in Snowball's face.

40

Instead of returning to his two-room compartment at the camp where he lived, Snowball went to visit Loomis.

Loomis snatched open the door wearing only his pajama bottoms.

"Set down, Snowball," he said nervously, as he eased himself down into a chair facing a lumpy sofa. On a coffee table were two glasses, one with lipstick on it, and three empty whiskey bottles.

Snowball looked toward the back and saw a half-naked woman running out the door.

"You got company?" he asked, embarrassed.

Loomis turned and looked over his shoulder, then quickly back at Snowball.

"Not no more," Loomis answered. ". . . Um . . . you didn't see who that was, did you?"

Snowball shook his head.

"Good. She a married woman. I can't tell you her name on account of if her man was to find out about her and me, he would take a brick and bust her brains out. She a happily married woman."

"Oh? If she happily married, how come she come to your house, Loomis?"

"Snowball, let me put a bug in your ear. When I love a woman,

she stay loved. These women around here ain't never had a
man like me. That one what just snuck off, I had socked it to
her best friend. Well, the woman bragged about me so much
this woman had to start to messin with me. I usually don't lay it
on married women. Shoot. I'm a Christian to the bone and I
have a lot of respect for marriage. I'm hot as a six-shooter now
on account of what Catty done to my cousin Yellow Jack. The
bitch. But the people around here call me the lover," Loomis
said, crossing his legs.

"That's why I'm here right now," Snowball whispered.

"I declare! Wait a minute now—" Loomis gasped, holding
up his hands. "I LIKE WOMEN ONLY!"

"Oh no—I ain't no sissy! I come here for advice." Snowball
was more alarmed than Loomis. "A man like you done probably had more than a million women, Loomis. You could prob'ly
tell me how I can get *one*. Can you?"

"Oh," Loomis sighed, uncrossing his legs. "What's the problem? You got the blue balls or somethin? Man, I had em last
year!"

"I ain't got no blue balls. I'm havin trouble with Mo'reen. I
been after her since I moved to Goons eight years ago and she
still don't like me. What am I suppose to do?"

Loomis scratched his chin and looked Snowball over thoroughly.

"Mo'reen ever give you any?" Loomis asked, with one eye
closed.

"Any what?"

"I declare!" Loomis exclaimed, slapping his thighs. "Is you
ever had you a woman?"

"Two. Ain't too many women want to lay up with a albino.
You know that, Loomis. Shoot."

Loomis looked at Snowball and shook his head.

"In the first place, Mo'reen been busted already. Bobby
Boatwright told me he got it down by the Blue Lake. So she
been experienced. She'll want her a man what know how to
love her the way he suppose to. Understand?"

Snowball nodded and leaned forward, listening.

"I want you to get you a French tickler and carry Mo'reen
off private. Put your piece in her pocketbook—"

"Slow down, Loomis. What's a French tickler?"

"It's a little doo-dad you slide on your piece and tickle your woman with. I wear em all the time. I'll lend you a few."

"Oh. And what's a pocketbook?"

"Goddamn, Snowball, don't you know nothin? A pocketbook is a coochie! A pussy, man! Damn! How you expect me to school you if you don't even know the basics?"

"OK. How long will it take you to learn me all I need to know so I can tickle Mo'reen in the pocketbook?" Snowball asked.

Twenty minutes later, Snowball was knocking on Maureen's door. She answered, opening the screen just enough to stick her head out.

"Mama Ruby ain't here," she snapped.

"I know. I seen Mama Ruby in the truck with Slim just now. I didn't come to see her, Mo'reen."

"Oh? Who did you come to see then?"

"You."

Maureen laughed.

"To talk to you about us—I . . . um . . . Loomis told me to say . . . listen—will you give me some pussy like you done Bobby Boatwright?"

"WHAT?!" Maureen shouted.

"Well . . . will you?" Snowball asked impatiently.

"He told?"

"Oh yeah, he told. Now listen here, I am even willin to buy you a bottle of pop," Snowball continued, fumbling in his pants' pocket to remove a fistful of coins.

Maureen stared at him.

"I ain't no rich man now. Don't be expectin more than two or three bottles of pop," Snowball said.

"You low-down, funky, no-color, dope addict you! Get outta my face! And when you see that low-down, funky Bobby Boatwright, tell him I'm goin to kill him dead!" Maureen shouted. She slammed the screen door shut and locked it, then threw herself on the sofa and sobbed.

41

Maureen lay on the couch crying for an hour. The sound of a car coming down the hill made her leave the sofa and stagger to the window. It was Yellow Jack's Cadillac, and Fast Black was driving. No Talk sat next to her and Ruby and Loomis occupied the back seat.

The car stopped but Fast Black did not turn off the motor. She got out and ran up on the porch.

"Oh, Mo'reen, Mama Ruby say for you to give me—" Fast Black stopped talking as soon as she got inside the door. "What you cryin for, Mo'reen?"

Instead of replying, Maureen's sobs intensified and she ran back to the sofa and fell forward.

"What's wrong, sugar?! Is you been raped?! Who done it?!" Fast Black asked, running to Maureen. "Talk to me, girl—who done it?!"

"Bob—Bob—Bobby Boatwright—" Maureen stammered.

Fast Black ran from the room back out to the car.

"Wait, Fast Black," Maureen shouted, jumping up behind her.

"BOBBY BOATWRIGHT DONE BROKE IN THE HOUSE, RAPED MO'REEN AND LEFT HER FOR DEAD!" Fast Black cried.

Ruby's face froze.

Fast Black got back in the car and turned it around.

"All he done was talk about me, yall—COME BACK HERE!" Maureen shouted. "Don't kill Bobby Boatwright!" But they could not hear her over their own loud, angry voices. "Oh, Lord, they fixin to go kill Bobby Boatwright!" Maureen said to herself. Instead of running up the hill, she took off through the bayou at the side of the house, a shortcut that would put her five minutes ahead of the Cadillac, enabling her to reach Bobby's house first.

The house Bobby lived in with his father sat in back of the Kaiser camp. It was a small, shabby cabin surrounded by palmetto trees. Bobby's bedroom was in back. His Mustang was in the backyard, so Maureen tiptoed up to his room and tapped on the window.

"What you want, you honky lover!" Bobby barked as soon as he raised the window.

"Help me in, Bobby Boatwright! I got to put a bug in your ear!" Maureen exclaimed. "Help me in the window!"

"Bitch! I'm goin to fuck the hell out of you this time," Bobby threatened as he helped Maureen climb in the window. He squeezed her breasts and buttocks angrily. "Get your juicy butt on in here."

Bobby's room was small and congested with a large bed, two chifforobes, and numerous pieces of stereo equipment. On one wall was a large poster of Malcolm X. Facing Malcolm X on the opposite wall was a large poster of a naked white woman.

Before Maureen could get a word out, Bobby had grabbed her and thrown her across his unmade bed.

"You don't two-time me with no cracker like John! You don't do that to me, girl!" he said, as his lips came crushing down on hers.

She bit his tongue.

"You wench!" Bobby spat, jumping up.

"Bobby Boatwright, you got to run and hide! They comin to get you! They comin to kill you dead! I come to warn you so you can get a head start!" Maureen shouted. "I declare, you got to run off somewhere! THEY COMIN FOR YOU!"

"WHO?! THE WHITE FOLKS?!" Bobby's eyes got big and his lips quivered with fright. "Why the white folks comin?!"

"Not the white folks, Bobby Boatwright! Ten times worse! Mama Ruby, Fast Black, Loomis, and No Talk!"

"WHAT?!"

"They got a notion in em you raped me and left me for dead!"

"I ain't raped nobody! Once I got you goin, you the one liked to raped me!" Bobby cried. "I ain't raped you, Mo'reen!"

"They didn't give me a chance to tell em!"

"Great balls of fire!"

Bobby lifted his mattress and removed a wallet and stuffed it in his back pants' pocket.

"What you goin to do, Bobby Boatwright?!"

"Girl, I'm fixin to haul ass! Soon as I get into Miami, I'm goin to ship out on the first vessel'll have me! Shit—goddamn! Them niggers get me, I ain't worth a shit no more!"

"I'll straighten em out! Give me at least a day! Don't haul ass yet!" Maureen wailed.

Bobby climbed out the window with Maureen, each running off in a different direction into the woods.

42

It took Maureen, Catty, and Yellow Jack to convince Ruby that Bobby had not committed any crime.

"I swear to God, Mama Ruby, Bobby Boatwright ain't done nothin to be ashamed of," Catty said.

"He sho nuff ain't. Honest to God, Mama Ruby, Bobby Boatwright been leadin a Christian life like you told him to. I seen him at that church on Brewster Street in Miami last night with my own eyes," Yellow Jack lied.

"I seen him too," Catty agreed.

"He can preach up a storm if you was to ax him," Yellow Jack continued.

"He sho nuff can, cause I seen him do it," Catty added. "That boy got more spirit than a little bit. I declare, I ain't never knowed no one boy with so much of the Holy Ghost in his soul," Catty added.

Yellow Jack gave her a sideways glance. He was still angry about Catty running off with the albums and letting them be destroyed.

They sat on Ruby's front porch. No Talk and Loomis sat in Yellow Jack's car holding blunt-ended sticks. Fast Black sat on the hood of the car shining a switchblade.

"Where is Bobby Boatwright now?" Ruby barked. "We went through his daddy's house with a fine-toothed comb yestiddy

and his Mustang caught afire as we was leavin. Accidental,"
Ruby said casually. She sat on the glider with her arms folded
across her chest. She held a can of beer in one hand and her
shotgun in the other.

". . . I think he at John's house," Maureen said.

"Bobby Boatwright's daddy sho nuff don't know what happened. He thinkin Bobby Boatwright went with John to fish in
Tampa Bay and they think a maniac broke in they house and
messed it up. We ain't told him it was yall," Catty said.

"You done right tellin him that, Catty. We don't want the law
down on us on top of everything else," Loomis said.

Ruby looked up at Catty's pleading eyes.

"Please, Mama Ruby. Don't yall do away with Bobby Boatwright. He play ball with us sometime and if he was to up and
disappear, we'll have to find another pitcher," Catty said.

"All I want to hear is the truth," Ruby said. She paused and
drank. "If the nigger busted in my house and raped my baby, he
ain't fit to live," Ruby declared, looking to Maureen.

"I swear to you, Mama Ruby. I swear on Virgil's disappearance . . . ain't nobody raped me," Maureen said.

"Is you certain?" Ruby asked quietly.

"Mama Ruby, everybody know how tough you is. What man
around here is goin to rape me?" Maureen asked, with a smile.

Ruby considered Maureen's comment and nodded.

"I see what you sayin. Ain't none of these men got that kind
of nerve. Certainly not Bobby Boatwright." Ruby sighed and
smiled. She then looked from Maureen to Yellow Jack. "Yall go
tell that child he can go on home. I ain't goin to mess with
him," Ruby said.

43

It rained continuously for the next four days. During this time, no one came to Ruby's house. But as soon as the weather cleared up, the usual visits resumed.

Maureen spotted Fast Black, Loomis, and No Talk strutting down the hill one afternoon. Fast Black entered the house first, snatching open the screen door without knocking.

"We want to see Mama Ruby," Fast Black told Maureen.

"Mama Ruby watchin *Lassie* right now, Fast Black. You know she don't allow nobody to mess with her when she watchin *Lassie*," Maureen said.

"This is important," Fast Black said.

"Sho nuff," Loomis interjected.

Maureen looked at him and studied his dry face.

"Well, so is *Lassie*, Loomis."

"Come on, Mo'reen. We got somethin for her. Go ax her to come out for just a minute," Fast Black pleaded.

"I ain't messin with Mama Ruby when she watchin 'Lassie,' I'm tellin you." Maureen placed her hands on her hips and shook her head.

Fast Black ran across the floor to Ruby's room and kicked on the door.

"Mama Ruby, it's me and Loomis and No Talk. Don't you want to see us?" Fast Black shouted at the door.

"Not unless yall want to talk to me about Jesus," Ruby replied.

"See," Maureen grinned. "I tried to tell you."

"Mama Ruby sent word by Yellow Jack she wanted us to help her settle a dispute between her and that A'rab down the road," Loomis said. "We want to get this mess the maniac done caused straightened out right now. Shoot. I want to get home to watch *Roller Derby.*"

"I don't know nothin about no dispute between her and that A'rab." Maureen shook her head again, looking toward Ruby's room.

"Some lyin foreigner done cut his throat. Them foreigners comin over here takin over and we fixin to put a stop to it," Fast Black declared. "Mama Ruby, come on out here!" Fast Black kicked the door a second time. "We fixin to bust Goons wide open!"

Ruby did not come out of her room until her television program ended, ten minutes later.

"Mama Ruby, can I put a bug in your ear?" Loomis began as Ruby floated across the floor.

"As long as it don't bite me," Ruby replied. She stopped in her tracks and looked at Maureen, recognizing the fright in her eyes. ". . . Um . . . Mo'reen, go pick me some blackberries," she ordered gently.

Maureen was glad to be dismissed. She grabbed the first bowl she saw in the kitchen, ran out the back door, and headed for the berry patch near the Blue Lake.

44

"Who is that in them bushes?" Maureen asked in a loud voice. "Who is that, I axed?" A moving blackberry bush by the Blue Lake had startled her.

"Is that you, Bobby Boatwright?" she asked. There was a sudden rustling in the bushes again and Maureen dropped the bowl she had brought with her, spilling berries all over her feet. Someone was hiding in the bushes trying to frighten her. She became angry, because whoever it was had succeeded.

First one, then two, three, and finally four white boys jumped from behind the bushes, where they had been hiding. Maureen clutched her bosom. In her bra, she carried the switchblade and the cross Ruby had given her on her thirteenth birthday. Maureen had never had to use the weapon and often forgot she carried it.

"What you doin out here by yourself?" one boy asked with a grin.

Maureen suddenly realized one of the boys was John French and she breathed a sigh of relief.

"Yall like to scared me to death," she said, talking in John's direction.

"What you doin out here alone? You pretty little ole brown hussy, you," John growled.

Maureen's eyes got big as she looked at him.

"I—I'm pickin blackberries to make my mama a . . . pie," she answered feebly.

John looked away, then quickly back at her.

"I like blackberries myself . . . especially the kind with hair," John smiled. "How about a black berry for me?"

Maureen looked at him and blinked.

"I got to go home," she said. As soon as she started to walk away, John jumped in front of her and grabbed her arms.

"You ain't goin no place," he informed her.

"I ain't?" she asked dumbly.

"Girl, I'm fixin to do what I should have done a long time ago," John told Maureen.

The other boys laughed and egged him on.

"Look-a-here, boy—"

"BOY?! Who you callin boy? How many boys you know who got nine-inch dicks like me?" John unbuckled his belt and unzipped his pants quickly with one hand, still holding Maureen securely in place with his other.

"Turn me loose!" she ordered, trying to pry his hand from her arm. She felt her bosom.

"What you got in your titties?" John asked, shaking her. "Huh? I axed, what you got up there in them pretty little ole brown titties?"

She pulled away from him and reached inside her bra to remove the switchblade.

"Hot damn!" one of the other boys shouted when Maureen clicked the blade open.

"Yall better leave me alone if you know what's good for you. I ain't scared to use this blade," she said, suddenly feeling more powerful.

The boys started to close in on her and she lost her nerve. Startled, she fell backwards and dropped the knife. All four of the boys piled on top of her.

Maureen fought with so much fury, two of the boys got tired and pulled back.

"Get a hold of yourself, girl, before somebody gets hurt!" John hollered as he slapped her face repeatedly. The two boys who had moved back stood and watched John and the fourth boy continue to wrestle with her. Maureen managed to get the knife back, and started slashing. She sliced John across his arm, forcing him to stand and attend to his wound. The other boy had his lips on her and was forcing his tongue in her mouth. She bit off the tip of the boy's tongue and sent him running from the berry patch screaming in agony. She spit the piece of tongue in John's face as he threw himself back on top of her.

Maureen screamed as John slammed his fist against her face.

The two remaining boys came and held her down, one holding open her legs and the other one pinning her arms down while John raped her. She closed her eyes and stopped screaming. She needed all her strength to endure the pain.

Afterward, she felt John rise, but the boys kept her pinned down.

Something was inserted inside her, not another penis, but the handle of her own knife. She fainted and when she came to, five minutes later, the boys were gone.

45

A sense of doom hung from the southern sky like the sinewy moss from the magnolia tree. From the front window in the upper room, Maureen looked up at the sky. It was just dark enough for her to piece together both the big dipper and the little dipper. A few other faint stars decorated the night like scattered marbles.

She lifted the window and leaned out, focusing her attention on Duquennes Road. The balmy air felt good against her face and neck. She had on her nightgown, which was low cut, flimsy and sleeveless. Her hair was plaited and pinned behind her ears.

Headlights from an oncoming car made Maureen widen her eyes as she gazed up the hill. Her heart began to beat rapidly when she realized it was a police car. The vehicle turned and started moving toward the house.

Big Red brought his dusty squad car to a stop in the front yard and he quickly climbed out. A long thick cigar hung from his lip. His melonlike belly and big butt gave his body a bell shape. His red hair was streaked with gray now. He paused for a minute, removed his hat to brush the hair back from his forehead, and looked up the hill before hastily rearranging his attire. His shirt was buttoned incorrectly and his belt was unbuckled. He retucked the shirt back down inside his pants without fixing the buttons and clumsily did his belt.

Big Red took his time moving to the back of the car, where he gallantly opened the back door on the driver's side and helped Ruby out. They stood close together and talked quietly. A few times Big Red placed his hand on Ruby's shoulder and nodded.

Ruby stood back on her legs with her arms folded. She had no shoes on and the long, flowered muumuu she wore had been Big Red's gift to her one Mother's Day. Suddenly they stopped talking and glanced around suspiciously. Ruby slapped Big Red on the back, then walked off toward the house. Maureen waited until Big Red returned to the car and started back up the hill before she left the upper room. As soon as he was out of sight, she ran down the stairs to the living room.

"Mama Ruby—" she started calling. Maureen stood in the middle of the floor looking out the window at Ruby fussing with a chicken on the porch. "Mama Ruby, please come in the house," she whimpered. "What done happened to me ought not to happen to a dog." Maureen's lips trembled as she watched Ruby continue to scold the chicken. Finally, Ruby snatched open the screen door and sauntered in. Maureen gasped. The front of Ruby's dress was covered with blood. "What happened to you?" Her first thought was that somehow Ruby had already heard about what John had done to her and had killed him. "Mama Ruby, you bleedin like a stuck pig! You got blood all over your good dress!" Maureen exclaimed. She remained in her spot, unable to move.

"I is, ain't I," Ruby said casually, gliding across the floor.

"Lord, Mama Ruby, what done happened this time?"

"Huh . . . just a little accident . . . nothin serious," Ruby answered, looking down at her dress. "I sho nuff hope this blood wash out."

"Mama Ruby, tell me what happened!"

"A accident, that's all. I had a little run-in with that ole motor-mouth A'rab what live down the road apiece," Ruby said.

"Old Abdullah? That ole A'rab? I seen him settin on his front porch yestiddy mornin, yestiddy afternoon, and yestiddy evenin. He is always settin on his front porch," Maureen said.

"He ain't settin there no more. . . ." Ruby nodded.

"This blood on you—you got blood all over your dress, Mama Ruby."

"Yeah, but it ain't my blood," Ruby replied. She turned to Maureen and blinked. Maureen stared in Ruby's eyes and bit her lower lip. She followed as Ruby continued across the floor to her bedroom.

"What you been doin while I was gone?" Ruby asked, as she pulled her muumuu over her head. She could not see the odd look on Maureen's face.

". . . Nothin."

"You get my blackberries?" Ruby tossed the muumuu on her bed.

"I forgot."

"You forgot? Where did you go when you left the house this afternoon with that bowl?"

"I ran into some girls from Kaiser camp and we got to talkin. I plumb forgot to get the berries. I'm sho nuff sorry, Mama Ruby." Maureen spoke with her head bowed.

Ruby smiled.

"Don't you worry about em. We'll get some another day and make us a pie. I declare, I love you to death, Mo'reen. You is such a Godsend. Jesus sho nuff is good to me," Ruby said proudly. She reached over and caressed Maureen's chin and became curious when Maureen's eyes refused to meet hers. "What's the matter?"

"Mama Ruby, is it *anybody* in the world you scared of?"

"Not a man, woman, beast, or spirit. Why?"

"I just thought . . . maybe there was somebody or somethin even you wouldn't go up against."

"I done cussed out the devil, kicked his ass, bound him to hell and you axin me if there is anybody or anything I'm scared of? Ain't nothin nobody can make or say that can scare me. Girl, don't you know I am the link between the Lord and the Dark One. Ain't nothin in between. Course, I get kind of squeamish when I think about Jews and rapists, but who wouldn't? Cept other Jews and rapists. Why do you ax?"

Maureen shrugged.

"I seen somethin on the news what kind of reminded me about you. A wild killer."

Ruby gasped.

"Why would a wild killer remind you about me?"

"I don't know. They said he was real tough and had kilt a lot of folks, like you."

"Yeah. Maybe so, we got that in common, but I ain't *wild*. Don't you never think of your mama as wild. That clear?"

"Yes, ma'am."

"What you gettin at, girl?"

"I just go to wonderin sometime. Sometime I worry about you when you leave the house with Loomis and Fast Black and No Talk to go chastize folks. I keep thinkin one day somebody is goin to get you back."

"Ain't nothin can kill me and don't you never forget that," Ruby said with conviction. She stood before Maureen in her half-slip and bra, both stained with blood.

"I seen John on my way home just now," Ruby said. She moved over to her bed and sat down hard and did not see Maureen tremble.

"What did he say, Mama Ruby?"

"He sho nuff was actin odd. Had his daddy's shotgun with him. Like he was lookin for trouble. Strange thing is, he took off runnin when he seen me settin in back of Big Red's car." Ruby looked at Maureen with a puzzled expression on her face. "White folks is so odd," she said, laughing. She paused as if waiting for Maureen to say something about John. "How come you actin so odd yourself, Mo'reen?"

"I ain't actin odd," Maureen mumbled. She moved swiftly across the floor and seated herself next to Ruby. "You say John had his daddy's shotgun in his hand?"

"Yeah. His hands was shaking like sumac leaves. Poor thing. Sometime I think John don't know what to do with hisself." Ruby smiled and cocked her head to the side. Suddenly she turned to face Maureen, placing her arm around her shoulders. "Now, tell me darlin, what you been doin while I was gone?"

". . . Nothin," Maureen said in a low, distant voice.

46

Ruby had never had a telephone installed in the house. "If anybody got somethin to say to me, let em say it to my face," she said. So whenever she or Maureen needed a telephone they walked up to one of the camps or into Miami to use a pay phone.

Maureen had been walking down Duquennes Road fifteen minutes when Big Red came speeding up behind her, his siren going. She stopped in her tracks and sighed with annoyance. Big Red pulled alongside her and jumped out of the car with his hand on his gun.

"Girl, what you doin roamin up and down this road by yourself? I bet Mama Ruby don't know where you at."

"I'm eighteen years old, Big Red."

"Well, act like it. You want some rapist or maniac to snatch you? I got enough on my hands with all them damn Cubans running loose. Shoot. I'll be bound!"

"I'm just on my way to visit a friend in Miami," Maureen replied tiredly.

"Who?"

"Nobody you know, Big Red." Maureen started to walk away.

"Look-a-here, girl. You get in this car and let me carry you on to the city. Your mama been awful tetchy lately." Big Red walked to the back door on the passenger's side of his car and snatched it open. "Get in this car!" he ordered. Maureen sighed and obeyed.

Big Red drove like a madman all the way into the city with the siren blaring.

"Where in Miami is you goin, Mo'reen?"

"Drop me off on Peach Street," she answered.

After he let her off, she took a bus to Patterson Street, where she got out in front of a saloon called the Black Hawk. The Black Hawk attracted mostly merchant seamen and prostitutes, being so close to the docks and the highways. Maureen went to one of two pay phones outside the bar.

She had not been in the booth a minute when several seamen approached and inspected her legs, flashing dollars in her face. She turned her back and pretended to be too involved in her telephone dialing to notice. Loud knocking against the booth made Maureen drop the telephone.

"What in the world—"

She turned to see Fast Black standing with her hands on her hips.

"Mo'reen, you got a dime I can borrow? I want to go in the Black Hawk but I ain't got no money," Fast Black said. She was plastered. There was plum-colored lipstick on her teeth and rouge that reached from her cheeks to her brows.

"A dime all you need to get in there?" Maureen asked.

"See, I'm goin to pay for a glass of water with it. They won't let you stay in there lest you buy somethin. I buy me a glass of water every time I come here until I can latch me onto a sugar man. I can sip on the glass of water till I make a hit."

"What if I give you a dime and you sip up all your water before you get a sugar man?"

"Then I'll ax somebody for another dime. You got a dime or not?" Fast Black said impatiently.

Maureen nodded and reached in her pocket, removed a dime, and handed it to Fast Black.

"Who you callin anyway, Mo'reen? A married man?"

". . . Um . . . no. I'm fixin to call that hairdresser on Bell Avenue to see if I can get her to do somethin to my hair. Put a wave in it or somethin," Maureen said, running her fingers through her naturally straight hair.

"Oh. Well, I'll be seein you," Fast Black said as she followed a mob of seamen into the bar.

Maureen quickly lifted the telephone again and dialed John French's number.

"Hello," a young girl's voice said. John had four younger sisters. Maureen recognized the voice as fifteen-year-old Sukey.

"Hello, Sukey. Is John there?" Maureen spoke in a deeper voice, hoping to divert Sukey's attention.

"That you, Bonnie Sue?" Sukey asked. Her voice was loud but Maureen could hear other girlish chatter in the background.

". . . Um . . . yeah. Can I speak to your brother?" Bonnie Sue was John's girlfriend, a seventeen-year-old blonde everyone expected John to marry. Bonnie Sue was a pretty girl with a passive nature, the ideal southern wife. She was also the daughter of a local politician.

"Hold on, sugar. Let me get him for you. How you been gettin along? We ain't seen you in a week. What's cookin, Bonnie Sue?"

"Oh, I been fiddlin around with them cousins of mine from the panhandle," Maureen replied, glad the gossip had reached Goons about Bonnie Sue's usual activities.

"You sound kind of funny today," Sukey commented.

"Must be this head cold I got. Can you get your brother for me now? Mama's waitin to carry me to the beautician."

"OK, darlin," Sukey said graciously. The next voice Maureen heard was John's.

"Hello there, sweet thang!"

"John, don't say nothin. Let me do all the talkin. This here is Mo'reen. Go get on yall's extension so you can talk private," Maureen instructed. John said nothing to her. She heard him tell Sukey to hang up the phone after he signaled her.

"What the hell you doin callin my daddy's house, girl?" John said.

"I'm in a heap of trouble and you the only one what can help me," Maureen said quickly, looking toward the entrance of the bar, praying Fast Black would not come out.

"Girl, if I'm the only one what can help you—you is in trouble!"

"Can you meet me in the bayou in back of my house in a hour? I got to see you, John."

"Uh huh . . . I figured you'd be wantin to see me again after that little party in the berry patch. Heh heh heh."

"This is not what you thinkin. I'm fixin to have a baby, John."

"By who?"

"By you, that's who. You the only one I been with in two months."

"What!—why you syphilitic black wench you! You think I'm goin for that?! The way Bobby Boatwright been fuckin you all over the place! Girl, you must be talkin through your asshole, cause your mouth knows better! You lyin whore!"

"You did get me pregnant. Now I want you to meet me in the bayou in one hour," Maureen said calmly.

"The hell I will!" John screeched.

"The hell you won't. You don't be there and I'm goin to blab what you done to me all over Dade County. You ain't had no business doin what you done to me, John. Beatin me and all."

"Girl, I just tapped you. I ain't hurt you."

"Oh yes you did."

"Listen . . . um . . . I ain't meant no harm. Look, when we goin to get together again? I sho nuff enjoyed myself. I see why Bobby Boatwright is so crazy about you! Wooo weee! But don't you call me talkin about havin no baby by me. That's frog shit! I ain't ownin up to no nigger baby. Me with Bonnie Sue fixin to be my wife and all. Her daddy won't be able to get hisself elected dogcatcher if you was to start blabbin this wild story around! You hear me?"

"Meet me in the bayou in a hour."

"Ain't you been listenin to me?!"

Maureen hung up on John.

47

John slapped Maureen down where she stood. She landed in a heap at the base of a palmetto tree deep in the bayou in back of her mother's house.

"Get up before I stomp a hole in you!" John yelled. He leaned over and slapped her face again.

"Aaaarrrggghh!" she wailed. They were too deep in the wilderness for anyone to hear.

She moaned and struggled to get up, holding onto the tree. Before she had full control of her senses, John pushed her back down with his foot. She landed on her back and he pressed his foot on her stomach and pushed.

"Aaaarrrggghhh!" she screamed, writhing in agony.

"Shet up!" John ordered. He fell to the ground and covered Maureen's mouth with his dirty hand. "There's quicksand all over the place out here. And in the swamps, there's gators! I'll shove your black ass in the quicksand or feed you to the gators if you don't shet up!" he threatened. Maureen nodded and John jerked her up by the arm and leaned her against the tree. "Don't you never call me on the telephone again with your nigger woman's lies!" he exclaimed, slapping her face hard.

"Please don't hit me no more, John," Maureen begged.

"I just come out here to get you straight. I ain't ownin up to no nigger baby. You go around tellin them lies on me and I'm goin to sic the Klan on you and Mama Ruby and all the rest of you niggers out here in Goons."

"I just need money," Maureen sobbed. "I don't want to have no half-white baby. I ain't got no money to get myself took care of . . . please help me. That's the least you can do."

"You is as nutty as a nigger-toes nut pie if you think I'm givin you money to get rid of some other man's baby."

"All I need is five hundred dollars. There's a use-to-be doctor in Miami what'll take care of me so I won't be pregnant no more . . . please."

John looked her in the eyes and shook his head, then turned to leave. He disappeared into a patch of bushes, and Maureen slid back down on the ground and drew her knees up against her chest. She sat for just a few seconds, listening. John's footsteps were loud and fast. Suddenly, she heard him scream.

"Have mercy—Mo'reen, help me. I'M IN THE QUICKSAND!"

Maureen took her time going to him.

"Mo'reen, I'm sinkin! Reach your hand to me!" John cried as Maureen stood over him with her arms folded. He was already in up to his waist.

"Help me, Mo'reen! Help me, Mo'reen!" His bugged-out eyes looked at her incredulously. He could not believe what was happening. Instead of reaching out a branch or her hand, she was just standing and staring at him.

"Aaarrrggghhh—Mo'reen, you can't let me die!"

"Why shouldn't I?" she asked softly, letting her arms fall to her sides.

"Mo'reen, I'll do anything you say!" John cried. His eyes refused to blink. His heart thumped so madly, he feared he'd have a heart attack long before the quicksand swallowed his body. If only Maureen would reach out her hand and help him to safety. She continued to watch him struggle. His eyes betrayed him; now he saw himself, his life flashing before him. He was dying. He was a child again. Not in a bowl of quicksand, but held protectively in his mother's arms.

"Mama?" he said, opening his eyes slowly.

"I ain't your mama, you nasty peckerwood, you," Maureen spat. "You lucky I'm a Christian. Otherwise, I wouldn't have dragged your tail out that quicksand just then." She let go of John abruptly and stood up. He watched her, tears in his eyes, as she slowly walked away, disappearing into the darkness.

48

After a restless night, when she had managed to sleep only three hours, Maureen was awakened by the sound of the screen door slamming downstairs. She tossed her bed covers aside and swung her legs over the side of the bed. Her stomach ached, as did her face. But John's beating was nothing compared to her future, now that she was going to have to suffer the consequences alone.

Downstairs, Ruby and Slim sat at the table in the living room, Slim sipping coffee and Ruby sipping beer. Maureen entered the room and found them shaking their heads, grim expressions on their faces.

"What's wrong with yall?" Maureen asked. She stopped at Ruby's side and folded her arms.

"I just got some sho-nuff bad news from Slim," Ruby replied, not facing Maureen.

"What is it this time, Slim?" Maureen asked, turning to him.

Slim looked up at her and did not blink his eyes during the whole two minutes he spoke.

"John French done up and got hisself kilt. I declare, them jailbirds don't live long. Fast Black and Loomis both got records a mile long . . . I suspect one of em'll turn up dead next. Poor John . . . dead as a Jew's tittie. The boy went and got hisself shot up last night. Tryin to rob one of them all-night stores in Miami. Went in there with his daddy's shotgun and axed the man behind the counter for five hundred dollars. Just like that. Not a thousand dollars, not five thousand dollars, but five *hundred* dollars . . . like that was all he needed. Poor John, I guess the boy had a problem he was tryin to work out and robbin was the only way he could. . . . I'd have borrowed the money from somewhere to lend him if he had only come to me. . . . I liked the boy . . . and he liked all of us . . . specially you, Mo'reen . . . told me so to my face."

Maureen's hands started to tremble.

"John dead?" she asked, leaning forward.

Ruby looked at her.

"We'll never know what was on the boy's mind," Ruby said sadly.

"You know, it just don't seem right. The boy knowed he could come to you, Mama Ruby. He always use to tell me you was like a mammy to him," Slim said.

Maureen felt as if the blood in her veins had frozen. Her situation was worse with John dead. Now there was no chance he would help her.

"What am I goin to do?" Maureen whispered, not loud enough to be heard.

49

Maureen's bruised and swollen face was easy enough to explain to Ruby. "I stepped on a pop-top on Zeus' porch and fell down the steps," she lied.

With John's funeral and tending the boy's bereaved family, Ruby had been too busy to pay much attention to Maureen's clumsiness.

"Hold a slab of ice to your jawbone, girl," was all Ruby said about Maureen's injuries. Sukey was at the house that evening. Maureen sat on her living room footstool while Sukey, swimming in grief, begged Ruby for help.

"Oh, Mama Ruby—I can't deal with it! I can't eat a bite! I can't sleep a wink! Two days since my brother was snatched away! Oh, I can't live with a death in my family!" The girl threw herself in Ruby's arms as Ruby lay stretched out on the sofa. Ruby ran her thick fingers through the frail girl's long blond hair and gently rocked her back and forth.

Sukey had spent the night there sleeping next to Ruby in her bed. The day before, each member of John's family had come to Ruby for consolation and a laying on of hands.

"Oh, Mama Ruby, lay hands on me again . . . soothe this pain!" Sukey wailed. She had been particularly close to her brother and had introduced him to his fiance, Bonnie Sue McFarland.

"Precious little ole white lamb you," Ruby soothed, placing a hand on Sukey's face, smoothing back her hair. "Just be thankful the good Lord didn't let the boy suffer none."

Maureen sat on the footstool with her stomach churning, and a knot in her throat that had been there off and on ever since the rape.

Five minutes after Sukey left, Ruby looked over at Maureen and Maureen quickly looked away. She ignored Ruby and looked out the window up the hill. Snowball was on his way and from the look on his face, he had a problem that required healing hands.

50

Maureen hid herself behind a stump until Catty and Fast Black had passed, walking down Duquennes Road.

"Wonder where ole Mo'reen been keepin her tail these days. This is the third time today we been to the house and she was gone," Catty complained.

"I know one thing, she been actin mighty odd these last few days. I bet you she foolin around with somebody's husband. Or some new man she don't want us to know about, huh?"

"Fast Black, you liable to hear about Mo'reen doin some of anything. Losin Bobby Boatwright to that high-yellow wench Jolene. I seen him with her at my weddin. Actin like lovebirds. Bobby Boatwright ain't got a bit of shame, carryin on like he done at my weddin."

Fast Black stopped and placed her hands on her hips.

"What's wrong with you?" Catty stopped and shaded her eyes to look at Fast Black.

"You bold hussy! The way you carried on at your own weddin, shamin my son, and now you talkin about Bobby Boatwright and Jolene."

"Look-a-here, you *old maid*—"

Catty was cut off by Fast Black's hand coming down across her face.

"What the hell's wrong with you, Fast Black?!" Catty slapped Fast Black back, harder.

"Aaarrrggghhh!" Fast Black cried, grabbing a handful of Catty's hair and pulling. "You keep on—you liable to make me lose my religion. I been—" Fast Black stopped pulling Catty's hair. "Lord, Catty, there go Reverend Tiggs! He see us out here actin like wild women he liable to preach our funeral—HOW YOU DOIN, REVEREND TIGGS?" Fast Black waved both hands at the passing preacher.

"Hi, Reverend Tiggs," Catty called.

Both waved until the preacher crossed the road.

"Wonder where he headed?" Catty said.

"Look like he on his way to Mama Ruby's house."

Maureen listened with interest. The women talked loudly and started walking again. Both were wearing starched jersey skirts and stiff plaid cotton blouses with the sleeves rolled up. Catty's hair was braided and Fast Black's was covered underneath a blue bandanna.

"Lord, I sho nuff hope Mama Ruby get them beer cans hid before he get there," Catty laughed. "I bet he goin to check up on Mo'reen. She probably sneakin around with a married man or somethin. What you think, Fast Black?"

"Oh, I do believe she got a new man. A foreigner, no doubt. I seen that Snowball hanging around the house last night. I bet he was waitin on Mama Ruby to go to bed so he could go in and coochie coo with Mo'reen, huh?"

"Probably so. From what I hear, Mo'reen sho nuff a hot mama," Catty laughed. "You reckon she messin with some foreigner? One of them greasy Cubans or one of them ole West Indians?"

"Either one of them or Snowball. You know how foreigners is when it come to women with long hair like Mo'reen got. I guess they like to wrap up in it, huh?"

"Me, I don't know and I don't care. All I know is, Mo'reen been actin right odd lately. Sound like to me she messin with a sho-nuff different kind of man. Not a foreigner yet. But at least a albino."

"Speak of the devil . . . Catty, look who drivin up Duquennes Road toward Mama Ruby's house."

Catty snatched her head around and shaded her eyes.

"Oh, Snowball and Mo'reen doin the hoochie coo. Look at the way he wheelin Yellow Jack's car."

"Wonder how long she been messin around with this all-white man, Catty?" Fast Black stopped walking.

"Ain't no tellin." Catty sighed and shook her head. You know somethin, Fast Black?" Catty stopped walking too.

"What's that?"

"It's a good thing me and you keep our eyes and ears open. How else would we know what was happenin around here?"

"You right. We got to find out everything on our own," Fast Black lamented, shaking her head. "Mo'reen and a albino. Now that's about the best piece of news I heard today."

"Sweet Jesus!" Catty made a wide, sweeping gesture with her hands, then stomped her foot. It was hot and humid. Both women were barefooted and perspiring profusely. Gnats played around their legs and sand stuck to their toes and ankles. They watched until Snowball went inside Ruby's house before they resumed their walk. "All the regular men in Florida and Mo'reen got to take up with a albino. Wooo!"

"Wonder how she could lay up with a un-black man? That's about as bad as layin up with a foreigner, huh?"

"Fast Black, what you call all them Cubans and crackers and West Indians you done laid up with? Shoot. And you even had the nerve to get yourself pregnant by a Chink. You talk about foreigners. Now I'm a woman what is scared of foreigners, sho nuff. Specially Cuban. I'd worry a scab on my brain tryin to figure out whether to feed him black-eyed peas and neckbones or Spanish rice and refried beans."

Maureen could barely hear her friends now as they had begun walking again and were almost out of hearing distance. The last thing Maureen heard was Catty saying, "Mo'reen could have done better than a albino—wooo!"

Catty's and Fast Black's comments gave Maureen an idea. She had considered telling a wild tale of a night of partying in Miami and waking up in the bed of a strange man. A man with coloring that might produce a light-skinned child; a Hispanic . . . or even an Oriental. Either Snowball or Yellow Jack, both the appropriate coloring. Everybody knew Snowball was crazy about

Maureen and as far as Yellow Jack was concerned, as close as he and Maureen were, it seemed natural that they would one day get together.

Catty and Fast Black had already condemned her. If they were fool enough to think she was low-down enough to involve herself in a secret romance with an albino, the least she could do was be fool enough to let them think that. It wasn't Maureen's fault. They were going to believe what they wanted anyway.

Maureen was five weeks pregnant and could not conceal her condition too much longer. Getting Snowball or Yellow Jack in bed was not going to be easy. She'd cussed out Snowball and he had vowed never to ask her out again. And Yellow Jack had never in his adult life shown any real interest in sleeping with her. She decided to try Yellow Jack first.

51

"Oooh, Yellow Jack . . . I been lookin for a man like you all my life," Maureen purred. Yellow Jack had come to the house and found her alone.

"What's wrong with you, girl?" he yelped, with a surprised look on his face.

". . . Um . . . you is my kind of man, *honey*," she said nervously. She grabbed the puzzled Yellow Jack by his hand, pulled him to the sofa and forced him down. "I done heard about you Chinamen. . . ."

"Is this some kind of a joke, Mo'reen? Cause if it is, it sho ain't funny. You up in my face, pullin on me. I tried to get you one time when we was kids and you like to got me kilt, runnin to ax Mama Ruby if you could give me some coochie. Shoot. You know I ain't about to mess with you since that day."

"Oh, honey, baby, I been thinkin about you for the past ten years. I still think about that day in the yard when you axed me to hoochie coo with you."

"And it took you all this time to get around to wantin to do it?"

"Yeah. You want to do it here on the couch?"

Yellow Jack stood up and stared at Maureen, his mouth hanging open.

"I come down here to borrow some bleach so I could wash

my car mats. I ain't come here to hoochie coo, Mo'reen. Shoot. Catty'll cut my nuts off if she was to find out. And Bobby Boatwright'll shit, if he was to find out. Mama Ruby'll shoot me! You crazy if you think I'm goin to take a chance on Mama Ruby!"

"Don't you like me, Yellow Jack? Don't you think I'm cute?" Maureen stood up, hurt.

"Girl, you sharp as a tack and you know it. Everybody know it. The thing is, layin up with a fox like you ain't worth me losin my nuts over. I ain't that crazy. I want to live to make somethin outta myself. I overheard Mama Ruby tellin Reverend Tiggs she suspect I'll turn into either a intellectual or a communist. That's how much sense folks say I got. I'm goin to be somebody. Lest Mama Ruby get my damn ass!" Yellow Jack declared, moving toward the door.

"Yellow Jack, don't go. Just do it to me, one time," Maureen begged, reaching out to him.

"Hot damn! Girl, I do believe somebody been feedin you Spanish fly! Get away from me—go on, Mo'reen! Turn my pecker loose, girl!"

Yellow Jack threw open the door and ran off the porch.

"Yellow Jack, come back!" Maureen hollered, stopping on the porch.

"You that hot, girl, I wouldn't do you no good. You need somebody like Loomis. A man use to hot women!" Yellow Jack jumped back into his car and sped up the hill.

Maureen couldn't hold back her tears as she stood and watched Yellow Jack's car disappear in a cloud of dust.

52

Another six days went by and Maureen still had no father for her unborn child. Only Snowball was left. He had stopped even speaking to her days earlier, and sometimes ran when he saw her coming in his direction.

Out of desperation, she went to his compartment at the camp and knocked on his door. Next door, Catty ran to her bedroom window and snatched it open to lean her head out.

"Mo'reen, what you doin knockin on that man's door? What you want with him?" Catty demanded.

"Shet up, Catty." Maureen spoke without turning around.

"Girl, you better tell me what you doin knockin on that man's door! Me and you been best friends since we was babies and I'm suppose to know. You can't go around knockin on men's doors and not tellin nobody why."

Maureen whirled around and faced her friend angrily.

"Catty, this ain't none of your business!" she said.

Catty gasped and covered her mouth with her hand as Maureen turned her back to her and knocked again. Snowball opened the door slowly.

"Whatyouwantfromme!" he said, running his words together. He repeated himself at his normal speaking rate. "What you want from me?"

"Can I come in?"

"I guess . . ." he said, opening the door wide enough for Maureen to enter. "What you want?!" he asked immediately after Maureen was inside.

"Remember that time you come to the house and axed me to . . . you-know-what with you?"

Snowball looked at Maureen and blinked. His room was dark and stuffy. He rarely opened his windows and seldom received guests. There was only one chair, a portable television on the floor, and a hotplate sitting on a gasoline can in his living room.

"I remember," he replied, puzzled but curious.

Maureen touched his arm.

"I been thinkin about you," she said.

Snowball just looked at her.

"What's the matter with you, Mo'reen?!"

"I just want a man—what's so wrong with that?!"

"You want ME?" the surprised man asked with a grin.

"Yeah, I want you, goddam it! Now you look here, you carry me in the bedroom and do it to me right now!"

Snowball moved back a step, shaking his head.

"All I do is go to work in the fields and shoot a little dope now and then. . . . I don't mess with no one. . . . Why you doin this to me?"

Maureen was amazed. Here she was trying to seduce a man who had made his feelings for her public and he was turning her down! Having Yellow Jack resist her had been bad enough.

"Don't you like me no more?" she asked, taking a step forward.

The frightened man held up his hand and moved back a step farther.

"Please go—please go and leave me alone. I never hurt you. I never hurt nobody. All I want to do is go to work and shoot a little dope now and then. I don't want no trouble, Mo'reen!"

Maureen lowered her eyes.

"You think makin love to me would be too much trouble?" she asked morosely. Her voice was low and hollow. It occurred to her that her problem was deeper than she'd thought.

"Please leave me alone, Mo'reen," Snowball begged.

Maureen opened the door and walked out slowly. Catty and

Fast Black were standing outside with their hands on their hips waiting for her.

Both women cursed as Maureen walked by without a word.

Ruby was concerned when Maureen came home crying.

"Who done messed with you?" Ruby demanded, rising from the sofa.

"Mama Ruby, I just want to go to the upper room," Maureen said. She stopped suddenly and faced Ruby.

"What's wrong, Mo'reen?"

"Nothin. Oh . . . I wish I had never been born, Mama Ruby!"

53

Another week went by and Maureen was still trying to figure out what to do. She avoided Catty and Fast Black, and Yellow Jack avoided Maureen. Snowball had been admitted to a Miami halfway house again, his drug problem worse than ever.

Ruby watched Maureen closely, following her every time she left her sight.

"Mama Ruby, I'm just goin to the toilet," Maureen said with disgust. "I don't need no escort."

"I know you don't, but you need me," Ruby insisted.

Instead of working in the fields, as she usually did this time of year, Maureen spent her days sitting in the living room watching television with Ruby.

Logan Hutchins, Snowball's cousin, came running up on the porch this particular Thursday afternoon, hysterical and calling for Ruby.

"MAMA RUBY—AARRGGHH!" he cried, snatching open the door and falling face forward on the floor.

"What in the world is goin on?" Ruby demanded, rising. She ran to Logan, who was struggling to lift himself off the floor.

"Mama Ruby—it's Snowball! Lord help us! Come quick! He done dropped dead and we need your healin hands to try to bring him back to life!" Logan cried.

"Dead?" Maureen mouthed, rising and running to Logan. "Who kilt him?"

"He overdosed on heroin!"

"Overdosed? I thought Snowball was in the halfway house again," Ruby said.

"He was. That's where he overdosed!" Logan informed them.

"Snowball done overdosed *in* the halfway house?!" Ruby asked. She grabbed Logan by the shoulders and shook him.

"Aaarrrggghhh!" he screamed. He pressed his face against Ruby's chest and wailed frantically.

"What is we goin to do now? You have to come and try to raise him, Mama Ruby!" Logan began beating Ruby's chest.

Ruby released Logan and turned to Maureen.

"Mo'reen . . . look like Satan done come to Goons and took up permanent residence," she said. "If anybody come lookin for me, tell em I went to try and raise a dead albino."

But Snowball was beyond help.

54

"Aaarrrggghhh—"

Everybody on the camps and everybody living in the houses throughout the camp area was awakened by Ruby's frantic screams that morning, three days after Snowball's funeral.

"Irene—Bishop," Ruby wailed as she ran up on their front porch in her housecoat. Irene snatched open the door and ran outside in her slip.

It was early on a hot Sunday morning. Dogs, made uncomfortable by the humidity, were already up, howling and biting at june bugs.

Ruby had awakened and prepared an elaborate breakfast for herself and Maureen. Reverend Tiggs had promised a special sermon and Ruby wanted to face the Sabbath on a full stomach. When Maureen did not come down for breakfast at her usual time, Ruby went to the upper room to find out why. Maureen was gone. Her bed had not been slept in and a crude note had been tacked to the door of her chifforobe.

Dear Mama Ruby,
I done run off on account of I am fixing to have a baby. By Snowball. A albino and a dead one at that. See, he overdosed, I think, on account of he knowed he was good as dead anyway. We figured you'd kill him dead and so what's

the use. Tell Slim not to get me nothing for my birthday on account of I won't be there to get it. Tell Catty she can have that transistor radio Bobby Boatwright gave me, it don't work no how.

Love, Maureen

"My child done left me!" Ruby cried, waving the note at Irene. Irene slapped Ruby's tear-stained face to silence her. Ruby closed her mouth but continued to wave her hands. Irene grabbed Ruby's hand and led her inside, where Bishop was sitting on the sofa in his pajamas.

"What done happened?" he asked.

"Mo'reen done run off cause she pregnant by that albino what died the other day," Irene answered, reading the note she had snatched from Ruby's trembling hand. Irene and Bishop looked at Ruby at the same time.

Ruby was wailing and her eyes were rolled back in her head as she stood in the middle of the floor.

"Bishop, run over to Roscoe's and call Big Red. This is sho nuff a po'lice matter," Irene said. Bishop obeyed, dashing from the house calling Roscoe's name.

Twenty minutes later Big Red came speeding down Duquennes Road with the siren blaring. He ran over six speckled hens in Irene's front yard as he brought the squad car to a halt inches away from the porch steps. He fell getting out of the car, making some teenagers double over with laughter. Ignoring the youngsters, Big Red ran up on the porch and on into the house.

"Come on in, Big Red," Bishop invited, as he stumbled into the living room with his hand on his revolver.

Catty entered from a back room wearing a housecoat and looking obviously annoyed.

"What's goin on out here?!" she asked.

Irene looked from Catty to Big Red.

"Mo'reen done finally got herself pregnant. Now she done run off on account of it's by that dead albino," Irene told Catty.

"I knowed it! I knowed it! Me and Fast Black said Mo'reen was messin around with Snowball!" Catty announced, bouncing up and down.

"Big Red, you got to find Mo'reen!" Ruby hollered. "Find

her and tell her I forgive her. I don't care who she pregnant by. Just bring her back to me! OH LORD!"

Fast Black entered holding a mason jar filled with pot liquor in one hand.

"I remember when Mo'reen was a itty-bitty baby," she sighed. "Now here she is fixin to have a baby herself."

"By a albino. Lord. Mo'reen might end up with a all white baby," added Bobby, who had entered the house immediately after Fast Black.

Big Red drove Ruby back to her house and within ten minutes Ruby's living room was filled with concerned friends.

When Maureen walked up in the front yard, she heard all kinds of chatter coming from inside the house.

"Yellow Jack, come out of Mama Ruby's ice box!"

"Slim, quit steppin on my foot!"

"Big Red, put that gun away."

"Catty, pull down your dress."

"Loomis, stop feelin on my legs!"

"I bet a maniac done kilt Mo'reen and fed her to the gators."

"Aaarrrggghhh!"

Maureen stopped, then walked quickly around to the back of the house. She listened and peeked in through a hole in the kitchen door. The kitchen was vacant. She quietly opened the door, let herself in, and tiptoed to the upper room. She unpacked the few items she had carelessly tossed in a shopping bag, returned them to her chifforobe, and went to bed.

Maureen had spent the night in the Greyhound bus station on a bench. By morning she was hungry and homesick and could not return home fast enough.

A few hours after her return, she left the upper room and went down to the living room. Irene and Bishop were the only ones left with Ruby, as everyone had gone out to search for Maureen.

"What's wrong with Mama Ruby?" Maureen asked.

Irene and Bishop gasped and turned around to face her. They stood over Ruby, who lay on the sofa in a catatonic state.

"Mo'reen, the whole world's out lookin for you," Irene barked.

Maureen rushed to Ruby and grabbed her hand.

"You get your big ole fat self up from there!" Maureen ordered.

Ruby opened her eyes and sat up to embrace Maureen.

55

Maureen's labor started before daybreak, one morning in the middle of March.

Ruby moved her from the upper room to the living room, where Maureen's twin daughters Loraine and Loretta were born at noon on the pallet Ruby had laid on the floor.

"What I have, Mama Ruby?" Maureen asked tiredly when she came to. She had had a fairly easy labor, but had passed out before the actual birth.

"Twin girls," Ruby said proudly. "Two beautiful little girls that look just like you."

"Just like me?" Maureen asked eagerly, afraid her children would take after their father.

"Just like you. Same nigger-toe color. Same straight black hair. Same looks. Everything, just like you."

". . . Um, they don't look nothin like Snowball?"

"Shoot. Them kids don't look nothin like that homely baboon." Ruby grinned.

PART
FOUR

56

It was fall, 1973. The Viet Nam war was over and most of the men from Goons who had participated in it had returned home. Still, there had been no word about Virgil. Ruby and Maureen prayed for the day another government car would come to the house carrying Virgil. They spent more time than ever looking out the window, up the hill.

Maureen sat on the footstool in the living room looking up the hill, shading her eyes with her hand. Ruby lay on the sofa with Maureen's six-month-old twins on her lap.

"Mama Ruby, come look out the window and see what I see," Maureen called over her shoulder, not taking her eyes off the hill.

Three slender white girls were walking toward the house accompanied by a gigantic black woman and a tiny black man carrying a suitcase. The white girls, all teenagers, had on shorts and flimsy blouses and were barefooted. The dust and the hot sun had turned their feet and legs brown. The big black woman wore a full-length muumuu and carried a large black purse. In her other hand she held a fan and was fanning her face. The man wore a dark suit, made from a fabric unsuitable for the weather.

"Look like Cousin Hattie, Sukey French, and some other white girls. And a itty bitty black man," Maureen reported.

"Have mercy," Ruby replied lazily, not taking her eyes off the children.

Maureen moved from the window and positioned herself on a hassock next to the sofa, pretending to be reading a Bible she had snatched off the coffee table. The crowd entered without knocking.

Hattie had opened the door and the others followed behind her in single file.

"Wooo wee!" Hattie exclaimed, grinning from one side of her face to the other.

"Cousin Hattie!" Ruby shrieked. She rose up from the sofa and ran to her cousin. Sukey took Loraine and one of the other girls grabbed Loretta from Ruby's arms and went to the sofa and sat down. Ruby embraced her cousin and kissed her about the face.

"What you doin in Florida, Cousin Hattie?" Ruby asked.

"Didn't yall get my letter?" Hattie replied, pulling away from Ruby.

The two girls accompanying John's sister Sukey were his other sister, fifteen-year-old April, and the girl he had planned to marry, eighteen-year-old Bonnie Sue McFarland. Maureen watched with disapproval as the white girls fussed over the twins.

"We was bringin you your mail, Mama Ruby," April announced. She left the sofa and sauntered over to Ruby and handed her an envelope she removed from her blouse pocket.

"It's a letter from Cousin Hattie!" Ruby laughed, waving the envelope postmarked three days earlier. In the letter Hattie informed Ruby and Maureen of her visit. Hattie had mailed the letter the same day she left Baton Rouge.

April often removed Ruby's mail from her roadside mailbox and delivered it to her. She'd use any excuse to get to Ruby's house and play with Maureen's beautiful brown babies, who reminded both April and Sukey of their cousin Charlotte's baby girl.

"Cousin Ruby, Mo'reen, meet my husband, Pharaoh Maze," Hattie said proudly. The man, who appeared to be shy, smiled at Ruby.

"How do," he said in a childlike voice.

"Lord in heaven, Cousin Hattie, you done finally got yourself married?" Maureen asked, coming over to shake Pharaoh's hand. "When you get married, Cousin Hattie?"

"Last Tuesday!" Hattie answered. "We met at a funeral and hit it off right off the bat!" Hattie took her husband by the hand and led him to a chair, then sat down on one of the sofas.

The white girls were interested only in the babies and seemed oblivious to the others in the room.

"I been blessed," Hattie sighed.

"Ain't it so. We all been blessed," Ruby insisted, looking at the girls with the babies.

"Mama Ruby, can we carry the babies for a walk?" Bonnie Sue asked.

Maureen ran to Sukey and hastily grabbed Loretta, then went to Bonnie Sue and snatched Loraine. Hattie leaped up from the sofa and took the children away from Maureen.

"These the little angels I done heard so much about!" Hattie squealed, frightening both twins, who looked at her wide-eyed. Though Ruby and Hattie were identical, Hattie's face was covered with several layers of heavy face powder and rouge, looking very unlike Ruby. The babies started crying.

"Cousin Hattie, you scarin em," Maureen said gently. She removed Loraine from Hattie's arm and handed her to Ruby. Sukey rushed over to Hattie and grabbed Loretta back.

"I just love these little babies so much," Sukey smiled. "They is so much like Charlotte's baby."

"Sho nuff is," Bonnie Sue added sadly.

"They goin to grow up and be heartbreakers like Mo'reen is," Hattie said with a laugh.

Maureen left the crowd fussing over the babies and returned to the window.

"Mo'reen, get back here! Where is your manners? Run get ice water for our company," Ruby instructed, walking toward her bedroom with the suitcase Pharaoh had carried in.

"How long yall plannin to stay, Cousin Hattie?" April asked.

"Not long, darlin. Just a few days," Hattie answered.

Maureen went into the kitchen and prepared a pitcher of ice water. When she returned to the living room carrying a tray with a pitcher and several glasses, everyone was outside in the front yard taking pictures.

"Come get in a picture with me, Mo'reen," Ruby yelled, shifting her weight from one foot to the other.

Maureen placed the tray on the steps and silently joined them, placing her arm around Ruby's waist. Hattie had a self-developing camera and three photos had already been snapped and set on the bannister to dry.

"Yall smile!" Hattie ordered.

Ruby grinned broadly while Maureen barely moved her lips. After the picture-taking session, the photos were passed around.

"Look at this one of Mo'reen . . . it's got a shadow on it!" April shouted, waving the picture at Ruby.

"Wonder what happened . . ." Ruby said, running her finger across a dime-sized shadow almost covering Maureen's face.

"Probably Bonnie Sue's thumb when she snapped it," Pharaoh suggested, looking at Maureen.

"Yeah . . . that must have been what it was," Maureen mumbled, with a hint of worry. She was confused and frightened. Before Virgil went into the army, Slim had photographed him. In one of the shots, Maureen had seen the same kind of shadow on Virgil's face.

It was much later that day that Maureen discovered the same kind of shadow on Loraine's face in one of the other photographs. Maureen was convinced it was not from Bonnie Sue's thumb.

57

On the second afternoon of Hattie's visit, Slim and Pharaoh left Ruby's house to go fishing in the Blue Lake. Maureen, Loraine, and Loretta were off visiting Catty, and Ruby and Hattie went to see Zeus for a card reading.

"Aaarrrggghhhh!" Ruby screamed as she fell from her chair in Zeus' living room.

"Get up off that floor, Ruby!" Zeus ordered, throwing the cards down on his coffee table. He stood up from the sofa and glared down at Ruby lying on the floor spread-eagled. Hattie left the sofa and ran to Ruby to help her up.

"I can't stand it! I can't stand it! I can't stand it!" Ruby roared as she staggered back to her chair.

Zeus sat back down and picked up the cards again.

"Now you wanted the truth and that's what I'm givin you!" Zeus said angrily. "I'm tellin you to your face, Mama Ruby, them kids ain't yours to keep. They all, Mo'reen, Lo'raine, and Lo'retta, goin somewhere and ain't never comin back!"

"Aaaarrrggghhh!" Ruby screamed, banging the coffee table with her fist. She leaped up and started to jump up and down, causing things to fall off shelves and the pictures on the walls to slide about. A chandelier hanging over the coffee table started to shake.

"Ruby, you tearin up my house!" Zeus shouted, clapping his hands together.

"Tell me them cards lyin! Tell me my kids ain't goin to leave me!" Ruby screamed.

Hattie grabbed her by the arm and forced her back down in the chair.

"Them cards don't lie! I ain't runnin one of them Mickey Mouse fortune-tellin games! You dealin with me, you dealin with a big-time operation! Shoot! I got white folks come all the way from Key Largo for me to read the cards for em. You know them cards ain't lyin about them kids of yours leavin you, Ruby!" Zeus hollered. "Now you get your big self on out my house before you tear it up! Shoot!"

Hattie took Ruby by the arm and led her home.

"Cousin Hattie, I got to make sure . . . make sure that the devil don't get his hands on my kids," Ruby whimpered as Hattie helped her to bed.

"You can't fight fate, Cousin Ruby. Like Zeus said, you dealin with a big-time operation when you got him readin the cards for you. You just can't fight fate."

58

"Oh, Mama Ruby, I was lookin out the window in the upper room just now, and I seen a soldier man comin down the hill!" Maureen exclaimed, running into the living room where Ruby sat on the sofa watching television with the twins, who were now five.

"We don't know no soldiers, Mo'reen. You must be seein—*soldier?*" Ruby jumped up and leaped twice in the air before running to the door. "PRAISE THE LORD— IT'S VIRGIL!"

Ruby and Maureen ran out the front door, leaving Loraine and Loretta bewildered.

Virgil, now a willowy veteran of thirty-five with sad eyes and a lined face, stopped in the front yard and smiled.

"VIRGIL!" Maureen screamed. She ran into him with so much force he fell to the ground, dropping the military bag that contained his possessions.

"This beautiful woman can't be none of Mo'reen!" Virgil cried. He rose quickly and embraced her. Turning to Ruby, he frowned, saddened to see that her weight had reached a dangerous level. She now weighed four hundred pounds.

"Thank you, Jesus!" Ruby cried, lifting her hands high above her head before grabbing Virgil and lifting him completely off the ground.

"Where you been, Virgil?" Maureen asked.

"In prison. I was captured and locked up and damn near forgot about," Virgil replied. "Well, ain't no more Viet Nam war . . . and I'm home to stay. Have mercy! I'm sho nuff glad to see yall!" He squeezed Ruby.

"I knowed you wasn't dead!" Ruby laughed, slapping Virgil on the back.

By now Loraine and Loretta had come out on the porch and were watching this reunion with their eyes shaded.

"Who is that man yall kissin and huggin on, Mama?" Loretta asked.

Virgil's breath caught in his throat and he looked from Loretta to Loraine.

"Whose little girls?" he asked, looking to Ruby.

"Mine," Maureen said proudly. "Ain't they pretty, Virgil?"

"Just like you is," Virgil teased, running his finger across Maureen's face. "You mean to tell me Mama Ruby let a man get *that* close to you, Mo'reen? You done got yourself married, girl?!"

"Hell no, Mo'reen ain't married. Snowball snuck hisself up on Mo'reen and got her pregnant, then he went and overdosed on dope," Ruby informed Virgil.

"Lo'retta, Lo'raine, yall come meet your uncle," Maureen invited, beckoning the children with her hand.

"My uncle dead. V-Eight Nam got him," Loraine said, eyeing Virgil suspiciously.

"He don't look nothin like you, Mama," Loretta remarked.

Virgil strode up on the porch and grabbed Loraine and then Loretta, holding them against his chest.

"I declare. A man go away from home for a few years and ain't no tellin what he might come home to," Virgil commented. "Lord, Mama Ruby, you get any fatter they liable to need a steam shovel to get you out the bed."

"Virgil, everybody in Goons been fussin at Mama Ruby for years to stop eatin so much. She don't listen to nobody. Just look at her feet. She ain't been able to wear regular shoes since nineteen and sixty-three. She have to wear mens' slides," Maureen complained.

"First thing Monday mornin, I'm carryin you to one of them diet doctors in Miami and see what we can do about you eatin up everything what ain't movin," Virgil informed Ruby.

"I ain't goin no place," Ruby pouted, removing the children from Virgil's arms. "Boy, you come on in this house so we can look at you some more. Mo'reen, drag them kids' things out Virgil's room and put em in mine."

"How come they can't move into the upper room with me?" Maureen asked, following Ruby as they all walked up on the porch.

"How many times I got to tell you, ain't nobody can stay in the upper room but you?" Ruby said over her shoulder. "Now Virgil back, I got to get him settled in and back to normal. And don't you keep gettin on me about my weight or no other mess. That clear?"

59

"What you mean, you got a place in Miami, Virgil?! This is your home! You ain't been home a month and already you talkin crazy! It's bad enough I've had to listen to Mo'reen talk about movin off to some foreign place called San Francisco. The last thing I need now is for you to start talkin about movin to Miami. With all them wicked folks runnin around loose!" Ruby shouted.

The house was full of friends, all of whom had given up hope of ever seeing Virgil Montgomery again. Virgil's welcome-home party had been going, off and on, for five days. Willie Boatwright and Catty were serving pretzels and glasses of pot liquor. Bishop was in charge of the record player and Loomis and No Talk made sure no nosy busybody wandered up to the upper room.

Maureen was outside on the front porch where it was quiet, getting acquainted with a man from Miami named Jack Roberts, another recently released POW who had returned to Florida with Virgil. To reduce the confusion between Jack Roberts and Jack Wong Harris, better known as Yellow Jack, Ruby promptly nicknamed Jack Roberts "Black Jack."

Though he had been home only three weeks, Virgil had secured a job in a Miami lobster factory and had become involved with a woman named Mary Davis who lived near the factory, much to Fast Black's dismay.

"I'm thirty-five years old now, Mama Ruby. I know you don't expect me to pick up where I left off. I don't want to stay out here in Goons no more," Virgil replied. "I done changed a whole lot since you last seen me before I joined the army. But from what I done heard, you sho nuff ain't changed. And, Lord, Mama Ruby . . . you near about as wide as a Mississippi road."

"Don't fuss at me about my weight. I know I'm a little on the heavy side. It run in my family," Ruby whined.

"The only thing that run in your family is yall like to *run* back and forth to the ice box, Mama Ruby—"

"Shet up! Now, like I said, you ain't movin to no Miami, Virgil!"

Virgil had pulled Ruby off to a corner. But her voice was loud, and everyone present could hear everything she said.

"I'm surprised Mo'reen is still livin out here in these swamps with you. Cooped up in that ole spooky upper room," Virgil told Ruby.

"Don't you never bad mouth the upper room no more," she hissed. "That room's sanctified, and Mo'reen'll be in it till the day she die!"

"Will she, Mama Ruby?" Virgil looked out the window at Maureen and Black Jack.

Outside Maureen heard what Ruby had said, and Black Jack heard her too. He looked at Maureen, this lovely brown slip of a girl with eyes that were mysteriously sad, and he sighed.

". . . Um . . . you got to excuse my mama, Black Jack. I think she goin through the change of life," Maureen apologized.

Black Jack smiled and glanced away, out toward the Blue Lake. Maureen gasped and shook her head when she turned and discovered Catty and Fast Black with their heads out the opened front window listening. She stuck her tongue out at them and returned her attention to Black Jack. She looked him over quickly but thoroughly. He was tall. A little thin, but a few Sunday dinners would fatten him up, she thought. He was dark and had a smile that lit up his face. His hair was a little too long, but Maureen was not going to worry about that just yet. She had more important things to work on first. Like matrimony. This man was in pretty good shape considering he had been locked away in a Viet Nam prison for more than a decade.

"And you didn't go into the army leavin no sweetie behind?" Maureen asked, trying not to appear coquettish.

Black Jack returned his gaze to her face and smiled.

"I did. When I got home my woman was married to my best friend and done had five kids." He laughed, adding, "Now she's almost as big as Mama Ruby."

"Married your best friend, huh. Ain't that a shame," Maureen purred. Fast Black and Catty giggled and left the window.

"I don't blame her. Would you have waited all these years?"

"I been waitin longer than that, Black Jack," Maureen almost whispered.

"What's that suppose to mean?" he asked, touching her cheek.

"I'll tell you one day," she answered, looking toward the lake. When she looked at him again, he was staring off toward the lake himself. She noticed his arms, which were muscular and long. As were his legs. He turned suddenly and noticed her looking him over. He smiled. He had already done the same to her. Their eyes met and she looked away, coughing to clear her throat.

"Can I come see you sometime, Mo'reen?"

"Uh . . . yeah." She was unable to hide her nervousness. She looked toward the house. Ruby was now in the window with her head leaning out. "Long as you don't do nothin to make my mama mad."

60

Virgil ignored Ruby's protestations. He not only moved to Miami, he married Mary.

"Mama Ruby, you better tie a can to Mo'reen's tail. I seen her roamin up and down the street with Sister Mary's Sister," Fast Black said one rainy Saturday evening as she and Ruby sat drinking beer on Ruby's front porch glider.

"Uh huh," Ruby grunted, belching.

"Next thing we know, Mo'reen'll be done run off again. With Black Jack. To that San Francisco . . ." Fast Black added.

"Shoot. Mo'reen don't want Black Jack. After havin a sport like Bobby Boatwright, she ain't about to take off behind a dull nobody like Black Jack. Shoot. Black Jack don't even drink," Ruby growled.

Maureen lay across her bed in the upper room while Ruby and Fast Black sat on the porch discussing her. A knock on her bedroom door interrupted her thoughts.

"Who it is?" Maureen called, rising.

"It's me, Mama," Loraine replied.

"Come on in, darlin," Maureen said, sitting up. Loraine entered, dressed in her nightgown and holding a coal-oil lamp.

"Hey, Mama, I heard Mama Ruby and Fast Black talkin about you again just now. They was talkin about Black Jack too."

"I don't care," Maureen shrugged. "They ain't got nothin better to do with they time, child. Know somethin, Lo'raine?"

"What's that, Mama?"

"One day I'm goin to give everybody in Goons somethin to talk about."

Loraine gave Maureen a puzzled look.

"Everywhere I go in Goons, they already talkin about you. Sayin you is sho nuff crazy bein so old and still livin with Mama Ruby. Catty said it."

"That wench got some kind of nerve. She is just as old as me, she still livin at home. Sometimes I think I'm the only person in this crazy town with a lick of sense. Just let em wait. One day I'm goin to haul ass."

"With Black Jack?"

"I don't know yet. All I know is, I ain't goin to spend the rest of my good years in this place."

"And I heard Boatwright say, you got a—"

"Lo'raine, don't tell me nothin else them crazy folks done said about me."

"OK. Mama, I won't mention it, but Mama Ruby even said you ain't got nothin no man would want."

"Oh? Next time I see Black Jack, I'm goin to ax him if I got anything he want. . . ."

The next evening, while Ruby, Loraine, and Loretta were at Roscoe's place, Black Jack came to the house.

Maureen served him pretzels and a glass of pot liquor.

"Black Jack, do I have anything you want?"

Black Jack choked on his drink. Maureen slapped him on the back as he coughed to clear his throat.

"What did you just say, Mo'reen?" he asked, looking at her incredulously.

"I got anything you want?"

"Now that you mention it," he started, then stopped, looking toward the door. "Um . . . you thought about what I said last week, Mo'reen? About movin to Miami, I mean."

"Yeah. I thought about it a lot."

"Well?"

"I am goin to leave Goons one day. First I got to give Mama Ruby time to adjust."

"Adjust to what?" Black Jack set his glass on the floor and placed his arm around Maureen's shoulders.

"Virgil movin out. She don't like livin by herself. There's a bunch of rapists livin out here in Goons."

Black Jack looked at Maureen for a long time before responding.

"I don't think Mama Ruby got anything to worry about. . . ."

"She told me she seen Zeus lookin at her the wrong way. And Bishop. And Boatwright. And some Cubans."

"Any of em tried to rape her yet?"

"No. But she say they want to. They just waitin to catch her livin by herself."

"Where did Mama Ruby come from?"

"Louisiana. Why?"

"What make her think the way she do? She got half of Florida scared stiff, and she believe one of these men out here might try to rape *her?* Mo'reen, I'm a man. I can tell you, there is very few men who would rape a woman like Mama Ruby. In the first place, she ain't young. She sho ain't pretty. And very few men would want to wrestle with a woman Mama Ruby's size, if you know what I mean."

"No, I don't know what you mean. What her size got to do with anything? She still a woman. She still got a you-know-what." Maureen removed Black Jack's arm from around her shoulders and gave him a sharp look.

"I had a fat woman once. It was like tryin to screw a piano," Black Jack complained. "Mama Ruby ain't—"

"I got to go change my blouse," Maureen said quickly, jumping up from the sofa and running to the upper room.

Inside the upper room, Maureen collected her thoughts. Black Jack had said a lot of things to her about Mama Ruby nobody had ever said. Things that were really making her see just how bad off she was, living with Mama Ruby. Maureen was crazy about Black Jack. He was what she needed to piece her life together. He was a strong, dependable man with a good job managing a service station in Miami. He had a nice, roomy apartment and money in the bank. He also cared about Loraine and Loretta.

"Mama Ruby'll kill Black Jack if she knowed he was tryin to

talk me into movin to Miami," Maureen said to herself. She stared out the front window for a moment. Yellow Jack's Cadillac went speeding down Duquennes Road toward Miami with Ruby, Loraine, Loretta, Fast Black, and Boatwright accompanying Zeus, who was driving. At least she would have time to pull herself together before Ruby's return. She turned around to see Black Jack standing in the doorway of the upper room.

"YOU CAN'T COME IN HERE, BLACK JACK. YOU IS A MAN! Mama Ruby say ain't no man but Virgil and Reverend Tiggs and Jesus allowed in here! She say if a man was to come in the upper room, he'll bring the devil with him!" Maureen exclaimed. She fell back against the wall and looked at Black Jack with wide eyes.

Black Jack smiled.

"I got news for you—by the time Mama Ruby get back to the house, the devil will have been in the upper room and gone," he said, moving toward her with a wicked smile.

"What? Listen here—WHAT YOU DOIN UNZIPPIN YOUR PANTS?!"

It was her first time with him.

61

As soon as Black Jack left, Maureen hurriedly filled a foot tub with hot water and took a bath and a douche. After cleansing herself, she returned to the upper room to make sure she had removed every trace of Black Jack's visit. She changed the sheets on her bed and sprayed the air with rose-scented deodorizer.

When Ruby and the children returned, Fast Black and Loomis were with them.

"Mo'reen, come down here and see what Loomis done bought for me!" Ruby yelled up to the upper room. Maureen ran down to the living room and gasped as soon as she saw Ruby.

Ruby had on a new set of false teeth. A pair so large she could not close her mouth all the way. Her face now displayed a constant grin.

"Good God!" Maureen exclaimed. She turned to Loomis. "Loomis, how could you do that to Mama Ruby?!"

"What's wrong with you, girl? Them choppers cost me fifteen dollars. Cash money!" Loomis shouted.

"I can't believe what I'm seein," Maureen said. She ran to Ruby and felt the teeth, which were also too white.

"Mama, I like Mama Ruby's new teeth. They look so funny!" Loraine laughed.

"Mama Ruby look like the cheshire cat," Loretta added.

"Mama Ruby look like a fool!" Maureen barked. She looked at Ruby, Fast Black, and Loomis all standing in the middle of the floor. "You all must be crazy. Just like Black Jack say you is."

"You just jealous cause you ain't got you no new teeth!" Loomis said with a smirk.

"And I'm gettin sick of hearin Black Jack's name. What you know beside Black Jack?" Fast Black shook her finger in Maureen's face before continuing. "If I was Mama Ruby, I'd put a stop to you runnin around with that Black Jack. Next thing we know, he'll be the cause of you backslidin."

Maureen ignored her and made herself comfortable on the sofa.

"Mama Ruby, when folks see you comin wearin them teeth, they will bust out laughin. You look like you smilin all the time—that ain't natural," Maureen told her.

"And what's wrong with smilin all the time? When you smile, the world smiles with you. But when you cry, you cry alone. Ain't that right, yall?" Ruby asked, looking from Loomis to Fast Black.

"Sho nuff," Fast Black nodded.

"Mama Ruby ain't never lied," Loomis replied. "Praise the Lord."

"Mama Ruby, is you a clown?" Loretta asked.

"Naw!" Ruby barked, reaching over to slide her knuckles down the side of Loretta's face.

"Mama Ruby, you know how kids is. Just like drunks. They believe in speakin they mind the way they see things," Loomis told Ruby. He went to the sofa and sat next to Maureen. "See Black Jack today?"

". . . Um . . . yeah. He stopped by for just a minute," Maureen replied.

"A *minute? I* would think the way he look at you, he'd want to spend more than a minute with you, girl."

"Loomis, shet up. Black Jack probably got better things to do with his time than set around with Mo'reen," Ruby said nastily.

"With other women, I bet," Fast Black said, folding her arms.

"Can't yall think of nothin good to say about Black Jack for a change?" Maureen asked angrily.

"Naw," Loomis said with a smile.

Fast Black and Loomis stayed for dinner. Afterward, Maureen eavesdropped from the kitchen as Ruby instructed both of them to keep their eyes and ears open as far as Black Jack was concerned.

To avoid a lot of unnecessary confusion, Maureen decided to confess her feelings to Ruby. As soon as the visitors left to take Loretta and Loraine for a swim in the Blue Lake, Maureen came out of the kitchen and seated herself on the footstool in front of the window.

"I'm twenty-four years old now," Maureen began.

Ruby turned to face her.

"So?"

Maureen had her back to Ruby.

"I'm gettin kind of restless. Like life is sho nuff passin me by." Maureen paused.

"And?" Ruby sat up on the sofa.

"And . . . and I got a itchin to move to Miami. Virgil say he can get me a job as a file clerk in the office at the lobster factory, and Sister Mary say she know a Jew what owns a building that's always got vacant furnished apartments and Black Jack say—" Maureen was cut off by a loud crash. The whole house shook. She turned around to see that Ruby had risen from the sofa and fallen out in the middle of the floor.

"What's wrong, sugar?" Maureen asked. She jumped up and ran to Ruby.

"You goin to leave me after all I done done for you?!"

"I have to leave, Mama Ruby. If I don't, I'll go crazy." Maureen tried to lift Ruby off the floor and had no success.

"You can't go, Mo'reen. I won't let you. You don't know what you sayin!"

"But, Mama Ruby, I have to go. I can't stay here for the rest of my life! I don't want to be like you!"

"AND WHAT'S WRONG WITH ME?!"

"Everything! You kill folks. You do all kinds of crazy things that I know can't be right. You run everybody's life. I ain't goin to continue lettin you run mine. You always tellin me I should be the happiest girl in Florida. Well I ain't! I ain't cause I want to get away from you. I want a life of my own. I want to be happy. If you love me, you should want me to be happy. I can't be happy livin here. Please try to understand."

Ruby pounded her thighs wrathfully and wailed.

"You stop that!" Maureen ordered, leaning over Ruby to remove the huge teeth. "Come on and get up, please!" Maureen grabbed Ruby's arms and forced her up.

"You want to leave me so you can go play footsie with that nigger Black Jack!" Ruby accused.

"I want to leave you for a lot of reasons. Can't you see I'm a grown woman now? I've been a grown woman for a long time."

"Aaaarrrggghhh!"

"Shet up, Mama Ruby, and listen to me. I don't like livin out here in Goons no more!"

"Aaaarrrggghhh!"

"I ain't got nothin to call my own. I hate that upper room. I hate this house. I hate the way you treat me!"

"Aaaarrrggghhh!"

"Will you stop all that hollerin?! I'm leavin this place if it's the last thing I do and there ain't nothin you can do to stop me!"

"Aaarrrggghhh!"

Unable to stand Ruby's screams, Maureen ran to the upper room.

62

Virgil's little house was on Davis Street. On one side was a Pentecostal church. On the other side was a saloon called the Come On Inn.

"I declare, Mo'reen. On a weekend we get loud singin and prayin from both directions. Church folks cryin the blues. Drunks at the saloon gettin beat up callin out to God. I swear, if the church folks went to the saloon and the drunks went to the church in the first place, it would make more sense!" Virgil laughed. Maureen sat with him and his wife, Mary, on his front porch. A pitcher of tea sat on the steps next to three empty glasses.

"Well, I think I would be much better off here in Miami," Maureen sighed. "I'm so de'pressed livin out in Goons anymore."

"Then why won't you leave?"

"I intend to."

"Mo'reen, you been leavin Goons since I come home. I been home four months now. You been foolin around with Black Jack tellin him all this mess about you movin on to Miami; how long you think Black Jack goin to wait on you to make up your mind?"

"I am goin to leave, I'm tellin you. I just got to wait for the right time, that's all."

"When is the right time?"

"When Mama Ruby realize she can live without me."

Virgil looked at Maureen so long she became nervous.

"What's the matter?" she asked, shifting in her seat.

"I don't think you really want to leave Mama Ruby."

"You just watch me. You can get away from her, so can I. You changed, I can too. You use to be so different. Somethin like Mama Ruby. Full of nerve. Kind of crazy. Bold. You don't seem like my same brother."

"What was he like before?" Mary asked, looking from Maureen to Virgil. Mary was a quiet and petite mulatto woman from Tampa. She had moved to Miami eight years previously to work in the factories. Her only sister, Sister Mary's Sister, so named because during the time her mother carried her that was the only title used, worked with her. Sister Mary's Sister was Maureen's age, unmarried, and living alone. She was Maureen's newest friend.

"Before I went to the army, I'd never lived nowhere else but with Mama Ruby. Everything she said was gospel. Lord knows she said and done a lot of crazy stuff. And I was right there with her. I started seein things different. I knowed I had to get away from her, lest I end up just as crazy as she was. I learned a lot shet up in that prison. I hate to say it, but Mama Ruby is as crazy as a bessie bug, and I'll tell her to her face," Virgil said.

"You ever thought about havin her put away?" Mary asked Virgil.

Instead of answering, Virgil looked at Maureen. They both laughed.

"I'd like to see the person who got enough nerve to try and put Mama Ruby in a nut house," Maureen replied.

"It ain't right for Lo'raine and Lo'retta to be growin up around somebody like Mama Ruby. Them kids is the main reason you need to leave, Mo'reen."

"Virgil, I declare, I am goin to leave her. Real soon. I can't stand the mess I'm in too much longer. I been havin headaches. I'm nervous. I can't sleep. I can barely eat. I'm goin sho nuff crazy, yall," Maureen complained.

"Mo'reen," Mary began, rising. She stood in front of Maureen and placed her hand on her shoulder. "Girl, we can help you. I got a piece of money from some property my daddy had.

Virgil got him a good job. We could get you one of them furnished apartments and help you and them kids out till you can do better."

"And you'll see more of Black Jack," Virgil added.

"You owe it to Lo'raine and Lo'retta, Mo'reen. Leave that place. Yellow Jack's fixin to move into a apartment on Wilson Street," Mary informed Maureen.

"Sho nuff? I declare." Maureen was really worried now. With Yellow Jack leaving Goons, she would have to depend mostly on Catty and Fast Black for company. She frowned at the thought.

"I got a feelin somethin sho nuff bad is goin to happen if you don't leave Mama Ruby soon," Virgil warned.

"Like what?"

"Just about anything. Wherever Mama Ruby is, strange things have a way of happenin."

63

Virgil, Mary, and Maureen left the porch and went into the living room. In the saloon next door Loomis, No Talk, and Fast Black shared a table in the center of the floor.

"Ain't that ole Boatwright comin this way?" Fast Black asked Loomis. They all looked toward a side entrance. Willie Boatwright was walking toward the table, leading a middle-aged, but very attractive, woman.

"Evenin, Boatwright," Loomis said, eyeing Boatwright's companion. "Who that you got with you?"

"I want yall to meet Othella Johnson from Silo," Boatwright said.

No Talk's eyes slowly scanned Othella's slim body. Loomis smiled and brushed off his lint-covered shirt. Othella smiled at the men.

"Howdy do, yall," Othella greeted. She had changed. Though her body was still youthful and firm, her once jet black hair was now completely white. Her skin was dry and spotted. Her eyes were vacant and her voice now trembled when she spoke. The years had been hard on her. Twenty years earlier all her children had perished in a fire that swept through her shabby house in Silo. Five years after that a jealous lover shot her in the foot, and she now walked with a noticeable limp. She had suffered two nervous breakdowns and had once been diagnosed as insane. Her current lover, a Silo dwarf called Midget, was Boatwright's half brother.

"Evenin, Miss Othella," Loomis grinned, clearing his throat. Fast Black kicked his leg under the table. No Talk pulled out a dollar and waved it at Othella.

"I declare," she giggled. "I never knowed Miami had so many fancy men!"

"This no-talkin fancy man belong to me," Fast Black pointed out, giving Othella a hard look.

"I don't see your name on him," Othella said, hand on her hip.

Fast Black gasped.

"How long you plannin to stay in this neck of the woods?" she asked.

"That depends," Othella said in a breathy voice, looking into Loomis' eyes.

"Shoot! You ain't got to worry about Othella takin your man, Fast Black. She my brother's woman. She is got too much class for somebody like No Talk anyway!" Boatwright interjected. "Othella is fifty-five years old!"

"I ain't worried about her takin my man. Can't no woman take my man, lest I let her. I'm just worried about these other women in here. Miss Othella is got a pretty good shape on her. Shoot. I hope my shape be that good when I'm fifty-five!" Fast Black exclaimed.

Loomis jerked his head around to face Fast Black.

"Fast Black, your shape ain't that good *now.*"

"Don't yall start no mess on my account," Othella begged, raising her hand. "I just want to have me a little fun and get on back to Silo. I don't like bein involved in no commotion. I'm fixin to find Midget—"

Just then Midget walked up.

"Othella, Boatwright, yall, we fixin to haul ass! Two niggers is fixin to cut one another up!" Midget announced.

Before anyone could respond, all hell broke loose. Glasses started sailing through the air. Shots rang out. Women screamed. Men cursed. Fast Black prayed. Loomis grabbed Othella's hand and followed Fast Black and No Talk as they climbed out a back window.

Virgil, Mary, and Maureen hit the floor next door.

"Sound like the gunfight at the OK Corral," Maureen chuckled. "I wouldn't be surprised to see Mama Ruby runnin out of there."

"Just listen to all that mess. There wasn't this much commotion on the battlefield." Virgil laughed.

"I seen Fast Black and her bunch goin in there earlier. I know they mixed up in the mess some kind of way," Mary said. "Mo'reen, run to the back door and take a look-see at my hens. Make certain they ain't got scared and run wild."

Just as Maureen ran from the room, Virgil got up and went to the living room door. Fast Black was banging away. He opened it just wide enough to lean his head out.

"What you want, woman?"

"We need a Band-Aid! Boatwright's brother's woman from Silo got hit up side her head with a ashtray!"

"I ain't got no Band-Aids, Fast Black."

"Dammit to hell! Oh, Loomis, put Othella in Yellow Jack's Cadillac. We'll carry her out to Goons where Mama Ruby can doctor her," Fast Black yelled as she ran off Virgil's front porch.

Virgil opened the door wide and went out to the porch. He felt his chest and held his breath. He recognized Othella immediately.

"Oh, Virgil, the hens is OK," Maureen yelled, running back to the living room.

Virgil returned inside and slammed the door shut. Mary and Maureen gasped and ran to him.

"What's the matter? You look like you just seen a ghost," Maureen whispered, grabbing his trembling hand.

"I did, Mo'reen. I just seen a ghost."

64

"I thought yall was goin to carry me to that Ruby woman's house, fancy man," Othella pouted. She lay next to Loomis in his lumpy bed, her legs wrapped around his.

"Shoot. I go messin with Mama Ruby this time of night, she liable to bust my brains out. Why don't you just go on to sleep anyway?" Loomis retorted.

"I knowed I should have gone on with Midget. You done brought me out here and made a fool out of me. I'm layin up here in this lumpy bed in the dark with a fool. You men is all alike. You. Midget. Boatwright. All men. I bet Midget about to worry hisself to death wonderin where I went. He suppose to carry me back to Silo in the mornin. Shoot."

"Goddamn it, woman. Didn't I tell you I'd carry you back to Silo myself. In my cousin's jazzy Cadillac. First thing in the mornin."

Othella was silent for a full minute before replying.

"I been thinkin. Fast Black say she'll lend me some clothes, if I wanted to stay in Goons a few days. I just might take a notion and stay here a little while. A few days at least."

"That's good. Now take your damn self to sleep. I got to work in the fields tomorrow."

Othella wrapped her arms around Loomis' waist.

"Fancy man, that Mama Ruby woman . . . what she look like?"

"Like fifty miles of bad road," Loomis grunted sleepily.

"I want to see her. I use to know a woman they called Mama Ruby. I want to—"

"Goddamn it, Othella! You been runnin off at the mouth for hours. Do you Silo women ever shet up?"

"I ain't no Silo woman. I'm originally from Shreveport, Louisiana," Othella said proudly.

Loomis sat up.

"That's the same place Mama Ruby come from," he told Othella.

Othella sat up.

"The more I hear about this woman, the more she sound like a woman I use to know."

"She could be," Loomis growled.

"Course they could just be two women with the same name, huh? I doubt if this the same woman I use to know. Maybe it's just somebody like her, huh, Loomis?"

"Let me tell you one thing. Nowhere on this planet is there another woman like Mama Ruby."

65

Roscoe ran what was considered a store in the living room of his compartment on the camp. In it he had an ice box and a counter containing items he sold. On the wall was a sign that read

No Credit	Beverages	Food
Mama Ruby	Beer	Gum
Bobby Boatwright	Pop	Popsicles
The Flatt Family	Pot Liquor	Beef Jerky
Fast Black	Buttermilk	Potato Chips
Loomis	Moonshine	Day-Old Tea Cakes

Maureen stood at the counter waiting for Roscoe to bag a six-pack of beer Ruby had sent her to pick up. He was taking his time.

"Roscoe, can you make haste? Mama Ruby can't get her day started without a beer," Maureen said, shifting her weight from one foot to the other impatiently.

"OK, darlin," Roscoe replied, not moving any faster.

Loraine and Loretta stood near the door inspecting the potato chip rack on the counter.

After handing Maureen the bag, Roscoe stood back and looked at her, then shook his head.

"What's the matter?" Maureen asked, feeling self-conscious.

"Where was you last night?"

"I spent the night at Virgil's house. Why?"

"Girl, when is you goin to slow down and get yourself married?" Roscoe placed his hands on his hips and gave Maureen a stern look.

"Slow down? Roscoe, if I slowed down any more I'd be dead. What would I be slowin down from? Who you think I am, Fast Black or somebody?"

"How old is you now? Thirty?"

"I'm twenty-five, Roscoe, and you know it."

"And you ain't never been married?"

"No. But I know my ship'll come in one day," Maureen smiled.

"Well if you was to ax me, I'd say your ship was the *Titanic*. I ain't never in my life seen no—"

"Thanks for the beer, Roscoe!" Maureen snapped, cutting him off.

Roscoe was only teasing her, and she knew it. He loved her and wouldn't do anything to hurt her. A widower for thirty years, Roscoe had no children of his own and had been eager to take in No Talk when he lost both his parents in an automobile accident at sixteen. When there was work, Roscoe worked in the fields, but he loved managing his little "store."

"Yall get off my counter!" Roscoe shouted at Loretta and Loraine. "These kids around here just keep my place in a mess." Roscoe moved over to the potato chip rack and rearranged it. Loretta and Loraine ran to the doorway, giggling.

"I'll be seein you, Roscoe. Come on, kids," Maureen said, on her way out the door. She smiled at Othella, who was entering.

"Howdy do," Othella said to Maureen. "Them your kids?"

"Yes, ma'am."

"They twins, ain't they?"

"Yes, ma'am."

"Twins run in my family. I had a twin brother. He died in the war. I had three uncles what had twins."

"Sho nuff?"

"Sho nuff. I had me a bunch of kids one time."

"Oh? Where they at?"

Othella looked down at the floor before replying.

"They burned up one night when my house caught on fire," Othella replied, looking in Maureen's eyes.

"I declare, lady. That's too bad. Can't you have no more kids?"

"I'd like to. The thing is, I'm a little long in the tooth to be havin babies," Othella laughed. "My last one was born dead. She was the prettiest little ole thing I ever had."

Maureen shook her head in pity and excused herself as she and the twins left.

Othella looked out the screen door at them walking toward Duquennes Road. Then she turned to Roscoe.

"Hi, Roscoe."

"Howdy, Othella. I see you made it through the night. After that commotion in Miami, I bet you rarin to get on back to Silo, huh?"

"I might hang around a few days. I kind of like Loomis and his friends. I'm glad now he brought me to your store to get that beer last night. I want to meet some of his other friends."

"Oh, we a nice bunch out here. We mind our own business. We Christians. We all got more than we need." Roscoe liked Othella. She was a pleasant woman with a nice smile. He could not imagine what she saw in a rogue like Loomis. "It sho nuff is good to see you again, Othella." Roscoe reached over his counter to touch her hand.

"Loomis sent me for more beer, Roscoe," she smiled.

"Comin right up!" Roscoe lifted his ice box top and removed the beer.

"I noticed your sign. What's them day-old tea cakes, Roscoe?"

"Mama Ruby cook me tea cakes for breakfast every mornin. What I don't eat, I sell the next day," Roscoe explained.

"Mama Ruby. I keep on hearin about a Mama Ruby woman. Loomis won't carry me to her house to meet her. Fast Black and No Talk won't neither."

"Ruby is my fiancee. We been engaged since nineteen and fifty-four. Ever since she come here."

Othella considered what Roscoe told her.

"This woman, tell me about her, Roscoe." Othella placed her elbows on Roscoe's counter and locked eyes with him. "I think I use to know her."

"Well, like I said, she come here in nineteen and fifty-four. Showed up from out of nowhere, it seem. That pretty gal what just left was her daughter Mo'reen."

"What this Ruby woman look like?"

Roscoe moved his tongue around inside his cheek and let out his breath.

"Can you picture Godzilla in a half-slip?"

Othella stared at him.

"Ruby Montgomery is got to be the biggest nigger woman ever lived. And the meanest! Wooo!"

"She got a boy named Virgil?"

"You *do* know her?" Roscoe gasped. "Yeah, she got a boy named Virgil. He just got back from V-Eight Nam a while back. He had been shet up in a prison."

Othella dropped her hands down to her sides and looked off sadly.

"What's the matter?" Roscoe asked, alarmed.

"Where she live?"

"Where who live?"

"This Ruby woman. I want to talk to her, Roscoe. I been wantin to talk to her for a long time."

"Straight down Duquennes Road you'll come to a road leadin down a hill. That ole shack at the foot of the hill is Ruby's house. Let me put a bug in your ear first. I hope you goin as a friend, cause she is one bad nigger. I heard she kilt a Klansman back in New Orleans and other folks in between! Whenever somebody come up missin, we look toward Ruby's house. She ain't your everyday woman."

"Ain't nobody out here'll go up against her?"

"I ain't. Shoot. That big woman'll come in here and tear my place up with me in it!" Roscoe laughed.

"Roscoe, forget that beer. I'll pick it up later. Right now I'm goin to pay this Ruby woman a little visit."

66

Othella stopped where the dirt road started down the hill to Ruby's and shaded her eyes with her hand. It was early afternoon and the sun was at its highest and hottest. She wiped perspiration from her face and shaded her eyes again so she could see the old house better.

The front door opened and Maureen came out, followed by Loretta and Loraine. They disappeared into the bayou off to the side of the house. Seconds later a gigantic woman wearing a long black duster opened the screen door and seemed to float out to the porch steps, where she stopped and looked up the hill at Othella, shading her eyes.

Othella's mouth fell open. Ruby had been obese when she'd last seen her. Her weight had almost doubled.

The two women watched one another for a long time before Ruby went back inside.

An hour passed. Ruby went out to the porch again and looked up the hill. Othella was still standing in the same spot, her eyes still shaded with her hand. An hour later, Ruby looked out her front window and saw her still standing at the top of the hill. This time Ruby was looking from the front window in the upper room. It was only then that Ruby knew who she was looking at. Othella made a salute and left.

When Maureen and the twins returned with a bucket of blackberries, Ruby was sitting on the front porch steps, her shotgun across her lap, looking up the hill.

"What's the matter, Mama Ruby?" Maureen asked, afraid Ruby might be waiting for Black Jack.

"Nothin," Ruby mumbled, not moving her eyes from the hill.

When Fast Black came to the house an hour later, Ruby was still on the steps and refused to acknowledge her presence.

"Mo'reen, what's the matter with Mama Ruby?" Fast Black asked, letting herself in the front door.

"I think somebody come by the house and raped her while me and these kids was gone," Maureen whispered.

Fast Black sat down next to Maureen on the sofa and breathed a sigh of relief.

"Oh. I thought somethin serious had happened." Fast Black reached over and patted Maureen's shoulder. "Girl, I couldn't get out the house fast enough. Loomis come by with his ole nutty woman from Silo."

"The one with that long gray hair? I seen her in Roscoe's today. She pretty, for a woman her age. She told me about her kids burnin up."

"And she had a mental problem ever since. Midget told me she throwed some potash in a girl's face one time and burned a hole in her. Woo!"

Maureen looked at Fast Black.

"You scared of her, Fast Black?"

"Hell no. Like Mama Ruby, I ain't scared of nobody. I just don't like her. She too crazy for me."

"I kind of liked her. She seem like a real nice lady."

"Mo'reen, you ain't got sense enough to know a crazy person when you come across one. I went up to Othella and axed her to help me hang out clothes. She told me to go to hell. Said she had too much sense to be workin."

Maureen laughed.

67

Virgil drove Big Red's squad car to Goons. It was well past midnight when he arrived, but he was not surprised to find Ruby still up. The look on her face told him the inevitable.

"Othella's in town," he said in a low, tired voice.

"I know. I seen her today," Ruby nodded.

Virgil walked on into the house and sat down on the sofa. Ruby remained at the door, looking up the hill.

"What you goin to do, Mama Ruby?"

"Wait."

"I knowed Goons wasn't far enough away. We should have gone north with Mo'reen. But no—no, you wanted to stay in Florida!" Virgil let out his breath angrily and glared at Ruby. She slowly turned to face him.

"And what was there to stop her from comin north?"

"Stop talkin so loud. You want to wake up Mo'reen and have her catch us talkin? Where she at anyway?" Virgil asked, looking toward the upper room.

"She in the upper room, where she belong."

"Mama Ruby, you done wrong," Virgil said, rising. He stood close to Ruby, who turned just enough to look at him out of the corner of her eye.

"I ain't never done nothin wrong in my life," Ruby whispered, blinking her eyes rapidly.

Virgil looked at her incredulously.

"You stole Mo'reen away from Othella. You don't call that wrong? The least you could have done was to let Othella know her daughter was alive. You could have mailed her a note or somethin after we first left Silo. Mo'reen grown now and her own mama don't even know about her. I bet if you had axed Othella to give you Mo'reen, she would have. Shoot. She already had her a mess of kids. What she say when you seen her today?"

"We ain't talked, yet."

"Fast Black and Loomis and No Talk run into her at the saloon next door to me last night. I heard em talkin about bringin Othella to you to get patched up on account of she got hit up side the head with a ashtray."

"They had brought that wench out here to me, she'd have got more than patched up."

"We got a mess on our hands. Like I said, you should have told Othella bout her baby bein live. You was wrong to keep Mo'reen like you done."

"I was only doin what the Lord wanted me to do. Why else would he make Mo'reen look dead when she first come? So I could get her off to myself, that's why."

"If the Lord wanted you to have your own daughter, how come he didn't let you get pregnant with one? How come he didn't make me be a girl?"

"Boy, we don't question the Lord's way. That clear? You keep forgettin I'm the one what give Mo'reen life. She *was* dead. My healin hands is what brought her to life. If that ain't the Lord workin through me. . ."

"I'm haulin ass. I ain't goin to be in this mess. What you goin to do when Othella bring the law here? Goons a small place with a lot of big-mouth folks. How long you think it'll be before Othella piece this mess together? All she got to hear is you livin here with a grown daughter named Mo'reen. Who just happens to look a hell of a lot like Othella. How you goin to explain to Othella you runnin off from Silo in the middle of the night? I bet before the week's out, you and Othella goin to have a showdown! Mama Ruby, you ain't got a chance. Ain't none of these Christians out here goin to respect you when they find out what you done! The devil's goin to finally get you!"

Ruby bit her bottom lip.

"Boy, how many times I got to tell you, I am the *devil.*"

68

That next afternoon, Othella sat on the ground in front of Loomis' house talking to herself, hitting at the blazing sun that had blistered her face.

"And the Lord will guide me . . . me and my children will be reunited. I declare, we will, huh Lord?" she said, looking up at the sky.

Yellow Jack, walking by, stopped and stood in front of her.

"You talkin to me, lady?" he asked. Afraid of his cousin's latest pick-up, Yellow Jack was glad he now had his own apartment in Miami where he had absolute privacy. He had a steady woman now and spent less time in Goons altogether. Yellow Jack had come to visit Maureen and argue the advantages of living in Miami as opposed to living in Goons.

"Is you the Lord?" Othella asked nastily.

"Naw." Yellow Jack shrugged.

"Then I ain't talkin to you," she said, tossing a handful of sand in his direction.

Yellow Jack hurriedly returned to his car, which was sitting in Roscoe's front yard with two flat tires. Catty, angry with Yellow Jack for not giving her his new address, had let out the air. Yellow Jack was now waiting for Roscoe to come out and help him repair the tires.

Othella jumped up and started running toward Duquennes Road and she did not stop until she reached Ruby's front door.

"OPEN THIS DAMN DOOR!" she shouted, kicking at the screen with both feet. "My kids *did* hear a baby cryin in your house like they said that day, when I sent em for some calamine lotion!"

"Hello, Othella," Ruby sighed, opening the door.

Othella rushed in and stood in front of Ruby as Ruby turned to face her.

Maureen and the twins were visiting Reverend Tiggs.

"You big, fat, lyin, kidnappin, no-good, backslidin black wench you!" Othella screamed. "No wonder you disappeared from Silo! I got suspicious sho nuff when you took off with me owin you a quarter! BITCH!"

"Now is that any way to greet a old friend?" Ruby asked in a calm voice, sitting down on the sofa.

"Friend?! You call yourself a friend? After all I done for you when we left Shreveport? Where would you have been without me in New Orleans?! None of them whorehouses would give us jobs on account of you, with your big, fat, black pie-faced self! I could have got me a job anywhere! All of em wanted me, but I wouldn't take no job cause they wouldn't give you one. That's the kind of friend I was."

"You lyin through your ass!"

"Am I?! Miss Mo'reen wanted me off the bat! She just took you on cause she felt sorry for you, like I did. Who wanted you? You was nothin but a big, fat black bitch then—and you still is! I made all kind of arrangements for you to meet men and everything. Then you thank me by stealin my baby! Bitch! It took me a long time, but I figured out this mess! You just made out like my baby was dead so you could keep her! You had this planned from the get go!"

"That ain't the way it happened!" Ruby shouted, rising. She stood in front of Othella with her hands shaking. "I declare, I did believe she was dead, just like you did. Honest to God, Othella. What kind of woman you think I am? I didn't know she was alive till later on that night! Honest to God. I wanted to bring her back to you! But the Lord wouldn't let me! He knowed how bad I'd been wantin me a baby girl! He give her to me! He made her look dead, till I got her away from you! Ax him!"

"Bitch! I ought to pop my blade in you right where you stand!" Othella waved her fist in Ruby's face.

"And I'll kill you dead," Ruby replied, nodding.

"That a threat?"

"That's a promise."

Ruby returned to the sofa and folded her arms.

"Just look at you! Just look at the way you set there like you got the world by the tail! Well, your world is fixin to come to a end. I'm carryin my daughter back to Silo with me—"

"Ain't nobody carryin Mo'reen nowhere! Not you! Not no fancy man with a fourteen-carat pecker! Not nobody! Mo'reen belongs to me!"

"We goin to see about that! I'll carry her away from this place if I have to carry her on my back—and kill you if I have to!" Othella paused and just stared in Ruby's face. "Why, Ruby? How could you do such a thing? I never would have done nothin like this to you."

"I didn't mean no harm," Ruby whispered. Tears filled her eyes. "All I wanted was somethin pretty. You had all them beautiful children. You was the prettiest girl in Shreveport. Othella, I ain't never been no bathin beauty. All I ever been was tough. I can get any man I want, but not on account of my looks, like you done. I'd give anything in the world to have somebody call me beautiful to my face. . . ."

Othella's eyes filled with tears.

"You ain't *that* ugly, Ruby," Othella said seriously. "There's a heap of women uglier and fatter than you."

"I thought that through Mo'reen I would know what it's like to be . . . beautiful. Can you blame me for what I done?"

Othella backed away and shook her head.

"You ain't gettin me to feel sorry for you no more. You done wrong, Ruby, and you goin to pay for it. I ain't goin to put you in jail. All I want is my daughter."

"Jail don't scare me. Ain't nothin in this world scare me like losin Mo'reen."

Othella shook her finger in Ruby's face.

"I'm goin to go up to your friends one at a time and tell em what you done. I can't let you get away with this. I mean, this ain't just one of them things. Everybody in Goons is goin to know what a no-good, low-down, funky, kidnappin wench you is! I'm goin to bury you!"

"You goin to tell Mo'reen on me?"

"You damn right! I can't wait to see her face when I tell her *why* you and her don't look nothin alike! I'm goin to sing like a Christmas choir!"

"Othella—please," Ruby begged. "I'll pay you! Name your price! I'll pay you the rest of my natural life! I got me two fancy men. Roscoe and Slim. Roscoe got his own store, he'll give me cash money. I get me a disability check every month. I'll pay you ten dollars a week from now on! CASH MONEY! All I ax is that you don't broadcast on me! Don't tell what I done! Don't ruin my life! Mo'reen can't never find out—"

"She bound to find out! How else am I goin to talk her into goin back to Silo with me? You think you can buy me off with a measly ten dollars a week? HA! You think I'm crazy or somethin?! You still got a nigger mentality! Shoot! I STILL got white folks' sense!"

"*Fifteen* dollars a week?"

"I don't want your money, Ruby! I want my daughter. But I ain't goin no place until I tell every man, woman, and child what you done! First thing in the mornin!"

Othella ran out the door back to Loomis' house.

69

Instead of returning home after visiting her preacher, Maureen went to Roscoe's. Catty had come to Reverend Tiggs' place and told her about the tires on her ex-husband's car and Maureen wanted to see Catty's vandalism. Loretta and Loraine had gone on home, taking the shortcut through the bayou.

After looking at the flat tires, Maureen went inside Roscoe's to get a Popsicle to eat on the way home. Before she could come out, Catty came to the door.

"Mo'reen, Loomis' ole crazy woman from Silo want to talk to you," Catty told Maureen.

"What about?" Maureen asked over her shoulder.

Roscoe looked past Maureen out his window at Othella sitting on the ground. He frowned, not knowing what to think.

"I don't know what she want to talk to you about," Catty answered, shrugging.

Maureen grabbed the Popsicle and went outside to Othella.

"What you want, lady?" Maureen asked amicably.

Othella stood up and Maureen realized she had a switchblade in her hand.

"Will you come back to Silo and live with me? You and them twins?" Othella asked. "I'll help you raise them kids real good. I'll make certain they get a good education and everything."

Othella faced Maureen, holding the switchblade up to Maureen's face.

". . . Um . . . I don't think I can do that, lady. I can't leave my mama for you. I don't even know you." Maureen turned away.

"Don't you turn your back on me too!" Othella shouted. She grabbed Maureen and snatched her around. Maureen's eyes got big and she held her breath.

"Lady, what's the matter? Why you want me and my kids to live with you? I heard you was crazy, but I didn't know you was *this* crazy." Maureen moved away. Roscoe was looking out the window. Catty covered her mouth with her hand. Maureen looked from Othella toward Ruby's house, unable to speak. Othella raised the blade high above her head and caught Maureen in the back when she tried to run.

70

Within minutes at least a dozen people from the camps and scattered houses had run to Roscoe's front yard, where Maureen lay bleeding.

"Aaaarrrggghhh!" Catty cried and fell to the ground.

"Yall give Mo'reen some air!" Boatwright shouted, pushing Bobby, Bishop, and Irene back out of the way.

"Somebody get Mama Ruby!" Roscoe ordered.

Othella, hiding behind Loomis' house, laughed as she watched the commotion she had started.

Yellow Jack was the only calm one in the crowd. He lifted Maureen and placed her gently on the backseat of his car. Then he took her home, his two tires still flat. The car could only move a few miles an hour, so the excited crowd reached Ruby's house before Yellow Jack's car.

"Mama Ruby—Mo'reen been kilt!" Bobby hollered, running down the hill.

Ruby heard him as she lay on her sofa reading the Bible. It took her five seconds to get from the sofa out to her front yard. Loraine ran out behind her, crying. Loretta followed seconds later.

Yellow Jack stopped his car a few yards away from the house, where Ruby had stopped in front of the car refusing to allow him to drive any farther.

"WHAT HAPPENED?" she roared, as she lifted Maureen's body.

"Loomis' woman from Silo done this, Mama Ruby!" Yellow Jack answered.

"Aaarrrggghhh!" Ruby wailed from the bottom of her heart.

Yellow Jack helped her carry Maureen into the house, then Ruby carried her to the upper room and slammed the door shut.

The whole crowd waited on the steps leading to the upper room for an hour before Ruby emerged.

"She's goin to be fine," Ruby said tiredly. She held the bloody knife in one hand and her Bible in the other. "Yall can go on home now."

Everyone left silently, returning to their houses to wait.

Fifteen minutes later, Ruby came thundering down Duquennes Road toward the camp area. Her teeth were clenched, spit oozed from the sides of her mouth. Her eyes were dilated.

"Look at that devilish grin," Irene whispered to Catty as they huddled at their front window.

"And them eyes. Like snake eyes," Catty added.

Ruby had lost both her shoes by the time she reached Loomis' house.

Roscoe was sitting in his front window watching as Ruby stomped up on Loomis' front porch. She stepped over a coon dog blocking her way and with her huge wide hand she gave the front door one push and it fell in, crashing on Loomis' living room floor.

Loomis and Othella looked toward the doorway at the same time. Ruby's eyes were on Othella, who stood glued to her spot in back of the room holding Loomis' telephone receiver away from her face.

"That better be Jesus you talkin to," Ruby said calmly to Othella as she started toward her. Othella looked at the telephone, then quickly and clumsily returned it to its cradle. She then reached inside her right garter and removed a straight razor she had stolen from Loomis.

"Oh shit!" Loomis gasped, holding up both hands. "Look, Mama Ruby, don't you come in my house startin no mess," he pleaded. Ruby ignored him and kept moving toward Othella.

"I been waitin on this day," Othella told Ruby. As soon as

Ruby was near enough, Othella slashed her across the face and blood spurted halfway across the room. Othella stabbed Ruby in the chest repeatedly. Not once did Ruby cry out.

"Die, die, you devil!" Othella screamed as she continued to slash Ruby, both hands on the razor.

"I be goddamn!" Loomis hollered. Ruby was covered with blood from her face down. "Othella, don't you kill Mama Ruby!" Loomis ran to them. With one hand Ruby swept him to the other side of the room. Loomis had just returned from Zeus' house and was unaware of Maureen's stabbing. "What is the matter with yall women?!" Loomis cried.

"I told you I was goin to get you, didn't I?" Ruby smiled at Othella. Othella sliced Ruby across her lips.

"You big motherfucker! Is you the devil, sho nuff?! Can't you die?!" Othella yelled, looking at Ruby incredulously. Seeing that the razor was having no effect on Ruby, Othella dropped it to the floor. Before she could get out of Ruby's way, Ruby's hands were on her throat. Ruby lifted her so high in the air her head knocked the ceiling. Unable to scream, Othella turned purple in silence as Ruby squeezed the life out of her body.

Loomis watched in horror as Ruby threw Othella's body out of his open back window, where it landed in a clumsy heap, her neck twisted and broken so that her head was all but on backwards.

Othella was buried in the cemetery off Duquennes Road and when Big Red came to investigate her disappearance, no two stories matched.

71

"Mo'reen, get back to the upper room. You want to brain damage?"

"I'm fine, Mama Ruby. I been stretched out for a week now," Maureen said weakly as she entered the living room. She joined Ruby on the sofa. A Band-Aid covered Ruby's facial wound. Other bandages had been applied to her bosom and arms.

"Mama Ruby, that crazy Silo woman cut you up real bad, didn't she? Just like she done me. You goin to heal good as new, you think?"

"Girl, it'd take more than a dull razor to get me down," Ruby coughed, touching a scab on her chin. Maureen reached over and touched Ruby's scab.

"Mama Ruby, that woman tried to kill you. Look at that cut on your arm."

"That little scratch? Shoot. I got bigger scabs on my feet from steppin on rocks," Ruby laughed.

Maureen sighed and looked away.

"I can't understand it. Why would that crazy woman want to kill me and you."

"Crazy folks can't be figured out. That's why they crazy," Ruby explained.

"I guess you right," Maureen nodded. "Where is Lo'raine and Lo'retta?"

"With Catty."

"What day is this, Mama Ruby?"

"Saturday. How come?"

Maureen went to the window and looked up the hill.

"Black Jack sent a bug by Yellow Jack to go in my ear. Say he comin to see me today. I might take a notion to spend Halloween with him."

"For what?" Ruby asked, annoyed.

"I am his lady friend, Mama Ruby. He suppose to spend some time with me."

Ruby rushed to Maureen and wrapped her arms around her waist.

"Mo'reen, last week I kilt a crazy woman over you. You think that nigger Black Jack would go out on a limb like that for you? He ain't like me."

"*Who is,* Mama Ruby?" Maureen gave Ruby a critical look.

"What is that suppose to mean?" Ruby released Maureen and moved back.

"Who in this world is like you? You need some kind of help. You need to see some trained white person what can help you straighten out yourself."

"Girl, the only thing wrong with me is you. I been bendin over backwards to give you a good life. You was happy till Black Jack brought his black self to town!"

"Was I happy?"

"Yeah. Up until then. You was in hog heaven. We all was. Now you done put this whole house in a uproar. Them kids struttin around here talkin about wantin to move off to Miami. There's all kinds of dangers in that city just waitin on Lo'raine and Lo'retta! Why just look what the wind blowed in last week. That crazy woman from Silo."

"We don't want to move to Silo. We want to move to Miami. That crazy woman wasn't from Miami."

"That's where Loomis picked her up. I'm tellin you, Miami is a wicked city. Worse than that San Francisco!"

"Mama Ruby, folks in Miami is scared to come out to Goons on account of you."

"Oh? Why?"

"See what I mean?" Maureen sighed. "You got some sho-nuff problems and can't even see em." Maureen returned to the sofa.

Black Jack did not come that day. By evening Maureen had

given up. Ruby left the house with Fast Black and No Talk, leaving Loomis with Maureen on the front porch telling her for the fifth time his version of Ruby's attack on Othella.

"Say Mama Ruby broke the woman's body clean in two, huh, Loomis?"

"She sho nuff did, Mo'reen. I seen her do it. I won't mess with Mama Ruby to save my soul!" Loomis laughed.

Now Maureen was afraid for Black Jack. She went home with Loomis and called Black Jack.

"Meet me in the blackberry patch by the Blue Lake tonight at nine, Black Jack. I need to talk to you," Maureen whispered.

"I'll be there," Black Jack promised.

"We got to talk . . . things gettin sho nuff hot around here. Especially after that commotion with that woman from Silo last week. I think Mama Ruby done went all the way crazy, Black Jack."

Black Jack waited before responding.

"How can you tell the difference?" he asked.

"Huh?"

"Never mind . . ."

"I need you more than ever now. Things is sho nuff closin in on me. I got to do somethin. And it seems like it's now or never. Please be at the berry patch tonight."

"Mo'reen, I'll be there," Black Jack said firmly.

They hung up, and Maureen looked around the living room for Loomis.

"Oh, Loomis, where you at?"

"In the back room. But don't you come in here, girl. I'm naked!"

"I just wanted to thank you for lettin me use your phone . . . bye," Maureen called. She let herself out the door and headed for Catty's to pick up the twins.

In Loomis' back room Ruby, Fast Black, and No Talk sat on the bed. Loomis stood with his ear against the door, listening.

"She gone?" Ruby asked, returning the extension to its cradle.

"Yeah. I heard the screen door slam," Loomis answered.

"What they say, Mama Ruby? What Mo'reen and Black Jack got cooked up?" Fast Black asked, rising. No Talk rose with her, but Ruby remained on the bed with her arms folded and her top lip twitching. "What we goin to do now, Mama Ruby?"

"Get him . . ." Ruby said.

72

"Virgil, you seen Black Jack?" Maureen asked.

"I ain't seen or heard from him in a week."

Virgil entered Ruby's living room from the kitchen and sat down on the sofa next to Maureen. Ruby sat on the other sofa, her Bible on her lap, watching television.

"No," Virgil said, looking at Ruby. "Ain't nobody seen him. He ain't been to work. His landlord ain't see him. Mama Ruby . . ." Virgil said, looking at the side of Ruby's head.

She turned slowly to face him.

"What?"

"You got any idea where Black Jack could be?" Virgil asked.

Maureen's eyes got big as she turned to Ruby and waited for her reply.

"I guess he's still on his honeymoon," Ruby said.

"WHAT HONEYMOON!" Maureen shouted. "Black Jack ain't married!"

"He is now." Ruby nodded.

Virgil looked from Ruby to Maureen.

"What is Mama Ruby talkin about, Mo'reen?"

"There is just no tellin, Virgil!" Maureen answered, jumping up from the sofa and standing in front of Ruby. "What you talkin about, Mama Ruby?! Black Jack wouldn't get married and not tell me!"

"Why wouldn't he? It ain't had nothin to do with you!" Ruby snapped, looking Maureen over from her feet up.

"Virgil, did Black Jack have other women?" Maureen turned around to face Virgil.

"Not that I know of, Mo'reen," Virgil replied, coming to stand in front of Ruby. "Mama Ruby, you know so much, who did Black Jack marry?"

"Some woman," Ruby shrugged, gently pushing Virgil from her view of the television.

"When did he get married and why didn't he tell me?" Maureen demanded.

"Well, for one thing, he left Miami in such a hurry I guess he didn't have time," Ruby said casually.

Maureen's hands trembled.

"That's why Black Jack didn't meet me in the berry patch that night! You went after him," Maureen whispered.

Loraine skipped into the room from the kitchen and interrupted the conversation.

"Oh, Mama. Can I go up by the Blue Lake and catch bugs?" Loraine asked.

"Go on, girl," Maureen said, waving the child away with her hand, not looking away from Ruby.

Loraine ran out, slamming the screen door behind her.

73

Maureen and Virgil badgered Ruby for two hours before they finally got the whole story.

Afraid that Black Jack was on the verge of taking Maureen away, Ruby had "introduced" him to some woman Loomis had just discarded and had Reverend Tiggs marry them at Slim's house one night.

"Some of my connections in Miami treated the newlyweds to two free weeks at a beach house near Miami Beach," Ruby added.

"You evil witch you!" Maureen shouted. "You run my man off? How come you couldn't be nice to him?"

"I was nice to him, Mo'reen," Ruby said levelly. "He ain't dead."

Virgil sighed and shook his head angrily, then turned to Maureen.

"You better get yourself away from this crazy woman before it's too late, Mo'reen! Somethin sho nuff bad is goin to happen if you and them kids don't get out of this crazy woman's house. I done told you I could get you a job at the lobster factory!"

"AAARRGGGGHHHH!"

The bloodcurdling scream from the front porch made Ruby, Virgil, and Maureen run outside.

Willie Boatwright fell into Ruby's arms.

"AAARRRGGGHHHH!" he screamed again.

"What's wrong, Boatwright?!" Ruby shouted.

Boatwright's body shook and went as limp as a rag doll. His eyes rolled back in his head and his false teeth fell out of his mouth onto the porch floor.

"What's the matter?!" Maureen yelled, slapping Boatwright's face.

"Oh Lord! Oh me! Oh Lord! OH YALL!" Boatwright wailed. "Lo'raine done fell in the Blue Lake and drowned!"

Ruby fainted and fell on Boatwright.

By the time Maureen and Virgil reached the Blue Lake a dozen people had collected on the bank. Slim and Bishop lay on the ground, wet and gasping for air. They had been the first to jump into the lake to try to save Loraine, but neither could swim. After Yellow Jack retrieved Loraine's body, he and Bobby Boatwright had jumped in to help Slim and Bishop.

Maureen stared in disbelief at her dead child, who lay in Yellow Jack's arms, her face blue and her body stiff.

74

The church was filled to capacity for Loraine's funeral. Ruby fainted twice during the service. The first time she fell, she fell across an empty bench and damaged it beyond repair. The second time, she fell on Bishop and broke his leg in three places.

No Talk played the piano. Reverend Tiggs' sister Ernestine came all the way from Boca Raton to sing "Sometimes I Feel Like a Motherless Child."

Bobby Boatwright showed up in an orange suit, white vinyl shoes, but no socks. Roscoe and Zeus, sitting by the entrance, commented on Bobby's appearance.

"I declare, that boy's a sho-nuff sport," Zeus whispered in Roscoe's ear.

"In a pig's eye. Sport my tail. That boy's a sho-nuff fancy man if ever there was one!" Roscoe insisted.

"Wonder what poor Mo'reen's goin to do now," Zeus continued.

"I ain't goin to mention it, but Yellow Jack put a bug in Fast Black's ear this mornin. Then she put that same bug in my ear."

"What the bug say, Roscoe?"

"Don't tell nobody I told you. On account of Mo'reen told Yellow Jack not to tell nobody but Fast Black and she made it her business to tell me. Roscoe, Mo'reen say she done had it sho nuff with Ruby. Mo'reen say she fixin to leave the upper room and ain't nothin goin to stop her. She say she fixin to move on to Miami. Look over there at Mo'reen. You ever seen such misery in a woman's eyes?"

Roscoe and Zeus looked at Maureen, sitting on a side bench facing the congregation. There was no expression on her face as she stared beyond the crowd, looking up alongside the wall.

"Roscoe, somethin tells me Ruby is about to go sho nuff crazy. If that girl do leave here, you'd be able to buy Ruby with a nickel, she'll be so worthless. . . ."

75

Only a handful of mourners accompanied Maureen to the burial. Ruby had been returned home, halfway through the funeral, in a catatonic state.

Virgil stood with his arms supporting Maureen as they watched Loraine's coffin being lowered into the ground.

"Virgil, how come it couldn't have been me?" Maureen asked.

"It wasn't your time."

"It ain't fair. It ain't fair that I keep livin in all this misery!"

"Shhhh . . . folks is lookin at us," Virgil replied. "We'll talk when we get back to the house."

"I can't . . . I can't go back to that house," Maureen wailed. "If I don't leave now—I never will!"

"Mo'reen, you is twenty-five years old. You ain't got to stay nowhere lest you want to."

"I'm scared Mama Ruby might commit soo-we-side if I go! She in bad shape, Virgil!"

"If Mama Ruby kill herself over somethin like that, she ain't got no business bein alive in the first place. You can't let her blackmail you like that. If you do, every time she want her way, she'll tell you she goin to commit soo-we-side. You can't live like that no more, Mo'reen. I want you to get away from Mama Ruby as soon as you can."

It suddenly started to rain and the burial proceedings were quickly concluded.

76

"Why you sittin out here in the dark by your self, Mo'-reen?" Ruby asked. She had come into the kitchen to fix herself a pitcher of ice water and found Maureen in her nightgown sitting on the back porch steps. It was close to midnight, six days after Loraine's funeral.

"I'm sittin here thinkin," Maureen answered. Her voice was hollow and low.

"Thinkin about what?" Ruby asked.

"Why I was born. Why Lo'raine had to die. Why nothing good ever happened to me."

"Look-a-here. It's a whole lot of girls what would just love to be in your shoes, Mo'reen."

Maureen sighed and turned around to face her. The light from the kitchen was dim and the huge shadows Ruby cast on the wall looked frightening. Maureen looked past Ruby to her shadow, then back to her face.

"Name three," Maureen said.

Ruby dropped her head and shifted her weight from one foot to the other.

"Come on in the house so we can talk," Ruby said.

Ruby sat on the living room sofa and Maureen sat on the footstool by the window.

"Close the door. Somethin tells me it's fixin to get sho nuff cold in here," Ruby said.

Maureen reached over, shut the door, and turned back to face Ruby.

"When my mama was pregnant with me, a strange preacher man come around on a wagon, sellin used Bibles. Mama wouldn't buy one, on account of she said they might be stole. Won't nothin bring the devil in a house quicker than a stole Bible. Anyway, the man come back later on and gave Papa one of the Bibles for free . . . that's how the devil got his foot in our door.

"Lightnin struck the house that night and I was born, premature. I had a full set of teeth . . . scales on my hands and feet like a serpent. I had webbed toes up until I was five and Mama got me operated on. They say when I got old enough to talk, I had the voice of a man. You see, Mo'reen, I was marked by that stole Bible. That conflicted with me bein a seventh daughter of a seventh daughter and havin healin hands. When I was two, I told Papa to his face I was the devil."

"You told me that same thing." Maureen coughed.

"I remember tellin you that, and I wasn't lyin. My bosom is a battleground for good and evil," Ruby said, placing her hand on her chest and pressing down hard. "All my life I been straddlin that thin line what divides good and evil. I got Jesus in front of me and in back of me but I got Lucifer on my right . . . and on my left. I axed God for me a second chance, to be born all over. He answered my prayer by givin me you, you is me all over again. You is my second chance. I axed him to make me beautiful the next time. Lord knows you is sharp as a tack. Havin you with me, I feel like I'm the beauty queen myself, you got so many good looks, Mo'reen. You is sort of like a special delivery to me from the Lord. Ain't no way I can let you go. If you ever do leave me, you'll be takin away a part of me . . . the part that keeps me alive. Don't you see why it's so important for us to live together, forever and ever?"

Maureen stood up.

"Mo'reen, now do you understand me better?"

"What about me? If God made me to be you all over, what I get out of this deal? I don't like bein you."

"You ain't heard a word I just said. You ain't no regular person. Just like Jesus wasn't. He was sent here for a special reason. He never married and nothin. He never had no girlfriend or nothin. He was happy."

"I ain't Jesus. I didn't want this. All I want is to live a normal life like other women. I want to get married and grow old and die like everybody else. I don't want to be no special person livin just so somebody else can have a second time. What about a first time for me?"

"Can't you see what I'm tryin to tell you? You wasn't born for the same reasons as Catty or Fast Black. You was a special order. I axed for you, special made. You have to live up to that. You have to, Mo'reen!"

"I'm fixin to go to the upper room," Maureen sighed. She left Ruby in the living room, but during the night, after Maureen had fallen asleep, Ruby entered the upper room and saw that Maureen had packed a suitcase and set it on the floor.

77

Ruby did not sleep that night. She did not even go to bed. When Maureen came downstairs the next morning holding Loretta's hand and carrying the suitcase, Ruby was on the sofa staring at the wall.

"Mama Ruby, we fixin to leave. Yellow Jack just drove up. He . . . he the one carryin me and Lo'retta to Miami. I'm takin that job Virgil been tellin me about and that furnished apartment. Virgil and Sister Mary paid the first and last month's rent for me." Maureen's hands trembled and her heart pounded against her chest.

A long silence followed and Maureen felt a chill as she waited for Ruby's response.

Ruby turned her head mechanically to face Maureen.

"I can't believe this! I can't believe you leavin me—"

"Mama Ruby, I am leavin you! I'm sho nuff gettin out of here for good! I want a life of my own!"

"A life of your own? AFTER ALL YOU BEEN TAUGHT?! How long you think you'll survive out there in that world without me?!"

"I don't care what you say. You ain't stoppin me, Mama Ruby."

"No, no, noooooo!" Ruby cried, shaking her head. She

slapped herself against the face with both hands, then started pulling at her hair. "Aaaarrrggghhhh!"

"Stop that!" Maureen shouted, stomping her foot. "You goin to hurt yourself! Please stop, Mama Ruby," Maureen begged, backing away, pulling Loretta, who was now in tears herself, with her. Ruby stood up, waving her heavy arms threateningly.

"Aaaarrrggghhhh—oooooooh!" Ruby cried. Her eyes crossed and she started walking in a slow, zombielike manner toward Maureen. With her arms in the air, Ruby was a gruesome spectacle. Loretta and Maureen looked at her with wide eyes, their mouths hanging open. Ruby began making low, guttural sounds, moving like a Frankenstein's monster. If it had not been such a serious situation, Maureen would have laughed.

"Mama Ruby, be reasonable," Maureen pleaded as she eased closer to the door.

"Aaaarrrggghhhh!" Ruby yelled. Loretta screamed and hid behind Maureen. Ruby was still moving toward them, now walking like a mechanical toy soldier.

"I declare, I ain't never seen you act like this. You done cracked up, sho nuff, Mama Ruby!" Maureen yelled. She turned to run. With Loretta close behind, she ran to the door, snatched it open, and fled, with Ruby still in pursuit.

"Oooohhhh!" Ruby shouted, now running with her arms outstretched. Loretta made it off the porch, but Ruby caught Maureen. Maureen dropped the suitcase as Ruby's arms went around her waist. "DON'T DO IT, MO'REEN! CAN'T YOU SEE WHAT IT'S DOIN TO ME? I LOVE YOU!"

"Turn me loose, Mama Ruby!" Maureen ordered, struggling with the madwoman. She managed to get free and off the porch. Yellow Jack started the car.

"Come on here, Mo'reen!" he screamed. "Mama Ruby'll kill us all!"

"Yellow Jack—help me!" Maureen cried, still running as fast as she could toward the car. Loretta had crawled into the backseat and was now huddled in a corner crying hysterically.

"Mo'reen, don't leave me. I'll do anything you tell me to do!" Ruby shouted. She was gaining on Maureen. Maureen almost made it to the car. When she turned to look at Ruby, she saw she had left her suitcase on the porch.

"Great balls of fire!" Maureen hollered, looking back to the car and Yellow Jack.

"Come on, Mo'reen!" Yellow Jack called.

"I got to get my suitcase!" Maureen replied. She had stopped running and was standing in one spot shifting her weight from one foot to the other. She ducked as Ruby reached out to grab her and started running back to the porch.

"Aaarrrgghhhh!" Ruby continued, close behind Maureen.

Maureen retrieved her baggage and jumped over the porch bannister to elude Ruby. Instead of running off the porch by way of the steps, Ruby jumped over the bannister as Maureen had. The big woman's agility made Yellow Jack whistle, and even more frightened. There was no limit to what a woman like Ruby could do; her size was not as much of a handicap as people believed it to be. Maureen leaped into the car over the trunk. She was extremely thankful that Yellow Jack's car was a permanent convertible. Maureen landed awkwardly in the backseat with Loretta, but quickly tumbled over the seat, where she installed herself next to Yellow Jack.

"DRIVE!" Maureen yelled. Yellow Jack stepped on the gas and the old car started to move, slowly easing up the hill with Ruby running behind.

"Aaaarrrggghhh!" Ruby cried. Miraculously, she caught up with the car and was running along beside it, reaching for Maureen. "YOU CAN'T GO! PLEASE DON'T DO THIS DO ME, MO'REEN! I'LL CHANGE! I'LL BE WHAT YOU WANT ME TO BE!"

"Faster!" Maureen shouted at Yellow Jack, pulling at his shirt sleeve. "She'll kill you if she catch us, Yellow Jack! You know she will!"

"Have mercy!" Yellow Jack screamed. He stepped on the gas some more. The car was temperamental and not in the best condition. He stomped on the gas pedal and this time the car shot off like a bullet, with Ruby still close beside it. It was too bizarre to believe. The gigantic woman ran like a gazelle, so desperate that she ignored the laws and confines of physical endurance. Finally, the car was far in front of Ruby. Loretta wailed, still huddled on the backseat crying. Maureen sobbed quietly as she watched Ruby running behind the car, until Ruby was no more than a big black dot.

78

The months came and went. Before Maureen realized it, she had been away from Goons six months. She had not seen or heard from Ruby. Too afraid to return home for a visit, she depended on Virgil and Yellow Jack to keep her informed of Ruby's activities.

"You certain you gave Mama Ruby my phone number and address, Virgil?" Maureen asked the Sunday before the Fourth of July.

"I axed Mama Ruby to her face when she was goin to call or visit you and she just looked up side my head. Then she said you wasn't never goin to have no good luck."

"I see," Maureen mumbled.

Bored with her job, and lonely in her dull apartment, Maureen spent most of her time with a neighbor and coworker, Gladys Goode, a plain unmarried Christian woman of forty-five.

"Sister Goode, sometime it seem like I went from bad to worse. My mama mad as a Russian cause I left and treat me like a in-law. My man gone off, married to some other woman. Folks don't bring me nothin but bad news."

"Mo'reen, it takes time for things to level out. Take this job here. I been filling lobster orders nigh on to ten years. It ain't no picnic. But before my life was a hog trough. The wrong men and bad company kept me in a pickle. Then I found Jesus. I ain't had the misery since."

Maureen looked at her friend for a long time. The lobster factory was located in a cul-de-sac on Preston Street near the docks. Assigned to a small office with a huge window, Maureen sat daydreaming off and on every day as she watched the ships come and go. Her friend Gladys and the two other women who worked in the same office had little in common with Maureen. Being considerably older and bitter, these women concentrated on the church and the lobster orders. Maureen was the only one with a child.

Loretta seemed as unhappy as Maureen. Maureen came home from work every day and found the girl staring at the wall.

"Lo'retta, do you like bein in the city?" Maureen asked one dark Friday evening.

"Naw."

"Do you miss Mama Ruby?"

Loretta shrugged.

"I think so. It was fun seein her beat up on folks. When we lived with her, I knowed wasn't nobody ever goin to mess with us. Now, I'm kind of scared. . . ."

Maureen also missed the security Ruby had provided.

"Well, we ain't done nothin to nobody. Ain't nobody got no reason to mess with us," Maureen replied.

79

Yellow Jack now worked as a truck driver, delivering fruit and vegetables from the camps to the produce markets in Miami. Sister Mary's Sister, an attractive woman with curly brown hair and light brown eyes, was Maureen's closest friend and Yellow Jack's latest love interest. He spent most of his free time at her apartment, which was a few blocks from Maureen's.

"Yellow Jack told me you done lost your job already, Mo'reen," Sister Mary's Sister said, sitting on a bench to Maureen's right, at Logan's Beach. Yellow Jack sat to Maureen's left.

"And they never really told me why. I axed Sister Goode what she knowed about it. All she told me was that the folks said I had to go." Maureen laughed dryly.

"What you goin to do about money?" Sister Mary's Sister asked.

"Virgil and Sister Mary and Sister Goode say they'll pay my bills until I find another job," Maureen answered. "You know somethin, Yellow Jack?"

"What's that, Mo'reen?"

"If I didn't know no better, I'd swear Mama Ruby had somethin to do with me losin my job. I been on a down slide ever since I moved to Miami." Maureen drank from a bottle of cola and turned to face Yellow Jack.

"Oh, I don't think Mama Ruby would do nothin that low-down and dirty," Sister Mary's Sister said.

Yellow Jack and Maureen looked at her at the same time.

"You don't know Mama Ruby," Yellow Jack said.

Not only had Ruby and Fast Black, Loomis, No Talk, and Big Red paid Maureen's supervisor at the lobster factory a visit, they had forced Maureen's landlord to give Ruby a key to Maureen's apartment.

"Day before yestiddy, I come home from the meat market and somebody done been in my place and broke my rented television and cooked a chicken and ate it—even left a sink full of dirty dishes! They cut up one of my good blouses and stole my Ray Charles album! Lo'retta told me one day she seen a man's legs crawlin out my kitchen window! Last week somebody went in there and left a pile of shit in my commode and didn't flush it, then ripped my phone out the wall!"

"This happened in broad daylight?!" Yellow Jack asked.

"Sho nuff did. Sister Goode say she seen a bunch of ugly folks leavin, walkin out my door like they owned half the world."

"Did you call the po'lice?" Sister Mary's Sister asked in a quiet voice.

Maureen shook her head slowly.

"Since when is the law got jurisdiction where the devil concerned?" Maureen asked.

They left the beach and returned to Maureen's apartment.

"Mama, come see what somebody done! I come home from the playground and stepped in a pile of mess in the kitchen!" Loretta hollered as Maureen, Yellow Jack, and Sister Mary's Sister entered.

"What in the world done happened now?" Maureen cried, rushing to the kitchen.

Four bushel baskets containing cow manure and chicken bones sat in the middle of the floor. Big piles of the manure had been carefully placed in front of the baskets.

"Great balls of fire!" Maureen sighed, almost laughing.

"Who could have done somethin like this?" Yellow Jack asked. He walked on in and went to the baskets to inspect the contents closer. "This is sho nuff crazy!"

Yellow Jack looked at Maureen and shook his head.

"Is we goin to move, Mama? It seem like every day somethin different happen!" Loretta said.

"I ain't goin no place," Maureen replied.

80

In September, Fast Black and Catty started visiting Maureen on a weekly basis, each time showering her with detailed accounts of their activities. Fights, robberies, and thefts were nothing unusual for Fast Black, so Maureen wasn't surprised when Fast Black revealed her latest activities.

"I went up side No Talk's head with a skillet the other night for goin through my pocketbook. He been jealous since I got me a job workin for Mama Ruby. We been sellin beer like Mama Ruby use to do when she first come to Goons," Fast Black informed Maureen.

"How is she?" Maureen asked tiredly. She stood leaning against her living room door as Catty and Fast Black shared the sofa.

"Doin real good!" Catty said quickly, looking at Maureen out of the corner of her eye.

"That's wonderful," Maureen replied with a smile.

"That's Jesus," Catty reminded. "If you ain't got Jesus, you ain't got nothin."

"Ain't it so," Fast Black added, clapping her hands and shaking her head.

"Mo'reen, when is you goin to come to your senses?" Catty asked.

Maureen gave her a surprised look.

"What you mean?"

"Mo'reen, you know what Catty mean. If you was my girl I'd have you put in a home! Runnin off like you done!"

"I'm a grown woman, Fast Black. Can't nobody do nothin to me," Maureen snapped.

Catty rose, grabbing the denim shoulder bag she brought with her.

"Mama Ruby said you done got too big for your britches. That brown-eyed wench Sister Mary's Sister done it to you. Bitch!" Catty spat.

"You just hate Sister Mary's Sister cause she got Yellow Jack sewed up, Catty!"

"I wouldn't have Yellow Jack!" Catty yelled.

"What's wrong with Yellow Jack?" Fast Black asked angrily, giving Catty a dirty look. "What's so wrong with my boy you don't want him, Catty?"

"What's wrong with him? Ha! I'd like to tell you what's wrong with your son, missy!"

Fast Black slapped Catty hard across the face and Catty grabbed a handful of her hair.

"Oh shit!" Maureen complained. "Hey! Yall get out of my house with that mess! You want Lo'retta to walk in on yall actin like fools?"

Fast Black and Catty stopped suddenly and started straightening their clothes and hair.

"Now. Like I was sayin, Mo'reen, that Sister Mary's Sister the one got you so high-and-mighty these days," Catty continued.

"Don't you be comin to my house talkin about my friend, Catty," Maureen warned, shaking her fist in Catty's direction. "You can leave right now!"

Catty and Fast Black gasped and stormed out the door, whispering and glancing back as Maureen stood on her front porch with her arms folded.

Several hours later, Maureen turned in for the night. She was depressed and lonesome. It had been weeks since she lost her job and so far she had been unable to secure another one. She cried a lot over Loraine and found herself missing Black Jack. She had awakened the night before clutching a pillow between her legs after having dreamed of him.

Music coming from a tavern at the end of the street sometimes kept Maureen from sleeping at night and she would wake up, off and on, sometimes getting only two or three hours' sleep. This particular night, the music had kept her up until one A.M. When she finally dozed off, she was awakened by the ringing of her telephone. She picked up the phone on the fifth ring.

"Hello," she said sleepily.

There was no answer.

"I said HELLO!" She spoke hard and held the receiver with both hands.

Her room was small and accommodated only her twin bed, the end table, and a three-drawer dresser. A picture of Jesus hung on the wall over her bed.

"Hello, who is this?"

There was still no answer, but there was someone on the other end of the telephone line. There was no heavy breathing or background noise, only the hollow, empty sound of loneliness. An odd voice, at first vague and unfamiliar, started to speak in a stiff, mechanical fashion.

"Verily, verily . . . I say unto you . . . 'GET THEE HENCE AND TURN THEE EASTWARD, AND HIDE THYSELF BY THE BROOK! AND IT CAME TO PASS AFTER A WHILE, THAT THE BROOK DRIED UP BECAUSE THERE HAD BEEN NO RAIN IN THE LAND!' " The phone went dead.

Maureen trembled as she returned the receiver to its cradle.

"Mama, who that you talkin to?" Loretta asked, running into the room.

"Nobody."

"I heard you talkin. I heard the phone ring. Was it one of them nasty men what call up ladies?" Loretta climbed into bed next to Maureen and slid under the covers.

"Naw. I don't know who or what it was, child."

She told nobody about the strange call from Ruby, but she became frightened. Ruby was constantly on her mind. It was not long before Maureen started seeing her everywhere she looked. Fat women, thin women, all began to look like Ruby. She saw her in stores where she shopped, peeking in windows at places where she had job interviews, loitering around outside her apartment building. Maureen thought she was losing her mind one night when she woke up and saw Ruby standing over her as she lay in bed.

"Mama Ruby?!" Maureen called out. The room was dark, except for a dim coal-oil lamp on top of the dresser. Before Maureen could become fully conscious, the vision disappeared. The music coming from the tavern suddenly got louder and kept Maureen awake the rest of the night. She did not get out of bed, but when morning came she discovered her front door wide open, and three empty beer cans on her coffee table.

81

Ruby was not an easy person to put out of mind. She made regular nocturnal telephone calls to Maureen and hung up on her immediately after quoting a scripture. Almost every time Maureen left her apartment she returned to discover that someone had let himself in and vandalized her property.

"How much longer you goin to let Mama Ruby and her gang torture you, Mo'reen?" Sister Goode asked, helping Maureen haul a foot tub containing corn cobs someone had left on her living room floor out to her trash can.

"I swear to God, Sister Goode, I ain't goin to let Mama Ruby get my goat!" Maureen vowed.

December was dragging by and Maureen's loneliness led her to spend several nights a week at the noisy tavern that caused her so many restless nights. On nights when her loneliness overwhelmed her, she brought home strange men who left her lonelier than ever.

"Sometimes I wake up during the night and I hear you talkin to somebody in your room, Mama. Who do it be?" Loretta asked one day.

"Huh?"

"Who be in your room sometime late at night? I hear em talkin to you. Men."

"Oh. Them. They just friends I meet here and there."

"How come they just come around at night?"

"Uh . . . they work days," Maureen lied.

"I wish we had another man like Black Jack comin around, Mama. He was sho nuff nice to us, huh?"

"Yeah, he was."

Maureen put Loretta to bed and slipped out to the tavern that night. After her visitor left, she cried into her pillow. "Oh, Black Jack, I miss you so much! And you, Lo'raine, why'd you have to go and drown?"

The darkness responded violently. A gigantic Bible Virgil had given her sailed across the room and hit the bedroom wall with a loud thud.

"MAMA RUBY, I KNOW THAT'S YOU!" Maureen shouted, leaping up from the bed. She ran and clicked on the light and ran to her living room. Loretta was already in the living room.

"What was that, Mama?!"

"I don't know!"

There was nobody else in sight, but the door was standing open again and they heard the sound of heavy footsteps running down the concrete road. Returning to her bedroom, Maureen found the Bible, as thick as the Miami phone book, had been ripped in half. She gasped and called Sister Goode.

"Can you run over here and spend the night with me and Lo'retta? We got a mess on our hands."

"I'm on my way."

Maureen called Yellow Jack and he arrived within fifteen minutes.

"What done happened now?" he asked.

"Somebody was here again," Sister Goode answered for Maureen. Maureen and Loretta sat on the sofa hugging one another.

"Who was it?"

"Don't know. Whoever it was, they got the strength of ten men," Sister Goode said. She picked up the torn Bible from the coffee table and shook it in Yellow Jack's face. "Ain't no regular person can do this here. . . ."

82

Yellow Jack and Sister Goode left early the next morning. It was a weekday and both had to report for work.

At nine A.M. Fast Black and Catty were banging on the door with their fists and feet.

"Open this door, Mo'reen!" Fast Black ordered.

Maureen took her time unlocking the two new locks Yellow Jack had installed before leaving. Annoyed beyond belief, Catty and Fast Black barked at Maureen as soon as they were inside.

"WE GOT TO TALK TO YOU!" Catty shrieked, waving her arms.

"WE GOT SOMETHIN TO TELL YOU!" Fast Black screamed.

Maureen held her hands up in front of her face.

"If it got to do with Mama Ruby, I don't want to hear it!" Maureen warned.

"BUT, MO'REEN! THIS IS THE BIGGEST NEWS SINCE THE PARTIN OF THE RED SEA!" Catty shrieked, tears streaming down the sides of her face.

"Goddamn it, yall! I have had it up to here with news about Mama Ruby! Can't I have some peace in my life?!"

"What's the matter, Mama?" Loretta asked, running in from her room.

"Nothin, Lo'retta. Go on outside and play. Catty and Fast Black just come to visit," Maureen said. She waved Loretta away.

Catty and Fast Black looked at one another and reluctantly sat down on the sofa. Maureen fell into a chair facing them.

"Oh, Mo'reen," Fast Black sobbed, shaking her head.

"I know I done upset yall, but I don't care. Shoot. I'm sick to death of Mama Ruby. I'd like to get through one week without hearin about her and her mess!"

"Mo'reen, this bad news sho nuff—" Catty said, rising.

"Catty, you just sit right on back down and shet up talkin about Mama Ruby. You or Fast Black say one more word about her and I'm puttin you out of here!"

Fast Black wiped her eyes with the tail of her skirt. Catty wiped hers with the sleeve of her blouse.

"This the worse mess," Catty moaned under her breath. "This the worse mess ever . . ."

"I been patient. I know Mama Ruby the one behind somebody comin in my house makin a mess. I don't care what she do, I ain't never goin back to her, long as she live!" Maureen spat.

Catty and Fast Black looked at one another and burst out crying louder.

"What's the matter with you two fools?"

"We want to . . . we . . . want to tell you . . ." Fast Black sobbed. She buried her face in her lap and rocked back and forth.

Maureen sighed.

"Catty, how you been doin?" Maureen asked, fanning her face with her hand.

"I been doin fine, cept, cept—OH!" Catty replied.

"Yall drunk or crazy or both or what?" Maureen asked.

"Mo'reen," Catty began, rising. "I need some air—Mama Ruby—"

"Don't mention that woman's name I said!" Maureen held up her hand.

"I need me some air too! Let's drag our tails to Logan's Beach," Fast Black suggested.

"Can we stop and get somethin to eat?" Catty asked. "Mo'reen, show us to the nearest rib place."

After purchasing three rib sandwiches Maureen accompanied Fast Black and Catty to the beach, where they sat for three hours watching the swimmers. Before leaving, they waded in the ocean to cool off before the walk back to Maureen's apartment.

"Mo'reen, we'll go back and set with you a little while before we start that long walk back out to Goons. Maybe that no-good boy of mine will show up and carry us home," Fast Black said in a tired voice. "The least Yellow Jack can do is carry his ex-wife and mama back home."

"He ain't good for nothin else," Catty added.

Back in Maureen's living room, Catty and Fast Black sat sphinxlike on the sofa, staring at Maureen.

"I wish I knowed what was wrong with yall. First you come here actin like wild women. Then at the beach you both act like the cat got your tongue. Now you both settin here lookin at me like I'm somethin good to eat," Maureen said, looking from one face to the other.

Catty leaned on Fast Black and turned her head to the side to look at Maureen out of the corner of her eye.

"Mo'reen, can I have them curtains out the upper room?" Catty asked.

"I don't care. I sho nuff don't want em." Maureen sat down hard on a hassock facing the sofa. Her face lit up when Loretta skipped in and sat on the floor next to her.

"What Mama Ruby do this time?" Loretta asked, looking from Catty to Fast Black.

"Darlin, she ain't done nothin," Fast Black almost whispered.

"Then what yall come here for? All yall come here for is to tell us somethin about Mama Ruby or ax for somethin or tell Mama how crazy she is," Loretta said.

"Lo'retta, your mama told us she don't want to hear nothin bout Mama Ruby no more!" Catty hollered.

"And I meant it," Maureen reminded, squeezing Loretta.

"Mo'reen, can I have that chifforobe out the upper room?" Fast Black asked.

Maureen shrugged.

"I don't care," she laughed. "You can have the upper room if you want that too. I won't be needin it. I'm stayin on my own."

"Can I have them end tables out the livin room?" Catty asked. "And that footstool that set in front of the window?"

"Can I have them couches? No Talk done ruined mine with them ole long toenails of his," Fast Black said.

"Yall can have what you want out the upper room. The rest of that stuff you'd have to ax Mama Ruby for," Maureen answered. "You know how crazy Mama Ruby is about all that junk in there."

"Speakin of junk, how come you got two locks on your door? Ain't nothin in here nobody would want." Catty said seriously, looking around the room.

"Catty, did you come all the way from Goons just to talk about my house?" Maureen asked, rising. She folded her arms and faced the women angrily.

"No. We came here to tell you Mama Ruby died in her sleep last night!" Catty said, then quickly covered her mouth.

83

Loomis borrowed a crane from a paper mill outside Goons to help Big Red remove Ruby's body from the upper room, where Catty and Fast Black had found her that morning when she failed to answer the door.

They had nervously kicked in the door and tiptoed to the upper room to find Ruby lying on her back on Maureen's bed, the whites of her eyes showing and her huge teeth sparkling in the early morning light.

"SHE DEAD!" Catty screamed.

Neither she or Fast Black was brave enough to get any closer than the door.

"MAMA RUBY DEAD! MAMA RUBY DEAD! MAMA RUBY DEAD!" Fast Black screamed, backing down the stairs, Catty on her heels. They ran out of Ruby's house and up the hill, shouting along the way, "MAMA RUBY DEAD!"

Bishop and Zeus, strolling down Duquennes Road on their way to the city, stopped in their tracks.

"MAMA RUBY DEAD?" Bishop asked, gasping for breath.

"MAMA RUBY DEAD!" Fast Black yelled, running toward the camps.

Bishop and Zeus started running down the hill to Ruby's house with Zeus screaming, "MAMA RUBY DEAD!"

84

"What they need a crane for?" Bishop asked Zeus as they sat on Ruby's front porch glider, several hours after hearing of Ruby's death.

"How else they goin to get that big woman out the upper room, fool? You ever tried to lift her?"

Zeus shook his head.

"She way too big to be put through the window. How they goin to get her out?" Bishop asked.

Zeus leaned back on the glider and scratched his chin.

"We goin to knock out the side wall of the upper room."

"Oh," Bishop said quietly.

In Ruby's living room two dozen people had gathered, sitting and standing around talking about Ruby.

"I wonder what is takin Catty and Fast Black so long to get back here with Mo'reen," Zeus said, looking at his watch. "They been gone all day. Everybody here but Mo'reen. Poor Virgil, he look like the world done come to a end. He locked up in his old room and won't say nothin." Zeus sighed and shook his head. He looked at Bishop.

"He ain't been in to see Ruby?" Bishop asked.

"Naw. I overheard him tell Boatwright he more scared of her dead than when she was alive!"

Bishop let out his breath and slapped his knee.

"I never forget how Ruby blowed into Goons like a hurricane nigh on to twenty-six years ago. Mean as a rattlesnake even then. You know somethin, Zeus?"

"What's that, Bishop?"

"I would sho nuff like to know what made Ruby the way she was. I ain't never seen or heard of no human bein tough as Ruby was!"

"Listen, Mama Ruby was the most dangerous woman alive."

"Ain't that the truth."

They got silent and looked up the hill again.

"Mo'reen better hurry on here. We got to hurry and get Ruby out that room before she swell up and bust." Zeus looked at his watch again.

Reverend Tiggs was in Virgil's old bedroom trying to console him.

"Leave me be, Reverend Tiggs. I know Mama Ruby had to die someday. Just like all the rest of us. But she wasn't sick or nothin. She wasn't that old. She grieved herself to death cause of Mo'reen leavin her!"

"Ruby was hopeless attached to Mo'reen. It's natural for a woman to be hopeless attached to her only daughter," the preacher said, pacing the room with Virgil, stopping and turning each time he did.

"She was such a strange lady. She done so many things! Lord, she goin to answer to God! She'll still be standin in line answerin a hundred years from now. Oh, Reverend Tiggs! I wanted so much for my mama to be saved when she passed!"

"Ruby *was* saved, boy!"

Virgil stopped and stood in front of the naive preacher.

"Reverend Tiggs, my mama done a lot of crazy things she hadn't been forgiven for. The worse was . . . was . . ."

"Was what?"

"Mo'reen . . . nobody know . . . Mama Ruby . . . I . . ."

"Virgil, if it's that hard for you to get it out, I don't need to know."

"I want to tell somebody! I can't die with it on my conscious! I been wantin to tell somebody! I ain't even told my woman!"

"What is it, boy?" Reverend Tiggs grabbed Virgil by his arms and shook him.

"Reverend Tiggs, I'm sorry. What I got on my mind is somethin I guess I'll have to keep there till I face my maker."

"You don't want to tell me?"

Virgil pulled away.

"I can't. Mama Ruby would have wanted me to keep it to myself to my grave. Like she done."

"Oh, Virgil—come out here! Here come Mo'reen down the hill with Catty and Fast Black and Lo'retta!" Irene yelled.

Virgil and Reverend Tiggs ran out to the porch.

"Psssst," Bishop said to Zeus, talking low so Virgil would not hear. "I'll be glad when this mess is over so we can go fishin."

"Me too. Big Red say he got a relation what's got a piano case we can use for a coffin," Zeus told him.

"That's good." They paused and waited. Maureen ran into Virgil's arms and he took her into the house. Catty, Fast Black, and Loretta followed.

Bishop and Zeus sighed and shook their heads.

"I sho nuff hope Loomis and Big Red got that crane figured out." Bishop looked toward the side of the house where Loomis and Big Red were trying to determine the best way to maneuver the crane sitting outside the upper room.

Inside the upper room, Maureen and Virgil stood over Ruby's body. Loretta stood in the doorway among the crowd that had come to look. Catty and Fast Black stood next to Loretta, crying. Others who had never even been on the steps leading to the upper room pushed their way in, looking around, searching for some clue to explain Ruby's mysterious rule.

"She dead, Virgil," Maureen whispered, crying, her face against Virgil's chest. "I kilt her!"

"You ain't done nothin of the kind! It was just her time to go!" Virgil replied.

Maureen pulled away from Virgil and leaned over Ruby. She closed Ruby's eyes with her fingers. Maureen did not hear the comments that followed.

"Jesus must be some good to send Mo'reen back home."

"Mama Ruby always said Mo'reen would come back to the upper room."

"Mo'reen can't survive outside the upper room."

"You reckon Mo'reen'll die now too?"

The room got quiet but the silence was short. A scream from the crowd distracted Maureen. Outside Loomis cursed and screamed at Big Red for falling off the roof.

"Big Red done fell off the roof!" someone shouted.

"Please, yall, everybody . . . go see about Big Red and let me and Virgil and Lo'retta spend a few minutes alone with Mama Ruby," Maureen pleaded. She turned to face her friends, the inside of her mouth dry as sand.

Bishop and Zeus still sat on the front porch glider talking. Neither moved when the crowd rushed out the front door and ran to the side of the house to see about Big Red.

"Fast Black, No'Talk, Loomis, and Catty won't have nothin to do with they spare time no more. They was like Ruby's shadows. And poor Big Red. He goin to be just lost without Ruby. From what I hear, Ruby was runnin the Miami po'lice department through Big Red. He had a lot of pull down there. Ruby havin so much pull with him, naturally had a lot of pull in the po'lice department," Zeus said.

"Ruby was near about runnin the state. I remember how stores what usually closed on Sunday use to be open *just* to do business with Ruby. Yeah . . . we goin to miss ole Ruby. She was one of a kind. And ain't no tellin how many folks we goin to lose without her healin hands."

"You got a point. I ain't been to no licensed doctor since Ruby came to town."

"And poor Roscoe and Slim, wonder what's goin to happen to them. Roscoe and Ruby bein engaged and all." Bishop sighed.

"Bein big a sport as Slim is, he'll have him one of them juicy butt women from one of the camps before Ruby get cold. Slim is sho nuff a fancy man. Know somethin, Bishop?"

"What's that, Zeus?"

"I ain't goin to mention it, but Roscoe told me to my face he ain't never had a woman what had what Ruby had between her legs. Said she had a pocketbook shaped like a guitar. And not a snap of hair on it," Zeus whispered in Bishop's ear.

"You don't say?" Bishop replied. He looked at Zeus for a long time, before they both chuckled. "Yep. We sho nuff goin to miss ole Ruby."

Yellow Jack and Boatwright came back from around the house carrying Big Red, who had sprained his ankle.

The crowd filed back into the house.

"Who helpin Loomis?" Bishop asked Irene.

She stopped and looked at him. Her eyes were red and swollen.

"No Talk on the roof with Loomis," she replied. "Ain't yall comin in the house? Don't yall want to see the upper room at last?"

Bishop gasped.

"Irene, yall in the upper room? Everybody? Even men?! Yall know how Ruby was about men bein in the upper room!" Zeus wailed, rising.

"What can she do about it now?" Irene asked, opening the screen door and letting herself back in the house.

Zeus and Bishop ran in behind her, stopping in the living room, where Virgil and Yellow Jack sat on the couch with Big Red.

"Virgil, can we go to the upper room too?!" Zeus asked.

"We ain't never been in it!" Bishop added, looking anxiously toward the stairs.

"It don't make no difference now," Virgil said.

85

Ruby's funeral was two days long. Reverend Tiggs' sister came to sing and Ruby's father preached for eight hours straight on the second day.

Already, people were talking about leaving town.

"I'm goin north, sho nuff, now!" Loomis announced.

"Me, I might take a notion to go to Atlanta and start me a business," Roscoe said.

"I'm goin to New Orleans. Get me a job as a fry cook in one of them fancy hotels," Zeus told everyone.

"A country girl like me, I couldn't live nowhere but in Goons. Shoot. I'm gettin old. . . ." Fast Black muttered.

Maureen listened and looked at them all as they talked, sitting in the living room of Ruby's house during a break from the funeral.

"What *we* goin to do now, Mama?" Loretta asked Maureen.

Everyone got silent to listen. Maureen looked up toward the upper room and sighed.

"Mo'reen, whatever you want to do, or wherever you want to go, you know I'll get the money for you," Virgil said. "That's the least I can do."

Maureen looked at Virgil a full minute before replying.

"Get me the money for two one-way tickets to San Francisco," she said.

THE UPPER ROOM

MARY MONROE

ABOUT THIS GUIDE

The following questions are intended to enhance your
group's reading of THE UPPER ROOM by Mary Monroe,
which deals with issues of racism, violence, unconditional and,
at times, blind devotion. National best-selling author of *God
Don't Like Ugly*, Mary Monroe once again delivers a classic tale
destined to be a perennial favorite. First published in 1985,
THE UPPER ROOM won critical acclaim and we hope you
have seen that such acclaim was well deserved.

DISCUSSION QUESTIONS

1. Do you feel that the people in Mama Ruby's life idolized her because they were afraid of her or because they loved her?

2. Before Maureen's birth, her biological mother, Othella, already had more children than she needed, and this made Mama Ruby jealous. If Mama Ruby had not kidnapped Othella's baby girl, do you think that Mama Ruby and Othella would have remained friends?

3. Knowing that his mother had kidnapped another woman's child, was Ruby's son, Virgil, wrong for not sharing this information with the authorities once he reached adulthood?

4. Should Virgil have, at least, told Maureen about her birth mother and the kidnapping once she reached adulthood?

5. Even though Maureen clearly loved Mama Ruby, do you think that Maureen would have left Mama Ruby sooner if Virgil had told her about the kidnapping?

6. When Maureen's birth mother, Othella, encountered Maureen, twenty-five years after her strange birth, she knew that Maureen was her missing child. Had Othella turned Mama Ruby in to the authorities—instead of confronting her and ending up dead—do you think Maureen would have chosen a relationship with her birth mother or supported Mama Ruby?

7. Despite Mama Ruby's morbid obesity and her violent nature, she had no trouble getting lovers. What do you think it was about Mama Ruby that made her attractive to men?

8. If Maureen had moved to another state instead of just a few miles away from Mama Ruby, do you think that Mama Ruby would have still stalked her?

9. Do you feel Maureen's leaving home contributed to Mama Ruby's death?

10. Despite her violent nature, her alcoholism, and her insane set of rules, Mama Ruby raised two great kids. People could count on her for spiritual guidance, emotional support, a good home-cooked meal, and advice. If a person like Mama Ruby entered your life, would you embrace her or keep your distance?